nowhere is safe enough...

EVERY STAR IN THE SKY

two sparrows for a penny · one

SARA DAVISON

Every Star in the Sky

© 2022 by Sara Davison

Three Dreamers Press

Guelph, Ontario

ISBN: 978-1-7770646-2-4

All rights reserved. Except for brief excerpts for review purposes, no part of this book may be reproduced, stored in a retrieval system, or used in any form without prior written permission from the publisher.

This story is a work of fiction. All characters and events are the product of the author's imagination. Any resemblance to any person, living or dead, is coincidental.

Scripture quotations taken from the (NASB®) New American Standard Bible®, Copyright © 1995 by The Lockman Foundation. Used by permission. All rights reserved. www.lockman.org.

The Author is represented by the literary agency of WordServe Literary Group, Ltd, www.wordserveliterary.com.

Cover Design: Roseanna White of Roseanna White Designs

WELCOME TO THE MOSAIC COLLECTION

We are sisters, a beautiful mosaic united by the love of God through the blood of Christ.

Each month The Mosaic Collection releases one faith-based novel or anthology exploring our theme, Family by His Design, and sharing stories that feature diverse, God-designed families. All are contemporary stories ranging from mystery and women's fiction to comedic and literary fiction. We hope you'll join our Mosaic family as we explore together what truly defines a family.

If you're like us, loneliness and suffering have touched your life in ways you never imagined; but Dear One, while you may feel alone in your suffering—whatever it is—you are never alone!

Subscribe to *Grace & Glory*, the official newsletter of The Mosaic Collection, to receive monthly encouragement from Mosaic authors, as well as timely updates about events, new releases, and giveaways.

Learn more about The Mosaic Collection at
www.mosaiccollectionbooks.com

Join our Reader Community, too!
www.facebook.com/groups/TheMosaicCollection

BOOKS IN THE MOSAIC COLLECTION

When Mountains Sing by Stacy Monson
Unbound by Eleanor Bertin
The Red Journal by Deb Elkink
A Beautiful Mess by Brenda S. Anderson
Hope is Born: A Mosaic Christmas Anthology
More Than Enough by Lorna Seilstad
The Road to Happenstance by Janice L. Dick
This Side of Yesterday by Angela D. Meyer
Lost Down Deep by Sara Davison
The Mischief Thief by Johnnie Alexander
Before Summer's End: Stories to Touch the Soul
Tethered by Eleanor Bertin
Calm Before the Storm by Janice L. Dick
Heart Restoration by Regina Rudd Merrick
Pieces of Granite by Brenda S. Anderson
Watercolors by Lorna Seilstad
A Star Will Rise: A Mosaic Christmas Anthology II
Eye of the Storm by Janice L. Dick
Totally Booked: A Book Lover's Companion
Lifelines by Eleanor Bertin

The Third Grace by Deb Elkink
Crazy About Maisie by Janice L. Dick
Rebuilding Joy by Regina Rudd Merrick
Song of Grace: Stories to Amaze the Soul
Written in Ink by Sara Davison
Out of the Storm by Janice L. Dick
Open Circle by Stacy Monson
The Heart of Christmas: A Mosaic Christmas Anthology III
Broken Together by Brenda S. Anderson
Every Star in the Sky by Sara Davison

Learn more at
www.mosaiccollectionbooks.com/mosaic-books

PRAISE FOR SARA DAVISON'S NOVELS

The End Begins

"The first book in Davison's Seven Trilogy grips the reader from page one and holds on until the very end... Thought-provoking, relevant, and suspenseful, *The End Begins* is a must-read."
— *ROMANTIC TIMES*, 4½ Stars, *Top Pick*

The Darkness Deepens (formerly *The Dragon Roars*)

"Sara Davison's second book in The Seven Trilogy brings together all the essential elements of a good suspense read—compelling story, fast-paced action, and believable characters... Readers will not be disappointed in Davison's second book in the trilogy; it delivers!"
— LUANA EHRLICH, Author of *Titus Ray Thrillers*

The Morning Star Rises

"Another thrilling read from Sara Davison. Thrust into the midst of intrigue, terror, and a heartrending love story, you will sit on the edge of your seat…"

— BONNIE LEON, Best-selling Author of the Northern Lights series

Vigilant

"In *Vigilant*, Sara Davison has created deep characters and a story that will grab your heart and keep you on the edge of your seat. Days after reading the story, the characters are still on my mind."

— PATRICIA BRADLEY, Memphis Cold Case series, Winner of Inspirational Readers' Choice Award

"*Vigilant* is a unique, boundary-breaking suspense full of emotional depth. Davison's thought-provoking style will leave you breathless as you grapple with tough moral issues long after the story is over."

— RACHEL DYLAN, Bestselling Author of the Atlanta Justice series

Guarded

"*Guarded* is an intriguing, emotionally-charged romance coupled with spine-tingling suspense, and filled with well-crafted, loveable characters. Her exceptional story-telling and stellar writing make Sara Davison an author to watch."

—ELIZABETH GODDARD, bestselling author of the Uncommon Justice Series

"*Guarded* kept me reading late into the night. The hero was noble, the heroine strong in the face of tragedy, but the little boy, Jordan, stole the show."

—ROBIN PATCHEN, award-winning author of fourteen novels

Driven

"Sara Davison delivers an emotionally charged, tension-filled, entertaining story I couldn't put down…"

~NATALIE WALTERS, author of Carol award finalist *Living Lies* and the Harbored Secrets Series.

"A story of faith and healing, with characters so well-crafted that they come alive with every turn of the page. This book is a reminder that even in the quiet, pain-filled moments of our lives, God is with us."

~ C.C. WARRENS, author of The Holly Novels

The Watcher

"Sara Davison has written a unique and powerful story of love, loss, and redemption that will touch your heart and feed your spirit. I highly recommend *The Watcher*."

~ NANCY MEHL, author of the Quantico Files Series

Lost Down Deep (Winner of the 2021 Carol Award for Romantic Suspense)

"If you're looking for a good mystery with a hint of suspense, a dash of sweetness, and whole lot of charm, then you've come to the right book. *Lost Down Deep* immediately plunges you into a mystery and keeps you guessing until the very end. With a picturesque small town as the backdrop, and charming characters to boot, this novel was quite a sweet read!"

~ CHRISTI F., Amazon Reviewer

Written in Ink

"Page after page, Ms. Davison raises the stakes, urging the reader on with challenges and danger—and faith. The brutal honesty of the characters, the unpretty unpolished human factor. The steadfastness of Father God, ever faithful, even to His unbelieving children.

"A powerful story of self-doubt and broken hearts, the depth of true love, and the reach of Divine love."

~ ROBIN E. MASON, Amazon Reviewer

To all those who risk their lives to rescue and support those caught up in human trafficking. As you have done it for the least of these, you have done it for Jesus.

And to every person who has been a victim of this horrific evil. El Roi—the God who sees—knows what you have been through. He knows your name. And he has never abandoned you.

You are always in his care.

Lift up your eyes on high And see who has created these stars, The One who leads forth their host by number, He calls them all by name; Because of the greatness of His might and the strength of His power, Not one of them is missing.

Isaiah 40:26

CHAPTER ONE

"Desiree's pregnant."

The words, whispered from girl to girl and accompanied by furtive glances around to make sure no one else was nearby, turned the blood ice cold as it coursed through Starr. *No.* How could this have happened? Whenever Brady brought a new girl in, the first thing he did was call for the doctor to come examine her and insert an IUD. Brady prided himself on running a clean house and on ensuring that none of the girls contracted any diseases. Or got pregnant.

Starr had known it to happen only once in the eight years since she'd been forced into service for Brady. *Bella.* She shuddered. Within hours of Bella whispering her secret to Starr between bouts of weeping and plaintive pleas for help, Brady and one of his men had dragged Bella from her room in the dark of night.

Starr never saw her again.

Grabbing a short, pink satin robe from her closet, she slipped into the hallway and crept toward Desiree's room. Somehow they had to keep Brady from discovering the truth before they could figure out what to do to help her.

Boots thudded along the hallway from the other direction. Too late. Starr stopped a few yards from Desiree's room and melded into a shadowy doorway. Her breath tangled in her throat. Brady and two of his men. They stopped outside Desiree's room, and Brady jerked his head at the door. One of the men with him flung it open, and the three of them disappeared into the room. Desiree cried out and Starr pressed her eyes shut. Her heart thudded against her rib cage. Was there anything she could do?

Several other doors along the hall slid open a crack, but no one else dared step out of their rooms.

"Starr!" Desiree's anguished cry as Brady's henchmen dragged her into the hallway spurred Starr into action.

She pushed away from the doorway and made her way toward the group on trembling legs. "Brady."

Brady stood with his back to her, arms crossed over his chest, as hard and unmoveable as an oak. "Stay out of this, Starr. It's not your business." His voice held a steel-cold warning.

Normally she would have heeded that warning, knowing what would happen if she didn't. Tonight, she couldn't.

With her light brown skin—an inheritance from her Filipino mother—and piercing blue eyes from a Caucasian father she'd never known, Starr was in high demand among Brady's clients. She earned him far more money than any of the other girls. Sometimes that meant she had a little more leeway than the rest of them to talk back to him.

Desiree yanked her arm away from one of the men and reached for Starr, her gold charm bracelet jangling against her wrist. The man grasped her arm again and twisted it behind her back. Desiree whimpered. Starr summoned up every ounce of courage she had. "Please don't do this, Brady. I'll take care of her, I promise."

"She was stupid enough to get pregnant; she deserves what she gets."

Heat rushed through Starr. "Stupid? Do you think she asked to have an endless line of disgusting men coming to her and—"

Even before he moved, she knew she'd gone too far. Brady uncrossed his arms and whirled around, his eyes as gold and hard as amber. "Stay with Desiree," he ordered the men over his shoulder as he started for Starr. Before she could get out of his way, he had wrapped his fingers around her elbow in an iron-tight grasp and hauled her along the hall to the doorway of her room. Starr bit her lip to keep from crying out at the pain that shot up and down her arm. Brady stopped and spun her around to face him. He looked like something out of Greek mythology—tall, blond, and muscular with a close-trimmed beard. His good looks and the charm he could turn off and on at will had lured more than one woman into this house. Of course, they found out quickly that the gorgeous exterior masked a cold, cruel monster. By then it was too late. "If you say one more word, I'll let the boys handle Desiree while you and I take a trip to the basement."

His face was so close to hers his breath brushed warm across her cheek. The intense fury roaring through her was doused immediately.

Brady did not allow drugs in his house. He preferred to use intimidation and fear to keep everyone in line, and he yielded both weapons with the deadly effectiveness of a Samurai warrior. Terror rose to take the place of anger, drying out Starr's mouth and throat so she couldn't have spoken if she wanted to.

Brady dug his fingers into bone. "Is that what you want?"

Starr held out for three seconds, her eyes welded on his, before shaking her head slightly.

"I didn't think so." Brady shoved her through the doorway.

"Do not let me see you again tonight or that's exactly what will happen."

He slammed the door. Starr stalked over and grabbed the knob. Then Brady's threat hacked its way through her muddled thoughts and she stopped, paralyzed. *The basement.* Slowly she let go and backed away. When she reached the wall, she slid along it to the floor, wrapping her arms around her legs and lowering her head to her knees.

Brady never made idle threats. If she opened the door to her room, he *would* take her to the basement. After what had happened there the last time, she doubted she would survive the trip. Even given her value to him, she had no illusions about her standing in this house—he wouldn't hesitate to kill her if she crossed another line with him, if only to make an example of her to the others.

Her elbow throbbed, and wave after wave of cold chills shuddered through her. *Jesus, help Desiree. I can't. Only you can.* Her chest ached, but she didn't cry. She'd wept almost every night the first year she'd been brought to this house. After Bella was taken away, she stopped weeping. What good did tears do? Only got her in more trouble if she was caught shedding them.

"Starr."

The heart-rending cry drifted along the hallway. Starr let go of her legs and buried her face in her hands. If she lived to be a hundred years old—which, given the life she'd been dragged into against her will, wasn't likely—she would never forget the sound of Desiree calling out her name in the night before she disappeared forever.

CHAPTER TWO

Cole Blacksky rapped on the frame, hesitant to enter the office even though the door stood partway open. "You asked to see me, Chief?"

His boss stopped writing and tossed his pen onto the large pile of paperwork on his desk. "Blacksky. Come in. And close the door." After Cole complied, the chief gestured to the black plastic chair across from him. "Sit."

Cole had no idea what this was about. He'd been with the Sudbury Police Force for seven years, five of them under this chief, so he was pretty familiar with the drill and didn't think he was in trouble. Of course, since his father's death six months earlier, he might have been a little less than a hundred percent focused. Part of the complex grieving process after losing someone with whom he'd had a … complicated relationship.

The chief crossed his arms over his massive chest. "I have an assignment for you if you're interested in heading to the city for a few weeks."

Hmm. Cole had done a bit of undercover work here, but

he'd never been tasked to do anything in Toronto. That could be interesting. "What's the assignment?"

"A few days ago, a young woman went to the Toronto PD. Told them that, when she was sixteen years old, she'd been lured into captivity by a trafficker in the city, a guy the PD knows only as *Brady*."

Cole scowled. Sex traffickers. Lowest form of life on the planet, as far as he was concerned.

The chief picked up the pen and tapped it on the pile of papers. "Ever hear of him?"

"I don't think so."

"He's on the province's top ten list, but we've never been able to make a strong enough case to bring him in. Apparently this woman, Carmen DeSoto—who went by *Bella* when she worked for Brady—discovered she was pregnant. Brady found out, and he and a couple of his men took her out of the city, beat her up badly, and left her for dead in the woods. Somehow she survived and got herself to safety. She never went to the police because she believed Brady would kill her."

"Which he probably would have."

The chief nodded. "In any case, she finally came in. Claims she couldn't take the guilt of knowing so many girls were still being forced to work for Brady. She wants to testify against him."

Cole's eyebrows rose. "Really." Although he hadn't worked many sex trade cases in his career, he was aware of how close to impossible it was to find anyone willing to testify against an active trafficker. The time the girls spent in captivity taught them a lot of things, chief among them to keep their mouths shut about what was going on or risk being beaten, tortured, or killed. Most women were too terrified—and had developed survival skills that were far too strong—to willingly put themselves in that position. Cole couldn't blame them—although, as someone in law enforcement whose hands were so often tied when it came to bringing these guys in and setting the women free, it was incredibly frustrating.

"What do they want me to do?"

"The Crown's asking for one more solid witness before the PD moves in on this guy. Someone who's more familiar with Brady's current operation. Carmen gave us the name of a girl who'd been in the house with her. Said she was a lot stronger than most of them, even tried to take care of the rest of them when she could. Carmen thinks that, if we can get her out of the house and take her somewhere safe, she might agree to testify. She's older, almost twenty-six, although she was seventeen when she was brought in."

Cole winced. Eight years as a slave in the sex trade. She'd have to be pretty broken, and more than likely an addict. How reliable a witness could she be? "You want me to meet with her?"

"Yes. Ms. DeSoto told us where to find Brady's girls online and the protocol for booking an appointment. The PD wants you to set one up as though you're a john and talk to this girl, see if she'd be open to the idea. If you can get a solid commitment from her, they'll extract her."

"It would take time to get her to trust me." If she ever did. Trust in a strange man would be nearly impossible to cultivate in a woman who'd been through what she had.

"Of course. Toronto is fine with moving slowly on this, as they're reeling in a big fish they don't want to slip off the hook."

"I'd have to pay every time I met with her."

"There's not a huge budget, given recent cutbacks, but you'll be able to pay for a few visits at least."

Going after one of the city's biggest sex traffickers was a leap from the types of cases Cole typically dealt with. "Why me?"

"Toronto needs someone who isn't on their force. Chances

are good Brady has a file on all their guys and would identify them as soon as they showed up, even if they used an alias, like you would." The chief touched the pen tip to a notepad in front of him. "Laken Jones, the lead guy on this case, recommended you."

Ah. Cole and Lake had met the first day of academy training, hit it off immediately, and been best friends ever since. They'd never worked together though. If Lake was heading up this task force, Cole was interested. "When would I start?"

"If you accept the assignment—and you're welcome to take a day or two to think about it—Toronto wants you to come in as soon as possible. Each day that Brady remains in power, girls suffer."

Cole exhaled. "I get it."

"All right, then." The chief tapped the top of the desk with his palm. "Let me know as soon as you decide."

"I will." Cole headed for the door. When he reached it, he turned back. "Can I ask the girl's name?"

The chief flipped over the page on the notepad. "They didn't use last names in the house, so Carmen knows her by only one name, probably not her real one. If you do go in, you'll be looking for a woman who goes by the name of Starr."

CHAPTER THREE

When Starr woke, dusk was falling over the city. Outside the window set high in the wall of the room she shared with Ruby, her best friend in the house, she caught glimpses of gray sky between the leaves and branches of a big maple tree.

Almost time to go to work.

She lay there for several minutes, not anxious to leave her bed—the one she didn't have to share with strangers. *Jesus, help me. Give me the strength to get through another night.*

During her time in the house, two girls had killed themselves—Jasmine, who'd used a chair to smash a hotel window and jump out after a john left and before the guard stationed outside her room could get in, and Ebony, who'd broken into the cabinet Brady kept under lock and key and downed enough medication to kill her long before they found her the next morning.

Starr got it. She'd nearly sunk to that level of desperation and hopelessness countless times. Two things kept her going. First, the other girls needed her. If she could offer them the slightest hope or encouragement, she wouldn't look for a way out. Second, her faith; God alone gave her the courage to leave her bed every evening and do what she had to do.

With a sigh, she tossed her covers off. Ruby's bed was neatly made. She must have gone to the kitchen to grab something to eat. Starr showered quickly and threw on a T-shirt and jeans before heading out of her room. To her right, the hallway led to the small area that served as a cafeteria for the twelve girls who lived in this house and were compelled, against their will, to work for Brady.

The aroma of stale coffee hung in the air when Starr entered the windowless room. Most of the girls sat around the tables staring into mugs of hot drinks or playing with the food on their plates. Few spoke, although most did offer a brief reply when Starr greeted them. This time of day—when they'd been yanked from the short reprieve that came with sleep and were mentally preparing themselves for what the next few hours would bring—was typically somber in the cafeteria. Starr poured a cup of coffee and checked the clock magnets on the front of the fridge. Hers was set to 7 pm, her first appointment for the evening. That gave her less than an hour to eat and get ready to go.

The latest addition to the house, a young girl named Willow who couldn't be more than sixteen, came over clutching an empty mug. Starr filled it for her before setting the carafe on the hot pad.

Willow had been with them only a few weeks. Unlike Starr, she hadn't been grabbed off the street. As she'd whispered over dinner one night, she'd been lured in through a dating site. After weeks of exchanging messages with a person she believed was a nice eighteen-year-old guy, she agreed to meet him. The *nice guy* dated her a few times before turning her over to Brady. Willow had witnessed the transaction, and the betrayal of the one she thought had cared about her seemed to have shattered her as much as what had happened in the house since.

Ruby's story was similar, and several other girls—those who were willing to talk about it—had told Starr the same sad tale. It was so easy for a predator with a computer—especially a professional like Brady with nearly unlimited resources—to deceive young girls. Particularly girls with little or no family support and a desire to find love and acceptance any way they could. Something like that might have happened to Starr, too, only she'd made it a lot easier for them.

For Brady.

Starr shook off the memory to focus on Willow. The initial terror she had given off in waves after arriving had abated a little. Although she seemed more resigned to her fate now, she hadn't yet adopted the air of utter defeat most of the other girls wore like a garment.

"Guess what I saw on the way to the hotel yesterday, Starr?"

The excitement in Willow's voice, an unusual sound in this house, had several of the girls glancing over.

Starr mustered a smile. "What did you see?"

"A baby in a stroller on the sidewalk outside my car window. She had on this sundress with flowers all over it and a pink bonnet. She was so adorable." Willow cradled the warm mug to her chest. "Someday I want to have a baby like that. Do you think I will?"

Starr met Ruby's gaze over Willow's shoulder. Ruby shook her head, a warning.

Starr couldn't bring herself to take it. She slid an arm around Willow's thin shoulders. The young girl's short, purple hair, starting to show blonde at the roots, brushed against Starr's arm. "Of course you will, sweetie. Someday you'll get out of here and meet a man who actually treats you well, and you will have lots of babies together."

Willow rested her head on Starr's shoulder. Starr ached at the perpetual confusion in the girl's jade eyes, as though she couldn't begin to comprehend what was happening to her. Was anyone looking for her? Brady was good at picking his girls. As far as Starr knew, none of them had family that cared about them and who would refuse to stop searching or let the police forget about them. Starr herself had run away from foster care the night Brady's men picked her up, although she'd seen the white van they had dragged her into in her neighborhood numerous times and suspected they had been watching her long before that.

She should stop talking. By unspoken house rule, they never mentioned the outside world. Not even their real names. For the first time since being brought into the house, though, Willow had a smile on her face. Several of the other girls did, too, and Starr felt a desperate need to go on, to shine a little more light into the darkness of their life.

She touched her head to Willow's. "One day all of this will be over, and you will be free. You'll be able to go shopping at the mall or see a movie, maybe take a trip to Hawaii and lie on a beach. Brady can't keep us here for—"

A palpable fear poured through the room like smoke after an explosion. Several girls stared at the doorway behind Starr. Her heart sank as she let go of Willow. Starr had let her guard down. Normally she situated herself in a room where she could see the door, prepared for Brady or one of his men to appear any time without warning. This evening she'd been so concerned about Willow and the others that she'd failed to take her usual precautions.

Now she would pay the price.

"Everyone go get ready. Cars start leaving in half an hour." Brady's voice held barely restrained fury. "Starr, you stay here."

The other girls scrambled to obey. Willow hesitated, but

Starr nudged her in the side gently and whispered, "Do what he says." The sooner Willow learned that rule, the better things would go for her. A couple of girls sent Starr a sympathetic look as they passed by, but most avoided glancing in her direction. Each one was careful to drop her plastic juice bottle in the blue recycling bin next to the door. Brady might not care about people, but he was inflexible when it came to saving the planet.

In seconds, Starr was alone in the room with him. A few drops of coffee splashed over the rim as she set her cup on the counter. *Jesus, help me.*

Brady crossed the room to her slowly, methodically. "Why are you filling that girl's head with talk of getting out?"

"I was trying to comfort her."

He reached her, grabbed her upper arms, and squeezed hard, yanking her to her tiptoes. "Save your *comfort* for the men who pay good money for it."

They don't pay me. The defiant thought was dangerous, since Brady had an uncanny ability to read that defiance in her eyes, as she'd found out the hard way countless times. "Why don't you let her go, Brady? She's just a terrified kid."

He abruptly released her arms. The backhand caught her across the cheek so hard Starr stumbled into the counter and had to grasp the edge of it to keep from falling.

"When are you going to learn to mind your own business?" He grabbed a handful of her long, dark hair and yanked back her head. White-hot prickles of shock radiated across her scalp. "If you can't do that, maybe you're the one who needs to go."

Starr was painfully aware that he didn't mean he would set her free—only that, like Bella and Desiree, she would be hauled away and never seen again.

Neither spoke or moved for a few seconds. Any word from her, any spark of insolence in her eyes, and he would hit her again. Repeatedly. Or maybe he'd simply issue the order for his men to take her. When she offered him neither, he exhaled, let go of her hair, and cupped her throbbing cheek. "Why do you make me hurt you, Starr? Do you think I enjoy it? I care about you and it's hard for me to have to punish you. You know that, don't you?"

It took everything Starr had not to recoil from his touch. Or to believe what he was saying. She'd known him far too long, seen too much. Brady was incapable of kindness. It was only another tool he wielded against them, keeping them off-balance and entangling them even more deeply in his web of control. Starr fought the pull. Kindness withered and died in this place. Even the girls, despite Starr's best efforts, were often cruel to each other, taking out their fear, self-loathing, and hopelessness on the easy targets around them.

So Brady's words sucked her in, mesmerized her for a few seconds like the eyes of a deadly cobra, until she was able to tear herself away.

He dropped his hand. "I hear you talking to Willow or anyone else like that again and you'll get far more than a slap across the face. Do you understand me?"

Too drained to fight him anymore today, Starr nodded. "Yes."

"Then go get ready. And for the next few days, until I tell you otherwise, go straight to your room in the morning and don't leave it until it's time to go to the hotel at night."

No food, then. And she hadn't eaten today, either. Starr glanced wistfully at the boxes of cereal and packets of instant oatmeal next to the cup of coffee she hadn't taken a sip from. How long would he make her go without this time? The record was six days. She'd have to warn Ruby not to try to sneak her anything, as Brady would be watching her roommate closely and they'd both pay for it if she did.

Starr stifled a surge of bitterness. Next to hopelessness,

bitterness was her biggest enemy. She had fought it every moment since arriving in this house. If she gave into it, as most of the girls had, she might never claw her way out, even if she did manage to get free of Brady one day.

Leaving behind the food and the untouched hot drink, she stepped around him and crossed the room.

"Starr."

She stopped in the doorway and faced him.

"So you know, if Willow or any other girl tries something stupid because of what you said, her blood will be on your hands."

The warmth drained from Starr's body. Brady always knew exactly where to stick the knife. She'd never known anyone to escape his clutches. Three girls had tried since Starr had been here. All three attempts had been thwarted and the consequences to the girls so horrific no one dared try again for years. What if the portrait of outside life Starr had painted for Willow resulted in the girl or anyone who'd overheard them deciding to go after that life?

Brady pointed. "Go."

Starr spun on her heel and made her way to her room. She'd keep a close eye on Willow and the other girls for the next few days and weeks, make sure no one was planning anything that could get her hurt. Or worse.

Brady was right. If anyone did try to escape, whatever happened to the girl when she was caught—likely a night of ice in the basement—would be entirely Starr's fault.

CHAPTER FOUR

This was one of the wildest situations Cole had found himself in since becoming a police office when he was twenty-three years old. In the seven years since, he'd often encountered women in the sex trade—on the streets, sometimes, but mostly at the station. He'd never approached one while working undercover as a john before, which was a whole new perspective. What would Starr be like? He'd paid two hundred dollars for twenty minutes with her, which suggested her services were in high demand. And he'd seen a picture of her on the site, so he had at least a sense of what she looked like, although he didn't trust that the photo hadn't been doctored.

He sighed as he pulled into the parking lot of the hotel and glanced at the digital clock on the dashboard. 9:56. His appointment was for 10 pm, and every ten-dollar minute counted, so he didn't want to be late. Especially since it had taken him four days to get an appointment with Starr.

After Cole had paid online with the card the PD had given him, he'd been given the room number and instructed to go straight up when he arrived, so he strolled past the front desk without stopping. His cheeks warmed a little. Did the clerk know what was going on upstairs? Had disgust crossed his face as he watched Cole head for the elevators?

Cole shook off the embarrassment. He knew why he was there—it didn't particularly matter what strangers thought. He stepped off the elevator on the fourth floor. Room 421 was easy to find, as a Latino man in a black T-shirt, muscles bulging across the chest and shoulders, pushed away from the frame as Cole approached. He gestured to a spot next to the door. "Hands on the wall."

Cole complied. The man ran his hands over Cole's torso and legs. He'd never been on the receiving end of a frisking before and suddenly had an increased empathy for anyone he'd arrested at the feeling of violation. Of course, given what the woman in the room he was about to enter went through on a nightly basis, he likely shouldn't use that word to describe his experience.

When Cole turned around, the man gave him a hard look. "No rough stuff."

"Got it." This Brady guy ran a tight ship. Although Cole doubted the man hesitated to use violence himself with the girls who worked for him, he clearly did not allow their clients the same leeway. Not with Starr, anyway.

The man pushed open the door, stepped into the room, and waited for Cole to go through. With barely a glance at the woman sitting on the edge of the bed, the security guard left the room.

Show time.

Starr sat, long legs crossed, her palms pressed to the mattress behind her as Cole walked over. His breath hitched a little in his throat when their eyes met. Although he knew from her picture that she was attractive, the photographer had failed by a long shot to capture how compelling she was. The piercing, sapphire-blue eyes combined with her light brown skin was a killer combination. It was more than that, though. Something shone in her eyes that Cole couldn't quite put a finger on. They hadn't gone empty and cold like those of other women he'd encountered who had been forced into this life. No sign that she was high or stoned either, which was encouraging.

Cole picked up the robe draped over a chair next to the bed and handed it to her. "Would you mind putting this on?" The pale blue teddy would not only be a distraction as they talked, but he needed to establish from the outset that he wasn't there to get what she thought he was, which might help her relax a little.

Her lips twitched slightly as she accepted the robe and slung it around her shoulders. "Putting more clothes on—that's a request I don't get often."

Was that *amusement* in her eyes? Cole didn't know what to make of this woman. How could she have kept a sense of humor through everything she'd endured? If he hadn't seen her picture, and the bodyguard outside her door, he'd think he had accidentally wandered into the wrong room.

She slipped her arms into the sleeves of the robe and knotted the tie around her waist. "Better?"

"Yes, actually." Cole shot a look at the door. How soundproof was this room? "Do you mind if I play music?"

She lifted slender shoulders. "It's your dime, handsome."

Cole flinched at the reminder that every man who came to see her had paid money to be there. Even with the stern warning from the Hispanic Rocky Balboa in the hallway, the type of men who would do that likely believed it gave them the right to do whatever they wanted to her. He hit a button to start one of his playlists and set the phone on the bedside table next to a box of condoms. Looked like Brady took other precautions to protect the women who worked for him. Cole pulled the chair nearer the bed.

The woman patted the mattress. "You could sit closer, you know."

"I'm good here." He shot another look at the door before leaning in. "It's Starr, right?" While that likely wasn't her real name, they were a long way from her being willing to share the one she'd been given at birth with him.

"That's right. Although you can call me whatever you like."

"I'm Cole." He held out his hand. It was a calculated risk, giving her his real name instead of the alias he'd provided on the website, but he'd do whatever it took to convince her he was telling the truth.

Her lips twitched again as she shook it, her hand small and cool in his. A barcode-looking tattoo on the inside of her left wrist caught his eye. Brady's mark. Cole swallowed. "I'm only here to talk."

"If that's what you want." She ran a finger along his arm. Her voice had gone soft and sultry. Cole had no trouble understanding why she was able to command the amount of money she was. Still, this close to her, he could see the tightness in her features, the hint of cynicism in her eyes, the sunken cheeks that suggested she might not have eaten for a few days—a common way for traffickers to keep their captives in line. And the discoloration on her face that looked to be a three- or four-day-old bruise. His jaw tightened. Was that the work of a john or compliments of Brady? In any case, this wasn't fun for her. She was clearly playing a role, and, while she was very, very good at it—enough that for a few seconds he'd almost forgotten what he was there for, and what he wasn't—she wasn't doing this by choice.

In that moment, resolve crystallized in him. Nothing would stop him from extricating this woman from the life she'd been forced into. Or from figuring out how to keep her safe after he did.

Except possibly Starr herself.

He had to talk her into agreeing to testify against Brady. And somehow he'd have to get her to trust him, or she wouldn't agree to go with him, no matter how many promises he made to keep her safe on the outside. Of course, he'd also have to figure out how to keep that promise. The Toronto PD had informed him they couldn't approve full witness protection, although they'd do their best to keep an eye on her.

Cole contemplated her. Their best wouldn't be good enough.

Starr's finger stilled on his wrist. "Was there anything in particular you wanted to talk about?"

This was the moment of truth. In addition to the fear of retaliation, it was common for girls to form a Stockholm-syndrome type of affectionate bond with their traffickers. And to demonstrate a loyalty to them that defied rational explanation. When Cole told Starr he was a cop helping the PD bring down Brady, she could easily call in the big guy from the hall and tell him what was going on, and Cole would end up in a dumpster before morning.

He clenched and unclenched his fingers, trying to dispel the pent-up tension. Her blue eyes gravitated to his fists, and she stiffened slightly.

Did she think he was going to hit her? Horrified, Cole flattened his hands against his jeans. Now or never. The music should cover any conversation, but still he lowered his voice. "Here's the thing. I'm a detective on undercover assignment for the Toronto PD."

Nothing changed in her expression. "Okay, you're a cop. What should I be?" She said the words lightly, almost teasingly, but Cole picked up on the current of weary resignation.

"No. I'm not playing games, Starr. I'm telling you the truth. I work for the PD. We're trying to bring Brady in and shut down his operation. But we need your help."

Starr stared at him a moment before her gaze flitted to the

door. When it settled on his face again, fear had sparked in her eyes. She straightened, clutching the top of her robe. "Why should I believe you?" The sultriness was gone from her voice.

Huh. Good question. "Technically, I have no way to prove it. I didn't think it would be a good idea to bring my badge with me. Or my gun."

Her smile was faint, almost non-existent. "No, it definitely would not have been."

"I could answer any questions on police protocol if you want to test me."

"A hardened criminal would know all that."

He offered her a wry grin. "Do I look like a hardened criminal?"

"No, but you don't really look like a cop, either."

Cole had been told that before, although he wasn't sure what it meant. At thirty, he was a bit younger than a lot of his colleagues, and he'd inherited his dark hair and eyes from his Anishinaabe grandmother as well as his mother—whom he'd never had a chance to meet—so maybe that was it. "I guess you'll have to trust me, then." Which wasn't likely. The last thing the woman in front of him would be inclined to do was trust any man.

She bit her lip as she studied him, no doubt running through the long list in her mind of all the terrible things that could happen if she did. "Why me?"

"A woman who used to work for Brady came to the PD recently, saying she wants to testify against him. She gave us your name as someone else who might be willing to be a witness if we got you away from him."

Starr narrowed her eyes. "I find that hard to believe. I don't know any woman who's left Brady and lived to tell about it."

"This one did. Barely."

"What's her name?"

"Carmen DeSoto. Although she went by *Bella* when she was with Brady."

Starr jerked as though a current of electricity had zapped through her. "Bella?" She whispered the name before pressing trembling fingers to her lips.

"Yes." Given her strong reaction, she clearly remembered Carmen, which was helpful. "She said she was taken to the woods outside the city five years ago by Brady and a couple of men. They beat her up and left her there, but she survived."

For a moment, Starr didn't respond, only appeared to be working hard to keep drawing in one breath after another. Then she lowered her hand. "I'm not saying I believe you, although I don't know how you would know about her if you weren't who you say you are. Even so, I'm not sure I'm willing to risk helping you get Brady. You heard what he did to Bella."

Starr had bent forward a little and lowered her voice to barely above a whisper, although there was no way anyone in the hall could hear them. Unless they'd placed a microphone in the room. Was that possible?

Cole exhaled. Anything was possible, given how successful Brady had been at eluding arrest to this point and how much money and power he'd amassed over the last decade. That was a chance he and Starr would have to take. A faint floral scent drifted from her, and Cole worked to stay focused. "I know what could happen, believe me. All I can promise is that we'll do everything possible to keep him from getting to you."

She gazed at him in silence for several seconds before drawing in a deep breath. "I'm not saying I'll do it, but, out of curiosity, what would be your plan if I did?"

"We'd take you out and then keep you safe somewhere until Brady's trial."

She tilted her head. The movement sent her long, dark hair cascading over her bare upper arm, not quite hiding fading bruises clearly left by someone's fingers. His jaw tightened.

"That's your entire plan?"

Cole reflected on his words. They did sound a little vague. His priority had been establishing contact with her, feeling her out to see if she would consider attempting an escape and being a witness against Brady. He hadn't thought out a lot of details beyond that. "So far."

"This isn't *Pretty Woman*, Detective, and I'm not Julia Roberts. I can't simply walk out the door and start my glamorous new life."

She didn't offer him even a faint smile this time, although she was clearly joking. Or maybe she wasn't. Of course she couldn't just walk away.

"I know that."

"Do you?" Any trace of humor was gone. "If Brady caught the slightest hint that I was even talking to a cop, let alone making plans to escape, he would not hesitate for a second to kill me. And that might be the best I could hope for from him." Her features remained neutral, but the quiver in her voice revealed her terror of the man who held her captive. Cole didn't want to think about what Brady had done to instill that kind of fear in her.

Or what he could do yet.

"I understand. And I swear I don't take that lightly. Before we make any move, I'll work out every detail for getting you away from him and for protecting you until the trial."

The skeptical look that crossed her face suggested she doubted his—or anyone's—ability to guarantee her safety if she agreed to cross Brady. "I haven't said I'd do it. I need to think about it."

"Of course. Take as long as you need. The PD is fine with moving slowly, making sure they have an ironclad case against Brady, so they can take him down for good." He propped his elbows on his knees and clasped his hands, imploring her to hear him. "I want you to know that, if you agree to this, I'll do everything in my power to help you get free of this life. And to free every woman Brady is forcing to work for him. You want that, don't you?"

Most of the women Cole had encountered in her position refused to make eye contact. In contrast, Starr stared so deeply into his eyes that for the first time in his life he fully understood the expression *windows to the soul*. He had to work not to squirm under her intense scrutiny.

"Of course I do, but the price of failure would be high, not only to me but to you."

"I'm willing to take that chance if you are."

"I'm not sure I am."

"That's fair. No one is going to force you." He hesitated. "Would you consider telling me where you're being held?" At the very least, they could watch the place, maybe catch Brady assaulting one of the women, something they could charge him with that might stick. It wouldn't keep him behind bars as long as they'd like, but it should give the PD the opportunity to move in and free the women.

Before Starr could answer, someone rapped on the door. "That's your two-minute warning." She rose and swayed a little on her feet. How long had she gone without food, anyway? Cole started to reach for her but stopped when she steadied herself on the bedside table. She inclined her head toward his gray shirt. "You might want to look a little less put together when you go out."

While Cole untucked and re-tucked the shirt a little less neatly, she pulled back the bedspread and rumpled the sheets. Warmth crept up his neck. Of course they'd have to make it look as though they'd done more than talk while he was in here. Those were the kinds of details he needed to include in his plan if he didn't want to put Starr in any more danger than necessary.

Starr slid off her robe and hung it over the chair. Cole stepped closer. "I give you my word that I'll put a lot of thought and effort into this, Starr. We'll work out a concrete plan that will involve the least amount of risk. And I'll come back as soon as possible so we can talk more."

She nodded. Then, as though afraid she might change her mind, she blurted out, "I don't know the number because there isn't one on the house, but it's a big place with yellow siding at the southwest corner of Lake and Huron Streets."

Cole blinked, amazed at her courage when she still had no idea if she could trust him. "That's extremely helpful. Thank you."

A buzzing sound indicated that someone had used the key card in the door. Starr ran her fingers through her hair as though straightening it as the big man from the hallway pushed it open. "Time's up."

Cole wanted to shoot her one last look but didn't dare. The bodyguard stayed where he was as Cole approached, so he had to brush by him to step into the hallway.

He felt the man's eyes on him as he strode for the exit. Did the guard suspect something? If he did, Cole could be throwing Starr to the wolves, leaving her alone with a man who would drag her straight to Brady if he thought anything was going on.

Given the precarious positions he often found himself in on the job, Cole sometimes wished he had a faith in a higher power. Never had he wished for that as hard as he did in that moment. Although he'd long rejected the idea of an authority figure in the sky glaring down at him in disapproval—he'd gotten more than enough of that from his father growing up —right now he desperately wanted to implore some kind of deity to watch over Starr until Cole could meet with her again. Because he couldn't protect her. Not yet.

And that thought sent far more fear coursing through him than he would have thought possible before he'd stepped inside Starr's hotel room twenty minutes earlier.

CHAPTER FIVE

Starr sat on the bed in the room she shared with Ruby, her back against the wall and her knees pulled to her chest. Her stomach growled, and she held a hand to her abdomen, trying to ignore the aching emptiness. Despite her hunger, the man who'd come to see her the night before dominated her thoughts. Cole. Had he actually been in her hotel room, or was her memory of his visit merely a hunger-induced hallucination?

If he *had* come, could she trust that he actually wanted to pull her out of this life? Was there a chance she could be free, that she could return to the world she'd described to Willow only a few days ago? Starr touched both palms to her cheeks. And was he telling the truth about Bella?

She threw a panicked look at the door, as though Brady might be able to read her thoughts from somewhere in the house and come storming in. Starr had often wondered if Brady *could* read her mind. He did seem to have extra-sensory perception when it came to her, as though he could discern every emotion, every fleeting thought. He'd even, on occasion, punished her for them before she uttered a word. If he had been telling the truth that day in the cafeteria—which she knew he hadn't been—that had to have been very *hard* on him. Starr rolled her eyes and immediately sent another terrified look in the direction of the door. Eye rolling brought more fury and violence raining down on the girls than any other action in this house, and she rarely allowed herself the luxury of performing it, even alone in her room.

The detective's visit had clearly infused her with a new level of courage and defiance she could not afford to indulge if she wanted to live long enough to at least hear his plan. Starr grabbed her pillow and wrapped her arms around it, trying to repress the intense longings surging up in her. For freedom from captivity. From fear. From having to do things every night that sickened and disgusted her. Most of all, from helplessly watching as the other girls, especially the young, confused ones like Willow, suffered with no hope of their unspeakable degradation ever ending.

What if she could change that—not only for herself but for all of them?

Starr rested her chin on the pillow. Longing was dangerous and, although it had sustained her since the night Brady's men dragged her here, so was hope. Normally she wouldn't have given that cop the opportunity to talk to her about what he was thinking of doing. He'd caught her at the right time, though, when her conversation with Willow was fresh on her mind.

And when she hadn't eaten in four days.

She'd been weak and vulnerable, or she would never have listened to a word he had to say.

Maybe he wouldn't come back. After he'd seen her in person—understood the kinds of acts she performed to avoid a beating, or worse—he might have decided she was not worth the risk. Which would be for the best. He'd stay away from her, and her life could return to the way it had been before he strolled into her hotel room.

Emotions sparked in her, as tangled as the Christmas lights her foster mother had pulled out of the box of decorations every year. Before Starr could try to sort them out, the doorknob turned.

Her head jerked in that direction. *Brady.* The door opened slowly. Ruby slipped through the opening and closed the door. Although Starr knew how risky it would have been for her roommate to bring her food, her heart sank at the sight of her friend's empty hands. Ruby walked over and dropped onto the mattress next to her. "Nine was loitering around the cafeteria, so I couldn't take the chance. I'm sorry."

Brady's men all looked and acted so similar, so much more like machines than human beings, that the girls simply referred to them by number. The men were all tall with the kind of muscles no one developed without regularly ingesting performance-enhancing drugs. Some were white, some black, some Latino, some Asian, but they all had hard faces, hard eyes, and hard fists.

Starr reached for her friend's hand. "I'm glad you didn't. I'm fine."

Ruby squeezed her fingers. "You're not fine. I don't know how he expects you to work when you haven't eaten for days."

Starr shrugged. Brady had countless ways to ensure she kept working—and kept her customers satisfied—regardless of whether she'd been allowed to eat. Every one of the rare times a john had complained about her, she'd been given the opportunity to experience a different one of those ways. Fed or not, she would do what she had to do that night, and she would do it well.

"Ruby." Starr bent her head closer to her friend.

"Yeah?"

"If something happens to me, will you promise me something?"

Ruby frowned. "What are you talking about? What do you think is going to happen?"

"Likely nothing. But if it did, would you keep an eye on Willow? She has no idea how things work around here. I'm worried Brady will do something terrible to her one of these days, and I honestly don't think she'd survive it."

Ruby's grip on her fingers tightened. "I don't know, Starr. I'm not like you. I'm not brave enough to stand up to him."

"No, don't do that." Ruby was so terrified of Brady she refused to say his name, only referred to him as *he* and then only if she absolutely had to speak of him. It wouldn't help Willow if Ruby got dragged into the situation, and it would only make things worse for Ruby. "I only meant that if you see her heading for trouble, warn her she shouldn't do or say something before it's too late."

Ruby bit her lip. "I'll try. But I don't know what I'd do myself if something happened to you. What would any of us do if—?"

Starr held a finger to her lips. Her muscles clenched at the sound of thudding boots in the hallway—never a good sign. Was it Brady? Had he somehow found out she'd talked to a cop? Before she could move, the door flew open, cracking against the wall. Brady's broad shoulders filled the doorway. Ruby's fingers, still clutching hers, went cold.

As they were expected to do, both scrambled to their feet and waited in silence for him to reveal the reason for his sudden appearance. Ruby stared at the floor, but Starr studied Brady's face. Did he know? He didn't look angry, but, as with everything when it came to Brady, she didn't trust that. She'd seen him appear perfectly calm at the start of an exchange, waiting until his intended target lowered her guard. Then he'd explode without warning into an all-consuming rage, the shock of it making the tirade—and subsequent punishment—that much more terrifying and effective.

Her heart thudded wildly. *Jesus. Jesus. Jesus.*

"Starr."

When he barked her name, she stumbled across the room, stopping in front of him.

"Go get your dinner."

It took a few seconds to process what he was saying, as the words were so opposite to what she was expecting. Then she nodded. He turned sideways in the doorway, waiting for her to go into the hall. When she reached him, he grabbed her chin and forced her to look at him. "You remember what I told you the other day?"

"Yes."

"You're going to keep your mouth shut?"

She nodded, slightly, since he held her chin in such a tight grasp.

"See that you do. Next time you won't get off so lightly." He let go and Starr brushed past him.

Her legs were weak from more than hunger, but, knowing Brady was watching, she made herself walk slowly and steadily to the lunchroom. Somehow he hadn't figured out that Cole worked for the Toronto PD, or Starr would have heard about it by now.

What did that mean, that they had checked him out and he passed whatever test they put him through? That it was safe for her to meet with him again to discuss the possibility of her freedom? The thought sent competing shivers of fear and excitement rippling through her. Or maybe he hadn't passed, and Brady was simply biding his time, waiting to catch them both in some trap that neither would be able to escape. She couldn't repress the shudder this time or keep from lifting shaking fingers and pressing them against the wall. Hopefully

Brady would attribute the sudden spell of weakness to low blood sugar.

Starr couldn't worry about what Brady did or didn't know. Right now, her priority was getting something to eat so she could think more clearly. And staying out of trouble for the next few days.

If Cole the cop came back to see her, she would hear him out. And then she would decide if the possibility of freedom was worth risking everything for.

CHAPTER SIX

Cole read the email over three times. When his father died, he left his small ranch outside Elliott Lake, the place where Cole had grown up, to his son. Which had been a pretty big shock. Cole wheeled the leather chair closer to the counter doubling as a desk in his Toronto hotel room. He had expected that, in death, his father would offer him what he had offered Cole in life—nothing.

His dad had always made sure his only child knew what a disappointment he was. Apparently the unforgiveable sin Cole had committed was causing his mother's death due to heart failure a few minutes after Cole was born—the result of a birth defect no one had known about. His father had raised him, provided for every material need, but physical affection or verbal affirmation—well, that was a different story. Cole could count on one hand the number of times his father had hugged or praised him for anything.

No idea what to do with the ranch or the emotional baggage that accompanied it, he'd contacted his father's neighbor, Tim Johnson, and asked if he would look after the place until Cole decided whether or not to keep it. He paid the man for his time, and all seemed to be running smoothly.

Now Tim had forwarded him an email from a real estate agent, inquiring about his willingness to sell the place. Cole tapped his fingers on the makeshift desk. Did he want to sell? What was he holding onto his childhood home for? Certainly not the warm memories. He sighed.

Although he'd always loved the four or five horses that would have been put down if his dad hadn't offered them a home in his stables, Cole had no interest in running a ranch, even one that was little more than a hobby farm now. And he definitely didn't want to bump into ghosts from his childhood every time he turned a corner. So what was he supposed to do with the place?

He closed his laptop. No need to decide tonight. He could sleep on it, consider the offer, and let the agent know in a day or two.

Cole switched off the desk lamp and stretched out on the bed, crossing his feet as he reached for the remote on the bedside table. After scrolling through the guide a couple of times with nothing capturing his interest, Cole turned off the TV and tossed the remote onto the mattress. Thoughts of the woman he'd encountered in the hotel room consumed him. Starr had been nothing like he'd expected. Even if she had been as broken and addicted as he'd anticipated, he'd still have done everything he could to get her out, but their encounter had given his mission a deeper, more personal urgency than he could have foreseen.

That urgency had driven him to head straight for police headquarters after leaving the hotel so he could meet with the team assigned to this investigation. They'd mapped out a preliminary plan to extract her from the hotel room but hadn't put a firm timeline in place. They needed to move carefully to avoid tipping Brady off as well as increase the chances of getting Starr out alive.

And keeping her that way.

Cole closed his hands into fists and smacked them against the mattress. As badly as he might want to smuggle a gun into his appointment the next night, grab Starr, and shoot his way out past the bodyguard at the door, he needed to rein in those impulses. Not only was Starr's life on the line, but so were the lives of all the women Brady kept enslaved. If they rushed the plan and Brady heard about it, he and the women could disappear, and it might be years before they were able to get this close to him again.

If ever.

On impulse, Cole rolled onto his side and snatched his phone from the bedside table. He hit a number and waited through three rings, until a cheerful "Hello" rang over the line.

"Hey, Grams."

"Cole!"

He flipped onto his back and bent one arm beneath his head. If anyone could drive away the cloud of discouragement and helplessness that swirled around him some days when he thought about all the people out there hurting and in need of help, it was his grandmother. Cole's father had sent him to her place every summer, Christmas, and school break. She was the one who had provided him with the unconditional love he'd craved as a child. That he still did.

"How are things in Arizona?"

"Hot. Sunny."

Cole glanced at the hotel room window. Rain pounded against the glass, streaming in rivulets to pool on the windowsill. Maybe he could take a quick trip to see her, spend a few days around a pool. That sounded a lot more appealing than taking on a human trafficker and his posse of armed and roided-out hoodlums. He tugged the spare pillow closer and rested his arm on it. No way he was walking away from this assignment, not when they were looking at the very real possibility of bringing down one of the biggest traffickers in the city, possibly the country. Not for all the sunshine in the world. "What were you up to today? Bingo? Knitting club?"

"Knitting club?"

Cole grinned. Even from two thousand miles away, her indignation rang through the line. "I've never knitted anything in my life. Today I helped at the church, serving lunch to the under-employed in the area. So much need, Cole. I feel as though I do so little to help."

"You do what you can, Grams. That's all any of us can do."

"I suppose that's true. You couldn't come for a visit, could you?"

"There's nothing I'd like more. Honest."

A short pause followed. "You're in the middle of something big, aren't you?"

The desire to tell her everything about the investigation, including an in-depth description of the woman he'd met with in the hotel room the other night, gripped Cole, but he wrangled it into the compartment in his mind reserved for classified undercover work. "Big enough that I won't be taking any trips south in the near future, I'm afraid."

"I understand. Don't you worry about me, Cole. I have my friends here and plenty to keep me busy. You focus on your work and on staying out of the line of fire, do you hear?" The slight tremor in her voice betrayed her. Although she never expressed it, he knew she worried about him. It was kind of nice to know someone in the world did.

"I will, I promise."

"I'll be praying."

"I know you will be." He did. His grandmother prayed for him every day. When he was staying with her as a kid, he often heard her through the thin walls, praying as she knelt next to her bed at night. He might not buy into everything she'd tried to teach him about God, but it did ease his mind, knowing she was thinking of him. If there was a God, his grandmother had as good a chance as anyone on the planet of getting his attention. And if there wasn't, what would it hurt, her saying the words that brought her comfort and peace every day?

"Giminadan Gagiginonshiwan."

Cole fished for the Ojibwe expression in his memory bank. Oh, right. "It was nice talking to you, too. I love you, Grams."

"And I love you. Be good and stay safe now."

Her customary sign-off. She rarely waited for him to respond—likely knowing neither was a foregone conclusion. Still, whenever he did find himself in a dicey situation or tempted to do something that went against the values she'd tried to instill in him, those words always rang through his head.

For several minutes after she ended the call, Cole stared at the device in his hand. He hadn't seen Grams since he'd taken a quick trip to Arizona a couple of months ago, and he didn't realize until he heard her voice how much he missed her.

Cole set the phone on the table and heaved himself off the bed. Might as well get a good night's sleep before his next meeting with Starr in twenty-four hours. If she agreed to commit to testifying against Brady, they could set the plan the team had devised into motion.

As the chief had said, every day they waited was another day she and the rest of the women in the house suffered at Brady's hands.

CHAPTER SEVEN

Starr held her breath as the key card buzzed and the door swung open. Number eight, a huge white guy with tattoos crawling all over his arms and neck, held it for her next customer. She bit her lip when she saw who it was. Cole.

It had been five days since he'd walked into her room and sent her life into upheaval. She still wasn't positive what to tell him. That would depend on the plan he had come up with to get her out of here safely. Or to at least minimize the threat to her life, which was likely the most he could promise her.

Starr studied him as he crossed the room. Now that she knew he wasn't there to get anything from her, she could assess him more objectively. She'd remembered he was good-looking, but, watching him as he drew closer—dressed in a black jacket and jeans—it struck her that he was even more attractive than she first thought. His hair was short and almost black, and the eyes that met hers were the color of rich, dark chocolate. With his high cheekbones, he reminded her of a younger Keanu Reeves.

Without a word, he lifted the satin robe from the chair next to the bed and handed it to her. A little of the stiffness left her shoulders—he still didn't want anything. Not in bed, anyway. Of course, he wanted her to testify against Brady. And if he did rescue her, maybe he'd want payment for that, too. No doubt he'd require something from her. Everyone did, eventually.

Repressing a sigh, she slipped on the covering as he tugged the chair closer.

"Hey, Starr."

She pushed her hair over her shoulder. "Detective."

He studied her a moment as though trying to read the answer to his unspoken question in her eyes. Then he pulled out his phone and tapped the screen until music rose from it. "Have you given any thought to what we talked about the last time I was here?"

Starr almost laughed. How could she have thought about anything else? "Yes. Quite a bit."

He set the phone on the table. "The last thing I want to do is pressure you. I'm only here to check in and see how you're feeling."

"That depends on you. Have you worked out a more detailed plan than you had the other night?"

"I've been discussing it with my team." He shifted the chair a little closer, until his knees were an inch from hers. "We think the best idea would be to take you from here, not the house, but we need more information. Besides the man at the door, does anyone come to the hotel with you? Any security either in the lobby or outside the building?"

Starr tightened the knot on her robe. "No. We all go out in separate cars at night. One guy drives me to whatever hotel I'm working in—that changes every few days—and waits outside the door until I'm done for the night. As far as I know, no one else does security in the building."

"Then that's how we'll approach this. If you decide you are willing to leave Brady and go into some kind of protective custody until his trial, then you and I will choose a night to move forward. While I'm in here with you, two members of my team will take out the bodyguard. We'll exit the hotel by the back door where a car will be waiting to take us to an undisclosed location."

Starr chewed on her lower lip. Although he'd fleshed out the plan a little, words like *some kind of protective custody* and *undisclosed location* sounded pretty vague. "I'm guessing you've still got work to do to figure out what you'll do with me if we're able to get out of the hotel?"

A sheepish look crossed his face. "It's a work in progress, I admit. But we'll nail down the details. Like I said, we won't rush this. I want you to be completely comfortable with the plan before we—" Cole's phone vibrated, and he reached for it and glanced at the screen. After a few seconds, his dark eyes connected with hers. "Does Brady ever come to the hotel when you're working?"

"No, never. Why?"

"We've been watching his place since you told us where it was. Brady and three other men left there a few minutes ago. They're heading in this direction. They could be going somewhere else, but—"

"They might have figured out who you are." Starr's throat tightened. "Which means…"

"It means you have a choice to make. We can stay here, and —if he does show up—you can plead innocence, claim you had no idea I was a cop."

"Even if he believes me, and I doubt he will, he'll take you away and kill you."

Cole shrugged. "My colleagues are following him. They'll be able to keep him from taking me anywhere."

"Maybe. Maybe not. He'll use you as a hostage. Best case scenario is a shootout that would put you and your fellow officers in extreme danger." Starr crossed her arms over her abdomen to push back a searing pain. "What's my other option?"

Cole pushed to his feet and strode to the window. He slid the glass up and pushed his palm against the screen.

Starr walked over to stand beside him. "We're on the top floor. We'll never be able to escape this way."

"It's only four stories." He angled his head to look up. "And there's a fire escape. If I can pull it down without alerting the guy in the hallway, we should be able to climb to the ground." Cole faced her. "The question is, are you willing to come with me right now?"

She dug her fingernails into her arm to hold back a surge of panic. *Willow.* The young girl's face, her eyes filled with terror and confusion, drifted through Starr's mind. If she could get out, testify against Brady and bring him down, Willow and Ruby and the other girls might be freed. The possibility of that was worth any risk. Her gaze locked with Cole's again. She barely knew him, but something in his eyes —what looked like kindness, even genuine concern—helped her to trust him. Slightly. And the truth was, whatever he might turn out to be like, he couldn't be worse than Brady.

"I'll go with you."

"All right, then. Let's do this." He still held his phone in one hand, and he typed something into it, hit send, then tapped on another button. Music filled the air again as he set the device on the windowsill.

Starr glanced at the phone. "Six minutes."

He nodded and shoved the screen with both hands. In seconds, he'd applied enough pressure to pop it out and tug it into the room. A cool breeze carrying the scents of fresh rain and damp earth wafted into the room. Starr shivered.

"Do you have clothes to change into?" Cole propped the screen against the wall

"Yes. I'll grab them."

Cole nodded and leaned out the window.

Starr hurried into the small bathroom and changed into the black yoga pants and pink hoodie she'd worn to the hotel. She stuffed her yellow teddy and robe into the trash can. If all went well, she would never dress in that kind of lingerie again. If it didn't, it was unlikely she'd wear it again anyway, unless Brady decided to bury her in it.

When she returned to Cole's side, he was leaning so far out the window that she grabbed the back of his jacket to make sure he didn't tumble out.

"Thanks." He stretched a couple of inches farther. "Got it." The sound of metal grating against metal sent tingles of fear skittering across her skin. It hadn't been terribly loud and had likely been masked by the music, but still she shot a terrified look at the hotel room door. When a loud knock echoed through the room, she jumped. Had Eight heard them? The door didn't open, so she assumed not. She checked the phone again. The last warning. "Two minutes, Cole."

Still leaning precariously over the window ledge, he hissed, "Does that knocking ever tick anybody off?"

Starr mustered a grim smile. "Surprisingly few. Believe it or not, most of my customers don't come here to cuddle."

Cole grasped the bottom rung of the ladder in fingers that had to be growing numb in the cool, damp air. The ladder came down a few more inches with another faint groan of rusted metal scraping against metal.

"Cole." The word came out as a low warning.

"I know. But I have to get it down." He tugged again. This time the rungs lowered a little more easily.

"A minute and a half."

He yanked on the ladder, and it dropped nearly to the ground. "It's down. Here." He let go, crouched, and linked his fingers together.

Starr didn't hesitate. She stepped onto his clasped hands.

He hoisted her up a couple of feet, far enough that she could swing a leg over the windowsill and reach for the ladder.

"Can you get to it?"

She nodded and grasped the wet metal railings to pull herself onto the fire escape. She descended a few feet. The ladder shook. Cole must have climbed out and slid a shoe onto the top rung. Starr forced herself to climb down faster. Any moment she expected to hear an angry shout from above, but none came. Starr jumped the last three feet onto the grass and waited for him. As soon as he reached the bottom, she whispered, "Thirty seconds."

"Let's go." Cole broke into a jog next to her as they headed for the parking lot behind the hotel. When they drew close to a row of vehicles, he tugged a remote from his jacket pocket and stabbed at the unlock button. Neither of them slowed until they reached the silver car with headlights that had flashed when he hit the remote.

Starr flung open the passenger door and jumped onto the front seat as Cole slid behind the wheel. He jammed the key into the ignition and started the engine. She barely had time to close the door before he backed out of the parking spot, shoved the transmission into drive, and stepped on the gas. No other vehicle entered the lot as he accelerated past the rows of parked cars and made his way to the exit. Clearly not having any interest in waiting around to see if Brady and his men would drive in, he spun the wheel and squealed out of the lot nearly on two wheels.

Starr didn't speak as he drove, only fastened her seatbelt and then held on to the door handle. A few times she peered over her shoulder but couldn't detect anyone following them. Cole checked the rear-view mirror several times but gave no indication he saw anyone. After ten minutes of quiet streets, her muscles slowly began to uncoil. "I don't think anyone's following us."

"I don't either."

Starr slumped against the seat. Was it possible? Could she be free of Brady? She clutched the seatbelt that crossed her chest. *Don't get ahead of yourself.* She wouldn't be fully free of him until he was safely behind bars. Maybe not even then. "What about this car? They'll be able to get the license plate from security footage and trace it to you, won't they?"

Cole signaled before pulling onto the 401 Highway that would take them out of the city. "It belongs to the PD. Untraceable."

She shifted a little to face him. "What do we do now?"

Cole sent her a weak smile she assumed was meant to be reassuring. Already she was coming to read him—his eyes, anyway—and she had no trouble figuring out the message they conveyed.

He had absolutely no idea.

CHAPTER EIGHT

"I have an idea." The thought had come to Cole suddenly, several minutes after Starr asked him what they were going to do now. It was crazy, and the last place he wanted to be, but it made perfect sense. He signaled and pulled over to the side of the highway. "I need to make a call. I'll only be a minute."

Starr nodded, although the look she shot behind them suggested she would far rather they keep going than sit here and wait for Brady and his men to catch up. Cole didn't want that either, but he couldn't keep driving around aimlessly. He shouldered open the door. It was almost midnight, and very few cars passed by as he walked to the front of the vehicle and leaned against the hood. After tugging the phone from his jacket pocket, he punched in Lake's number. Lake had worked closely with him on the plan to extract Starr. A plan that had been blasted to pieces tonight. They'd have to start from scratch and figure out where to go from here. And in a few minutes instead of the weeks they thought they'd have to piece together the perfect strategy.

At least Cole had a temporary solution to offer. He doubted the PD would officially assign him to stay with Starr, since Lake had made it clear they weren't able to pay for full-time protective custody. Still, Cole wanted to keep in touch and let them know that, if Starr agreed, he would take her to his father's place until someone came up with a better idea.

As the phone rang, he studied the signs attached to an overpass fifty yards ahead. They had almost reached Highway 400, the one that would take them north. On some level, had he known that was the direction they needed to go?

"Jones."

"Lake. It's Cole."

"Cole! What's happening?" Lake had been the one to send the text warning him Brady was heading in their direction. No doubt he'd been pacing ruts in his office waiting to hear from him.

"We got out of the hotel without seeing Brady or any of his guys."

"We?"

"Yeah. Starr is with me."

"Okay." Lake said the word slowly, as though that scenario was sending all kinds of thoughts spinning through his head.

"If no one has a better idea, I can take her to my dad's place outside Elliott Lake. I doubt anyone would be able to find her there."

"Hold on. Let me run it by my detective-sergeant."

Cole waited through the sound of footsteps thudding along a hallway and a rapping of knuckles against a door. The murmuring of voices suggested that Lake was holding the phone to his chest while he explained to his boss what was going on. Cole kicked at pieces of the gravel scattered across the cement shoulder of the highway as he waited. The tiny stones pinged off the stone divider and bounced back to land in front of his shoe. *Come on. Come on. Come on.*

Three minutes later, a door closed. "Okay, Cole." Lake came back on. "I told Sarge what was happening. Unfortunately, he won't agree to officially task you to watch Starr. We just don't have the budget with all the cutbacks we've had the last few years."

"I get it. I still feel this is something I need to do. If Starr doesn't go into hiding, it won't take Brady long to find her and kill her."

"That's probably true. The DS did agree to cover basic expenses like food and other necessities. Not sure for how long, but likely a few weeks, at least."

"That will help. My dad's estate takes care of the farm expenses, and we won't need much beyond that." Cole's head whirled as he attempted to fit the pieces of this new puzzle together. "I have a bunch of vacation time coming to me. I'll use that up, and then we can see where things are at."

Another door closed on Lake's end. Likely he'd reached his office and gone inside. Cole waited through a pause, until Lake's chair creaked, and he spoke again. "Are you sure about this, Cole? I mean, you don't know this woman. She's undergone serious trauma, which could be a lot for both of you to handle."

Cole wasn't sure, at all. But what choice did he have? "I'm the one who put her in this situation; I can't abandon her now."

"I understand that, but it could get really complicated. If she was actually going into protective custody, we'd provide a female officer to stay with her."

"I know." Cole twisted his upper body toward the cement divider, averting his face as a transport truck roared past, a cloud of hot air and diesel fumes enveloping him in its wake. He stifled a cough with his fist before continuing. "But since I'm all she's got, we're going to have to deal with the situation the best we can. Hopefully you guys will be able to bring Brady in soon and keep him locked up so that it will be safe for her to get her own place."

"That would be the best-case scenario. We do have several officers on their way there as we speak. For now, I know you won't officially be working for the PD, but I'll keep you up to date on what's happening and support you any way I can. And I'll put in a call to the chief in Elliott Lake so he knows what's going on in case you need him."

"I appreciate it." Cole pressed his palm to the cool metal hood. "Hopefully Starr will agree to go with me. After everything she's been through, I don't imagine she'll be thrilled at the idea of some guy she barely knows taking her to the middle of nowhere. So far she's proven to be a lot stronger than I expected, though."

"That's good. She'll need to be. Want to meet somewhere so we can exchange cars?"

"That would be great. I'm at the 401 and 400. I don't want to make the switch anywhere that might have security cameras Brady could get his hands on. Can you come to the York Regional PD parking lot on Major Mackenzie Drive?"

"On my way."

"Thanks." Cole ended the call and rounded the front of the car. He climbed behind the wheel and glanced at his passenger. Her features were neutral, but the way she clutched the door handle, knuckles gleaming white in the moonlight, suggested she wasn't as calm as she appeared. "Are you okay?"

"You mean other than the fact that I'm in a car with a complete stranger fleeing a ruthless human trafficker who would kill me in a second if he found me?" She sent another look out the rear window.

Cole smiled grimly. "Yeah, besides that."

"Then yes, I guess I'm okay." Starr faced forward. "Will the police go to Brady's tonight?"

"They're already on their way."

"Good."

He turned the key in the ignition. "We're going to drive a

few kilometers up the 400 and then switch cars so I have mine."

"Then what?"

Cole eased onto the highway and merged with the light traffic. "If you're all right with this, I told the PD I would take you to my dad's ranch."

For a few seconds, she didn't answer. When she spoke, her voice was strained. "What will your dad think of that?"

He put himself in her place. No doubt she was wondering how many strangers—how many men—he was taking her to stay with. "He won't be there. He ... passed away six months ago."

She let go of the door and faced him. "I'm sorry."

The compassion in her voice floored him. How was she capable of such empathy for others after everything she had been through?

"Thanks, but I'm okay. We weren't that close."

"Still, he was your father."

That was true. And Cole certainly didn't hate the man. His father hadn't been abusive or anything. Although he wasn't opposed to using his belt on Cole's backside occasionally, he never did so excessively or without reason. The reason typically being that Cole had been attempting to get his attention by whatever means necessary. "I guess so."

She cocked her head as though she wanted to pursue that further. Instead, she asked, "So it will only be us at the ranch?"

"Will you be all right with that?"

In the dim moonlight, she scrutinized him as intensely as she had the first night he'd gone into that hotel room and told her who he was. Even when he returned his attention to the road, he felt her gaze on him. After several long seconds, she exhaled softly. "I suppose."

That was more than he'd expected, so he'd take it.

Starr ran a finger along the window frame. "What if Brady

identifies you from the hotel security footage? Won't he be able to tie you to your father that way and figure out you might be at his place?"

A fair question, but one with an answer too complicated to get into at the moment. Hopefully she'd accept the short version. "I don't go by my father's last name. We had a falling out over a decade ago, and I legally changed mine to my mother's maiden name."

"Ah." That two-letter word might be worthless in Scrabble, but she'd managed to load it with a lot of meaning and a hint that she was filing the information away. Thankfully, she didn't push it, not even to ask what that name might be. "Who is bringing your car to you?"

The slight tremor in her voice was the only clue that the idea of meeting up with another stranger at one in the morning threw her a little.

"My friend Laken Jones, or Lake, as I call him. He's another cop working this case with me, a great guy. I've known him since we were at the police academy together."

She didn't answer.

Cole sent her another sideways glance. She was staring out the front window again. "Starr."

She blinked but didn't look at him. "Yes?"

"He's safe. I promise."

Although she didn't answer, her shoulders relaxed a little. They drove in silence for a few minutes until Cole directed the vehicle onto an exit ramp. Starr didn't move, but he felt it in the atmosphere of the vehicle when her apprehension ratcheted up. Nothing he could say would fully convince her she could trust Lake—or him—so he didn't comment as he drove to the police station where they'd arranged to meet.

All Cole could do was keep proving to her that he would never do anything to hurt her. And that he would do everything he possibly could to make sure no one else did, either.

CHAPTER NINE

A few minutes after Cole turned off the engine, another car pulled into the lot. "I'll be right back." He climbed out of the vehicle.

Starr gripped the door handle, hard enough her fingers ached. *He's a cop. And a friend of Cole's. He's safe.*

She struggled to put her full faith into any of those statements. She never had seen concrete proof that Cole was a detective; how could she blindly believe that his friend was? Maybe the two of them worked for another trafficker, or were traffickers themselves, and had teamed up to steal her away from Brady so they could use her for their own nefarious purposes.

Starr glanced around the lot, empty except for a row of cruisers parked at the other end, near the entrance to the building. She mentally calculated the distance to the entrance. Could she make it to the doors before either of them stopped her? If they were cops, they could come in and explain the situation to whoever was working there, and then she'd know for sure. If not, they wouldn't follow her inside and she would be safe.

Except that she wouldn't be. She couldn't stay there forever. Someone—a man, probably—would take her into a little room and force her to tell her story over and over. Then they would either arrest her or turn her loose. Either way, it wouldn't take Brady long to track her down.

Her body went cold, and she let go of the door and shoved her hands into the pocket of her hoodie as she stared out the window. Cole stood talking to his friend, who leaned against the driver's side door of his car, arms crossed. In the lampposts that lit the parking lot, she studied him. He was tall, like Cole, and, from what she could see in the dim light, his skin was darker and his hair shorn close to his head. He wore a brown leather jacket and jeans. Neither of them looked like any of the cops she'd encountered. They were good-looking, but Brady had been, too, and he … Her fingers curled into fists in her pocket. What were they talking about?

Starr glanced to her left, away from the two men and the station. A row of trees lined the far end of the parking lot. If she climbed over the console and slipped out Cole's side, she could be halfway to the row or farther before either of them noticed. That might be her best bet, to lose herself in the dark streets, alleys, and back yards that had to lie beyond the trees. With any luck, the men would give up trying to find her before the sun rose. Plenty of girls could testify against Brady. Why did it have to be her? The police knew where the house was. They could take Brady into custody and have eleven women who would share everything that had happened to them.

Except they wouldn't. Starr leaned the side of her head against the glass. Ruby would be far too terrified and so would Willow. She ran through the list of girls who had lived in the house with her. She couldn't think of any who might be willing to stand up in court and tell strangers what Brady had done to her, not knowing that he would be there and would somehow find a way to exact revenge, even from behind bars.

Like she had agreed to do.

Shudders convulsed her body. She couldn't do it, either. She had to get away from Cole and whoever this other guy was. What had she been thinking, agreeing to show up in court in an attempt to free not only herself but all the women Brady had stolen? What made her think she could be a savior to the rest of the girls? There was only one Savior, and it wasn't her. A little of the ice-cold tension paralyzing her eased at the reminder, and she closed her eyes. *Jesus, I have no idea if I'm doing the right thing here. Help me to know. Keep me safe.*

A soft rapping on the window near her head startled her, and she jerked away from it. Cole opened her door slowly and crouched, as though he understood that towering over her might freak her out. "I'm sorry. I didn't mean to frighten you."

Her throat had gone dry, and Starr struggled to swallow. "It's okay." She lifted her gaze over his shoulder. The guy who'd been talking to Cole had disappeared. Where had he gone? Was he circling around to come at her from the other side? She berated herself for not jumping out when she had the chance. Now it was too late.

"Laken is right there." Cole spoke quietly as he nodded toward the station. His friend waited on the sidewalk at the corner of the brick building, fifty feet away. "He'll stay there until we're in my car."

Starr eyed Cole's vehicle. It sat three spaces over, maybe twelve or fifteen feet. When she met his gaze, he was watching her intently.

"Here." He reached into the inside pocket of his jacket. She stiffened, but, instead of the weapon she'd half-expected, he withdrew a plastic holder that he flipped open and held up. "He brought my badge from the station."

Did that mean he'd brought Cole's gun, too? She didn't like

the fact that he was armed and she wasn't. And the badge might not be real. Or his. She glanced at it and then back at him. He didn't shrink from her probing gaze. If he was hiding something, he was exceptionally good at it. Nothing in his eyes suggested he was capable of hurting her or that he had pulled her out of one horrific situation only to plunge her into another one. All she could detect was compassion. She drew in a shuddering breath. Time to trust.

Cole slid the badge into his pocket. "Are you okay to come to my car with me?"

Despite the urgency of their situation, he sounded relaxed, as though he was perfectly fine to wait until she felt at ease enough to leave the vehicle and accompany him to … Where were they going again? His father's ranch? Another round of shudders threatened, but she willed them away. *Enough.* "Yes."

He offered her a slight smile before straightening and moving back. Starr stepped onto the concrete parking lot. Cole nodded toward the vehicle. "My car's unlocked."

Starr sent a wary look in Laken's direction. He lifted a hand but didn't move any closer. She walked to Cole's car, tugged open the passenger side door, and slid onto the seat. Laken had left the keys in the drink holder between the seats. Everything in her longed to hit the lock button, but that would leave Cole standing outside the car and the three of them in a ridiculous standoff. She wedged her hands under her thighs to keep from doing it anyway.

Cole climbed behind the wheel and stuck the key in the ignition. "Are you good?"

It touched Starr that he kept asking, as though he genuinely cared, but she steeled herself against softening. That would mean letting her guard down, and she couldn't do that until she knew he was safe. "I'm good."

"Good." He flashed her a grin in the dim interior. "Then we're off." He drove out of the parking lot and onto the highway. Starr watched the rear-view mirror, but, as far as she could tell, Laken wasn't following them. No one else appeared to be, either.

Gradually they left behind the streetlights. The darkness around them thickened as the distance between buildings lengthened. Starr stared out her window. Thousands and thousands of golden lights pinpricked the sky. "There are so many stars."

Cole ducked a little to peer out the front windshield. "Yeah, as soon as you get out of Toronto it's a lot easier to see them." He shot her a look. "Have you been out of the city before?"

"No, never. When I was little, my mom talked about us going for a drive in the country some time, but she was too busy working, and then she got sick and ..." Starr dug her nails into the door handle. *You're telling him too much.* "We never went."

With the tip of her finger, Starr outlined the shape of one particularly bright star. Words from the song her mother had sung to her every night when she was a child floated through her mind. *Star light, star bright, first star I see tonight. I wish I may, I wish I might, have the wish I wish tonight.* She touched her finger to the glass, holding the bright star in place. *Jesus, I know it isn't the first star, but could I have a wish anyway? I wish all of this could be true—that I am actually free of Brady, that I can trust Cole, and that I will be safe. Oh, and that Ruby and Willow and the other girls can be free, too. I know that's more than one wish, but ...*

"That's pretty," Cole said, softly, as if he knew she'd been lost in thought and didn't want to startle her again.

Her face warmed. Had she sung the words out loud? Her gaze still focused on the bright star, she murmured, "My mother sang it to me when I was little, and then my foster sisters and I gazed out the window at the stars every night."

The heat in her cheeks deepened. Why was she talking about life outside the house again? Hadn't she learned her lesson the other night? And why was she telling this stranger so much? For eight years, she'd mostly kept her mouth shut. Except when she was angry or fighting for one of the other women, she'd chosen her words carefully, testing each one to make sure it wouldn't get her in trouble. The filter that had saved her from even more violence than she had to endure appeared to have been removed with the arrival of Cole the cop in her life.

And that scared Starr more than anything else that had happened that night.

Keeping one eye on the quiet highway, Cole studied the woman in the passenger seat. The back of her head, anyway. Foster sisters. Something had happened with her parents, and she'd ended up in the system. Not surprising. Traffickers loved to target girls with no stable families watching out for them. Made them easy prey. His fingers clenched around the steering wheel. Should he try to get her to open up about how she landed in care? Or at least a little more about her foster sisters? It sounded as though she might have had a decent relationship with them, so maybe it would help her to talk about them, get her mind off everything that was going on.

Or maybe it would make things worse, bringing up her past. Cole was in over his head here. He'd gone through only rudimentary training at the academy on how to deal with people in the throes of a mental or emotional crisis. He was not equipped to help a woman who'd endured years of unspeakable trauma. Any question could trigger her, and she might lose it completely. Then what? They couldn't walk into a healthcare facility and ask for help. Brady would be on them the second they left the building.

Before he could decide on a course of action, Starr turned toward him. "Where is this ... ranch we're going to?"

"Right. Sorry. It's just outside Elliott Lake."

When she only stared at him blankly, he added, "About five hours north of here." He hid a wince. Until he said it, he hadn't thought about how taking her that far from everything familiar and into the isolation of northern Ontario might feel to her. "I hope you don't mind going that far."

She shrugged. "The farther the better."

That was true. If they could get to the ranch undetected, the chances of Brady being able to find them were slim. Not none, but slim. Cole tapped a finger on the steering wheel. "If you need to ... stop along the way, just let me know."

"I'll be fine." Starr shoved her hands deeper into her hoodie pocket. "You stop if you want to, though."

It would be best if they didn't. Security cameras at every service station or coffee shop would capture their images if they did, increasing their risk. Which was unfortunate because he could use an extra-large double-double at the moment. "I'll be all right. Why don't you get some rest?"

"What about you? I'm used to being up all night. Will you be okay to drive for five more hours?"

Cole had no idea. So far, the adrenaline coursing through him since he'd gotten the text from Lake in the hotel room was keeping him going, but, if that wore off, exhaustion could hit him hard. "I think so."

"I'd offer to spell you off, but I can't."

"You don't drive?"

"No. My foster mother was going to teach us, then she ..." Starr bit her lip. "Well, it didn't happen."

And then Brady had taken that young girl who hadn't even had a chance to get her license and stripped her of the last of her youth and innocence. The surge of rage that tore through Cole, while it did ramp up the adrenaline that had started to dissipate, scared him. He couldn't get emotionally involved in this case. If he was going to keep Starr safe like he'd promised, this could not get personal for him. He focused on the few feet of concrete visible in their headlights and the white lines flashing by on either side. "Try and sleep."

For a few seconds, he felt her gaze on him. Then, as though she sensed the change in his attitude, she rested her head against the window. Everything in him wanted to look over, ask if she was comfortable, but he forced himself to stare straight ahead. Starr was a witness. Someone in his protective custody, if unofficially. Add to that the fact that she was coming out of years of being tormented and used by men, and the very last thing she needed was to think that he looked at her the same way any of them had.

All very, very good reasons for him to quell any interest beyond the desire to watch over her. And to make sure he was able to deliver her safely to the courthouse so they could finally toss Brady and everyone who worked for him behind bars and out of commission for good.

CHAPTER TEN

"Starr."

Although the voice was gentle, Starr jerked upright. Was she late for work? If so, Brady would ...

"It's okay. We're here. At the ranch."

She blinked to bring the man speaking to her into focus. Blood pounded in her ears, but the terror eased a little as memories of everything that had happened that night flooded over her. She was free. Free of Brady, at least. She straightened and stared out the window at the brick farmhouse, silhouetted against a lightening sky. She had landed someplace she'd never been and was stuck here for the foreseeable future with a man who was a virtual stranger. It remained to be seen whether she had found true freedom. *Jesus, help me. Keep me safe.* Starr pushed open the door and stepped outside. Strange odors filled the air. Not entirely unpleasant, but nothing she had experienced before.

Cole rounded the front of the car to stop next to her. "A good country smell, my dad used to call it." His grin slowed the rapid beating of her heart slightly. "If you haven't been out of the city before, it might take a bit of getting used to."

"I guess." Starr's fingers trembled, and she wished she had something to hold on to. They'd left in such a hurry that she hadn't been able to bring any belongings—not that she had many. What would she wear while she was here? How would she brush her teeth or her hair? Everything in Starr longed to sit down on the cement steps leading up to the house and burst into tears, but she steeled herself against showing any emotion.

"Shall we go in?" Cole held out a hand toward the front door.

Starr nodded and followed him to the porch stairs. When he stopped and nudged aside a rock in the flower bed with the toe of his running shoe, she glanced at the windows on the second story. Would one of those be her room? Would Cole expect her to share with him? She swallowed. He crouched and picked something up. When he straightened, he held it in the air. "Key's still here."

Without waiting for a response, he started up the stairs, pulled open the screen door with a creak, and slid the key into the lock. "No one's been in the house for a few months, so I apologize in advance for any dust or spiders." He opened the heavy wooden door, stepped inside, and held it for her as she sidled past. "Not afraid of spiders, are you?"

Starr had been, when she was younger. After the terrors she'd faced over the last few years, spiders felt pretty tame. "They don't bother me, no."

"That's good." Cole closed the door and flicked the lock. The clanking of metal against metal echoed in the stillness of the front hallway. They were alone in the house.

Starr shoved away tingles of apprehension. At some point, she was going to have to trust Cole, or she'd drive herself crazy trying to guess what he might do. He'd put himself at great risk by crossing Brady, which suggested he wasn't helping her on a whim or trying to get something for himself. Still, he was a man ...

"Are you hungry?" Cole switched on the hall light and peered in the direction of what must be the kitchen.

She shook her head. Although she couldn't remember the last time she'd eaten, her stomach was far too knotted to even contemplate food.

"Just as well. I doubt there's anything edible here other than maybe a few canned goods. I'll go out in the morning and grab a few groceries and some clothes."

Right. He hadn't planned on driving here tonight, so he wouldn't have anything with him, either. "Okay." Starr studied him in the dim hallway light. Dark shadows rimmed his eyes. "You must be exhausted."

Cole rubbed the back of his neck. "I admit I was getting pretty tired the last few miles. I'll be fine after a few hours of sleep. Although coffee will be top of my list when I go into town."

So he'd be leaving her alone in the house? Cold fingers slid along her spine, but she ignored them. Obviously it wasn't safe for her to go out in public, not when Brady was no doubt using every resource he had to find her. And they needed supplies—Cole was going to have to go to the store sometimes. And maybe he'd need to return to work. She couldn't expect him to risk his job for her. She swayed a little on her feet. It was all too much to think about tonight.

"Here." Cole hit another light switch, this one at the base of a long, curving set of stairs. "I'll show you to your room."

That sounded promising, as though he planned to allow her a room of her own. Starr took a deep breath of warm, stagnant air before following him up. They passed one closed door on the right before he opened the second. He stepped back so she could walk into the bedroom. He hadn't been exaggerating about the dust—a thin layer coated the long dresser along one wall and the little table next to the double bed. Cole walked over and switched on a lamp. The soft glow of the light, the multi-colored quilt on the bed, the plush white area rug, and the rocking chair in the corner—a knitted afghan tossed over one arm—gave the room a warm, inviting feel.

The pink rose of the waning sunrise filtered through the large window. Later in the day, this room would no doubt be filled with bright sunlight. Starr reflected on the small, high window in the room she'd shared with Ruby. Like the rest of Brady's house, very little light penetrated the darkness, so this sunlit room would be a pleasant change.

"Here." Cole crossed the room to push open another door. "Your bathroom. I'll see if I can find clean towels in the linen closet and bring them to you. Why don't you get settled while I'm gone?"

Starr nodded but glanced at her empty hands after he'd left and almost laughed. It wouldn't take long to settle, since she had nothing to put away. She lifted the quilt and shook it out. In the small beam of light piercing through the early morning clouds to fall in a puddle on the floor, a cloud of dust hung in the air. Starr tossed the quilt onto the bed. She could sleep in her clothes, but she would love a toothbrush. Although she hated to ask him for anything, maybe Cole wouldn't mind picking one up when he went into town. She jumped at the soft tapping on the door.

"Sorry." Cole stood in the doorway, a sheepish look on his face. "I seem to have a knack for startling you."

"It's fine." Starr waved a hand through the air. "I'm a little jumpy. It's not your fault."

"That's understandable. It's been an eventful few hours." Cole set a couple of folded towels on the dresser. "I found these in the closet." He dropped a toothbrush still in the package, a tube of toothpaste, and a bar of soap wrapped in paper onto the dresser next to the towels.

Those few items suddenly felt like absolute luxury.

"Oh, and here." He tugged a bottle of water from the pocket of his jacket and carried it to the bedside table. "I found a case in the kitchen. Very little else, unfortunately, so this will have to do until I go for supplies."

"No problem." Starr eyed the bottle, suddenly intensely thirsty. "I'm used to going without food. Don't rush into town on my account."

A shadow flitted across his face, as if he understood what she was talking about. How could he? Had he suspected the first time they met that she hadn't eaten in a few days? He was a detective; no doubt he was adept at picking up on those kinds of details. Which meant it likely wouldn't be easy for her to keep anything from him.

Whatever his thoughts were on what she'd said, Cole kept them to himself. "I'll pick up some clothes for us when I go. What size do you wear?"

A frown creased her forehead. She didn't like the idea of owing him any more than she already did. As though he understood that, he added, "The PD offered to foot the bill for necessities like that. For both of us."

Oh. That did help. "I'm a size six. Or small, depending on what you're getting. But I don't need much."

"Got it." Cole walked across the room. "My room is the last one on the left if you need anything." He turned in the doorway and leaned against the frame. "Look, Starr. I can't imagine what you've been through the last few years. I want you to know you're safe here." He touched the knob. "There's a lock on the door, so feel free to use it if it makes you feel better, although I won't come in your room again. This is your space, and I promise I will respect that."

She nodded, her throat tight.

Cole pushed away from the frame. "I hope you can find rest here. And peace." He took a step into the hallway.

"Cole?"

He stopped and faced her. "Yes?"

"Thank you." The words sounded so tiny, so inadequate. She was referring to so much more than the water or towels or the place to stay. He'd risked his life tonight to free her from captivity, and she would never be able to thank him for that.

"You're welcome. Get some sleep." He tapped the door frame with his palm a couple of times before disappearing into the hall.

Starr waited a moment, until his footsteps had faded down the stairs, and then she walked on slightly shaky legs over to the door and closed it. After a slight hesitation, she turned the lock in the handle. Something deep inside told her she could trust Cole, but so much had happened in the last few hours—so much had changed—that she had no idea how much weight she could give her intuition.

She pressed her back against the door and surveyed the room, lighter now with the rising of the sun. As Cole had suggested, for now all she wanted was to rest. And maybe experience a little peace for the first time in as long as she could remember.

CHAPTER ELEVEN

The smell of coffee and frying bacon roused Starr from a deep sleep. When she opened her eyes, it took a moment to get her bearings. Then their escape from the hotel room and mad flight north came crashing back. Starr ran her fingers over the colorful quilt. Who had made it—Cole's mother? His grandmother?

Bright light flooded the room, and she tossed the covers off. Although the room was already hot from the summer sun, the wood was cool beneath her bare feet as she padded over to the window. The air was musty from the house being closed up so long. Starr worked the lock loose of paint and rust until she could maneuver the small lever to the right. Then she wedged her palms under the top of the wooden frame that surrounded the lower pane of glass and shoved upward. The window groaned a little but slid open a few inches, ushering in a chorus of birds singing and that *good country smell*, as Cole had called it. A heady mixture of fragrant flowers, warm earth, and something she couldn't identify.

The breeze wafting into the room loosened something

that had been tightly coiled in her stomach. She could open the window whenever she wanted fresh air.

Or needed to escape.

She perused the area outside the window. Was there a way to get down if she had to leave quickly? A trellis covered in vines was attached to the wall next to her window. She could reach it, but she doubted the old wood would support her if she attempted to climb it. A large maple tree stood a few feet away. Maybe she could launch herself from the windowsill and catch hold of one of the thick branches. She'd have to be desperate, as the chances of her falling to the ground were as high as they were of being able to successfully swing herself onto the limb.

Starr fought her instinct to map out an escape route. *Rest and peace.* Cole's words echoed through some place deep inside. She longed for both so strongly it terrified her. She had to keep her emotions in check. Everything Cole said and did sparked hope in her, and hope was dangerous. Allowing herself to believe him—to believe that any of this was real—would cloud her judgment and leave her vulnerable.

Starr rested her forehead against the cool glass, damp with condensation. What was happening in Brady's house? Had he returned there after going to the hotel and taken out his wrath on the girls before the police could arrive? A guttural moan escaped her. If she found out she'd been the cause of more suffering for any of them, she would never forgive herself.

What if Brady hadn't returned to the house? He could have lost the police and slipped out of the city. Maybe even now he was on his way here.

Starr lifted her head. She'd lived in fear of Brady far too long—it was time to stop. She gazed through the glass. Beyond the maple tree and the gravel lane, fields spread out as far as she could see, dotted with more trees. The rutted mud was covered with a low stubble. Corn stalks, maybe? Or straw? She'd never seen a farm field before, so she could only guess. The vastness of the land and the blue sky stole her breath away. The rays of sun—high overhead now—caught the stalks, turning them a brilliant gold. Had she ever seen anything so beautiful? And she could look out her window and admire it any time she wanted.

At the edge of the field, light sparkled on the surface of a pond next to a red, wooden barn. Did they have animals here? Cole said his dad died six months ago, so any livestock must have been taken away. Or did someone come here to care for them? She stuck her thumbnail between her teeth. If Cole forgot to mention to whoever it was that they were here, or if he didn't want to manage the place himself, did that mean some stranger could show up any time?

Before her trepidation could spiral into panic, Starr turned away from the glass. Given the smells emanating from downstairs, Cole had already gone into town and returned. The aroma of hot grease alerted her to the fact that she was ravenous.

Starr went into the small bathroom off her room. She'd left the toothbrush, paste, and soap on the counter the night before, and she used them to freshen up now. Having no other clothes yet, she smoothed the front of her pink hoodie and then ran her fingers through her hair. She paused, her hips against the countertop as she gazed at her reflection in the mirror. Since she hadn't been able to apply fresh makeup, the faded bruise from the backhand Brady had given her was visible, and she touched it lightly with her fingertips. Was it possible no one would ever hit her or torture her or use her for their own twisted pleasure again? Despite what she'd said to Cole the night they'd met, maybe she *had* been able to walk away and start a new life like Julia Roberts in *Pretty Woman*.

If so, what would that new life look like? She thought

about the man downstairs, frying bacon for the two of them in the farmhouse kitchen. How did he play into all this? Would the Toronto PD find another place to hide her soon so Cole could go back to his own life?

The prickling sensation in her chest frightened her. *You can't count on him or anyone else,* she admonished the reflection staring at her. *You need to do this on your own.* Starr shoved away from the counter. *You can do this.*

Fortified by the lecture, she made her way downstairs. Cole stood at the stove, his back to the doorway. He'd been wearing a black shirt the night before, and today he had on a long-sleeved burgundy T-shirt, so he'd obviously gone shopping. For himself, anyway. Would he have felt comfortable picking out items for her? Her gaze flitted to three plastic bags on the kitchen table.

Cole clicked off the burner beneath the frying pan and turned to reach for the plates he'd set on the island. He paused when his gaze landed on her. "Oh, hey. I didn't hear you come down."

"I followed the smell of frying bacon. Hard to resist."

He smiled. "There's coffee, too, if you drink it." He waved a spatula in the direction of a coffee maker on the counter, a few drops of grease splattering onto the marble top of the island. "Help yourself."

"Thanks." Starr padded across the linoleum and grabbed the carafe. A blue mug with large white polka dots sat on the counter next to the coffee maker, and she filled it with the hot liquid, drawing in a deep breath when the mocha-scented steam drifted past her nose.

Cole chuckled as he grabbed a plate. It clinked lightly against the other one as he lifted it. "A coffee and bacon lover. A woman after my own heart."

Flustered at the wording, Starr reached for the carton of cream beside the mug and splashed a little into the coffee, relieved when he focused on dishing up the scrambled eggs and bacon. Two pieces of toast popped up from the toaster next to the stove, and she set her mug on the counter. "I'll get them."

"Thanks." When she walked over to stand next to him and reach for the toast, he nudged a pound of butter closer to her with the spatula. "Silverware's in the drawer in front of you."

Starr nodded and slid the drawer open to grab two knives and two forks. After closing the drawer with her hip, she buttered the toast and set a piece on each plate. Her mind whirled as she grabbed her coffee and followed Cole to the table. When was the last time she'd eaten bacon and eggs? The girls fended for themselves for meals. One of Brady's men stocked the makeshift cafeteria with quick and easy processed foods the women grabbed and ate before they headed out the door and again after returning from the hotel. The last time she'd had any kind of home-cooked meal had to have been at her foster mom's before…

Starr pushed away the thought and the nostalgic pathway it had started to lead her down.

"Sit anywhere." Cole circled one of the plates in the air, gesturing to the six chairs around the table.

Starr pulled out the one across from his place, and he leaned across the massive table to set a plate in front of her.

"Thank you." She handed him a knife and fork, and he nodded as he took them.

No doubt Cole was as hungry as she was, unless he'd grabbed something in town. From the way he was digging into his eggs, she guessed he hadn't.

He paused with the fork halfway to his mouth. "How did you sleep?"

"Really well, actually. The bed was comfortable."

"Good. No spiders in the night?" He stuck the forkful of eggs into his mouth.

"Not that I saw." She bit off a piece of bacon. The taste was every bit as good as she remembered, and she barely repressed a moan of pleasure. "How did it go in town?"

Cole balanced his knife on the edge of the plate and reached for his mug. "Pretty well. I didn't see anyone I knew, which I was happy about. Not that I know many people around here anymore, since I've been gone a few years." He nodded at the bags on the table. "I picked up a few things for you that I hope are all right. I had to guess at what you might like."

"They'll be fine. I'm not planning on hosting a dinner party anytime soon."

The dark eyes that met hers were smiling. "Probably best." He set the mug on the table, his face growing serious. "By the way, Lake called this morning. Brady's in custody."

"Really?"

"Yeah. They know more about him now, including that his last name is Erickson. And he did go to the hotel last night. They staked the place out, but somehow he slipped past them. Thankfully, they caught him at a roadblock they'd set up on the way to the border."

"He was heading south?"

"Yes. Which means he doesn't know we came this way, or he would have followed."

"That's good."

"It is good. And with him behind bars for now, you can relax."

Starr didn't miss the *for now*. How long would they be able to hold Brady? He likely had access to virtually unlimited funds. Unless he was denied bail, he'd be out of prison before she had time to unpack the bags of things Cole had bought her.

He rested a hand on the middle of the table between them. "You okay?"

Starr took a deep breath. Brady had taken enough from her; she wouldn't allow him to steal her peace of mind now. Not when they were likely somewhere even he wouldn't be able to find them. "Yeah, I'm okay."

"Hey." Cole waited for her to meet his gaze before pulling back his hand. "I told you I'd do everything in my power to keep you safe, and I meant it. The PD also wants you safe, so you have a lot of people looking out for you."

"I know, and I appreciate it." Starr glanced around the large country kitchen. The bright sunflowers dotting the cream-colored curtains at the window and the apple-red toaster and kettle offered splotches of color that gave the room a cheerful feel, bolstered by the sunlight pouring through the glass. "Do you have any idea how long we'll be staying here?" Despite the angst swirling through her, she did feel relatively safe on the ranch. The thought of moving somewhere and having strangers watching over her made the few bites of breakfast she'd gotten down churn in her stomach.

"I'm not sure. Lake said he'd get back to me with any updates. I did tell him we can stay here as long as necessary, though."

"You did?"

"Yeah. If you agree, that is."

Starr nodded. "I'd like to stay here. But what about you—don't you have to work?"

"For now, this is my work. I called my chief in Sudbury this morning to let him know I wouldn't be in for a while. He knows how important this case is, so he was good with that."

"I hope so. I don't want you getting in trouble because of me."

"I won't." He pointed to her plate with his fork. "Go ahead and eat before it gets cold."

A distant memory, of bowing her head before meals,

prompted her to set her toast on the pile of scrambled eggs. "Do you mind if I say grace?"

He blinked as though the question had caught him off guard. Then he lowered his fork to the plate again. "Of course not."

Starr said a simple prayer, thanking God for the food and asking him to watch over her and Cole and the girls in the house, wherever they were now. By the time she said *Amen*, her stomach had settled a little, and she scooped a spoonful of eggs and a piece of bacon onto her toast and took a bite. Everything tasted amazing—Cole was a good cook. Speaking of which ... "If we're going to be here for a while, I could do some of the food prep."

He pushed his chair away from the table. "You cook?"

"Actually, no. Not at all." She took a sip of lukewarm coffee. "But I could learn."

He grinned before walking over to the coffee maker. "For now, I'll take care of it. However, you are more than welcome to help with the chores."

"Chores?"

"Yeah." He carried the pot of coffee and the cream over and set the carton on the table. "More coffee?"

"Yes, please."

He filled her cup before pouring more into his own. Starr added a little cream to hers, but he lifted a hand when she held it out to him. "Black for me." He returned to the fridge, grabbed a bottle of water, and divided it between two glasses. "Ice in your water?"

A shudder rippled through her. "No, thanks. I don't like ice."

He glanced over. Had something in her voice given her away? "I'll remember that."

Starr lowered the carton to the table. "What kind of chores did you have in mind?"

Cole set a water glass at each of their places before resuming his seat. "When I lived here, we had a bunch of animals. In recent years, my dad got down to a few horses he'd saved from the slaughterhouse. They need to be fed, of course, and exercised. And their stables have to be mucked out."

"Mucked out?"

"You know, shoveling their … messes?"

"Oh." Her face warmed. "Got it."

He chuckled. "You really never have been out of the city, have you?"

"I really haven't." She brushed her hands together, sending a sprinkling of toast crumbs over her plate. "Who's been taking care of the horses the last few months?"

"My dad's neighbor came over every day." His eyes met hers and he added, quickly, "I called to let him know I'd be staying here for a bit, so he didn't need to come by."

Starr wasn't sure whether the fact that he seemed able to read her mind comforted or disconcerted her. "Any other chores that need to be done?"

"Looks like they've brought the hay in, which means we're heading into the quiet time of year. No one's been stockpiling wood, so if we end up staying more than a few weeks, I'll have to chop enough to get us through winter. Then there's repairing fences and painting any outbuildings that need touching up. Probably a few things to fix around the house as well, especially since it's been sitting quiet for months."

Her lips twitched. "And this is the quiet time of year?"

"Absolutely. Likely only eight or ten hours of work a day instead of twelve or fifteen."

When her eyes widened, he laughed. "Don't worry. I didn't bring you here so you could perform free labor. You can do as much or as little as you want."

"I'd like to help out, although I don't know how much use

I'll be in a barn." Starr used her knife to corral the last bit of bacon and eggs onto her fork. Even cool, they were the best things she'd eaten in a long time. "I can do dishes, though." She set the cutlery on her plate and stood.

Cole took the plate from her. "For today, you can be the guest. Go unpack your bags. Whenever you're ready, I'll give you a tour of the barn and the rest of the property." The cell phone he'd set on the table buzzed, and he glanced at the screen. "That's Lake. Hold on." He picked up the device, hit a button, and lifted it to his ear. "Lake. What's up?"

He listened a minute and then shot a look at her. Was Brady out already? Her knees went a little weak, and Starr pressed a palm to the table to support herself.

"Okay, thanks. Keep in touch." Cole stuck the phone in the back pocket of his jeans. "They found the security guard who was outside your room last night."

"Found him where?"

He hesitated. "In an alley near the hotel."

"Dead?"

"Yeah."

Her mind whirled. Eight was dead. Because of her. How many more people would suffer as a result of the rash decision she'd made the night before?

"Starr."

She forced herself to meet his gaze.

"It's not your fault. Brady is making these choices. He's the one who treats human beings like garbage to be used up and tossed away, not you. All of this is on him."

She nodded woodenly.

Cole set the plate down and came around the table, stopping in front of her. She stiffened slightly, although he didn't touch her. "Look, my colleagues might not appreciate me saying this, but you don't have to testify against him. If it's too much for you, you can walk out that door any time. You're not a prisoner here, and no one can force you to do anything."

His words broke through the cloud of haze swirling around her. "Thank you for saying that, but I do have to do this. I can't stand by and let Brady continue to get away with the things he's done and maybe hurt more people."

"Okay, but remember that you can change your mind any time."

"Thank you." Starr reached for the bags. "I'll go put these things away, and then I'll be ready to mock out stalls or whatever you need."

He laughed. "*Muck* out stalls. And sounds good."

Starr walked along the hallway, the bags banging against her leg. She paused when she reached the front door. *You're not a prisoner here. You can walk out that door any time.* She touched the wood lightly with the tips of her fingers.

Of all the things Cole had done for her the last twenty-four hours, those words were the greatest gift of all.

CHAPTER TWELVE

To demonstrate the task to Starr, Cole shoved the pitchfork under a pile of straw and ... other things and hefted it into the wheelbarrow he'd parked on the cement walkway outside the opening. The simple prayer she had offered at breakfast filled his thoughts. She believed in God? The last few years hadn't driven her faith in a benevolent being from her? How was that possible? Starr talked to God like Grams did—as though she knew him and believed he actually cared about what she was saying. Were the two of them fooling themselves, or had they figured out something he hadn't yet?

Cole did talk to God occasionally, mostly when diving for cover as a suspect fired at him or when he was trying to keep a meth addict or accident victim alive until the ambulance arrived. Those conversations largely consisted of urgent pleas from his end and radio silence at the other end—but, still, he tried. In case God might deign to respond at some point. Was that why Starr and Grams prayed? Just in case? Somehow it felt like a lot more than that to them. And, of course, he never had been shot. So there was that.

Cole shook his head to clear it of the confusing thoughts

and focused on the task at hand. "That's pretty much all there is to it. Want to give it a ..."

Starr didn't appear to be listening. She stood in the walkway in front of the stall next to the one he was working in, gazing at Cocoa, the large, brown Arabian who'd been his father's favorite. Cole walked over to her, his dad's old rubber boots clumping on the straw-strewn cement. "Ever been this close to a horse before?"

"No, there aren't many opportunities to interact with farm animals in Toronto. I have seen police officers riding horses, and the parades I went to as a kid had them, so I've seen them from a distance. I've always thought they were the most magnificent animals."

"They are that."

"It's very cool that your dad rescued them from being killed."

"Yep." They were heading into dangerous territory, and his nerves started to tingle.

Still gazing at the horse, Starr added, "He must have been a caring man."

If he was, it wasn't me he cared about. Not a conversation he wanted to have right now. "I guess." Cole planted the tines of the pitchfork on the walkway and nodded toward Cocoa. "Go ahead and pat her on the nose. She's incredibly gentle."

"Really?" Starr tilted her head, a skeptical look on her face.

"Really." Cole grabbed one of the apples he'd brought from the house and set on a shelf and held it out to her. "Here. Try giving her this."

Starr took the apple from him. "Just hold it out to her?"

"Set it on your palm and keep your hand flat. She won't hurt you."

For a few seconds, Starr hesitated, and then she held out the apple. When Cocoa's wide lips parted and she snatched the apple and crunched it in her large teeth, Starr dropped her hand and turned to Cole, her blue eyes wide and her mouth forming a perfect *o*.

Cole contemplated her. How had she not let her time in captivity rob her of the capacity for wonder and joy? She radiated both at the moment, and it took everything he had to remember the commitment he'd made the night before to keep his thoughts about her completely professional. He cleared his throat. "You have a friend for life now."

She swung her attention to the animal. He could almost see her summoning courage as she slowly lifted a hand and touched the small white shape on Cocoa's forehead. "It looks like a star." She traced the outline of the mark gently before resting her palm on the space between Cocoa's eyes. "So soft."

After a moment, she lowered her hand. "Sorry. You were showing me how to mack out the stalls."

Oh. Right. That's what he was meant to be doing. "It's *muck* out the …" He caught the gleam in her eyes and stopped. "You're messing with me now, aren't you?" Shaking his head, Cole carried the pitchfork into the stall. Starr followed him but stopped in the opening. He shoved the tines under the straw again, and then faked throwing it toward her. She let out a little squeal and jumped out of the way. Cole chuckled and carried the load out to dump into the wheelbarrow. "Sorry. Couldn't resist."

"Very funny." She held out her hand. "I think I've got it."

He didn't move. "How do I know you won't get back at me by dumping manure on my boots?"

A small smirk crossed her face. "That's a chance you're going to have to take, isn't it?"

With a sigh, he handed her the pitchfork and then retreated behind the wall. What she might have lacked in physical strength, Starr made up for in sheer determination. In ten minutes, the pile in the barrow next to Cole had grown considerably, and almost none of the nasty stuff had landed on his feet. He stepped into the stall. "Pretty impressive for a first attempt. I'll finish now." He reached for the fork, and she surrendered it without arguing.

Starr swiped an arm across her forehead. "How many stalls are there again?"

"Only four in use now. Cocoa's and the other three horses'. That big black one is Coal Miner. The other two are Beau and Matrix."

"And they all have to be mucked out every day?"

"Yep." He tossed another load into the wheelbarrow. "Rethinking your offer to help out around the place?"

"Not at all. It might take a while for me to develop farm muscles, but I'll get there." She held up a bent arm as though showing off her biceps.

Cole had no doubt. He was beginning to think there wasn't anything this woman couldn't do if she set her mind to it. He threw the last load into the barrow and leaned the pitchfork against the wall. "That's it for today. Now we get to wheel this out to the manure pile behind the barn."

Starr eyed the barrow. "Looks kind of tippy."

"It can be if it isn't balanced right. Want to give it a go?"

"All right. But if this all goes horribly wrong, it's on you."

"Hopefully not literally."

Starr laughed. "No promises." She positioned herself between the handles. "I just..."

"Lift and push."

She nodded and hoisted the handles to the height of her hips. Nothing happened when she pushed until she stepped back with one foot, bent her legs, and really leaned into it. When the wheelbarrow lurched forward, she let out a small, triumphant cry and wheeled it toward the rear exit. Halfway there, the barrow lurched a little to one side, and a pile of straw and manure slid onto the walkway. Cole grabbed the side and helped straighten it. She lowered the handles until the wheelbarrow rested on the cement and cast a stricken look at him. "I'm sorry."

The tiny dart of fear that crossed her face contracted his stomach muscles. How had Brady or his lackeys reacted to minor accidents to cause her to instinctively respond that way? A number of choice words directed at the low-life trafficker passed through his mind. "Don't be. It's an easy fix."

Cole snatched a shovel leaning against the wall, shoved it under the straw, and tossed the load into the wheelbarrow before propping the shovel against the wall again. "You're safe here, Starr." He would tell her that over and over, a thousand times if he needed to, until she finally believed it.

He'd said the words quietly and so low he wasn't sure if she caught them, but she seemed to. She pushed her shoulders back and lifted the handles again, this time managing to get the wheelbarrow out the back door, across the packed dirt of the yard, and to the base of the large pile of manure thirty feet from the building. When she set it down, she turned to him, her eyes bright. "Now what?"

"We dump it. You take one handle and I'll take the other."

She nodded and moved around to stand on the far side of one of the handles. Cole took hold of the other one. "Ready? One, two, three."

They lifted at the same time, and the heavy load slid onto the pile. When they lowered the wheelbarrow to the ground, she stepped back and swiped her hands together to brush off the dirt. "That was incredibly satisfying."

"That's farm work. I'd forgotten how good it feels to do a little manual labor."

"A little?" She offered him a look of mock indignation as she raised both palms in his direction. "I have blisters, Cole. Actual blisters."

He leaned closer. She did have a couple of raised red spots

on both hands. A stab of guilt shot through his chest. "I'm sorry about that. I shouldn't have—"

She shook her head. "No, you're right. It felt incredibly good to clean out that stall. What other chores need to be done?"

"I still have to sweep the floors and spread fresh straw in the stalls, but maybe you should go inside and take it easy. I think there are bandages in the medicine cabinet in the main bathroom on the second floor."

Starr waved a hand dismissively. "I can do that later. Where do you keep the broom?"

"Are you sure?"

Her eyes met his. "If I say something, I'm sure about it."

"Good to know." He grasped the handles of the wheelbarrow. "All right, then. Come inside and I'll scrounge up a couple of brooms."

Cole parked the wheelbarrow before grabbing a bale of straw and carrying it to the first stall, which he'd already swept clean. He dropped it in the walkway and reached into his pocket for a jackknife. After prying open the largest blade, he slid it under the bailer twine and sliced through it.

Starr's eyebrows rose. "That's a cool little tool."

"A farmer's best friend, believe me." She seemed interested in the knife, not put off by it, so obviously not a trigger for her. "Here." He strode to a shelf, dug through a basket, and retrieved a small jackknife that would fit comfortably in the pocket of her jeans.

"For me? Really?" She took it and tugged open one of the blades.

Cole smiled. "Really. You never know when it will come in handy around here." He left her examining the other blades and carried an armful of straw into the stall. By the time he emerged for more, she'd grabbed one of the several brooms scattered around the barn and was sweeping out another stall. Cole could only see the top of her head, her dark hair gleaming in the glow of the cobweb-covered light hanging above her. He tore his gaze away and headed to the mow to grab another bale, sending himself a stern warning as he went.

Professional.

CHAPTER THIRTEEN

When she and Cole finished cleaning the stables, Starr practically skipped into the house. Every part of her ached, but, as she'd told Cole, it had felt extremely good to work hard. Maybe the thrill of spreading straw or shoveling manure—which she'd quickly figured out had been the source of the smell she hadn't been able to identify that morning—would wear off at some point, but she'd never done anything like it before. Not to mention that she'd had fun—something that was such a distant memory it took her a few minutes to realize that was what was happening.

Cole made them a dinner of chicken, potatoes, and vegetables, and every bite tasted heavenly. Shortly after they finished the dishes, Starr yawned and excused herself to go to bed.

She closed the door of her room and stared at the lock for a moment before turning it. Her mother had taught her that if something seemed too good to be true, it likely was, and Cole definitely seemed to be too good to be true.

Starr reflected on the quiet words he'd spoken to her that afternoon—that she was safe here. Although she hadn't responded, the assertion had sent warmth coursing through her body, which meant that his kindness was getting to her. Part of her was grateful for it, even longed for it, but the other part warned her that the longing was dangerous. If he was anything like Brady, he'd use that kindness to lower her guard, and she couldn't let that happen.

He's nothing *like Brady.*

The fierce thought took her by surprise. It also served to prove her point—she was becoming far too comfortable with Cole. Years of having to fend for herself, of fighting every single day to survive, should have taught her better. If she was losing the ability to protect herself, the lock on the door would have to do it for now.

Two of the plastic bags still sat on the bed. After carrying them to her room following breakfast, Starr had pulled out of the first bag two pairs of jeans, two pairs of yoga pants—black and navy—four T-shirts in various colors, and a hooded sweatshirt. Not wanting to hold Cole up from going out to the barn, she'd changed into the jeans, a T-shirt, and the hoodie and left the other two bags to open later.

Starr wandered over to the bed and tugged one of the bags closer. She reached in and withdrew an item at a time—socks, two packages of underwear, two pairs of pajamas, even a bag containing four sports bras in soft, pastel colors. Her cheeks warmed a little, although she was happy to have them. Had Cole been uncomfortable picking them out or paying for them at the cash register? A bit of the wall she'd erected around herself crumbled slightly, and she shook away the thought.

From the third bag, she pulled out a pack of razors, deodorant, bottles of shampoo and conditioner, a hairbrush, a pack of ponytail holders, hand lotion, and even a box of tampons. Although she didn't need those with the IUD, she did appreciate Cole being willing to purchase them. If the bras hadn't mortified him, the feminine hygiene products must have—but, still, he'd done it.

Underneath all the practical items, she discovered a candle, a lighter, three large bars of chocolate, and two novels. Clutching those things to her chest, Starr sank onto the bed. Who was this guy she suddenly found herself living with? While he'd included pretty much everything she might need, he'd also been thoughtful enough to think of things that would comfort her and help her feel at home.

How could she not trust a man like that? Starr studied the items in her arms. The candle and chocolate did stir up dark memories of the night Brady had called her to his quarters. He'd used those things to soften her up, to mess with her head until she didn't know what or who to believe anymore. Was that what Cole was doing?

You're safe here. The words flowed through her mind like a light breeze, driving the dark thoughts away before it. No. Cole wasn't like that. She didn't know how she could be so certain, but she was. *Jesus, if I'm wrong about him, help me to know it. If not, help me to trust.* With a soft sigh, Starr set the candle and lighter on the bedside table and the books next to them. Sliding open the top drawer, she dropped the chocolate into it. She was too full from Cole's dinner to eat any of it tonight, but she would.

Should she go thank him? He might have assumed she had opened all the bags earlier and wondered why she hadn't acknowledged his gifts. She bit her lip at the thought that he might be disappointed—that was the last thing she wanted. Before she could second-guess the move, Starr hopped off the bed, crossed the room, and unlocked and opened the door. Light shone from beneath Cole's bedroom door. When she reached it, she stopped, took a deep breath, then knocked lightly. "Cole?"

Something creaked, as though he'd been sitting on the bed

or a chair and gotten up. Seconds later, his footsteps thudded across the floor. Starr swallowed as the knob turned and he pulled open the door. She was relieved to see he still wore his jeans and T-shirt. And that he smiled when he saw her. "Hey. Everything okay?"

"Everything's fine. I just finished unpacking the things you bought me, and I wanted to thank you for everything—especially the candle and chocolate and books. It was really kind of you to think of getting those for me."

"It wasn't any trouble. Well, one or two of the things caused me a bit of trouble, but that was okay. Like I said, I didn't see anyone I knew in the store." He offered her a sheepish grin.

Although she tried to steel herself against it, that grin wormed its way past her defenses. Brady would never have been able to manufacture anything that genuine or real. His eyes would have given him away every time. Cole's were warm in the soft glow of the overhead light in his room, and Starr couldn't keep from smiling in return. "Well, I appreciate all of it."

"Worth every bit of embarrassment, then." He leaned his forearm on the door frame.

She caught a glimpse of posters on two of the walls. Wayne Gretzky and Sydney Crosby. Of course. Every good Canadian boy's heroes. A shelf of gleaming gold trophies hung on a third wall above a small desk where he'd likely done his homework as a kid. "You played hockey?"

He glanced over his shoulder and then back at her. "Oh, yeah. For years. I was a Sudbury Wolf for a couple of seasons before a knee injury ended my brief career."

Wow. The Ontario Hockey League. Only a step below the NHL. "A few of the Toronto Marlies went to my high school. My friends and I thought they were pretty cool."

Amusement flitted across his face. "Are you saying that, if

we'd gone to the same high school, you'd have been a groupie?"

Warmth crept up her neck. "Who knows? I'm sure you had plenty of those at your school."

"Well, you know," he blew on the tips of his bent fingers and rubbed them on the front of the burgundy T-shirt, "I did all right."

"I'm sure you did."

His smile widened. "What makes you say that?"

She'd walked right into that one. The warmth in her neck flamed across her cheeks. Before she could fumble for an answer, he saved her with a laugh. "Don't answer that. I'm teasing you." He pushed away from the door frame. "Will you be able to sleep?"

"I can't imagine I'll have any trouble after all that fresh air and the work we did today."

He sobered. "That reminds me, how are your hands?"

She turned them over and examined them. "They could use a bit of toughening up, but I'll be fine."

"Here."

Starr stepped back as he came into the hallway and crossed to the room opposite his. Reaching inside, he flicked on a light before disappearing into what appeared to be the main bathroom he'd mentioned earlier. Starr stopped in the doorway. Cole opened the mirrored door of the medicine cabinet above the sink and pulled out a box. He tapped a couple of small bandages onto his palm and then replaced the box.

When he came back to her, he said, "May I see?"

She hesitated and then lifted her hands to show him. He studied the red marks but didn't touch her. "Skin's not broken, so you shouldn't need antibiotic cream." He held out the bandages. "You likely don't need these tonight, but if you're planning to do more work tomorrow, you'll want to protect those areas."

She took them from him. "Thanks. And I'm definitely planning to work tomorrow. I had fun today. And I want to earn my keep while I'm here."

He switched off the bathroom light. "Well, I enjoyed your company, but you're under no obligation to work while you're here. You don't have to earn anything, Starr."

Somehow the simple words conveyed far more than the lightness in his tone suggested. "Thank you for that." She held up the bandages. "And these."

"You're welcome."

"See you in the morning?"

"I'll be here."

Starr nodded. When she reached her room, she closed the door and slumped against the back of it. After a moment, she pushed herself away, turned, and locked the door. Even as she did it, she knew the gesture was futile.

It wasn't her bedroom door that Cole the cop was seriously threatening to breach but something much more terrifying—the walls she'd spent the last eight years carefully constructing in order to minimize every possible threat.

CHAPTER FOURTEEN

Starr grew more and more comfortable with Cocoa and spent a lot of time grooming her and leading her around the corral outside the barn the way Cole showed her. One warm, early-September afternoon a couple of weeks after they'd arrived at the ranch, she caught a movement out of the corner of her eye and glanced over at the fence. She hadn't realized Cole was there, but he stood, one booted foot on the bottom rail, his arms folded on the top one, watching her with Cocoa. When she met his gaze, he lowered his foot. "How do you feel about going for a ride?"

Starr jerked her gaze to the horse. Was she ready for that? Although Cocoa had proven how gentle she was, she did tower over Starr, and, even though the horse was getting old, every movement was a testament to her strength and agility. "Um…"

He climbed over the fence, dropped lightly onto the dirt floor of the corral, and made his way to her. "You don't have to do anything you don't want to do, but I promise you Cocoa is the perfect horse to start on." He rested a hand on the horse's gleaming side, and Cocoa whinnied softly. "She rarely moves faster than a walk."

"Would you go with me?"

"If you want. I could take Coal Miner. Since he broke his leg badly before coming here, he can't go much faster than Cocoa. Even so, I've always been partial to him because we share a first name, even if it isn't spelled the same."

Starr's laugh was cut off by the sound of a vehicle approaching on the road that ran past the farm. Her gaze darted in that direction, and she watched, her stomach tight, as a black pickup approached the driveway and continued past, trailing a cloud of dust. The truth that cast its dark shadow over what might otherwise have been a time of pure happiness for her was that Brady had made bail shortly after being arrested. She'd figured he would but had still prayed fervently for two days that the judge would refuse to grant him that option. The fact that he was no longer behind bars made it hard for her to sleep at night.

"Hey." Cole waited until she met his eyes over Cocoa's back. "You know Brady's under house arrest until the trial, right?"

Her throat had thickened, so she nodded and ran her hand over Cocoa's soft neck.

"The PD is watching him closely, and he has an ankle bracelet; if he does try to leave the house, they'll be on him in minutes."

A lot can happen in minutes. Starr buried her fingers in the horse's long mane. "I know." She did know it in her head. And even if Brady escaped, there was no reason to think he would be able to find her here. Most of the time she could rest in that and in her belief that God was watching over her. Then something would happen—even something small like a vehicle driving past the ranch—and the fear came rolling in again.

"You're safe here, Starr."

How many times had Cole said that to her since they'd arrived here? Every time, the quiet words untangled the knots forming in her stomach.

"The girls are okay?" She'd asked him that before, more than once, but felt driven to hear his answer again.

As always, he responded calmly, as if he understood her need to hear the words over and over. "Yes. They were all released, and they're being given lots of support. They're in good hands."

The faces of Ruby and Willow and the others drifted through her mind. *Jesus, be with them. Watch over them and let them get the help they need so they can start living that life Willow and I talked about.* The idea comforted her as much as Cole's quiet promise. "Any news from Laken on when the trial might be?"

"No. The wheels of justice move slowly, unfortunately. It could be weeks or months before it starts."

As much as she would love for the trial to be over and for Brady to be behind bars, Starr couldn't bring herself to wish that her time here at the ranch would pass more quickly. She loved everything about the place—the view of rolling farmland from her bedroom window, working around the horses, spending time with Cole. While she wasn't quite ready to analyze why that last one brought her so much joy, she did know that her trust in him grew every day. She'd even stopped locking her door at night although, the first time she had left it unlocked, a couple of nights ago, she'd only done so after standing in front of it debating for ten minutes.

She exhaled through rounded lips and then patted Cocoa's back. "Will you show me how to put a saddle on this beautiful girl?"

"Absolutely. Hold on, I'll get it." Cole disappeared into the barn and returned a couple of minutes later with a blanket over one shoulder, his other hand gripping the saddle resting on his hip. He tossed the blanket over Cocoa's back before setting the saddle in place and walking Starr through how to properly do it up.

In a lot of ways, her education in how to prepare for the real world had stopped at seventeen. The skills she'd learned in Brady's house weren't any she cared to remember or use in her new life. Cole never seemed to mind when she didn't know how to do something but simply rolled up his sleeves and showed her.

After he cinched the strap under the horse's belly, he returned to the stable to get Coal Miner, the jet-black horse Starr hadn't worked up the nerve to approach yet. When she studied him from a distance, his power and spirit excited her, and she could understand why he was Cole's favorite. Personally, she preferred the steady presence of Cocoa.

A few minutes later, Cole strode outside, holding on to the reins of the massive animal. The big horse snorted and tossed his head, but Cole kept him in check as he led him to the fence. After looping the reins around the top rail, he returned to Starr. "First, stand on Cocoa's left side, facing away from her head." Cole grabbed the triangle-shaped piece of metal dangling from a strap along the side of the horse and twisted it. "Slide your left foot into the stirrup, then grab the saddle horn." He tapped the part of the saddle sticking in the air. "Lift yourself up and throw your right leg over Cocoa's back."

It sounded straightforward enough. Starr grasped hold of the saddle horn and then maneuvered her left foot into the stirrup while Cole held it still. When she tried to haul herself up, she failed to get her leg over, and her right foot landed on the ground. Hard.

"Are you all right?" Cole stood so close behind her she could feel the warmth of his body, but he didn't make contact. He hadn't touched her since he'd brought her to the ranch, not even a simple nudge in the arm or a brushing of their fingers when he took something from her. Starr appreciated that almost more than anything else he had done.

"Yep." She took a firmer grasp of the horn and, when he stepped back, shoved off the ground as hard as she could. She managed to throw her leg over the saddle this time and land on it with a slight thud.

"Well done!" Cole adjusted the stirrups to a comfortable length for her legs. "Hold on a minute—I'll get Coal Miner and join you."

He crossed the corral and pushed open the large gate before returning to untie the big horse's reins. In seconds he had pulled himself astride the massive animal as though it were the easiest thing in the world and ridden to her side.

"Show-off." Starr wrinkled her nose at him.

Cole chuckled. "I've been riding these horses since I was a kid. You did amazing for your first time."

"I haven't moved yet. We'll see how amazing I do once Cocoa gets into gear."

"Let's give it a try. Let go of the horn and hold the reins in one hand." He waited until she had, reluctantly, released her death grip on the saddle and taken the reins. "That's it. Now dig your heels gently into her sides and she'll start to walk."

Starr tapped Cocoa's sides with her sneakers, barely touching her. Cole grinned. "You might have to press a little harder. Don't worry—you won't hurt her."

When she did, Cocoa ambled forward. The rocking motion felt strange, and Starr nearly grabbed the saddle horn again, but she wanted to do this right. After a couple of minutes, she adjusted to the unfamiliar motion and was able to go with it instead of fighting it. They weren't exactly racing like the wind, but the sensation was glorious and liberating. She swung her gaze to Cole, riding at her side. "I'm doing it! I'm riding a horse!"

When his brown eyes met hers, they held something she couldn't quite discern but that stole away the breath she'd been about to take. Then he smiled, and the moment passed. "I see that."

Starr returned her attention to the movement of the horse beneath her, the light breeze brushing across her warm cheeks, the ring of trees around the corral—still mostly green but with a sprinkling of orange leaves that hinted at a brilliant autumn display.

"Want to try a short walk outside the corral?"

Starr straightened in the saddle. "If you think I can handle it."

"I'm pretty sure there isn't anything you can't handle." She glanced at him. He looked a little sheepish, as though he hadn't meant to say that out loud. He nodded at the reins in her hand. "If you want to go right, move the reins to the right. When Cocoa feels them against the left side of her neck, she'll turn right. If you want to go left, move the reins to the left. Pull on them both if you want her to stop."

Cole kept Coal Miner at a walk as they directed the two horses out the gate and onto the gravel laneway. Three smaller white buildings and a larger one lined the gravel driveway on the far side of the barn from the pond.

Starr gestured to them with her free hand. "What's in those buildings?'

"Nothing much now. When my grandfather ran the ranch, it was a much bigger operation. He used those cabins to house workers he hired for the season. My dad did the same for a while, but massive farming operations, often run by corporations, started taking over in the area, eventually making it impossible for him to make a living. He sold off a lot of the property and scaled it back to a hobby farm. I only call it a ranch now out of habit."

Starr narrowed her eyes a little, imagining this place with

workers everywhere and children playing by the pond or riding bikes up and down the driveway. Like Cole must have done. She could see him—a dark-haired nine-year-old racing his bike to the end of the lane or running to catch the school bus. She realized suddenly that a smile had crossed her face, and she sobered before he could ask what she was thinking.

By the time they reached the road, dark clouds had scuttled across the sun. Starr shivered at the sudden drop in temperature. Cole reined in Coal Miner. "Let's get them home and into the barn before it starts to rain."

Starr succeeded in turning Cocoa around, and Cole smiled encouragement as they started toward the corral. "Want to try a trot?"

She measured the distance to the gravel driveway warily. "How fast is a trot?"

"Slightly faster than a walk."

That didn't sound too intimidating. She bit her lip. Could she do it? Cole's quiet assertion—that he didn't think there was anything she couldn't handle—gave her a boost of confidence. "How do I get her to go faster?"

"You can give her another nudge with your heels. And try accompanying that with a clicking noise, like this." He made a sound with his mouth open, tongue pressed to the roof of his mouth.

Starr copied his movements. After a couple of attempts, she reproduced a noise that sounded a bit like the one he'd made. Close enough for Cocoa, who started moving a little faster beneath her. After a couple seconds of panic, Starr reminded herself not to fight the motion but to allow her body to move along with the horse. They trotted all the way to the corral, Cole keeping pace perfectly beside her. They reached the gate, and Starr guided Cocoa through it before pulling on the reins to get her to slow and then stop.

"Hold on." Cole pulled Coal Miner to a halt, slid off, and

tied the reins to the fence again. Then he strode over to stand on Cocoa's left side. "Dismount like you got on—keep your foot in the stirrup and swing your leg over her back and to the ground. I'm right here. I won't let you fall."

Somehow Starr knew he wouldn't. She took a deep breath and swung her leg over Cocoa's back and to the ground. She stumbled a little as her foot came out of the stirrup. Cole's fingers pressed lightly against her shoulder blades, but he dropped his hands as soon as she regained her balance. "You good?"

"So good. That was amazing."

"You did great. You were born to ride."

A drop of rain landed on Starr's cheek. He lifted a hand, and for a second she thought he might wipe it away. She held her breath, not sure what she hoped he would do. Instead of touching her again, he reached past her and patted Cocoa's side. "Better get them inside and brushed down." He gathered up the reins and held them out to Starr.

After he'd freed Coal Miner and walked him into the barn, Starr followed. Her heart beat out an erratic rhythm in her chest. Whether that was a result of the lingering triumph of her first horse ride or Cole's nearness, she wasn't sure. *Steel yourself.* Protecting her was an assignment for Cole. She couldn't let her heart get involved or it would only end in more pain for her, which was the last thing she needed.

Those moments of being one with the beautiful animal she rode, the way the darkness pressing around her seemed suddenly pricked with tiny dots of light—like the night sky she'd gazed at in wonder when driving out of the city for the first time—gave her hope. Which didn't scare her the way it had when she was at Brady's.

Shivers tingled along her spine.

A hope that didn't frighten her might end up being the most dangerous hope of all.

CHAPTER FIFTEEN

Cole scanned the screen of the disposable phone Lake had given him when they'd met up to exchange vehicles. He'd handed his over to Lake to remove the chip and battery so it couldn't be traced. Hopefully, once the threat against Starr was neutralized, he'd get it back. For now, this one was safer. He sighed and tossed the device onto the bedside table.

The police were keeping a close eye on Brady, but so far he hadn't made any attempt to escape the dark hole that had been the place he'd held all those women captive. How the man could live with himself after what he had put them through was beyond Cole. He fervently hoped that, now that Brady *was* forced to live with himself, he was haunted night and day by the oppressive darkness shrouding the place—a darkness woven out of the suffering and pain of everyone who'd been forced to exist under that roof.

On the off chance God might listen to anything he had to say, Cole shot a look at the ceiling and hissed, "Can you hear me? If so, could you possibly direct a little of that wrath and judgment of yours Brady's way? If anyone on earth deserves a smiting from almighty God, it's that pathetic excuse for a human being. If you could make him pay for everything he did to those girls, to Starr, that would be really great."

The fury that always consumed him when he thought about everything Starr had endured surged through him now. His chest clenched so tightly he had to rub a palm over it before he could draw in a breath. The fury intensified with every day he spent with Starr. She embraced every new experience that came along with a joyfulness he couldn't comprehend, given her past. Every time she turned to him, those sapphire eyes huge and filled with excitement, his resolve to keep his feelings professional weakened further.

He'd never met anyone like her, and—although he was aware he was sliding one foot after the other slowly, slowly across ice that grew thinner with every step—he couldn't bring himself to either put up a wall to keep her out or talk to Lake about the wisdom of finding another situation for her. Instead Cole had spoken to the real estate agent—let her know his place was off the market for the foreseeable future. He would call her if that changed.

In the meantime, he and Starr would—

A moaning sound disturbed the stillness that had draped over the farmhouse, and Cole bolted upright in bed. Was that Starr? A soft cry echoed along the hallway, and he thrust away the blankets.

His bare feet thumping on the cold wooden floor, he crossed the room, yanked open his door, and hurried toward Starr's room. When he reached her door, he stopped and listened. She cried out—mumbled words punctuated by the only two he could understand, *night* and *ice*—and Cole rapped lightly on the door. "Starr?"

The only response was another cry. Should he go in? He'd promised her he wouldn't, but it sounded as though she was in deep distress. Taking a deep breath, he slowly turned the handle. It wasn't locked. He stored that bit of information to scrutinize later and slowly pushed open the door. "Starr?"

She flung herself onto her back, struggling with the sheets. Again she mumbled something about ice, and he frowned. Why was she dreaming about that?

"Brady, no!"

The sharp, desperate cry dispelled any hesitation Cole had about going to her, and he strode to her bed and dropped to a crouch next to it. Perspiration beaded on her forehead. "Starr?"

She moaned again. Abandoning his resolve to never touch her, Cole rested his hand on the fingers that clutched the colorful quilt his dad's mother, who died years before Cole was born, had made. "Starr. It's Cole. Can you hear me?"

She didn't open her eyes, but the fingers clutching the quilt relaxed beneath his and her body stilled.

He pulled his hand away before she woke up and saw it.

After a few seconds, she opened her eyes, blinking a few times as though trying to orient herself. The eyes that met his still held wildness, but, as he watched, that faded. "Cole?"

"Yeah. I apologize for barging in here, but you sounded like you were having a bad dream."

"Oh." She drew a trembling hand across her forehead. "I'm sorry."

"Don't be. I was just worried about you. What were you dreaming about?"

Starr hesitated and then said, "I don't remember."

Clearly that wasn't entirely true, but Cole wasn't about to force her to open up to him if she wasn't ready. "Want some water?"

"Yes. Please." She sat up, clutching the quilt to her chest, and leaned against the headboard.

Cole grabbed the bottle from the bedside table and held it out.

"Thanks." The bottle shook, but she managed to take a few swallows before setting it on the table.

He sat back on his haunches. "Do you get nightmares a lot?"

She shook her head, the long hair she usually wore up in a ponytail tumbling over her shoulders. "I've never had one like that."

So she remembered how bad it was, even if she couldn't recall all the details. Interesting that she would start having terrible nightmares now, when she had escaped her horrific situation. He was no psychiatrist, but maybe that was *why* she was having them—her mind was finally free to start processing everything that had happened to her. Which meant they could occur with greater frequency.

"I'm sorry I woke you."

"You didn't. I was awake, but, even if I hadn't been, I wouldn't have minded at all."

"Well, thank you. It helped a lot, you being here."

"I'm glad." Cole clambered to his feet. "Do you think you can go back to sleep?"

She yawned and covered her mouth with one hand, her eyes somehow laughing. "Does that answer your question?"

"Good. Call if you need me, okay?"

"I will. And thanks, Cole. I mean it."

He nodded and left her room. He would have preferred to leave the door open in case she cried out again and he didn't hear her, but it was a pretty huge deal that she wasn't locking it. Leaving it open would no doubt make her feel far too vulnerable. He pulled it shut and trudged to his room. As a concession, he left his open a crack, hoping that would help.

After Cole crawled into bed and tugged the blanket to his chin, it struck him again how in over his head he was. As dumbfounded as he so often was at Starr's capacity for joy, clearly she had underlying issues. He should talk to Lake about the possibility of the PD paying for her to talk to someone. Hopefully someone she could meet with over the phone, so they didn't have to reveal her location.

In the meantime, he would stick close. Even if he didn't have much experience dealing with serious mental or emotional issues, he did know that being there for her, night or day, was what she needed most.

So that was exactly what he planned to do.

CHAPTER SIXTEEN

"I have a present for you."

Starr looked up from the book she'd been reading—the second of the two novels Cole had given her along with the candle and chocolate. He dropped onto the far end of the couch and rested a large bag on the cushion between them.

Starr leaned over to set the book on the coffee table. "Cole."

He held up a hand. "Compliments of the Toronto PD. Don't worry."

She contemplated him a moment before reaching for the bag and tugging out a thick purple winter jacket, black wool hat, scarf, gloves, and a box that held a pair of black, fur-lined winter boots. As uncomfortable as she was with other people buying her things when she had no way to repay them, she set the box on the coffee table and hugged the warm clothes to her. "These are beautiful."

"You'll need them if you're going to keep going outside over the winter. There's snow in the forecast for the weekend, which isn't that unusual around here, even this early in October."

Snow. Starr had seen the stuff before, of course. It did snow in the city, although in the winter it was dark before they left Brady's house and still dark when they returned in the early morning hours, so she'd only caught glimpses of it in the light that pooled at the base of the lampposts.

Something Cole had said snagged in her brain like a fishhook caught in weeds. *Over the winter*. Was he planning on them being here until spring? How was he able to put his life on hold for months? She lowered the clothes to her lap. "Don't you have anyone in your life who might not like you being here with me that long?"

He cocked his head. "You mean like a girlfriend?"

"Well, yeah, or family members or friends. You haven't seen anyone in the weeks that we've been here."

"First of all, I don't have a girlfriend. I was in a fairly serious relationship a couple years ago, but that ended. My family is all gone except for my grandma. She moved to Arizona a few years ago because of her arthritis. I talk to her on the phone every week or two. As for friends, most of mine are on the force in Sudbury or Toronto, and they know I'm on assignment, so, other than Laken, no one's expecting to hear from me for a while."

The word *assignment* stung a little, but it was a good reminder to Starr of her place in his life. What about the woman he'd been seriously involved with, though? Had they been engaged? She refused to put a name to the spark of dark emotion that ignited deep in her gut because of what it might mean about her feelings toward him. Instead, she ruthlessly extinguished it.

Cole shifted to face her. "Speaking of Laken, I spoke to him earlier today, and he gave me the number of a woman you could talk to over the phone if you want to."

Starr tightened her grip on the purple coat. "You mean a therapist?"

"Yes."

Did she want to? The thought of every memory she had worked hard to bury deep inside being dredged up and discussed turned her skin ice cold. "I don't know if I'm ready for that."

"It's fine. If you ever feel you are, just let me know."

"Okay." She forced herself to unclench her fingers as she scrambled to find a safer topic of conversation. "Tell me about your grandmother."

"Grams?" Warmth filled his eyes. "She's the best. My mother died after giving birth to me, and Grams, her mother, really filled that void. She and my grandfather, who passed away when I was twelve, had a farm not far from here, and I spent a lot of time there. My dad let me go for weekends and school holidays, which is what saved me."

"Saved you?"

He looked a little flustered, as though he hadn't meant to say that. Then he sighed. "Yes. Like I told you, I had a difficult relationship with my father. I think he always blamed me for my mother's death. He wasn't abusive, but he never showed me any affection, and he was critical of everything I did. I wasted a lot of years trying to win his approval before finally realizing it was never going to happen. As soon as I turned eighteen, I changed my last name to my mother's. I liked the fact that it was Grams' last name, too—made me feel even more connected to her as well as to my culture."

"What name is that?"

"Blacksky. My mother was Anishinaabe, which is a native tribe in this area. So is Grams, although my father and grandfather were Caucasian."

Cole Blacksky. The name suited him. "How did your grandparents meet?"

"Grams left the reserve where she'd grown up, not far

from here, when she was eighteen. She went to Toronto to find work and was there for only a few weeks before she went to the Yonge Street Mission one night for a meal. She met my grandfather, who was volunteering with a group from his church. As she tells it, they pretty much fell in love the moment they met. They were married a few weeks later, and Gramps took her to his family farm to live—the one where I used to spend summers and holidays."

"So you're one quarter Anishinaabe?"

"Actually, half. My grandmother was pregnant when she arrived at the mission. Gramps adopted my mother after she was born."

"Do you speak her language?"

"*Enh, ndi anishnabem bangii eta go.*"

Her eyebrows rose and he laughed. "It means, *yes, a little*. Grams tried teaching me when I was a kid, and some of it stuck. Mostly that line and *Ikidon miinawaa*, or *Please say that again*, which is usually what I have to say when Grams tries to speak to me in her native tongue."

Starr ran her fingers over the faux fur lining the hood of the purple coat. "I can see it."

"See what?"

"You as a seven- or eight-year-old running around on your grandparents' farm."

His smile sent warmth wafting through her, into places that had been cold for so long she didn't realize they were until they began to thaw.

"I had a lot of fun with her. Still do. She's this amazing seventy-five-year-old woman who spends every free moment serving meals at the drop-in center in town or working with the homeless. I admire her more than anyone I know. As a kid, I always looked forward to spending time with her. Although it made going home that much harder."

Starr wrapped her arms around the plush purple coat, her heart hurting for him. "I'm sorry life with your dad was so hard."

His eyes met hers. "Thanks."

"Did you ever reconcile after your falling out?"

"Not really. I still tried to come see him every month or two. We were polite to each other, but not much more than that."

"Do you think you've forgiven him?"

Cole stared at the flames flickering in the woodstove a moment before blowing out a breath. "I've never really thought about it. I guess I'd have to say no because thinking about it stirs up a lot of anger and resentment."

Starr got that. Hearing Brady's name brought the same emotions crashing over her. For a long time, she'd felt that way about her own father, too. She'd only been able to come to a place of forgiving him with God's help. If she was ever going to let go of her bitterness and anger toward Brady, she'd need God's help with that as well, but she wasn't nearly ready. Did Cole have a faith that might help him let go of his resentment toward his dad?

"Do you believe in God?"

He huffed a short laugh. "Not holding back tonight, are you?"

Starr bit her lip. "You can tell me to shut up any time you want."

He sought out her eyes again. "Starr, I've been waiting and hoping you'd open up and talk—really talk—to me since the night we met. I will never tell you to shut up. You can ask me anything you want, and I'll tell you the truth. And I'll never get angry over anything you say."

How did he always know her deepest fears before she could voice them? She'd had to guard her words for so long and been punished so often for something she'd said that Cole's invitation to talk to him about anything she wanted without fear of retribution felt like chains falling off her wrists. The freedom was exhilarating but a little frightening, too, as though more bricks were tumbling from the walls she'd built around her heart. How many more could fall before he began to see everything she kept hidden and locked away? When he looked at her, he already seemed to see more than anyone else ever had. She pulled the coat closer, needing the warm comfort of it.

A log fell in the stove, sending up a cloud of sparks with a hissing sound. Cole rubbed his forehead. "I guess I'd say that my relationship with God is like the relationship I had with my father—complicated. And maybe it's unfair, as though I've let everything I've always felt for my dad, the way he treated me, get all wrapped up with my concept of God. Grams has the most incredible relationship with God—she talks to him as though he's her best friend and sitting right next to her. It hurts her that I don't have that, but I'm not there yet."

Yet. Starr drew comfort from the word. Not that anything was happening between her and Cole, but if he didn't share her faith, it never could.

"You do, don't you?"

She loosened her hold on the coat. "I do what?"

"Believe in God."

"Yes. I could never have made it through my mother's or foster mother's deaths or my time in Brady's house without him. And I could never have forgiven my own father without God's help. That's why I asked about your faith; I believe there are things and people we can never forgive on our own strength."

"Are you telling me you've forgiven Brady?" His eyes, warm and soft a moment before, grew hard.

"No, definitely not. But someday I hope to. Carrying around that kind of hatred and bitterness doesn't punish the person who wronged you—it only slowly eats you up inside, destroys you. I don't want to give Brady that kind of ongoing power to hurt me."

The hardness in his eyes softened. "I guess I get that. And since you put it that way, I do hope you'll be able to forgive him one day, since I'd never want that for you, either."

"And I hope you can forgive your father."

In the warm glow of the fireplace, something arced between them. Something deeper and stronger than anything that had passed between them before. Neither of them spoke or moved for several seconds. Then Cole shook his head, as though intentionally breaking the spell. "How would you feel about learning to drive?"

Starr grabbed the bag and stuck the purple coat into it. "Drive?"

"Yeah. I could give you a few lessons in the laneway. If you pick it up as quickly as you did horseback riding, you'll be an expert before you know it."

It took Starr a moment to switch out of the conversation they'd been having into something much lighter, but she was grateful to Cole for taking them there. The thought of driving sent the same mixture of excitement and apprehension swirling through her she'd felt when he suggested trying to ride Cocoa, but that had turned out pretty well. "I'd love it, if you're willing."

His easy grin vanquished the last of the hardness that had briefly settled in his gaze. "I'm completely willing. I checked with my agent to make sure my life insurance was paid up and everything."

"That's hilarious. How much damage can I do driving up and down the laneway?"

"I guess we'll see tomorrow." Cole slid to the edge of the couch and stood. "In the meantime, *ninoondezgade*. Which means *I'm hungry*. That's one phrase that is firmly planted in my mind because I said it so often to Grams. Still do, whenever I see her, because she's the best baker in the world."

Starr stuffed the rest of the clothes into the bag. She'd hang them on the hooks in the hallway before going upstairs later. "I'll set the table. *Gutom na ako*—which is *I'm hungry* in Tagalog, my mother's native tongue." She bit her lip. Why had she brought up her mother? Would Cole push Starr to talk about her? She wasn't sure she was ready for that, and she definitely wasn't sure she could handle another intense conversation. Not tonight. She hurried into the kitchen and flung open the cupboard doors, hoping that dinner prep might distract him from what she'd said.

When she closed the cupboard door, he was standing on the other side of it, watching her. "I know what you're doing."

"What do you mean?" Starr injected as much innocence into her voice as possible.

"You're avoiding me because you're afraid that, since you mentioned her, and since I opened up to you about my dad, I'm going to push you to talk about your mother."

When she didn't respond, he took the plates from her. "I will never pressure you to do or to talk about anything you don't want to. I promise. Okay?"

She exhaled. "Okay."

"Having said that, since it helped me to talk about my dad, I am going to ask you about her. Soon. But if you're still not ready, you can simply say so and I'll drop it. Deal?"

"Deal."

"Good." He carried the plates over to the table.

She reached into the cupboard for two glasses. If Cole's dad had been as hard on him as he claimed, his grandmother must have made the absolute most of the time she'd had with him. Not that the previous men in her life had set the bar very high, but, from what Starr had seen, Cole Blacksky had grown up to become a kinder and more decent man than she had allowed herself to believe existed.

CHAPTER SEVENTEEN

When the old farm truck jerked to a stop and stalled out—for the third time—Cole had to press his lips together to keep from laughing at the look of consternation Starr gave him.

"I will never be able to do this."

"You will. It just takes practice." He'd considered letting her off the hook and teaching her on his car, which had an automatic transmission, but his dad had drilled into him the importance of learning to drive a stick first.

As much as Cole might not have appreciated his father's parenting methods in general, he had to admit that the man had raised him to not shy away from doing hard things. Starr may not thank him now for giving her this skill, but one day she would. Hopefully. "Put the gear into neutral." He ran through the steps again.

Starr did everything he'd told her to, and the truck lurched forward.

"That's it. A little more gas. Good. Now press on the clutch again and move it into second."

The forward movement of the truck smoothed out and she glanced at him, her eyes glowing with that familiar, triumphant gleam they held whenever she tried something new or accomplished a difficult task. Cole swallowed. After their conversation last night, and the intense moment they'd shared, he was deeply aware of how rapidly the situation was spiraling out of his control. Or at least how much his feelings were. He absolutely should look into finding Starr another place to stay.

He couldn't do it, though. The thought of asking her to go to an unfamiliar place with strangers felt like cruel and unusual punishment. And she'd suffered through more than her fair share of that already. She was happy here. Even in the few weeks since they'd pulled into the driveway, the light shone more brightly and more often in her eyes, and the darkness that had occasionally swirled around her like a cloak had done so less and less.

She had come so far, and he couldn't ask her to start that journey again with someone new. Or ask anyone else to be there for her in the night, when the ghosts of her past were set free to roam through her psyche, stirring up memories. Memories so vivid that—given how he could only rouse her with difficulty and that, for a long time afterward, a deep trembling gripped her—must have seemed to her like living those horrors all over again.

Every time, he assured her that she was safe here, with him. So it wouldn't be fair to her to shuffle the responsibility of keeping her that way to someone else.

Who are you trying to kid, Blacksky? He wasn't keeping Starr here for her benefit. Not entirely. The thought of her leaving was becoming more and more unthinkable with every day that passed. If she was gone, much more than the house would seem empty and dark. His life would as well.

Cole rested his arm on the window frame. Enough. She was here now, and she was safe. If his heart wasn't, that was his problem, not hers. He wouldn't upheave her life to protect himself from getting hurt. "Okay, slow down. We're almost at the end of the lane."

Starr eased the truck to a stop.

"Excellent. Now shift into neutral and I'll tell you how to back up and perform a three-point turn so we can return to the yard."

The exercise turned into more of a thirteen- or fourteen-point turn, and, by the time the old pickup was bouncing along the rutted gravel driveway toward the barn, they were both in stitches. She laughed with abandon, as though her laughter had been held in captivity as long as she had been and was now set free. Which was likely true.

An hour later, the last tendrils of orange and rose streaks in the sky had nearly faded, but she'd gone up and down the lane a dozen times without stalling once. When she slid the transmission into neutral the final time and turned off the engine, she touched both palms to her cheeks. "I can't believe it. I can drive."

"Yeah. And most of the time it will be a lot easier than that."

She turned in the seat to look at him. "What do you mean?"

"You just learned on a standard. Most vehicles, like my car, have an automatic transmission. That means no clutch—you simply turn the engine on, put it in drive, and hit the gas. The car automatically shifts through the gears, so you don't have to."

Her mouth dropped open a little. "Why didn't you teach me to drive on your car, then?"

"Because this is a good skill to have, and now you have it. Next time we can switch to my car, and you'll see how it will be most of the time when you're driving."

Starr tilted her head. "Did your dad make you learn on a standard?"

"Yes."

"So some of the lessons he taught you were worth passing on."

He had to agree, grudgingly. "I suppose so."

"What else did he do right?"

Cole reflected on that. Looking back, his dad had done a lot of things for him—more than he'd ever acknowledged. As Starr was watching him with an expectant look on her face, Cole guessed she wasn't going to allow him to decline to acknowledge them now. "All right. He instilled in me the value of hard work. Taught me everything I know about fixing things and respecting the land. How to take care of my money. Passed along his love of animals and nature." Blood pulsed in his ears as the memories flew at him faster and faster, like snow driving against his windshield in a blizzard. "And he was a great cook and showed me the way around the kitchen." More memories brought a smile flitting across his face. "He took me fishing in the pond over there pretty much every Saturday in the summer, and in the winter he built a rink on it and taught me how to shoot a puck." He inclined his head toward the pond at the edge of the field, too dark to see now in the waning daylight and the long shadow of the barn.

"Then, he wasn't all bad."

He had to give her that. In fact, the more he thought about it, the more things came to his mind. A sick feeling struck him. Had Cole ever thanked his dad for everything he had given him, or had he spent all his time resenting what he couldn't? "No, of course not."

As though she could sense his growing discomfort, when she spoke again, her voice was low and quiet. "He must have loved your mother very much, since he never got over losing her."

Another revelation. Cole had spent the first eighteen years of his life with a man overcome by intense grief and hadn't even realized it, let alone shown him any grace. Had his dad kept a desert of emotional distance between them only because he was afraid of loving someone else that much and possibly losing him, too?

His eyes pricked and he shoved open his door. "I ... need some air." He rounded the front of the truck and slumped against the hood, his thoughts whirling like the wind had the day a tornado had roared through the property when he was seven. Cole dug his fingertips into his temples. His dad had risked his life coming after him that day. Racing through the forest that lined the far end of the hayfield where Cole had been building a fort, calling his name until Cole heard him and answered, then picking him up, tossing him into the truck, and barely making it to the house in time for the two of them to scramble down the steps into the cellar.

The tornado had missed the farmyard but razed a straight path down the center of the forest, obliterating the fort Cole had been working on.

He didn't realize Starr had climbed out of the truck and stood next to him, leaning against the hood, until she spoke, her voice as soft as the moonlight gleaming off the foot of chrome bumper between them. "If your dad was here now, are there things you'd like to say to him?"

When his dad was alive, so few words had passed between them that Cole hadn't given much thought to what he might want to say after the man was gone. Now he realized there were things, buried deep, that Starr's gentle but persistent questioning had stirred up like the mud at the bottom of the pond when he waded into it in his rubber boots. "Yeah, I guess there are."

"Where is your dad buried?"

Cole sent her a sideways look. "In a small cemetery down the road. Why?"

"It's dark out. I doubt anyone will see us if we go there. Do you want to drive over?"

What he wanted was to gather her in his arms and hold her until the cold rippling through him like waves on a January lake eased, but even driving down the road to talk to his dead father seemed a wiser idea. Far less pleasant, but wiser. And maybe getting a few things off his chest would help.

Although, would it be safe to take Starr away from here? Cole pulled the phone from his jacket pocket. "Let me check with Lake first, make sure everything's okay."

The soft glow of the lamppost in the yard fell across her face as she nodded. He focused on the screen as he typed a quick message: *Everything quiet there?*

Twenty seconds later, the device vibrated against his palm: *The turkey vulture hasn't tried to leave the nest. Nothing yet on legal proceedings. All well with you?*

Yes. Just checking in.

Okay. Any new developments, you'll be the first to know.

Thanks. Cole dropped the phone into his pocket. No real reason not to go. And likely Starr would appreciate getting off the property, even if it was to visit a cemetery in the dark. "Nothing new. You sure you want to do this?"

"I'm sure. I don't want to push you, though, if you're not."

"I'll likely never be sure, so tonight's probably as good a time as any." Which was true. If he chickened out now, he might never summon the courage to go.

Starr lifted her hand, the truck keys dangling from one finger. Cole took them from her. With a long exhalation of breath, he pushed himself away from the truck and made his way to the driver's seat. His fingers trembled, and it took a couple of tries to insert the right key into the ignition, but soon they were bumping along the lane. Neither spoke as they turned onto the gravel road, headed for his father's final resting place.

Cole appreciated Starr giving him time and space to try to rein in his whirling thoughts, to organize them enough that he'd have some idea of what to say when he stood in front of his dad's headstone. By the time they reached the small, fenced-in area surrounded by trees and farmland, his thoughts had settled a little. Starr's quiet presence helped. Kept him from performing his own three-point turn and driving home and forgetting the whole thing.

He entered the small parking lot and stopped the truck. When he switched off the engine, the lights died as well, leaving the hundred or so tombstones spread out before them bathed in the soft glow of a half moon and countless stars. His heart thudded, but he reached for the door handle.

"I'll wait here."

Cole nodded and shoved open the door with his shoulder. He hadn't been here since the day his dad was laid to rest, but thankfully it was a small cemetery and he found his dad's plot after a minute of searching. Careful not to stand on the grave, Cole planted his feet, shoulder-width apart, to one side of the stone and crossed his arms as he stared at the simple epitaph. *Kurt Caldwell. 1950-2021. With the Lord.* Funny, if Cole had bothered to read the inscription the day they brought his father here, the last few words hadn't sunk in. *Was* his father with the Lord? They'd never really talked about faith or religion although, now that he thought about it, his dad had occasionally read Bible stories to him from an old book of his mother's. When Cole was really young. Why had he stopped?

Maybe those words were simply ones the engraver—or whatever you called a person who designed headstones—automatically inscribed if not given other instructions, in which case they could mean nothing.

Anyway, he hadn't come here to try and figure out what

his dad's religious beliefs might have been. He'd come here to unload on the man lying six feet beneath his feet. Feeling a little silly, he glanced around the area before focusing on the headstone again. "Dad? It's Cole." He shuffled from one foot to the other, trying to acclimate to this strange situation. "A friend of mine suggested I come here and say some of the things I'd want to say if I had another chance to talk to you."

Friend? Was that what Starr was? He had lots of friends, and none of them made him feel the way she did. Forcing his attention to his father, he uncrossed his arms and rested a hand on top of the stone, grounding himself.

"I guess what I most want to ask is *why*? Why was I never good enough for you? I tried. I got good grades and helped with chores and did what I could around the house without being asked. That was all for you. Whenever I brought home a report card or made dinner to surprise you when you came in from the barn or went out to feed the animals at five am in the middle of winter without complaining, I did it because I hoped you would say one nice thing to me. That you would compliment me or thank me or in some way affirm that you cared about my accomplishments. Or me, for that matter." His throat thickened a little, and he cleared it before continuing. "I loved you, Dad. I suppose all I really wanted to hear from you was that you loved me, too."

Cole rubbed his forehead with his fingers, not realizing until he touched his head that they were shaking. He shoved his hand into his jacket pocket. "Starr got me thinking tonight. She said maybe you were too grief stricken over losing Mom to be able to love anyone else. Or to express that you loved them, anyway. I guess, if you were capable of that much love, maybe you did have a little of it for me, even if you couldn't say it. And maybe I should have been more understanding about how torn up you were about losing the love of your life. I'm sorry about that. Sorry she died giving life to me."

His voice cracked a little, and he swallowed hard. "You carried that bitterness around all your life, and I saw what it did to you. While I've followed in your footsteps in a lot of ways because of everything you taught me, that's one path you walked that I don't want to follow. Like Starr said, that kind of anger and resentment can eat you up inside, destroy you. And I don't want that."

Cole tipped his head to gaze at the night sky, awash with millions of golden lights. "Are you there, God? Starr says some things can't be forgiven without your help. And I want to try and forgive my dad. Could you help me?" He waited a moment, although he had no idea what he was waiting for. Something big, maybe, earthshattering. Instead, he felt a slight, almost indiscernible sensation of something sliding free, like a pair of handcuffs snapping open when Cole inserted the key and turned it. He pulled his hand from his pocket and rested both palms on the smooth, cold marble stone. "All right, here it is. I'm letting go of all of it—the hurt, the anger, the bitterness. I can't carry it around anymore. It's too heavy a load." He ran both palms across the top of the stone. "I guess what I'm trying to say is"—he stopped and took a long, jagged breath—"I forgive you, Dad."

No flash of lightning split the sky at the pronouncement. Only a cool autumn breeze brushed by him, sending a few dry leaves cartwheeling over the nearby graves. Still, something gave a little in his chest. And a sense of serenity wafted in like the smoke that unfurled in the air when he opened the wood-stove door.

"I also want to thank you for loving my mother so well. That gives me hope that she had a happy life. And although I never knew her, that matters to me." Cole patted the stone with both hands before shoving them in his pockets. "Goodbye, Dad. I hope that, wherever you are, you're resting in peace. I truly mean that." For several long minutes he stood there, gazing at the stone, then he nodded and made his way on unsteady legs to the truck.

After he'd climbed behind the wheel, he stared out the front window for a moment, until a light touch on his arm roused him. Cole glanced down. Starr's fingers rested on the sleeve of his jacket. Even through the fabric, he felt the warmth of them, absorbed the comfort she offered before she pulled her hand away.

"Are you okay?" The interior light was still on and the blue eyes watching him intently glowed in the soft illumination.

"You know what?" Cole took a deep breath, testing the effects of his newfound lightness. "I am. I think that really helped."

Her smile warmed him more than the heat blowing through the vents. "That's good, Cole."

"Yeah." He shifted the truck into reverse. "It's good." Which was something that, until he met Starr, he never thought he would be able to say about a conversation with his dad.

CHAPTER EIGHTEEN

Starr stood at the window in her room, gazing out over the field covered in snow from a mid-October dusting. Not quite a blanket, as only an inch or so had fallen from the pewter sky that day. An afghan, maybe, like the one hanging over the arm of the chair in the corner of her room, the holes allowing the stubble to poke through.

The first star twinkled near the moon, and Starr pushed the tip of her finger to the glass. *Jesus, can I make a wish on that star? I wish that you would watch over Ruby and Willow and all the other girls. I don't know where they are tonight, but you do. Be with them. Please.*

Did the other girls have bad dreams like she did? Every few nights she woke up drenched in sweat and struggling for breath, dark figures still reaching for her even as they slowly faded. Every time, Cole was there, watching her with concern etched deep into his forehead. It helped, him coming into her room, being there when she struggled to consciousness.

Cole. She ran her finger down the glass, wiping away a little of the condensation near the bottom. *I know I'm only supposed to get one wish, but could you also be with Cole? Help him to know that you love him. He's such a good man, but he needs you. We both do.*

Cole's dad had kept a bunch of movies on a wall of shelves in the living room, and after dinner Cole asked her if she wanted to watch another one tonight. It scared her how much the idea of a movie-and-popcorn night thrilled her. Kind of like a date. But not a date. She needed to be very clear about that in her head. Starr was an assignment to Cole, someone he was being paid to keep safe, and she had to remember that.

She traipsed down the stairs and into the living room. Flames roared behind the glass of the woodstove. Cole stood in front of the floor-to-ceiling shelves of books, games, and movies. He looked over his shoulder. "What are you in the mood for—comedy? Western? Classic?"

"A classic would be good."

"Any one in particular?"

Starr dropped onto the sofa. "I don't care. You choose." Other than the couple of films they'd already watched—*Sabrina* and *The Maltese Falcon*—she'd never seen any classic movies. She'd loved both of those and enjoyed Humphrey Bogart. Obviously Cole's father had, too, because when Cole stuck a video into the player, Bogart's name flashed across the screen again, along with the title—*Casablanca*.

He settled onto the cushion at the other end of the couch and set a big bowl of popcorn between them. "I think this one's my favorite. It's got a bunch of famous lines in it and, in my opinion, the best movie ending ever."

"Don't tell me."

"Of course not." His dark eyes glowed warm in the flickering firelight. "Not knowing how the story is going to end is the best part."

Starr stuck a few kernels of popcorn into her mouth. Was he talking about the movie or about the two of them? So much lay ahead of them, and it was impossible to guess what would happen in the future. They'd already been here two months with no indication that Brady's trial would start anytime soon. When it did, there was no way to predict how it would go. Or what their lives would look like after it was over. Would she be safe then? Would they go their separate ways? With everyone she loved gone, where would she live when she left the ranch? She would be completely alone.

Starr grabbed a pillow and wrapped her arms around it. She hadn't even thought about that.

You'll never be alone.

The thought softened her rigid muscles. Of course she would never be alone. Whatever happened, God would be with her.

She pushed all thoughts of her uncertain future out of her head and relaxed into the movie. As Cole had said, the film had a bunch of great lines, and it was a lot funnier than she'd expected. Sad, too. She could hardly believe it when Rick gave Ilsa up in the end.

Starr stared at the screen until the last credit scrolled by, emotions roiling. When the TV went dark, she finally uncurled her legs and reached for the popcorn bowl to take it to the kitchen. Cole was watching her, and she paused, her hand resting on the edge of the bowl.

He tapped the other side of the rim with one finger. "What did you think?"

"I liked it."

"Just liked it?" He looked a little disappointed, which made her chest ache.

"I loved most of it. The acting was great, and it was really funny, but the ending was sad. My heart broke for Rick, having to give up the woman he loved."

"Yeah, that part's definitely sad. But his sacrifice helped defeat the Nazis, and he did end up with a good friend."

"That's true. And maybe that's how it is sometimes—no

matter how much you love someone and want to be with them, it's better for both of you to let the other one go."

His eyes probed hers so intently she couldn't look away. Did he think she was talking about the two of them? *Was* she? She couldn't be. They didn't love each other. And he'd given her no hint he was thinking about a life with her after all this was over. She wasn't thinking about that, either. They had a professional relationship that neither of them had sought out or committed to long term. And when the reason for it ended, so would the relationship.

As much as that might send a dart of pain through her chest, it was true. She grasped the bowl and stood. "Thanks for the movie night. I'll take this to the kitchen, and then I think I'll head upstairs. I'm tired."

"Okay."

Starr crossed the living room but stopped when she passed a small table by the window. "I didn't realize we had a computer."

Cole had been following her with their glasses, and he stopped next to her. "Neither did I until this afternoon. I found it in my dad's office."

"Is it okay to use it?" People could track you through a laptop, couldn't they? Slivers of ice dug into her skin.

"It's fine, as long as neither of us enters any personal information. No one can trace it to us if we don't. So go ahead and look something up on the Internet or whatever, but make sure you never log into a site with your name or any other contact information."

Hmm. Interesting. She'd love to research taking care of horses, since she hated pestering Cole with questions. And when it was closer to the time for her to go, she could search for a place to stay and maybe a job.

Before her thoughts wandered to the future again, she carried the bowl across the hall to the kitchen, dumped out the kernels, and washed it before leaving it upside down in the dishrack to dry. Cole waited until she was done to take her place at the sink and wash the glasses.

"Well, good night." Without looking at him, she started for the door.

"Starr."

She half-turned. "Yes?"

He hesitated and then said, "Good night. I hope you sleep well."

She offered him a weak smile. "You too."

Before he could say any more, she escaped up the stairs to her room and closed the door. Tears threatened, but she blinked them away. Crying wouldn't help her here any more than it had helped at Brady's.

Briefly she considered locking the door, but it wouldn't help. While nightmares from her past would no doubt terrorize her in the dark of night—the shadows of their grasping fingers hovered around her periphery even now—what frightened her even more was the deep longing rising within her for a future she could never have.

CHAPTER NINETEEN

Cole opened the door of the smallest cabin and stepped inside. The air was musty, which wasn't surprising since no one had been in here for at least eight months, maybe longer. Nothing a little fresh air, a good dusting, and a coat of paint wouldn't fix. He felt his way in the dark, trying to remember the layout of furniture. After a few seconds, the tips of his fingers brushed the shade of a lamp, and he reached beneath it and pressed the switch. Soft light flooded the place, illuminating an old plaid couch, a braided floor rug, a small table and two chairs against one wall, and a single bed in the far corner.

Cole dropped onto the couch. Things seemed to have returned to normal with Starr, especially when they were working side by side in the stables. Even so, a week after the movie night, their exchange at the end of the film still sent him into a tailspin.

What had Starr been referring to when she said that sometimes it was better for two people to let each other go, even if they loved each other? Was that a commentary on the film's ending, or could she have been talking about them? Had the possibility of her and Cole becoming romantically involved crossed her mind like it had his?

Was she ready for a relationship with a man? Would she ever be? He groaned and propped his elbows on his knees so he could lower his head into his hands. What was happening to him? He had never felt this strongly drawn to a woman, this deeply connected. Not even with Eve, his last serious relationship, and he'd entertained thoughts of asking her to marry him before he realized what a mistake that would be. The fact that his heart had chosen this woman—someone who had been through so much and who was still obviously deeply wounded, someone for whom he should only feel a professional responsibility—was bad timing at best and unconscionable at worst. Although she wasn't a child. She'd proven to be a strong, capable, intelligent woman, and, if she made the decision on her own to get involved with him, was there anything indictable in that?

He groaned again as he straightened. He needed to talk to Grams. Cole snagged the phone from his jacket pocket and hit the number. She answered after one ring, as though she'd been anticipating his call.

"Cole!"

"Hi, Grams."

"What's wrong?"

Despite his inner turmoil, he had to laugh. "Sometimes I just call to say hi, you know."

"I know. But you use a different tone of voice for those calls."

That was news to him—he'd thought he only had one voice. "Well, nothing's wrong per se, I just needed to hear your voice. How are you doing?"

"*Nminoyaa gwa.*"

He nodded. She was fine, which he was always happy to hear. "What did you do today?"

"Saturdays I help out at the food bank, as it's their busiest day. All those people in need, Cole. It would break your heart."

Yeah. So many hurting people in the world. It broke his heart all the time, the things he saw at work. His heart had never been as shattered by any of it as it was when he thought about Starr and the other women and what they had endured at the hands of Brady. His fingers tightened around the device. "I'm sure it would."

"Enough about that. What's on your mind?"

He drew in a breath. Given the ongoing investigation, he shouldn't disclose much. "This is all confidential, Grams. I'm not supposed to talk about what I'm in the middle of, but I could really use your wisdom."

"You know whatever you say will remain between the two of us."

"Yeah, I know." Cole rubbed the back of his neck. "I'm staying at Dad's place."

"That's a good thing. It's what your dad would have wanted. And your mother. But aren't you working?"

"Technically, I'm on leave. But I've been here a couple of months with someone I'm trying to keep safe until a trial."

"Ah. And how is she doing?"

He lowered his hand to rest it on his jean-clad knee. "What makes you think it's a woman?"

"Cole."

All right, maybe he had a voice for that, too. "Okay, it's a woman. And the person she's testifying against was her sex trafficker."

"Oh, no. That poor, sweet girl."

"How do you know she's sweet?"

"Because I know you. You wouldn't have to fight feelings for her so hard if she wasn't."

He didn't bother asking this time. Grams knew him better

than anyone. And she had the collective wisdom of her people and a direct line to an all-seeing, all-knowing God on her side. Cole didn't stand a chance. "All right, yes. She's sweet. Also funny and smart and she has this incredible ability to embrace life, which is all pretty incomprehensible, given what she's been through."

"She has a faith."

It wasn't a question. "She does. I have no idea how she kept holding onto God through everything that happened to her, but somehow she did."

"Cole, she didn't hold on to God; he held on to her. That's how she made it through."

"Well, whatever it was, she's the most amazing person I've ever met."

"Then what is the problem?"

"I'm afraid of hurting her. She has these nightmares all the time, so I know she's dealing with a lot of trauma, and I have no idea how to help her. Plus, even if I haven't been officially hired to protect her, the best course of action would be to stay focused and professional. What if allowing myself to fall for her somehow impairs my judgment? I'd never forgive myself if I let anything happen to her."

"You were always one for bringing home strays, Cole. Every time you walked in the door, I held my breath a little, waiting to see what you might have tucked into your shirt or what you were about to pull out of your pocket. Remember that turtle with the scraped shell? Or the robin that had fallen out of its nest?"

"Are you suggesting she is only another stray I've brought home?"

"Of course not. I'm suggesting that maybe God gave you those assignments when you were growing up to prepare you for the greatest one of all—taking care of and protecting the precious, deeply wounded heart, mind, and body of this beautiful child of his."

"Why would God choose me for that? I don't even believe in him."

"Don't you?"

Cole didn't answer. He never had been able to lie to his grandmother.

"Cole, you can't be that mad for that long at a God you don't believe in. Even you aren't that stubborn."

"I don't know. Maybe. She has gotten me thinking about God more than I have in a long while. She even talked me into going to Dad's grave and talking to him. And I prayed while I was there, that God would help me let go of the past so I could move forward."

"And?"

"I was able to tell Dad I forgave him. So, I won't rule out the fact that maybe God is out there, and maybe he does hear me when I talk to him like the two of you insist he does."

"I'm really happy to hear that. As for why God chose you for this, that's between you and him. And I think you know there's only one way for you to find out."

"Which is?"

"Ask him."

After another silence, she added, "Don't make the mistake of thinking you can fix her though, *ngwis*. That's not your job."

Ngwis. My son. Cole had always loved when she called him that, as though she was not only speaking for herself but for his mother. The word filled a hole in him with a rush of warmth.

"Only God and a trained professional and this sweet girl herself can heal the deep hurts in her mind and soul. But you *can* ask him to do that for her, and you can allow him to use your love, patience, kindness, and commitment to her to help bring healing into her life."

"More praying, huh? I guess I can give it a shot."

"You should. And remember that I said patience, Cole."

He almost laughed at the don't-you-dare-eat-any-cookies-before-dinner tone in her voice that he'd heard countless times growing up. "Yes, ma'am, I heard you. So you don't think I would be a terrible man or cop if I let this get personal?"

"If God has brought this woman into your life, then no, absolutely not. God doesn't make mistakes."

"Okay, Grams." Cole brushed a piece of straw off his jeans. "I promise I'll think about everything you've said."

"Good. You know I'll be praying for you."

"I do. And I appreciate it."

"*Gi zah gin.*"

"I love you, too."

"Be good and stay safe."

This time she didn't ring off immediately after saying the words, as though she needed to hear his confirmation.

"I'll do my best." Cole disconnected the call and stuck the phone into his pocket. Talking to his grandmother inevitably clarified any issue for him. What that might mean for him and Starr, he wasn't sure. That was up to her. He would respect however she felt and whatever she wanted to happen or not happen between the two of them.

He studied the small room. An idea began to form, and he stayed where he was for a few minutes, allowing himself to fully visualize it. This room would work perfectly, and it would make Starr happy.

Whether or not she decided she wanted their relationship to go any deeper, if doing this for her would ensure her happiness, he'd get started on the project right away.

CHAPTER TWENTY

Although Halloween was still a few days away, winter typically came early in this part of Ontario. Today the season of cold and dark was rudely shouldering autumn aside and barging its way into the area. Snow pelted the windshield as Cole backed the old farm truck up to the cabin to unload the supplies he'd picked up that morning. Thankfully, his dad had kept a stash of cash in a safe in his office. Cole had almost forgotten that, but, when he was wondering how to pay for the supplies he needed for this project without using a credit or debit card Brady could track him with, it had come to him. As had the combination when he started to turn the knob. The stack of twenty-dollar bills would keep them going for a while, allow them to make the occasional purchase he couldn't charge to the Toronto PD.

Work on his secret project was going slowly, mostly because he didn't want Starr to suspect anything, so he could work out here only when she was occupied inside, reading in front of the fire or before she woke up in the morning.

Today he'd headed out first thing to catch the hardware store as soon as it opened. Hopefully he'd be able to transfer everything into the cabin and be in the kitchen making breakfast before Starr came down.

When he finished, he pulled the truck around to the side of the barn. Through one of the large windows that lined the side wall, movement inside the building caught his eye, and he shook his head. It was getting harder and harder to rise before Starr. She'd slept until eight or nine the first few weeks at the ranch, but lately it wasn't that unusual for her to be out with the horses by seven. Time with Cocoa appeared to be deeply therapeutic for her. After she'd spent an hour or two brushing the big horse or trotting through a field on Cocoa's back, happiness emanated from Starr like the warm, familiar smells of leather and horse hide, which made Cole equally happy. At least.

He slammed the truck door and strode to the opening of the barn. When he stepped inside, Starr's back was to him as she swept the walkway, and he took advantage of the opportunity to study her. She seemed so at home on the ranch. It was nearly impossible to comprehend that she hadn't set foot outside the largest city in Canada until a couple of months ago.

What if they stayed?

Cole propped a shoulder against the door frame. He'd used up his vacation time, and now he was on a leave of absence from the Sudbury PD. If that went on for too long, he'd have to start dipping into his savings. His boss had offered to talk to the Elliott Lake police department, see if they would be interested in accepting him on transfer, which Cole was open to. Even part-time work here would help. But it might turn into full time, and then there would be no reason not to give up his apartment in Sudbury and live here indefinitely. And maybe Starr would want to stay with...

He shoved away from the frame. That was putting the cart so far ahead of the horse the animal might never catch up. He couldn't even think about anything long term for them yet, not until he knew what she was thinking about the future.

He took a step toward her and froze at the sight of something in Starr's path. *God, no!* Although rattlesnakes inhabited this region, they rarely came onto the property. Not into the buildings, anyway. Cole had seen only two of them out here in his lifetime. Both times his dad had calmly walked over in his high rubber boots, lifted the snake with a pitchfork, and carried it out to the fields. Given the recent drop in temperature, the reptile was likely seeking the warmth of the barn and had no intention of harming anyone. Still, if Starr got a step or two closer, chances were good it would strike.

She preferred to wear sneakers when she was riding, and Cole realized with a sick twist in his gut that she hadn't pulled on her rubber boots before coming out here, leaving her legs vulnerable even through her jeans.

Cole took another step forward. "Starr." He forced his voice to stay low and even so he wouldn't make her jump. "Don't move."

She stopped sweeping. He knew the second she spotted the snake because she tensed, dropped the broom to the cement floor with a clatter, and then snatched a shovel leaning against the wall. Lifting it high into the air, she brought it down on the snake. She hit it three times before Cole could reach her. "Okay, okay. You got it. It's dead."

"Are you sure?" Starr lowered the shovel but kept a tight hold on it, as though the snake might lift its completely crushed head and lunge toward her.

"I'm positive." Cole tugged the shovel from her gently. His heart thundered so loudly he could barely hear his own voice, and he concentrated on taking several deep breaths as he picked up the broom and carried it and the shovel over to lean them against the wall.

After grabbing a pitchfork, he returned to her side. "What, exactly, do the words *don't move* mean to you?"

"In this case, with a rattlesnake three feet from my shoes, they meant stand there and let it sink its fangs into my leg."

"If you hadn't moved, it likely wouldn't have struck."

"I preferred not to take that chance."

Cole sighed. Although he liked seeing her stand her ground and make decisions for herself—something most former sex slaves had had beaten out of them—sometimes, like it had with the snake, that kind of defiance could endanger her, which terrified him. It did suggest she was coming to trust that he wouldn't get angry if she talked back to him, which was a good sign. "For the record, I try not to kill snakes when I see them, especially the Massasauga rattler, since they're a protected species in Ontario. I pick them up with the pitchfork and carry them out to the field."

"Well, for the record, I always take a shovel and crush the heads of the venomous snakes I encounter."

Cole's lips twitched. "Encountered a lot of venomous snakes in the city, did you?"

"No. This is my first one. That's how I know I crush them every single time. Only way to deal with a snake, as far as I'm concerned."

A little of the terror lifted, and he chuckled. "I'll give you that, for a city girl, you do know how to take care of yourself."

"Who else is going to?"

Cole's smile faded. She'd clearly meant to say that lightly, but a thread of pain wound through the words. And truth. At least, the truth as she had lived it until a couple of months ago. "I would have, if you'd given me time." He stuck the tines of the fork under the dead reptile, picked it up, and headed for the door. "I'll be right back."

After tossing the snake into the long grass at the edge of the field, Cole slammed the pitchfork into the soil and leaned against the implement. A cold north wind bit into his face and neck, but he barely noticed as he gazed out over the white field to where it met the edge of the gray horizon. He reflected on the first thing that had crossed his mind when he realized what was happening in the barn. It hadn't been a blasphemous thought—he'd said it like a real prayer. And he'd done it without thinking, as though maybe it was becoming instinct. Was that possible? And had God answered his fervent plea by not allowing the snake to bite Starr? "God, if that was you watching out for her in there, thank you. If you're as all-knowing as Grams says, you don't need me to tell you I'm in over my head here in more ways than I can count. Please help me. And please keep watching over Starr. I don't know what I'd do if something happened to her."

The wind rustled the grass at his feet. Otherwise, no audible response came to him. Not that he'd been expecting one, even if Grams did seem to hear exactly what God was saying to her. Cole didn't have her years of practice, so even talking to someone he couldn't see or hear felt foreign to him. A little less each time, so maybe that was the secret. "Thank you." He nodded toward the horizon and added, "Amen." He wasn't sure what that meant, but it was how Grams and Starr ended their prayers, so it must be right.

Cole took a deep breath as he made his way to the barn, hoping he'd be calm enough by the time he reached Starr that she wouldn't detect how much her close call had, well, *rattled* him. When he stepped inside the building, Starr had grabbed the broom again and calmly returned to sweeping the floor.

Cole wandered over. "Are you okay?"

"I'm fine."

"It didn't scare you, facing down a snake like that?"

She stopped sweeping and lifted slender shoulders. "I've faced down worse."

Which was probably true. The sick feeling in his stomach intensified. "You're really something, do you know that?"

She took another swipe at a scattering of straw in the walkway. "I'm no one special."

"Do you truly believe that? Starr, I've encountered a lot of women through my work who went through something similar to what you did, and no one I ever met came out of it as strong as you have or as full of life." Cole barely resisted the urge to grab her hands to ensure his words were getting through. "Even so, you're not on your own anymore. I'm here, and more than anything I want to be there for you, to try and keep you safe any way I can."

A small smile crossed her lips as she met his eyes. "You're very dedicated to your job."

"You have to know this stopped only being a job for me a while ago." He grimaced. That had slipped out before he'd had time to think it through. "I mean, I care about you. And I care very much about keeping you safe and making sure nothing happens to you. But you have to help me do that. I need you to promise that you'll trust me when I ask you to do something, that it's for your own protection, and that you'll do it."

For a few seconds, her gaze probed his, as though she was deciding whether she could do what he asked. He got it—she'd been in survival mode for so long, with no one to stand up for her against Brady or his goons. It would require a momentous act of will to surrender that kind of control to him. He wasn't sure she would be able to do it. Then she nodded. "All right. I'll try."

"Thank you." Cole held out a hand for the broom. "I think we've both earned breakfast. Let's go in and I'll make something for us."

"That does sound good."

After propping the broom against the wall, he followed her out the door into the crisp morning. When they reached the truck, he opened the passenger door and grabbed the paper bag of groceries, which he'd picked up partly because they needed them and partly because he didn't want Starr to wonder why he'd driven to town.

She tugged the black wool gloves from the pocket of her purple coat and slid them on. "Feels like winter."

"It is coming. It's going to get a lot colder and snowier than this in the next month or so."

They passed the small cabin he'd unloaded supplies into that morning, and Cole held his breath. Hopefully she wouldn't ask for a tour—not until he was ready to show her what he was working on inside. He released it in a puff of white air when she didn't glance at the building. Her attention was on the small shed to their right. "Will we have enough wood for the winter?"

Cole had chopped quite a bit since they'd gotten here, but not enough to get them through the coldest months if he wanted to keep the thermostat low. "I'll chop more before the heavy snow comes."

"Could you teach me how?"

"If you want me to."

"I do." She rubbed her hands together as they approached the bottom of the stairs. "But first, coffee."

"Definitely." He'd been up for three hours and hadn't had his first cup yet. Cole followed her up the steps.

Starr pulled open the screen door and reached for the knob, but it didn't turn. "It's locked." She looked up at him and touched two gloved fingers to her lips. "It must have been locked when I pulled it closed. I'm sorry."

"Don't worry. It happens."

"Do you have a key?"

"Actually, I don't. I put the one my dad kept under the rock on my set of car keys and left them hanging up inside when I took the truck to town."

Her eyes widened. "What are we going to do?"

Cole set the bag of groceries on the small table between two wicker chairs on the front porch. "There's always more than one way to get into an old house. Come with me. I'll show you what to do if it ever happens when I'm not here."

She let the screen door close. Cole strode around to the back of the house and shoved aside several long, reaching branches. "There's a window hidden behind the bush that my dad always left open for situations like this."

Cole pushed past the evergreen branches until he stood in front of a small window, barely big enough for an adult to climb through to get into the laundry room. He planted his palms at the top of the lower frame and shoved upwards. The glass slid easily, revealing an opening with no screen.

Starr squeezed into the small area next to him. "Want me to go in?"

"I don't mind."

"I'll fit through more easily."

He held a hand toward the opening. "Suit yourself."

The bottom of the frame was about hip high, so Starr was able to swing a leg over the sill and then lower herself onto the floor on the other side.

Cole peered through the opening. "You good?"

"Yep." She headed for the laundry room door. "I'll let you in the front."

Cole pushed the window down as tightly as he could before shoving aside the branches of the bush, its needles pricking his fingers through his thin wool gloves.

By the time he climbed the steps and grabbed the bag of groceries, Starr had unlocked the door. "Thanks." Cole held the screen open with his elbow, and she let go and stepped out of his way. "I think that's enough excitement for one morning, don't you?"

"Never a dull moment at the ranch, is there?"

"Not with you around, there isn't." Cole carried the groceries to the kitchen. If they were lucky, killing a snake and getting locked out of the house would be the most excitement they'd face between now and the start of Brady Erickson's trial.

CHAPTER TWENTY-ONE

Cole set the wooden bar in place on the double barn doors, locking them for the night. When he turned, headlights slashed across the yard. He melted into the shadows at the side of the barn. Who would be dropping in unannounced? He shot a look toward the house. Starr had gone in ahead of him and was somewhere inside, alone. If the occupants of the car had malicious intent, they would be between him and Starr, and it was unlikely he could get to her before they did.

The driver's door swung open, and Cole tensed, prepared to run at whoever it was if they appeared to be a threat. His muscles relaxed when a woman stepped lightly to the ground. Cassandra White.

Cole stepped out of the shadows. "Hey, Cassie." Cassandra was a lawyer who worked as legal counsel for the police department in Elliott Lake. His dad had introduced them when Cole was home for Christmas last year, and Cole had asked her out to dinner a couple of times. Enough to know that, although he liked her and considered her a friend, there was no spark between them that could grow into anything more.

"Hi, Cole." She met him at the end of the walkway leading to the front porch.

"What brings you all the way out here tonight?"

"I had to see for myself if the rumors were true."

Were people talking about him and Starr? The more they did, the greater the chance the wrong people might catch wind of her presence. "What rumors?"

"That you're keeping a woman here in protective custody."

Cole shot a look in the direction of the house. "That's not meant to be common knowledge."

"So it's true."

"Where did you hear that?" *And what business is it of yours?*

"Why are you evading the question?"

Cole expelled a breath. "I am protecting a witness, but, like I said, that's supposed to be confidential. The more people who know, the more danger she is in. Can you tell me who told you?"

"Relax. Since you've brought her here to our jurisdiction, the chief and I have been discussing the case. It's all strictly confidential."

"This is an official visit, then? A little late in the day for that, isn't it?"

She rested a hand on her hip. "It's an unofficial call. I was driving by and thought I'd stop in and see how you were. This is a dangerous assignment, Cole, and I'm concerned about you. I don't want to see you get hurt."

Somehow, he didn't think she meant physically. "I'm doing my job."

"Is that all it is?"

He contemplated her. "Why are you really here, Cassie?"

She took a step closer. The light scent of spicy perfume drifted from her as she tossed her long, auburn hair over one shoulder. "Talking to the chief got me thinking about you, that's all. I thought you and I had something, but I haven't heard from you in months."

Cole gestured toward the house. "As the chief told you, I've been busy."

"Is that all it is? If so, I can wait. But I'd like to know I wouldn't be wasting my time."

He repressed a sigh. As far as he was concerned, he'd made it pretty clear after their last date that he wasn't interested in pursuing anything more. "Look, Cassie, I like you. We're friends. But I don't see it being anything more than that between us. I'm sorry."

Her features hardened. "This is about *her*, isn't it?"

He frowned. "Who?"

"This woman you're supposedly protecting. She's becoming more than an assignment to you, isn't she?"

"This has nothing to do with her. I told you after the last time we went out that I didn't see us going anywhere."

The screen door creaked open. "Cole? Dinner's ... Oh."

Even in the dim light, Cole caught the trepidation that flashed across Starr's face. He lifted a hand. "It's okay. This is Cassandra White, legal counsel for the police department."

Her shoulders relaxed a little, but Starr pressed a hand to the wooden porch post as though she needed the support. Not surprising. Cassandra was the first person other than Cole she'd seen since coming to the ranch. Anger simmered in his gut like a pilot light. Cassie ought to have known better than to show up here without warning, given the circumstances.

In the warm glow of the porchlight, Starr offered their visitor a faint smile. "Nice to meet you, Cassandra. Do you want to come inside? You're welcome to join us for dinner."

Having Cassie around for hours was the last thing Cole wanted. He shook his head. "She was just leaving."

Cassandra took a deep breath. "That's right. I need to get going. Thank you, though."

Starr nodded. "Good to meet you."

"You too."

Cole waited until Starr had disappeared into the house before returning his attention to Cassandra. She was watching him intently. "Seriously?"

"Seriously what?"

Her hazel eyes bore into his. "She is a *hooker*, Cole. Do you have any idea how many men—"

The simmer exploded into an inferno. "Stop. Do not say another word. She is not a hooker." He shot a look in the direction of the house before leaning closer and grinding out, "She was the victim of a human trafficker. Have you no compassion?"

Her shoulders slumped. "You're right, of course." She rested a hand on his chest. It took everything Cole had not to step back, out of her reach. "I care about you, Cole. I don't want to see you get hurt. In any way."

"I'm a big boy. I can take care of myself. And her."

"Because she's your *responsibility*."

"Exactly."

She withdrew her hand. "All right, stick to that story. But if you aren't going to be honest with me, you might try being honest with yourself. And her." When he didn't respond, Cassie climbed behind the wheel and Cole closed the door. She lowered the window and rested her arm on the frame. For a few seconds, she only stared through the front windshield. Then she met his gaze. "I can see why you're drawn to her; she's lovely. Not what I expected at all."

Not what I expected, either. The heat in his chest cooled a little. "Like I said, I'm only doing my job."

A small smile played around her lips. "If you say so." She leaned forward and started the engine. "I'll tell the chief you have things well in hand."

"You do that."

"And I apologize for what I said; you're right, it was uncalled for and unfair."

"I accept your apology."

"Thank you." Cassie's eyes, when they met his, held sadness. "Be careful, Cole."

"Always." Cole nodded and watched as the car bounced down the driveway and turned onto the road. Then he strode across the front yard, heading for the house. Although he'd accepted Cassie's apology, her words still echoed in his ears, pelting him like stones. *Please God, if you're out there somewhere, don't let Starr have heard them.*

Cole found her in the kitchen. She was tossing salad in a wooden bowl on the counter and didn't look up when he came in. He studied her. She didn't look upset, but no one knew better than he did how well she could hide her emotions. Eight years of working for Brady had drilled that into her. "Hey."

She managed to flash him a brief smile without meeting his eyes. "Hey."

Knots formed in his stomach. He'd made stew in the slow cooker earlier, and the comforting aromas of simmering meat, veggies, and gravy wafted on the air. He inhaled. Some other smell mingled with the stew. "Are you *baking* something?"

"I thought I'd make biscuits for dinner."

"Wow. I didn't know you baked."

"I don't. Felicity tried to teach us, but I was definitely the worst at it. I wanted to try, though, so I watched a YouTube video."

"They smell good."

"I hope they will be."

Cole washed his hands at the sink and then walked to the island. "Anything I can do?"

"You can set the table if you want." She refused to look at

him. The salad was well tossed, but still she dug into it with both wooden tongs.

Cole's chest clenched as he flattened both hands on the top of the island. "You heard, didn't you?"

"Heard what?"

"Starr."

She stuck the tongs into the lettuce. "All right, yes, I heard. I'm sorry. I didn't mean to listen in on your conversation. I only wondered who she was."

"I told you she's the legal counsel for the force."

She cocked her head and met his eyes for the first time since he'd come into the kitchen.

Cole blew out a breath. "All right. I guess I would call her a friend. And we did go out for dinner a couple of times. But there was nothing there."

"For you, maybe." She picked up the salad bowl and carried it to the table.

Was that a hint of jealousy in her voice? Hope sparked deep inside. "Starr." He waited until she set the bowl on the table and looked at him. "There was nothing there."

"It really isn't any of my business, Cole." Starr walked back over and reached for a bottle of salad dressing on the island.

Cole slid a few inches closer to her. She let go of the bottle. He stopped a foot away. The air between them vibrated until he could practically hear it humming. Everything in Cole longed to reach out and touch her, but he forced himself to keep his arms at his sides. After all she had been through, if anything ever happened between them, she would have to make the first move. "It could be your business."

She stared intently at the bottle of dressing. "No, it couldn't."

"Why not?"

Starr faced him. "Like I told you, I heard what your friend said. The question is, did you?"

He narrowed his eyes. "What does that mean?"

"She was only being honest. I *am* a—"

His head jerked. "Don't say it. Don't say that word."

"Not saying it doesn't make it less true."

"That is not what you are."

"Cole." Starr clutched the edge of the island. "I had sex with men for money. What else would you call it?"

"Did *you* get money for it?"

She blinked. "No, but—"

"Then that's not what you are. Or were." Cole ran a hand over his face. "Look, I hesitate to use the word *victim* with you, since nothing about you suggests that's what you are, but that is what you were. You were a scared kid when Brady took you, and whenever he or one of his men hit you, or you were forced to do things with a stranger in a hotel room, you were a victim. You weren't responsible for any of it. None of it was your fault."

Starr sighed. "And none of that is going to matter to people once my past gets out."

Cole wanted to protest that it wouldn't, but that was wishful thinking. At some point she was going to testify at Brady's trial, which would be covered by every major news outlet in the country. Everyone would know her story then. "Does it matter what a bunch of strangers have to say about you?"

"Not about me, no."

"I don't care what they say about me, either."

Starr's ocean-blue gaze met his. "I do."

For a moment, neither of them moved. His arms literally ached to hold her, but he'd been so careful not to touch her since bringing her here. For years she'd been subjected to men touching her without her consent, often violently. He was determined to show her that every man was not like that—that they didn't all see her as an object to use to fulfil their own base desires or property to be beaten into subservience.

Now, though, the electricity that arced between them was so strong that Cole struggled to keep that commitment. Given the look in her eyes, he wasn't sure she would object. Maybe—

The timer on the stove buzzed.

Starr whirled around and opened the oven door.

"Here." Cole pulled open a drawer and tugged out a pair of oven mitts. After sliding them on, he bent down, retrieved the baking sheet, and set it on the stove. Starr closed the door. When she straightened the towel hanging on the handle, her fingers shook slightly, and he berated himself for letting things get too intense between them. "These look amazing."

Starr touched one with the tip of her finger. "You're being kind. They don't look anything like Felicity's—hers were so big and fluffy."

"She likely had years of practice. These look pretty great for a first attempt."

"I guess the test will be how they taste." Starr grabbed a lifter and transferred several of the biscuits to a plate before carrying it to the table.

Cole scooped stew into bowls for them and set one at each of their places. They sat, and Starr lowered her head a moment. He sent up his own silent plea for patience and wisdom as she finished praying. The biscuits were hard and a little salty, but Cole slathered butter on his and wolfed it down.

Starr only downed half of one before setting it on her plate. "These are awful." She sounded so dismayed that he almost laughed.

"They're not awful at all. I think they're great."

"Wow. You must really"—she stopped and cleared her throat—"be hungry if you believe that."

What had she been about to say? That he must really care about her? "I was, but honestly, they're not that bad."

She pressed a finger to a crumb on the table and dropped it onto her plate. "I'm sorry. I wanted to do some of the baking and cooking so you wouldn't have to make everything."

"I'll teach you. It's not hard."

"Would you?"

"Of course. I don't have a huge repertoire, but I can show you what I know." When she looked at him like that, her eyes shining, there wasn't much he wouldn't happily agree to.

Maybe nothing.

"That would be great." She held his gaze for a few seconds. Then, as if she could sense the intensity building again and wanted to head it off, Starr finished her last spoonful of stew and pushed away from the table. "I think I'll head upstairs, read for a while."

A little distance was probably a good idea. They both needed to figure out what was going on between them and what they were going to do about it. She carried her bowl and plate to the sink. When she set them down, they rattled a little against the stainless steel. Cole stood and picked up his dishes. "Leave them. I'll do the clean-up tonight."

"Okay, thanks." The smile she offered him was a little shaky. "See you in the morning."

"I'll be here."

She nodded before disappearing into the hallway. Cole set his dishes on the counter before propping a hip against it. Was it possible Starr felt the same way he did? And how, exactly, *did* he feel? He pushed away from the counter and turned on the hot water. He knew exactly how he felt. He was falling for her, hard. The truth filled him with equal amounts of excitement and fear.

Starr had been through so much. Would she ever be able to give her heart freely and fully to anyone? Should he even ask her to? Likely not when he was supposed to be focusing on keeping her safe. He scrubbed a plate hard with the dishcloth. He wouldn't let Brady be the reason they weren't together. The man had stolen eight years of Starr's life; no way would Cole allow him to steal another minute.

He set the dishes in the rack, thoughts whirling through his head like pieces of his fort caught up in the tornado that day. Sometime soon, he would have to broach the subject with Starr. They couldn't keep dancing around it like they had tonight. After that, whether or not they moved forward with anything was entirely up to her.

CHAPTER TWENTY-TWO

Starr closed her bedroom door and leaned against the back of it, her heart racing. What had happened down there?

She'd heard more of Cole's conversation with Cassandra than she'd let on. Not only had she overheard what Cassandra had called her—her fists clenched against the door—but she'd caught Cole's ardent defence of her, too. Did he truly not see her that way?

She pushed away from the door. It didn't matter how Cole saw her. She'd heard what he'd said about that, too—that he was only doing his job. Despite his words in the barn that day —that she had to know this had become something more to him—the fact remained that she *was* his assignment. Maybe there was an attraction between them, but that didn't mean they were destined to live happily ever after. At some point during her years with Brady, she'd resigned herself to the fact that she would never have that kind of relationship. What decent, self-respecting man would marry a woman who'd done the things she had?

Starr sank onto the edge of the bed. Was that all it was? An attraction? Cole had never looked at her like the men who used to come into her hotel room. And he had never tried to touch her. Still, she knew he was drawn to her, like she was to him. The problem was, since she couldn't deny the growing chemistry between them, she couldn't stay here any longer. It wasn't right.

When Starr entered her teens and boys started paying a lot of attention to her, her mother talked to her often about God's design for relationships, which definitely did not include living in the same house with a man she was attracted to—a man for whom she had strong feelings—but who was not her husband.

Felicity had echoed her mother's advice when talking to Starr and her foster sisters about dating. She had strict rules, but she lovingly explained the reasons and the dangers inherent in the girls not following the boundaries laid out for their physical, emotional, and spiritual protection.

Although Brady and everything that had happened in the intervening years had destroyed Starr's plan to save herself for marriage, the desire to honor not only God but the two women whom she'd loved and respected so much still ran deep.

She slipped off the bed and onto her knees, folding her hands and resting them on top of the quilt. "Jesus," she whispered. "Help me to know what to do now. Where to go." She rested her forehead on her clasped fingers. Where *could* she go? She had no job, no money. Could she get one in town? "Show me the way. Please. And take away the feelings I have for Cole. Nothing can happen between us, and I don't want to get hurt. More than that, I don't want to hurt him."

How much did a small apartment cost, anyway? Starr twisted to glance at the door. Cole's footsteps had passed by twenty minutes earlier. He likely wouldn't hear her if she left her room. Not that he'd mind, but she didn't want him figuring out what she was thinking of doing until she could make definite plans. Starr pushed her palms into the mattress and rose, then tiptoed across the room. She turned the knob carefully and slowly pulled open the door so it wouldn't creak. When she didn't hear anything, she crept down the stairs.

Starr settled herself on the couch in the living room, the laptop resting on her knees. There weren't a lot of real estate listings in Elliott Lake, but a couple of apartment ads did look promising. If she could find a job, it shouldn't take too long to earn enough for a deposit and the first month's rent. Starr checked a couple of job sites while she was at it. She'd worked in a coffee shop for a year before Brady ... while she was in high school. Maybe she could do something like that again. Except she had no resume, no references, and no recent work experience. Nothing she could share with a prospective employer, anyway.

With a heavy sigh, she closed the laptop. It wasn't likely she could get either a job or an apartment, but she had to try. Cole wouldn't like it, but she'd do what she could to make him understand. Maybe he'd be relieved not to have to worry about her every minute. They'd been here for weeks. If Brady had been able to figure out where she was, he'd have escaped and made his way here by now. Or sent a couple of his punk security guards to exact revenge for him. Acid burned the back of her throat, and she set the laptop on the coffee table.

An image of Brady's computer, sitting on a large oak desk in the suite of rooms he'd invited her to one night, sent waves of cold rolling through her. Even if Brady hadn't tried to leave the house, that didn't mean he hadn't been working diligently night and day on his computer. He could have hired private investigators and sent word to his extensive network of contacts in an effort to find her and stop her from testifying against him. And, in the process, punish her for betraying him. A death like that would be long and torturous. A bullet through the head or running her down with a vehicle would be a mercy from him, and she could expect no mercy.

Starr forced the thoughts from her mind. God was watching over her and so was Cole. Even if she moved into town, he'd be able to stop by occasionally, make sure she was okay. And she'd pick up a disposable phone and promise to call if she needed him. That might ease his mind.

Starr sent up another fervent prayer for guidance as she climbed the stairs to her room. When she went into the small bathroom and squeezed toothpaste on her brush, she caught her reflection in the glass and touched her fingers to her lips. Tonight, in the kitchen, had Cole thought about kissing her? Would she have wanted him to?

Starr braced herself on the counter as chills pricked her arms. Maybe it would be dangerous for her to move out and get a place on her own.

But after tonight, it felt a lot more dangerous to stay here alone with Cole.

CHAPTER TWENTY-THREE

Cole poured himself a cup of coffee and carried it into the living room. He peered through the bay window, trying to see if Starr was outside. He hadn't heard her moving around, so maybe she was still sleeping. Personally, he'd tossed and turned in bed, going over and over what had happened in the kitchen the night before.

He lowered himself to the couch and drove the fingers of his free hand through his hair, longer than he usually kept it as he hadn't attempted to get a haircut since they'd arrived in the area. Slipping in and out of the grocery store was one thing, but a barbershop was usually the hub of all gossip in town, and he had no desire for them to become the subject of any of it.

Cole took a sip of coffee. It was just as well the oven timer had gone off when it did. Not that he would object to something starting up between them. After he'd talked to Grams, the idea had taken root in his mind and wouldn't let go. But until he knew for sure how Starr felt, he shouldn't do anything that might further complicate their already complicated situation.

To get his mind off her, he set his mug on the coffee table and reached for the laptop. A brown leather Bible sat next to it. Starr must have found it in the study and carried it out here. Another indication that maybe his father had more of a faith than Cole realized. Probably he should read it himself more often.

Cole left the computer and picked up the book. The leather was worn slightly along the edge, as though someone had opened it often. He flipped idly through a few pages. Handwritten words in one of the margins caught his eye, and he lifted the book closer to examine them. The writing was small and neat, definitely not his father's looping scrawl or Grams' curving, open style. Then who …?

He turned to the pages at the front. After reading the name inside the cover—Winona Joy Blacksky—he closed his eyes. He was holding his mother's Bible. Touching the same cover, the same pages her fingers had touched. How had he never seen this book before? When he opened his eyes and leafed through the pages, reading the words the woman who had sacrificed her life for his had penned next to numerous passages of Scripture, tears pricked his eyes. Cole ran his fingers over one of her notes before closing the Bible and setting it on the coffee table. He'd take his time going through it, reading every word she had written. Already he felt as though he knew her better, and he looked forward to delving deeper into who she was and what her relationship with God had been.

For a few moments, he gazed at the flames flickering behind the glass, absorbing the emotions seeping deep like an underground spring. Then he reached for the laptop to check the weather. If snow was in the forecast, he'd spend a few hours chopping wood this afternoon. Maybe give Starr that lesson he'd promised her.

Two tabs were already open, and he frowned when he

realized what they were—a site that advertised apartments for rent and another with job listings. Starr hadn't used a computer in years. Likely she thought she'd exited out of them, but she'd only minimized them. Why was she looking at those pages?

Cole groaned. He knew exactly why she was looking. He'd freaked her out the night before, and now she felt as though she needed to leave. What did she think, that she was no longer safe with him? The sip of coffee churned in his stomach. *You are an idiot, Blacksky.* At what point had he stopped thinking of Starr only as his responsibility and started thinking of her as something else entirely?

If he was honest, he'd never gotten over being thrown by their initial encounter. Likely he hadn't had a completely detached attitude toward her since he'd caught a glimpse of the humor that, incomprehensibly, she'd been able to display with him even when she thought he was there as a customer.

The truth was that Starr wasn't like any woman he'd ever met. Cole rested his head—which suddenly felt as though it weighed a hundred pounds—on the top of the couch and stared at the chandelier hanging above his head, wisps of cobweb trailing from the crystals.

God, can you help me out here? Maybe Grams and Starr are right, and you actually can hear me. And possibly you even care about what I'm going through. I know you have to care about Starr because, well, how could you not? I agree with you—keeping Starr safe is the most important thing in the world. Help me to remember that and, if they frighten her at all, to set aside my feelings so I can convince her I would never do anything to hurt her. Please.

Soft footsteps padded down the stairs and Cole straightened. After snapping the laptop closed, he returned it to the coffee table and reached for his mug. He followed the sounds of a cupboard door closing and a drawer sliding open. A beam of sunshine poked through the kitchen window to fall on the gleaming hair Starr had pulled into a ponytail, and he paused in the doorway to watch her.

When she started to turn, he stepped into the room and walked over to pour her a cup of coffee.

Her smile looked a little uncertain as she greeted him. "Good morning."

Cole added cream before holding the mug out to her. "Morning. *Makademashkikiwaaboo?*"

She blinked as she took it. "I'm sorry, what?"

He grinned. "That's *coffee* in Ojibwe. It literally translates to *black medicine water.*"

Starr laughed. "That's perfect." She took a sip of the steaming liquid.

"It's a fun language. A lot of words form a picture like that. Another one is *naabese*. It means rooster in English, but the literal translation is *one that struts like a man*. Those are the words Grams used, anyway. There are a lot of variations, partly because Ojibwe was originally an oral language and partly because a lot of the language was lost when generations of kids were sent to residential schools and not allowed to use it."

Starr winced as she set her cup on the island. "That's tragic."

"Yes, it is. A lot of people are working on bringing the language back, though, which is encouraging." Cole settled onto the stool across from her at the island. "How did you sleep?" She hadn't had a bad dream in the night, not that he'd heard, so maybe she hadn't been as freaked out as he thought. Although she was thinking of leaving …

"Pretty well. Longer than I'd intended."

"You're entitled to that once in a while." He hesitated. Should he bring it up? A faint warning bell sounded—either God's or Grams' voice in his head, he wasn't sure—but he ignored it. If she was planning to bolt, he needed to know. "Were you up late for some reason?"

She eyed him over the rim of her blue, polka-dotted mug. "No reason in particular."

"Are you sure?"

Starr set the mug on the island, hard enough that a few drops sloshed over the rim and onto her hand.

"Here." Cole strode to the sink. After running cold water on the dish cloth, he carried it over and handed it to her.

Starr took it and rubbed her hand, but her blue eyes were fixed on his. "Why are you asking me that?"

"I just …" He just what, needed to monitor everything she did so he could grill her about it?

"I'm not a fan of games, Cole. If you have something to say, go ahead and say it."

This is not going to go well. The warning bell grew louder. "Maybe we should discuss this later."

"No, I think we should discuss it now. You saw what I was looking at on the computer, didn't you?"

No way to avoid the conversation. He'd waded into a big pile of sludge, and he had no choice but to slog through to the other side. "I didn't mean to, but the tabs were open when I went on it a few minutes ago."

"You said it was okay for me to use the Internet."

"It is, but I'm a little concerned about what you were using it for."

"I didn't realize there were rules about what I could look at."

Cole repressed a sigh. He hadn't heard that tone in her voice before, and he didn't like it one bit. Why had he thought it would be a good idea to question anything she did after he'd told her repeatedly she was free to make her own choices, something she hadn't experienced in years? "There aren't any rules, no. But if you are considering leaving the ranch, I think it's something we should discuss."

"I'm not seriously thinking about it yet, but I wanted to at least look into the possibility."

"Starr. You know you can't leave here."

As soon as the words left his mouth, he knew they'd been a mistake. Too late, he put himself in her shoes and heard how they must sound.

She pulled herself up to her full height. Eyes flashing, she ground out the words, "I *can't* leave?"

Cole tried backtracking. "That didn't come out right. I only meant that it wouldn't be safe for you to go. Like I told you before, you're not a prisoner here."

"So, to clarify, I'm not a prisoner; I'm just not allowed to leave."

When he didn't answer, she grabbed her drink, marched to the sink, dumped out the coffee, and dropped the mug onto the stainless-steel bottom with a loud clunk. "I'm going to the barn." She whirled to face him. "That is, if I have your permission to go outside."

He winced. All right, maybe he deserved that. Still … "You don't need my permission to do anything."

"Just checking." She stalked across the room.

Desperate to repair at least a little of the damage he'd done, Cole met her at the end of the island. "Wait." Without thinking, he reached out, intending to lightly touch her sleeve as she passed by. She flinched and ducked away from him. Cole dropped his hand. Did she think he would hit her? The idea sickened him more than anything that had happened that morning.

Starr stormed past him and disappeared into the hallway. Seconds later, the screen door slammed.

Cole backed up to the nearest bar stool and dropped onto

it. Propping his elbows on the island, he lowered his forehead to his palms. *God, didn't I ask you to help me out there?*

Even if he didn't know God terribly well yet, Cole didn't need an audible response to know exactly how God would respond to that. He'd warned Cole—twice—to keep his big mouth shut and let Starr come talk to him when she was ready.

It wasn't God's fault that Cole hadn't had the sense to listen.

CHAPTER TWENTY-FOUR

Cole waited half an hour before following Starr to the barn. When he pulled open the heavy wooden door, she was shoveling out a stall, her back to him as she dumped one furious load of muck after another into the wheelbarrow. When it was full, she tossed the pitchfork onto the cement walkway with a clatter, dug into the back pocket of her jeans to retrieve the jackknife he'd given her, then yanked open the blade and sawed through the binder twine on a bale of straw until it gave way beneath the intense pressure with a snap. Cole grimaced. Definitely not the time to continue their earlier conversation. He set a takeout mug of coffee and two apples—one for her and one for Cocoa—on the top of the wall of one of the empty stalls inside the door and slipped out into the cold morning.

The light layer of snow they'd gotten a few days ago was gradually melting in the wan November sunlight, but frost still glazed the blades of grass that crunched beneath his boots as he made his way to the cabin where he'd been working on the surprise for Starr. He had a couple of boxes of supplies to unload, and then the place would be ready for her to see.

But when would she be ready to see it?

Cole dropped onto one of the benches he'd set in the center of the room. Now what? He stared at the blank wall in front of him for several minutes before pushing to his feet. Pulling out his own jackknife, he sliced open the two boxes he'd carried in here the day before and scrounged around in them until he found what he was looking for—a two-foot-high ornate metal cross. Cole snatched the hammer and one of the nails he'd left on the small table at the front of the room, pounded the nail into the wall, and hung up the cross.

The pounding helped a little, but the sight of the cross helped even more. Cole wasn't sure why, but a lot of the tension that had turned his muscles to steel that morning eased when he contemplated it, and he took the first deep breath he'd been able to draw in since opening the laptop an hour earlier. He sank onto the bench again, mesmerized by the ornate scrolling on the piece of art. It was only a symbol, yet it held a kind of power he couldn't explain.

"I don't get it yet, God, but I want to. Can you help me?"

A slight warmth flowed through his chest, accompanied by an almost indiscernible movement, like the wind rippling through Coal Miner's mane when Cole took him for a ride. Was that God letting Cole know he was there? That he heard him? Cole fervently hoped so because he needed divine guidance today.

For the rest of the morning, he unloaded the boxes and placed everything where he'd pictured it the day he sat on the couch in this cabin and imagined what it could look like. When he finished, he stood by the door and surveyed the room, nodding in satisfaction before switching off the light and heading outside.

Starr didn't come inside the house while he was making lunch, so he threw together a ham and cheese sandwich, washed it down with a glass of lemonade, and headed out to the woodshed. Obviously she was still angry with him, and he didn't blame her. Hopefully being with Cocoa was helping her. Or maybe she'd discovered the punching bag hanging in one of the empty stalls. Cole hoped so, since that bag had helped him deal with a lot of stress and resentment growing up.

He set a piece of wood on the stump, grasped the axe in both hands, and then raised it over his head and brought it down on the piece of wood. A couple of hours later, he'd worked out a lot of the frustration he'd been feeling—with himself, mostly—and added quite a bit of wood to the pile for winter. He lowered the head of the axe to the ground and swiped his other arm across his forehead.

"Hey."

Cole spun in the direction of the voice. Starr stood at the edge of the woodshed, clutching the reusable cup he'd left in the barn earlier. She lifted it in his direction. "Thank you for this."

"It was the least I could do."

She wrinkled her nose as she came over and sat on one of the pieces of wood that ringed the firepit Cole's dad had dug in the yard. "You don't have to feel that way. I know you were only concerned about me. It's possible I'm a little oversensitive to people telling me I can't leave a place." She offered him a wry grin.

"That's understandable." Cole leaned the axe against the stump he used for cutting and walked over to sit next to her. "But it was wrong of me to push you to tell me what you were thinking. I should have waited until you came to me yourself, when you were ready."

"Which I would have done."

"I know. The thought of you leaving scared me, though, and I wasn't thinking clearly."

"I know I wouldn't be as safe in my own place, but I'd be

careful. And I could get a disposable phone to call you if I needed you."

The desperate fear of her going away, somewhere apart from him where he couldn't keep constant vigil, was beginning to mingle with a growing feeling of hurt. Was it him she didn't want to be around anymore? "Don't you like it here?"

Starr set the coffee cup on the ground and clasped her gloved fingers in her lap. "I love it here. These months on the ranch have been the happiest of my life."

"Then why do you want to leave?"

She bit her lip. "I just ... don't think it's the best idea anymore, you and me being here alone."

"Why not?"

She shrugged. "I just don't. Can we leave it at that for now? I promise I won't make any rash decisions—I'll talk to you before I make any kind of move."

"All right. Thank you." After what had happened that morning, he wasn't about to push her to share anything she wasn't ready to share. Hopefully she would come to him when she had a better idea of what she wanted to do and why, and they could discuss it. In the meantime, he'd pray she would have a change of heart and be content to stay here. Especially since she'd admitted she was happier than she'd ever been. Another piece of information he stored away to analyze later.

"Are you still willing to teach me?" Starr nodded at the stump where he'd propped the axe.

"Sure." Cole stood and walked over. "Stay there and I'll show you."

He grabbed a large piece of wood and set it on the flat surface. When it was balanced, he stepped back, planted his feet, and eyed the spot where he wanted the blade to land. When he lifted the axe and brought it down, the piece of wood fell into two perfect halves. Cole nudged one piece off before standing the other half on its end and slicing it in half.

He did the same with the other until he had four pieces of wood pretty much the same size and shape.

Starr grabbed two of the pieces to set on top of their growing pile. "Pretty impressive."

Cole offered her a mock bow, a piece of wood in each hand. "Thank you very much." He stacked the wood and then picked up the axe and held the handle out. "Want to give it a go?"

"Absolutely." Starr pulled off her gloves and stuck them in her pocket before reaching for it. Cole hefted a piece of wood onto the stump, made sure it was solidly in place, and moved a few feet away.

Starr studied the wood for a few seconds before raising the axe over one shoulder. Cole held his breath. As long as she didn't miss the stump entirely, she would be okay. Hopefully. She took a deep breath and then brought the axe down on the wood. She didn't hit it very hard, and the blade bounced off the top of it. "Hmm. It's harder than it looks."

"Like most things, it takes practice. Want to try again?"

"Of course." She adjusted her stance before lifting the axe. This time she swung it a little harder, and the blade sank into the wood, stopping halfway down. She lifted the axe and the wood came with it, the head buried deep inside. Starr sent him a helpless look. "Now what?"

Cole strode forward. "Here." He took the axe from her, lifted it embedded in the wood, and brought it down hard enough on the stump that the piece of wood split in half.

"Well, sure, I did the hard part for you."

He chuckled. "Yes, you did."

"Can I try again?"

He handed her the axe and set one of the half pieces of wood on the stump. This time she studied it for a good minute, walking around it like a golfer planning out her final shot at the Masters.

Cole pressed his lips together. Finally she stopped, planted her feet, and brought the axe down on the wood. One piece toppled onto the stump and the other landed on the ground with a thud.

"Ha!" She let out her trademark triumphant cry. For ten more minutes, she hacked away at pieces of wood and tossed them to Cole to stack on the pile. She laughed easily at herself when she missed or couldn't strike hard enough to penetrate the wood, something that happened more often as she grew tired. The wind ruffled strands of hair that had come loose from her ponytail, and her eyes were bright with exertion and fresh autumn air.

Cole struggled to tear his gaze away and not get caught watching her. They'd barely gotten back on even footing—he didn't want to do anything to drive a wedge between them again.

Or add fuel to her desire to leave the place.

At last she surrendered the axe to him, rubbing her upper right arm with a rueful look. "I'm making progress with the farm muscles, but I think chopping wood must require a whole other set."

"You did great. That's enough wood for today, anyway. I'll go out and bring in the horses for the night, and then I'll start supper."

"Sounds good."

She started for the house. Cole leaned the axe against the stump. As much as he didn't want to drag them back to that morning, something still weighed on him, and he needed to deal with it before any more time passed. "Starr?"

"Yes?" She stopped on the bottom step of the porch and faced him.

Cole walked over and stopped a couple feet in front of her. With her on the step, they stood pretty much eye to eye. It would be great if they saw the topic he was about to bring up the same way. "You know I would never, ever hit you, don't you?"

Her shoulders slumped. "I do. Honest. I'm sorry I reacted like that this morning—it was pure instinct."

"I get it. But it killed me, thinking you could ever be afraid of me."

Starr shook her head, her ponytail swishing across her shoulders. "I'm not. The opposite, in fact. When I'm with you, I feel completely ... safe."

That went a long way toward healing the hurt of their earlier exchange. "Good. That's how I want you to feel. Because you are."

She gripped the stair railing. "I did a lot of thinking while I was working in the barn, and I might be ready to call that woman you mentioned."

Relief surged through Cole, but he worked to keep it off his face. "All right. I'll look up her number as soon as I come in."

She nodded and offered him a smile before heading into the house. Cole stood for a long moment, staring at the screen door, before making his way to the stables. Somehow he had to convince Starr to stay. Not only because he wouldn't be able to keep her safe if she left, although that was still his top priority, but because he couldn't imagine not being able to greet her in the morning, her sleepy sapphire eyes meeting his over the rim of her coffee cup. Or hearing her voice drifting along the hallway when she stood at the window and sang the song her mother had taught her when she was a child. Or lying in bed listening for her cry so he could go to her room and comfort her. Who would do that if she moved away?

Cole shook his arms as he wandered past the horse stalls, trying to rid himself of the melancholy. If Starr called the therapist Lake had recommended, the woman might be able to help her work through whatever it was that was driving her to take off.

In the meantime, everything was good between them. And maybe, if he dedicated himself to making them even better, Starr would change her mind about ever leaving here at all.

CHAPTER TWENTY-FIVE

Starr shoved both palms against the bathroom counter and stared at her reflection. *What are you doing?* Out by the woodshed, she'd come close to admitting her growing feelings for Cole. Had he picked up that she didn't feel she could stay here any longer because she was falling for him? The last thing she wanted was to leave the ranch—and him—but her fear of staying was intensifying. Part of that was because it seemed inappropriate when she was coming to think of him as far more than the man assigned to protect her. So much of what she'd had to do in Brady's service had left her feeling sullied and tainted before God, but she hadn't had much choice then.

This she did have a choice in. And now that she was free of the life she'd been forced to live for most of a decade, she was determined to stay pure in her thoughts and her actions before God. Which meant not living alone with Cole, spending so much time with him.

The other part was that her survival instinct was kicking in. Her feelings for Cole left her vulnerable, and she had felt vulnerable for far too long. If she allowed herself to give in to what she felt for him deep down, she would open herself up to unspeakable heartache. And she couldn't put herself through that—not when she was already dealing with so much.

The only way to prevent having her heart shattered was to leave here. To leave Cole. Even if that meant making herself more of a target for Brady. Neither choice was appealing, but in many ways it felt riskier to stay on the ranch than it did to leave. Physical pain she was used to and could handle, but emotional pain was much more devastating.

Starr pushed away from the sink. She'd do a little more research into jobs in town as soon as she could get on the computer without Cole around. She hadn't promised she wouldn't keep looking into the possibility of leaving, only that she would let him know if she made any decisions. Which she would.

She left the bathroom and walked to the large window overlooking the fields. The thought of not being able to see this view whenever she wanted to, of being alone in the world again, dug out such a gaping cavern in her chest that she had to hold the heel of her hand to it so she could draw in a breath.

This life on the ranch felt like looking out the tiny window of the room she had shared with Ruby—the ever-changing beauty on the other side of the glass close enough to see but with a barrier between her and it that couldn't be breached. Being here, with Cole, was the same. It had given her a brief, breathtaking glimpse into a world that was beyond her grasp. And while it had brought her joy and hope, the longing it had sparked within her was slowly destroying her.

She had to leave.

The north star glimmered on the horizon. Starr touched the cool glass with the tip of her index finger. *I can't have him, I know that. So please help me to let him go. To walk away while I still have the strength to do it.*

For a few seconds, she gazed at the bright star, reflecting on the words of her fervent prayer. *Did* she still have the strength to walk away? The thought of it made her physically ill, but she'd forced herself to do a lot of things that made her physically ill in the past. She could do it again.

Maybe.

Starr spun away from the window and made her way downstairs. While she was here, she would enjoy every moment with Cole and with Cocoa. She'd soak in the beauty of this place so that, when she was gone, she could hold everything she'd experienced here in her heart as precious memories that would sustain her through whatever lay ahead.

The smell of hot grease lured her to the kitchen. Cole stood on the far side of the island, chopping vegetables. Behind him, something sizzled in a frying pan. He looked up and smiled as she wandered into the room. He wore jeans and a black T-shirt, and the combination of the way he looked, the smile, and the great cooking was severely testing her resolve to stay strong. *Jesus, protect my heart.*

"Something smells good. Can I help?"

"Sure." Cole scooped up a handful of chopped carrots and celery and tossed it on top of a bowl of lettuce. "What do you know about grilling?"

"Grilling?"

"You know, on the barbeque? I was about to throw on a couple of steaks."

"Um, pretty much nothing. I'm not sure I've ever barbequed. Funny enough, not something most people in the city do."

"Then it's time. Come out to the back deck."

He carried a container to the glass doors that opened to a wooden deck. Once Starr had stepped outside, he followed her and slid the door closed. Smoke seeped from the sides of the closed lid of the barbeque. Obviously Cole had already started a fire in it—or whatever you did with barbeques. He set the container on a flat surface extending out one side of the barbeque and removed the lid. The aroma of spices wafted from the meat. "I've already marinated them and preheated the barbeque." He lifted a pair of tongs from a hook attached to the end of the flat area and used it to reach into the container and lift out one of the two steaks. Clutching the tongs in one hand, he lifted the barbeque lid with the other and set the steak on top of a row of thin round bars. The meat hissed when it hit the hot metal, and another waft of spices rose on a cloud of steam.

Starr breathed deeply. The aroma was already incredible, and it hadn't cooked yet. "Smells amazing."

He held out the tongs, handle first. "Want to put the other one on?"

She accepted the utensil and then slid the tongs around the remaining steak. When she transferred it to the grill, the same hiss greeted her offering, which sent an inordinate rush of satisfaction through her.

Cole slid the lid onto the empty container. "Are you okay to keep turning them every three or four minutes while I finish dinner?"

Her trepidation must have shown on her face because he laughed. "You'll do fine. If you drop one or burn them, it's not the end of the world—I have more in the freezer."

That helped. The fear of doing something wrong and being punished for it was deeply ingrained in her, but every time Cole said something like that, the fear loosened its grip a little. "All right, then. I'll give it a go."

His smile was warm in the glow of the back deck light. "Great. I'll check on you shortly." Cole retreated into the house but left the glass door open.

For a few minutes, Starr concentrated on the steaks. When she finally looked up from the grill, her throat went a little dry. While Cole had been there, next to her, she hadn't noticed how dark it had become, how heavy the blackness hung over the lawn and, beyond that, the farmyard and fields. The lone lamppost near the barn did little to penetrate the darkness. The moon was a tiny sliver in the sky, and all the stars had disappeared behind heavy clouds. A cold northern wind brushed past Starr, carrying bits of ice that tingled against her face, her throat, her bare fingers. She shivered as the wind moaned through the evergreen trees on the property.

The back of her neck prickled. Anyone could be out there, watching. Backlit by the lamp next to the door, she was an easy target. Something rustled in the underbrush, and all the warmth drained from her. Starr backed toward the house, holding the tongs in front of her, a pitiable defence against anything—or anyone—that might come lunging out of the dark.

"Starr?"

She let out a small scream as she whirled around, still brandishing the tongs. Cole stood in the doorway clutching a plate, his forehead deeply grooved. "It's okay. It's me. Are you all right?" He stepped onto the deck and scanned the darkness surrounding them. "Did something happen?"

For a moment she couldn't answer, the pulse pounded so thickly in her throat. Everything in her wanted to throw herself at him, let him hold her until the pounding stopped, but she stayed where she was. When she spoke, the words came out in a breathless rush. "Only in my head."

His face softened. "I'm sorry. I didn't realize how dark it was out here. I shouldn't have left you."

She lowered the tongs to her side. "It's fine. I'm not a child. You should be able to leave me alone for ten minutes."

"Even so …" He held out his hand. "Here. The steaks

should be done. I'll put them on the plate, and we can go inside."

The tongs shook in her fingers when she held them out to him. Cole didn't comment, only took them and nodded toward the house. "It's starting to sleet. Go on in. I'll be right there."

Unwilling to let him out of her sight, Starr stepped into the living room but waited inside the sliding doors. Cole transferred the steaks to the plate, twisted a knob below the barbeque, closed the lid, and returned to the house. She stepped out of his way as he came through the door and then slid it closed behind him. He turned the lock with a decisive click. "There."

Her heart still skittering around in her chest, she followed him to the kitchen. Cole set the plate of steaks on the island. "These look perfect."

Her knees were weak, and Starr sank onto a chair. Cole put a steak on each of their plates. He added a scoop of the potatoes he'd fried on the stove and carried the plates to the table. He had already set sour cream, steak sauce, and the bowl of salad on the table. Everything smelled incredible, but Starr held a hand to her abdomen, not sure if her stomach was ready for food.

Would it always be like this? Would terror attack without warning, even when she was doing something as innocuous as cooking food? How did she think she could live on her own if the sound of the wind in the night sent such cold chills rippling through her that she screamed when someone said her name?

"Can you eat?"

She wasn't sure she could keep anything down, but he'd worked hard to prepare their meal, and she didn't want to disappoint him. "I think so."

"Want me to pray tonight?"

She blinked. In all the time she'd been here, all the meals they'd shared together, Cole had never offered to pray, although he had also never objected when she did and always bowed his head. She'd assumed that was out of respect for her, not because he was also praying. They hadn't talked about their faith in weeks, not since the night he confessed his relationship with God was complicated. Had something changed? "I'd love that."

"Okay, then." He propped his elbows on the table and clasped his hands before bowing his head. Starr did the same, although she couldn't keep from peering at him through half-closed eyelids as he spoke. "God, thank you for this food. Please watch over Starr and me. Keep us safe, and help us not to be afraid. Give us wisdom to make the right decisions about our future. And thank you for being here with us tonight. Amen."

The prayer was simple, but Cole spoke the words earnestly. They convicted her, and warmth flooded Starr's cheeks. She added a silent prayer of her own. *Forgive me for being so afraid. For forgetting that you are with me always, even in the dark and cold. And even when Cole isn't.*

Their eyes met when she lifted her head. "Thank you."

He nodded as he picked up his knife and fork. His phone sat at the other end of the table, and he pointed to it with the fork. "By the way, the therapist's name is Stephanie Brown. I added her number to the contacts. She's expecting to hear from you, so feel free to call anytime to set up an appointment."

"What makes you think I need to talk to someone?" Starr reached for the salad bowl. "Isn't every rational adult terrified of the dark?"

Cole smiled at that, but the deep lines that had been etched across his forehead when he stepped out onto the deck hadn't eased. "We can all use someone to talk to."

Starr used the tongs to transfer salad onto her plate. "I know. And I will call her. Soon."

Somehow, despite what had happened on the deck, she had flipped the steaks enough to keep them from burning. In fact, they had turned out perfectly, melting like butter on her tongue after she dipped them in the tangy sauce. "That might be the best steak I've ever had."

"That's on you. You cooked them."

"I think it might have had something to do with the way you prepared them but thank you." Starr took a bite of potatoes and washed it down with a sip of water. "I didn't realize you prayed."

Cole wiped his mouth with a paper napkin. "Until a few weeks ago, I didn't. Not since I was a kid." He tossed the napkin onto his empty plate. "Something's changed since I met you. Grams raised me to believe in God, but none of it really sank in for me. Then you came into my life, and I saw how you were able to believe in God, that he was good, even after everything you had gone through. And that's had a profound effect on me. I've been talking to him more and more, figuring out where the two of us stand."

His words pattered against her skin, as warm and gentle as the sleet had been cold and hard. "That's amazing, Cole."

"I think so."

His eyes held hers, and although she knew she should, Starr couldn't look away. After a moment, Cole reached for her plate and set it on his. "Could I show you something?"

"Of course."

They carried the dishes to the sink, and then Starr followed him into the hallway. Cole lifted her purple winter coat from the hook and handed it to her. "What I want to show you is outside—is that okay?"

As long as he was with her, she wasn't afraid to step into

the cold and dark. Starr nodded. She zipped up her jacket and tugged on her hat and gloves.

"Here." Cole wrapped the black wool scarf around her neck and tied it loosely. "It's freezing out there."

Starr struggled to keep her breathing even. It may be freezing outside, but with him standing a few inches in front of her, tucking one end of her scarf under the other while his brown eyes probed hers, she doubted she would feel the cold at all.

CHAPTER TWENTY-SIX

Cole walked across the icy driveway in the direction of the cabins. He'd almost reached for Starr on the deck after he'd frightened her by coming out, barely remembering in time his resolve not to. Now he stayed close but forced himself to keep his hands at his sides instead of taking her arm to ensure she didn't lose her balance on the slippery surface. Maybe he should have waited until morning to bring her out here, but, after they'd talked at dinner about how much his relationship with God had changed, now seemed like the right time.

Would she like what he had done? He'd been so sure she would, but maybe she'd see it as a manipulation, a ploy to try and make her stay at the ranch. Which it wasn't. He'd had no idea she was thinking of leaving when he conceived the idea for the project. Still, if he were completely honest, a small part of him did hope that when she saw it she would be less inclined to leave, and he would have a much greater chance of keeping her safe.

And keeping her with him.

Her boot slipped on a patch of ice, and he shot out a hand, stopping short of grasping her elbow. "Careful."

She nodded, her gaze fixed on her boots as she maneuvered across the slick surface. They reached the step to the small porch in front of the cabin, and Cole stopped. "I don't want to leave you out here alone, so can you close your eyes while I get everything ready?"

"Okay." Starr braced herself with a palm against one of the porch posts as she stepped onto the painted boards.

Cole crossed the porch to the door. "Don't look."

Starr laughed and covered her eyes with one hand.

Grinning, Cole pushed open the door. "Okay, the opening is right in front of you." He guided her with his voice until she stood in the room and a little to the right of the doorway. Then he stepped in and closed the door. He went quickly around the cabin, switching on lights and preparing everything for her to see it for the first time. He wanted it to be perfect, but he also didn't want to leave her standing there with her eyes closed for long. Although he couldn't have asked her to wait outside, not after she'd been so terrified when he found her on the deck earlier. His grin faded. What had happened out there, anyway?

He shook away the thought. "Okay, you can look." His heart thudded a little. *God, help her to like it. I want this to be a special place for her.*

Starr lowered her hand and opened her eyes. Her mouth formed a perfect *o* shape, the way it always did when she was overcome with wonder. After a few moments, she turned to him, her eyes huge. "Cole. This is the most beautiful place I've ever seen. What is it?"

"It's a chapel."

While she surveyed the room, he followed her gaze. Candles flickered on small tables at the front and back of the room. He'd strung mini lights around the rafters, which suffused the room with a warm glow. Four short wooden benches sat in the middle of the room, two on either side of a narrow aisle. He'd even asked an antique dealer in Elliott Lake if he had a prayer bench in stock. The man didn't have one, but he'd tracked one down in a nearby town and had it shipped over for Cole to pick up. Cole had set it in front of the small table that sat beneath the cross he'd nailed to the wall. Soft music played from the iPod he'd picked up in town, and warm cinnamon and vanilla scents wafted from the candles.

The overall effect was one of peace. It felt that way to him, at least, and Cole prayed that she could feel it, too. If anyone deserved peace in her life, it was Starr.

When she swung her gaze to him again, she had tugged off her gloves, stuck them in her pocket, and clasped her hands beneath her chin. "You did all this?"

"Yes."

"Why?"

"For you."

In all the time he'd known her, Cole had never seen Starr cry. Not even when he came into her room after she'd had a terrible nightmare. She didn't cry now, but her eyes glistened as though she was on the verge. Was that a good thing?

"No one has ever done anything like this for me. Can I look around?"

"Of course." Cole slid onto the bench closest to the door while she wandered around the room, examining the lamps and candles he'd placed on various surfaces and trying out the prayer bench. When she finished, she joined him, keeping a couple of feet of distance between them.

Her eyes glittered in the candlelight when they met his. "I don't know what to say. I can't believe you did this."

"It was my pleasure. And I don't want you to think I did it so you would stay. I only wanted you to have a place to go where you could find peace and forget about everything that was going on in the world for a little while."

"That's exactly how I feel here. It's the most peaceful place I've ever been."

"Good."

"And I know you didn't do it so I would stay." She folded her fingers on the back of the bench in front of them. "About that, I know I didn't give you a good reason before, when you asked me why I wanted to leave, and I feel you deserve that."

Cole nodded. "I'd appreciate you telling me. I always want us to be honest with each other."

Starr studied her fingers. "I want that, too. The thing is, I have feelings for you. Before I realized that, when I was only an assignment to you and you were the person tasked with keeping me safe, it felt okay to be here. But now that I've realized I'm falling for you, it doesn't feel that way anymore."

Cole could barely breathe. She was falling for him? They'd shared moments of deep connection, but he'd been terrified to let himself hope it could be more than that for her. Like it was for him. Much more. Sitting next to her, in this place of peace, a place dedicated to God, he could no longer deny the truth. His overwhelming desire for her to stay with him wasn't only because he was desperate to keep her safe. It was because he loved her. Cole wasn't sure when it had happened, but his feelings were so tightly woven through the deepest part of his being they might have always been a part of him.

He opened his mouth to tell her, but something stayed him. A sense she wasn't ready to hear it yet. That, as he had needed to tell her over and over she was safe, he had to show her how deeply he felt every moment they were together until she finally came to the place where she could accept it. Believe she was worthy of that kind of love.

"Starr." Cole waited until she shifted on the bench to face him. "I feel the same way. The moment I met you, I thought you were one of the most beautiful women I'd ever seen. But it was more than that. You captured my heart from the beginning. I couldn't believe you were able to laugh, that a light could still shine in your eyes, that you could show so much compassion when I told you about my dad, after everything you had endured. I think you're the most incredible person I've ever met."

Her lower lip quivered. "Maybe that's all the more reason I should move away from here."

What could he say to convince her to stay? The answer came to him less as a revelation and more as an unveiling of the answer he'd long known but hadn't fully acknowledged. Grams was right. Even if the PD hadn't officially assigned him to protect her, someone had. He felt that deep in his bones. And the only way he could truly do that was to keep her here, with him.

"What if we got married?" It wasn't a new thought—it had hovered like a soft shadow around the periphery of his mind almost since the night he had brought her here. This was the first time he had allowed the image to fully form, to take on shape and definition. The first time he had allowed himself to indulge in imagining what a life with her could truly look like. What it would *be* like.

Her eyes widened. For a few seconds, she didn't say anything. He tried to read what she was thinking in her eyes, but in the dim lighting it was difficult to discern. Finally, she said, "You don't want to marry me. I'm a mess."

"We're all a mess. As Grams would say, that's what we need God for."

Her lips twitched slightly. "That's true, but you know what I've been through, what I've done..."

God, give me the words to say. To convince her she is precious, not only to you, but to me. "I don't care about any of that. You didn't choose that life; you were forced into it. And somehow, through the grace of God, you have come out of it one of the strongest and most amazing people I have ever known." He searched her blue eyes. "You told me once that you were going to try and forgive Brady because you didn't want him to have ongoing power over you. Well, you can't let him rob you of joy in life, either, or keep you from being with the person you're meant to be with. That's only giving him another kind of power."

Her eyelids flickered. Was he getting through to her?

"The thing is, I don't know if I …" She looked away from him and stared at her hands. "If I can be with you … like husband and wife."

"I get that. I'm willing to wait as long as it takes. Nothing will change with us, physically. Not unless you want it to. You can still have your own room, and I promise I will never push you to do anything you aren't comfortable with or ready for."

"What if I'm never ready?"

Cole took a deep breath and pressed his palms to the bench on either side of him. "All I know is that I want you in my life. Being with you these past few months, seeing you every day, has brought me more joy than I've ever experienced."

"Really?"

"Really. So, what do you think? Will you marry me, Starr?"

She hesitated and then said, "Tala."

His forehead wrinkled. "What?"

"My real name. It's Tala."

His breath caught. He'd figured *Starr* was an alias, but he hadn't been sure if or when she would trust him enough to give him her true name. "Tala." He tried it on his tongue. It was beautiful and exotic and suited her perfectly.

"Yes." She smiled faintly. "Tala Tangalou. My mother's last name."

"It's beautiful. Thank you for giving it to me."

"You're welcome." She fell silent, gazing at the ornate metal cross at the front of the church as though seeking wisdom.

Cole studied it, too, the sight of it filling him once again with that inexplicable peace.

A light touch against the side of his hand drew him from his meditation. Although she still faced forward, Starr—uh, Tala—had slid her hand across the distance between them to rest her baby finger lightly against his. Deeply aware of the sacredness of the moment, Cole didn't move. He barely breathed, blown away by the profound courage it had to have taken for her to be the first to reach out to him. They sat like that, candlelight flickering off the walls, soft music playing, her finger soft and warm against his, for several minutes, until she drew in a breath. "Okay."

Joy flowed through him. Until those few moments of silently waiting for her answer, he hadn't realized how desperately he wanted her to say yes. How much he wanted her to be his wife.

Whatever that looked like for them.

Cole wasn't a fool. He knew it wouldn't be easy. Tala had suffered more trauma than he would ever know, and it would take time—maybe a long, long time—for her to heal. If she ever fully did.

But he knew something else, too, as surely as he had ever known anything. Tala Tangalou was worth waiting for. His grandmother's words—that his assignment was to cherish and protect Tala's precious, hurting heart, soul, and body—fluttered through his mind. Whether or not his wife ever got to the place where she could give herself fully to him, Cole would dedicate his life to doing exactly that.

CHAPTER TWENTY-SEVEN

They walked side by side to the farmhouse. At the bottom of the stairs, Tala turned to him, her eyes glowing. "Thank you, Cole. I know I shouldn't ask you to do this, but I'm incredibly happy."

"You didn't ask me, I asked you. And I'm glad you're happy. That's all I want for you, to be happy and safe. I hope you know that."

"I do. It's what I want for you, too." Her smile was warm. "I'll see you in the morning?"

"I'll be here."

He watched until she reached the top of the stairs. Then Cole tugged the phone from his back pocket and made his way to the living room, where he sank onto the couch. The joy that had coursed through him when Tala agreed to marry him hadn't diminished. She didn't seem to be having second thoughts, either. Not yet, anyway.

Although the proposal had been spontaneous, Cole wasn't second guessing it. Not even close. As soon as the idea came to him, he'd known it was right. They hadn't talked about when they would do it, but he hoped soon. Even if they wouldn't exactly be having a honeymoon, he wanted to know there would be no more talk of her leaving the ranch. Or him. Ever.

With what he was pretty sure was a goofy grin on his face, he punched in his grandmother's number and glanced at the screen while it rang. Ten o'clock. A little late for a phone call, but Grams had always been a night owl. She'd be up, and she would want to hear his news. When she answered, her voice was so cheerful he knew he hadn't disturbed her.

"Cole!"

"Hey, Grams."

"You sound happy."

Cole shook his head. How she was able to pinpoint his emotional state with only those two words every single time he would never know. "As a matter of fact, I am."

"Because of that sweet girl you were telling me about?"

"Yes, actually. I wanted you to be the first to know that I asked her to marry me tonight, and she said *yes*."

"Oh, Cole." Grams paused. Although he'd detected elation in her initial response to his announcement, her voice, when she spoke again, contained a gravity he wasn't sure he'd ever heard in it before. "It won't be easy."

He rested against the cushions of the couch. "I'm well aware."

"I know you're a good man, so I don't need to tell you this, but you will have to be more patient and understanding with this woman than you have ever been in your life."

"I will be, Grams. I love her. I would never do anything to hurt her."

"I know you wouldn't, intentionally. But as strong as you say she is, I can assure you that a part of her is extremely fragile. And I say that because, to a small degree, I understand it."

Cole's eyes narrowed. "What do you mean?"

Grams drew in a quivering breath. "I never told you about

the weeks after I left the reserve and went to Toronto and before I met your grandfather at the Yonge Street Mission, but it was a very dark time. I was basically living on the streets, and …"

Cole closed his eyes, terrified of what might be coming.

"A lot of things happened that I never shared with anyone except Gramps. And the police." A hint of bitterness crept into her voice.

Cole's stomach twisted. "You mean you were …"

"Raped, yes. More than once. And assaulted numerous times."

He leaned forward, propped his elbows on his knees, and pulled the phone away from his ear, clutching it in both hands and pressing the edge of it to his forehead. *God, no. Not Grams.*

She waited patiently through the long silence. Finally, Cole held the phone to his ear again. "Grams. I'm so sorry. I had no idea."

"I never saw any purpose in telling you. Until now."

"What did the police do?"

"Nothing. They told me I shouldn't have left the reserve, but that, since I had, I'd asked for what I got."

Cole drew in a few deep breaths, pretty sure he was about to throw up on the living room carpet. "You must hate that I became a cop."

"Cole, no. I love that you're a cop. Things are changing. Very, very slowly, but they are changing. Incredibly brave women, and men, too, are standing up and refusing to accept that kind of treatment any longer. And good cops like you who treat everyone with the dignity and respect they deserve help as well."

He massaged his forehead with the fingers of his free hand. "How could you still believe in God after he allowed that to happen to you?"

She sighed. "I didn't know God at the time. I was

completely alone those first few weeks. It was an incredibly dark time that I don't like to think about. But then, as you know, I wandered into the Mission looking for a meal one night and met your grandfather who was there volunteering with a group from his church. He—all of them, actually—showed me so much grace and acceptance that it was impossible not to be drawn to them. And to the God they all believed in and loved."

A terrible thought struck Cole. "Was my mother …?"

"A result of rape? No. I was already pregnant when I left the reserve, although I didn't know it then. Your biological grandfather was my high school boyfriend. And since we're talking about him, if anything ever happens to me and you decide you want to find him or any other of your family members, my lawyer has the information you'd need to get started."

Cole had never entertained that possibility. Or given serious consideration to the fact that he had a grandfather and likely aunts and uncles and cousins out there somewhere. He filed that away in the back of his mind to think about another day. "Did you ever tell him about my mother?"

"I did. He wasn't a bad guy, although he refused to come with me when I left, and, when I called and told him I was pregnant, he let me know he was definitely not ready to be a father."

Cole blew out a breath. "I'm so sorry you had to go through all that."

"I am, too, although it brought me to your Gramps and the wonderful life I had after meeting him. He was so good to me, Cole. I struggled to give myself to him completely, not only my body but my heart, after everything I had been through. But he was kind and patient and understanding, and eventually I was able to fully accept the love he wanted to offer me and to see myself the way he saw me. The way God saw me. It took time, though."

"I understand."

"I hope you do. Have you told her that you love her?"

"No. I started to tonight, before I proposed, but something stopped me. I sensed she wasn't ready to hear it yet."

"Trust those instincts. It took me a long time to be able to accept it when Gramps tried to tell me how he felt about me. It took him proving his unconditional love for me with his actions before I could hear what he was saying."

Cole rested his elbow on a forest green pillow propped against the arm of the couch. "That's my plan."

"I love your girl already and can't wait until it's safe to meet her."

His girl. A small smile crossed his lips. "Neither can I."

"Do you know when you'll get married?"

"No. We haven't discussed details. I'm sure it will be soon, though." Cole rubbed his palm over the rough fabric on the arm of the couch. "I … told her nothing would change between us. Not until she is ready. I promised I wouldn't push her, and I won't." It wouldn't hurt for him to make the promise to someone else. Someone he respected and never wanted to let down.

"That's good, Cole. If you are patient and wait for her, I believe she will come to you eventually."

"I promise you I will."

"You know I'm praying for you. And her."

"I do. I'm also praying."

"That's the best and most powerful thing you can do."

"I'm beginning to see that."

"*Ndi mnowaangozi.*"

He smiled. "I'm happy, too."

"Be good and stay safe."

"I will."

Grams ended the call and Cole tossed his phone onto the coffee table. Burying his face in his hands, he reflected on everything she had told him. Somehow he'd never considered the possibility that she had gone through such terrible trials before she met Gramps. With everything he'd seen, he should have suspected that an eighteen-year-old girl—a young, pregnant, Indigenous woman alone in the city with no support and no resources—might have run into serious trouble, but he'd chosen to believe she had been okay. That she had met the love of her life and gotten married and lived a beautiful, happy life on their farm. Which she had. But before any of that happened, she'd gone through at least a taste of the hell that Tala had. He pressed his eyes shut again, unable to bear the thought of how the two women he cared about the most in the world had suffered.

When he lifted his head, a tear had started down one cheek and he swiped it away. While he would never have wanted either of them to endure what they had, they had both survived. More than that, they had emerged strong women with unshakeable faith, humor, and deep empathy for others.

And Gramps had given Grams a life full of love and laughter and the chance to heal and move forward, leaving the past behind her.

Cole's hands closed into fists. However long it took, however challenging it might be, with God's help, he would do the same for Tala.

Tala stood in front of the window, gazing at the dark sky punctured by countless golden dots as far as she could see. What had happened in the chapel tonight? A proposal was the last thing she'd expected from Cole.

He'd told her she couldn't let Brady keep her from finding joy or from being with the person she was meant to be with. Was that truly how he felt—that he was that person? If he meant it when he said he'd experienced more joy since he'd met her than he ever had in his life, then, yes, he must believe that.

And she felt the same way. Although she'd been terrified to admit it, even to herself, she'd felt their connection from the moment they met. And that feeling had only grown stronger each day she spent with him.

Tala traced the outline of the big dipper with one finger. She and Rose and Jae, her foster sisters, had gazed out at the stars most nights, making wishes on the first one to appear and trying to identify various formations. Quite often Felicity joined them. Her husband had taught her a lot about the stars, and she passed along the names and the stories behind many of the constellations. The thing she had said about the stars that struck Tala the most, though, was that God had put every one of them in place. "And you know every star by name," she whispered. The idea that God knew every star in the sky—every star in every universe, billions and billions of them—by name, was more than she could wrap her mind around.

"And if you know every star by name, you must know every one of us by name." When no one around her, not even friends like Ruby, knew her real name, Tala had clung to the truth that God knew it, that it was engraved on the palm of his hand. Without that knowledge, she would have been afraid her name might be lost, since she was so determined not to let her true one slip out to Brady that even in her own mind she had become *Starr*. But God had kept her name in trust for her until Cole freed her, and now God had given it to her again. She hadn't planned to tell it to Cole tonight, but something had nudged her to. Had assured her it was safe. That *he* was safe.

Cole knowing her name felt deeply intimate. He'd thanked her for giving it to him, as though she'd offered him a precious gift.

That sense, that he valued not only her name but her, was part of the reason she had accepted his proposal. The thought of a home and maybe even a family someday had drawn her as well. And his insistence that her past—the things done to her and the things she had done to survive—weren't insurmountable barriers to him, as she'd assumed they would be for any decent man. He had to care deeply for her to be able to say that, didn't he? Maybe even love her?

Something in her resisted that thought. He couldn't. Not after everything she had done.

Still, sitting in the chapel, gazing at the gorgeous cross Cole had hung on the wall, she'd admitted to herself that she loved him. His kindness, his patience, the way he could always make her laugh, his willingness to risk his life for her, his ability to make her feel safe. How could she not?

But more than any of that, the sense of rightness that filled her when she called out to God in that sacred place Cole had created for her had helped her let go of her fear and agree to commit herself to him for life. And she had no regrets.

Tala ran her finger over the cool glass before turning away from the window. A sharp crack brought her around again, her heart jumping and fluttering. What was that? Had someone thrown something at the window? If anyone was out there, she would be visible through the window for miles with the bedroom light on. And now whoever it was knew which room was hers.

Ducking to the side of the window, she leaned against the wall for several seconds. Then, staying low, she made her way across the room and hit the switch to turn off the light. Darkness as thick and black as the pond at midnight fell over the room as she crept to the window. When she reached it, she stood to one side of the frame and peered cautiously around the curtain. A brisk wind swooped through the branches. Bare limbs swayed in the breeze, sending moonlit shadows skipping across the lawn in a mournful dance.

Chills skittered across Tala's skin. Nothing else moved outside, but, in the pale light reflecting off the snow, a person could easily hide in the bushes or the shadows lining the house or barn. Another gust of wind swept across the yard, and the tip of a branch scraped across the glass. Was that what she had heard? Maybe, although it had seemed much louder, possibly because she'd been deep in thought.

Or because her nerves were still on edge from what had happened on the deck.

Terror flickered again, but she ruthlessly shoved it away. She would call the therapist tomorrow. If she wanted a future with Cole, she needed to do everything she could to deal with the past.

Starting with refusing to let fear steal her joy. Tala straightened her shoulders. Brady was under constant surveillance. Even if he did somehow escape, he wouldn't be able to find her. She needed to let go of the ever-present worry that he might one day show up here.

It was impossible.

Still, for the first time since she had arrived at the ranch, Tala reached up and pulled the blind down over the window and then yanked the curtains closed.

Of course, locking her door had done nothing to keep Cole from breaching her defenses. And if Brady did track her down at the ranch someday, determined to make her pay for her betrayal, blocking the view from her window would do nothing to stop him, either.

CHAPTER TWENTY-EIGHT

Tala dropped two pieces of bread into the toaster. The coffee maker gurgled, releasing a puff of mocha-scented air that she breathed in deeply. Clutching her blue mug, she walked over to stand in front of the machine. *Come on. Come on.*

"It won't brew faster because you're standing there waiting for it." Cole's voice held laughter.

Tala whirled around. She hadn't heard him coming down the stairs or along the hallway. A fluttering rose in her stomach. Was that excitement at seeing him or apprehension that he might, after sleeping on it, regret their hasty decision? "I know. Years of trying haven't changed that, but I continue to hope."

Cole strolled to the cupboard, took down the gray-and-white-striped mug he used every morning, and then came over to stand beside her. "Maybe if we combine our mental forces, we can hurry it along."

"Worth a shot."

With a final hiss of steaming water, the machine fell silent. "Done." Cole reached for the carafe and filled her mug before sloshing the steaming liquid into his own. "Apparently we make a formidable team."

Was he only talking about the coffee or about their future? Tala reached for the cream. No sense trying to analyze every word he said or the way he said it. Sooner or later, they'd have to talk about what happened the night before. Then she would know where they stood. The fluttering morphed into a slight churning. The toast popped up and, thankful to have something to keep her occupied, Tala took a sip of coffee before setting the mug on the island and going over to grab the toast and slather butter and jam on it. "Toast?"

"Sure, thanks." Cole slid onto a stool on the far side of the island as Tala dropped two more slices into the toaster.

When she finished, she took the one across from him. "Sleep okay?"

"Like a rock. You?"

"Me too." It felt as though they were dancers meeting on the floor for the first time, feeling each other out before clasping hands and waltzing across the room.

Cole set his mug on the island. "Tala."

The toast popped up, and she hopped off the stool. "I'll get it."

She took her time buttering the toast and spreading strawberry jam over it. If Cole was about to retract the offer he'd made in the chapel, she wanted a couple more minutes to indulge in the fantasy that maybe she really could have this life. Here, with him.

When she couldn't delay any longer, she resumed her seat and slid a plate across the island to him.

"Thanks." Cole didn't look at the toast. His eyes probed hers, so intently that Tala had to force herself not to look away. "How are you feeling today about what we discussed last night?"

Was that a trap? If Tala told him she was all in—that, even

if not much would change on the surface, she couldn't wait to marry him—what would he say? What if he responded that he felt the complete opposite today? "How do *you* feel?"

One side of his mouth quirked up. "Exactly the same as I did last night. I want you to know I didn't make that proposal lightly. I meant it. I really do want to marry you. But if you have any second thoughts, I want you to share them."

Tala shook her head. "I don't. I didn't accept your proposal lightly, either. I want us to do this."

His shoulders relaxed a little, as though he'd been as worried as she had been. He pulled the plate of toast closer. "All right, then. What do you think about getting married in the chapel?"

Her thoughts drifted to the tranquil space. "The chapel would be perfect."

"Okay. I'll drive into town this morning, see if I can talk to Grams' pastor. I've met her a couple of times and she seems nice. I'll explain the situation and find out if she'd be willing to come out here in the next week or two, unless that's too soon for you."

The sooner the better. "It's not." Tala set down the piece of toast she'd been about to bite into. "What about witnesses?" Was there anyone they could trust enough to invite? She pressed her palms to the cool marble.

Cole tapped his fingers on the island. "I could ask Cassandra White, since she already knows you're here. And maybe Lake."

"So your ex-girlfriend and the guy who's paying you to carry out your assignment in a completely professional and detached manner. Those are the two you want to ask to be our witnesses?" Tala said the words lightly, teasingly, although the conversation she'd overheard between Cole and Cassandra still stung a little.

Cole set his toast down as well. "First of all, she's not my ex-girlfriend. We had a couple of dinners together, and I knew pretty much right away that it wasn't going anywhere." His lips twitched. "On the charge of not being detached, I admit I have no defense. I am no longer detached when it comes to you, if I ever was." His face grew serious. "I want you to know that becoming personally involved in this case—involved with you—has not made me less vigilant. If anything, it's made me more alert, more determined than ever to make sure nothing happens to you."

"I know that. And I was only giving you a hard time. I can't imagine that Cassandra would want to watch you marry someone else. If she's willing, though, it does make sense, since she knows I'm here and has an obligation to keep that confidential." She scooped up a splotch of strawberry jam with her finger and stuck it in her mouth. "What do you think Laken and the PD will say when you tell them?"

"Lake will be happy for me." Cole hooked a finger through the handle of his mug and pulled it closer but didn't lift it to his mouth.

A twinge of apprehension worked its way through Tala. "And the police department?"

He hesitated before blowing out a breath. "I have a confession to make. I haven't been completely transparent about this arrangement. The truth is, the PD didn't have the budget for full-time protective custody for you."

Tala tilted her head. "Then who's been paying you?"

"No one. I mean, they have covered some expenses. Our groceries and basic supplies, your winter clothes, stuff like that." He ran a finger around the rim of the mug. "My dad's estate has taken care of pretty much everything else."

"So you weren't assigned to protect me?"

"Not officially, no. Although they did support the idea and have helped out where they could, especially Lake."

Tala's thoughts whirled. "What about your job?"

Cole winced slightly. "I took a few weeks of vacation time. When that ran out, I asked for a leave of absence. My boss knows what I'm doing here, and he's been extremely understanding. I can probably take another month or two off. By then, hopefully we'll have a better idea of what is happening with Brady."

When Tala didn't respond, Cole met her gaze. "I'm sorry I didn't tell you all that from the beginning."

"Why didn't you?"

"I thought you would refuse to stay here if you realized I was doing it on my own, not with the police department."

"You were right; I would have."

He lifted his hand, palm up.

She didn't answer, and he lowered his hand to the island. "Are you angry with me?"

Was she? "I'm trying to be."

He let out a short laugh. "Only trying?"

"Yes. I mean, you lied to me. And brought me here under false pretenses."

Cole sobered. "That's true. And you have every right to be upset about that."

"Yes, I do. Although..."

His eyebrows rose.

"It does mean a lot to me that I was never just an assignment to you. That you chose to be here with me."

His face softened. He splayed his fingers on the island between them as though reaching for her. "Yes, I did. And I will keep choosing that. Every day." His hands slid closer. "Are we good?"

She sighed. "We're good."

"Good." The tips of his fingers brushed hers, so lightly she wasn't even sure they had, before he pulled his hands back. "I'll head into town then, talk to the pastor and Cassie. Hopefully I'll return in time to help you with the chores." He flashed her a smile that left her a little weak in the knees before he carried his dishes to the sink, rinsed them off, and set them in the rack to dry.

Tala watched as he left the kitchen. By the time Cole returned, other people would know about this crazy thing they were planning to do—it would no longer be something the two of them were only thinking about.

The thrill that sent coursing through her confirmed what Tala already knew. No matter what anyone else had to say about it—and she suspected some people would say plenty—she hadn't been wrong to say yes to Cole.

CHAPTER TWENTY-NINE

Cole walked out the door of the small church Grams had attended when she lived in the area. The conversation with the pastor had gone well—better than he'd expected. His and Starr's...

He paused halfway down the stone steps at the front of the church. Not Starr's, Tala's. It would take a bit of getting used to, calling her by another name. He wanted to, though. Starr was the name Brady had called her, the name that represented the life she had been forced to live before she and Cole met. The life of torment and slavery he wanted so badly to help her heal from. Calling her by the new name—her true name, the one that everyone in her life who loved her had called her—could very well be part of that process.

Cole clutched the metal railing as he continued down the stone steps. His and Tala's situation was unique, no question, but after he'd explained what he could to the minister, whose compassionate eyes and gracious responses compelled him to open up more than he might have, she'd agreed to marry them the following week. Cole had asked if the kissing-the-bride part was a requirement, and she'd assured him it could be left out. Not that he would have minded it being included, but he was determined to keep his promise to himself, Grams, and Tala never to pressure her.

On the way to his truck, he walked past the legal office where Cassandra worked and ducked inside before he could change his mind. The lobby was surprisingly posh for the small, unpretentious town. Rich oak paneling and expensive-looking works of art gave the place the hushed atmosphere of a museum, and he practically tiptoed to the reception desk.

The young man sitting behind it looked up as he approached. "Good morning. Can I help you?"

"I was hoping to speak with Cassandra White." Cole rested his palms on the marble counter.

"Do you have an appointment?"

"No. This isn't an official call. I'm a friend of hers."

"May I ask your name?"

"Cole Blacksky."

The young man held up a finger. "Give me a moment."

Cole wandered around the lobby, examining the prints on the wall while the young man made a phone call. Thirty seconds later, he rose from his seat. "Mr. Blacksky?"

Cole swung around. "Yes?"

"Ms. White will see you. I'll show you to her office."

Cole followed the man down a long hallway lined with closed doors. Near the end of the hall, the man stopped at one and rapped lightly.

"Come in." Cassandra's voice floated toward them. The man opened the door and then stepped back to allow Cole to go by.

Cassandra rose from her desk, a warm smile on her face. "Cole. Good to see you." She gestured to the armchair across from her desk. "Sit. Please."

The receptionist closed the door as Cole made his way across the expansive room. Cassandra's office mirrored the rest of the building with leather furniture, dark wainscoting, vases of fresh flowers, and more beautiful prints on the walls.

Cassandra resumed her seat. "I'm glad you're here."

"You are?"

"Yes. I've gone over and over the conversation we had in your driveway, and I feel sick about it. I don't know what possessed me to say what I did. I feel terrible."

"Don't. You offered an apology and I accepted it. It's done. Forgotten."

"Thank you." Cassandra clasped her hands on the desk. "What can I do for you?"

"I came to ask a favor, but, before I do, I want you to feel absolutely free to refuse if you're not comfortable."

A small smile played around her mouth. "All right."

Cole leaned forward and lowered his voice. "You were right about one thing that day. The woman I'm protecting is more than a job to me. Much more. In fact, I've asked her to marry me."

"Really."

"Yes. And she has accepted. We're getting married next week."

For a few seconds she only stared at him, and then her face softened. "That's wonderful news, Cole, truly. I'm happy for you. A little sad for me, but I guess I've always known, on some level, that you and I were not meant to be."

"I do want us to be friends."

"We are. So how can I help?"

Cole ran his palms over the soft leather arms of the chair. Exactly how far could he stretch the bounds of their new friendship? "As you know, you are one of the very few people who are aware she's at my place. We need two witnesses at the wedding next Wednesday evening, and I wasn't sure who else to ask …"

Cassie held up a hand. "Say no more. I'd be glad to do it."

"Are you sure?"

She grinned. "Well, *glad* might be a strong word. Watching you marry another woman may not be my first choice of how to spend my day, but, as I said, I am happy for you. And although I only met your fiancée briefly, she struck me as quite exceptional. I only hope she deserves you."

"Pretty sure I'm the one who doesn't deserve her. But if you're willing to do this, we would both deeply appreciate it."

"I am, honestly." She tilted her head, studying him.

"What is it?"

"How can she get ready for a wedding if no one else in town knows she's here? Does she have a dress?"

Cole frowned. He hadn't considered that. Even if the wedding was small and somewhat unconventional, he did want to make it special for Tala.

"You haven't given that any thought."

"No, I guess I haven't."

Cassandra straightened a pile of folders on her desk. "Why don't you let me help with that, too? I can find a dress for her."

"I don't know, Cassie. That's an awful lot to ask. Maybe we could order something online." Even as he said it, Cole knew they couldn't. Not without entering personal information, which would be far too dangerous. As would him dress-shopping in this small town. Word would get around fast.

"That's not a good idea. You don't want a delivery person coming onto the property, right? Plus, it might not arrive in time. Besides"—she spread both hands in front of her—"you're basically looking at a professional shopper. Might as well take advantage of my skills."

Cole's shoulders relaxed. "If you're sure …"

"I am. Although your fiancée might want some say in the dress, so I'll pick up two or three and she can choose the one she wants. I assume you're not thinking of a formal wedding gown?"

"No. Something simple but beautiful would be perfect."

"Any suggestions for color?"

"Blue." He answered without thinking about it. "She has these incredible blue eyes, so that would be ideal."

"Okay. Any idea what size she wears?"

"Six." Cole leaned forward to pull out his wallet. "I can give you the cash to buy it."

Cassie lifted a hand again. "Would you allow me to make it a wedding present?"

"That's not necessary. You're already doing far more for us than we have a right to ask."

When she spoke again, her voice was soft. "It is necessary. For me. If I do this for her, I'll feel a lot better about what happened." She twisted her fingers together. "Did she hear what I said?"

Cole hesitated. "She did, actually. But she's a remarkably forgiving person. She doesn't hold it against you."

"Still, I want to apologize to her as well. And I truly want to do this for her. Please."

"All right. Thank you."

"I'll call you when I have them and we can arrange a time for me to bring them to her."

"Tala."

Her perfectly shaped eyebrows rose. "Pardon me?"

"Her name is Tala." Maybe he shouldn't tell her, but she'd hear it at the wedding.

Cassie smiled. "Tala. That's pretty."

"Yes, it is." Cole stood. "Thank you, Cassie. All of this means more to me than I can say."

"I'm happy you thought to come to me. That means more than *I* can say." She walked him to the door. "I truly wish you and Tala all the best, Cole."

"I believe you."

"Good. See you soon." She closed the door softly behind him.

Cole nodded at the receptionist before heading to his car. For a long moment he sat behind the wheel, bracing himself for another difficult conversation. Then he reached for the cell phone he'd set in the cup holder and tapped in the number.

"Jones."

"Lake? It's Cole."

"Cole, hey." Something creaked in the background, as though Lake had leaned back in his desk chair. "Everything okay there?"

His voice, brusque when he answered, had warmed, which helped, although Cole still had no idea how to broach the subject of his upcoming wedding. "We're fine. Still quiet in the city?"

"Seems to be. We're monitoring the house carefully, but no movement so far."

"Good."

"What's up?"

"I, uh …" Despite the thin coat of ice on the windshield, Cole swiped a beat of sweat away that had started down his temple. "I need to discuss something with you."

"All right. Personal or professional?"

"Both, I guess." He'd blurred the lines between the two pretty well, so it was a challenge to differentiate between them. He'd never been more thankful that the PD hadn't officially tasked him to protect Tala, as this conversation—and their situation—would be a lot trickier if they had. "I thought I should give you the heads up that Tala and I …"

"Tala?"

"Yeah, sorry. Starr's real name is Tala Tangalou. She only told me last night." He heard a scratching noise, as if Lake was taking down that information. "Anyway, we …"

"You've gotten involved." Lake didn't sound shocked, which was good.

"Yeah. How did you know?"

"Well, beyond the obvious, that you're two single, attractive people thrown together and left alone in the middle of nowhere for months, I got the sense after the first time you met her that she had already gotten to you."

"You're right, she had. And that's only grown. She's amazing. Even after everything she's been through, she's strong and caring and has a great sense of humor. She constantly blows me away with her capacity for joy and her wonder at trying new things."

"So, basically, you never stood a chance." Laughter rippled through Lake's words.

"No, I didn't."

"Okay, then." Another creak and a thunk as his desk chair snapped into place. "Let's circle back to the two of you being involved. What does that mean, exactly? Anything that might have crossed moral boundaries?"

Cole's neck warmed. "We haven't done anything I'd need to go to confession for, if that's what you're asking."

His friend laughed outright at that. "Good to know. Especially since, last time I checked, you weren't Catholic."

"No, I'm not, although …"

"Although what?"

"Tala has a strong faith, and she's got me thinking a lot about my relationship with God." Lake was a believer; he'd get it. He talked to Cole about it sometimes, although Cole hadn't had a lot to say on the matter.

"Ah. Interesting. I'm liking this girl more and more."

"Me too. In fact, I'm in love with her." Cole took a deep breath. "I asked her to marry me last night and she said yes."

He closed his eyes and waited through a long silence. To Lake's credit, when he spoke, his voice conveyed no emotion. "So, pretty deeply involved, then."

Cole let out a short laugh. "You could say that."

"Did you set a date?"

"A week from Wednesday, here at the ranch."

Lake exhaled. "As your friend, I'm really happy for you, man. As someone working with you on this case, I will have to file a report. Since you're not officially on assignment, the department doesn't really have a say in what you do in your personal life. However, you have received money to cover part of your expenses, so I need to keep the detective-sergeant updated on the situation."

"Got it."

"On your end, I don't guess you need me to tell you it will be very complicated."

"No, I don't. She's worth it, though."

"I believe you. And I really am happy for you."

"I'm glad to hear that." Cole scratched at a spot on his steering wheel. "Because there's something else."

"Okay." Lake drew out the word, as though he wasn't sure he wanted to hear it.

"We need another witness. Any chance you'd be willing to stand up with me?"

"Hold on." Another pause, then, "Sorry, checking my calendar. I believe I can make that work."

"Really? That'd be great. Thank you."

"Thanks for asking me. Although I know the list of people you could have asked was incredibly short, I'm still honored."

"Even if it hadn't been, you're the one I would have wanted next to me." Which was true. Cole couldn't imagine having anyone else standing with him when he got married.

"That means a lot. I assume it won't be black tie?"

"Black tie, no, but I do have a friend picking out a dress for Tala, so some kind of tie would be appropriate."

"Done. Text me the details and I'll be there."

"I will. And Lake?"

"Yeah?"

"Thanks for not trying to talk me out of it."

"Would I have been able to?"

"No."

Lake chuckled. "That's what I figured. I trust you to know what you're doing. Tala does sound like a remarkable woman. I'm looking forward to getting to know her better."

"I'm looking forward to that, too. We'll see you on Wednesday." Cole tossed his phone onto the passenger seat. That had gone better than anticipated, although he'd known Lake would be supportive.

He cast a glance in the direction of a small jewelry store, the only one he knew of in town. As much as he would love to purchase decent wedding bands for them, he couldn't go there. The owner was an old friend of his dad's and not exactly known for his discretion. For now, they'd have to settle for the ones he'd picked up at a chain store in town. Sometime in the future he'd upgrade them to something better, more permanent.

And maybe, by then, Brady Erickson would be behind bars, and they could stop living with the constant threat of him showing up and destroying their life together before it even began.

CHAPTER THIRTY

Tala scrubbed the frying pan long after the last of the food had been scraped away. "Cassandra's still coming here tonight?"

"Yes." Cole eased the pan from her grip. "She'll be here in a few minutes. You said you were okay with it, right?"

"Of course."

He propped a hip against the counter as he swiped the dish towel over the pan. "Then why do you seem so wound up at the thought of her being here?"

Tala dried her hands on the other end of the towel. Why *was* she so wound up? "I'm not sure. Maybe because Cassandra is the first person I've met in years who might become a real friend. It feels as though there is a lot more riding on this evening than simply trying on a couple of dresses."

He set the clean pan on the stove. "Try not to put too much pressure on yourself. Despite what happened the last time she was here, which she feels terrible about, Cassie's a really nice person. If you're yourself around her, she'll have no choice but to love you."

She shot him a look, but Cole busied himself with drying the last of the dishes in the rack and didn't meet her gaze. Tala had been herself around him—was he saying that he loved her? Did she want him to say that? She wanted to want him to, but that wasn't exactly the same thing, was it?

Tala repressed a sigh. Why was she torturing herself by asking questions for which she had no answers? Couldn't she rest in the fact that he was going to marry her in two days so she could stay at the ranch with him without feeling as though she was in any way compromising her moral standing before God?

Tala squeezed the water out of the dishcloth and tossed it over the faucet to dry. She still wrestled with the idea that, given her past, she could ever stand before God clean and pure. Maybe that was less about God and more about her inability to fully embrace his mercy and grace. She was working on that as well. In the meantime, right or wrong, something deep inside wouldn't allow her to live with Cole unless they legitimized their relationship. Something more than her mother's or Felicity's voice in her head.

As she'd promised herself—and him—Tala had called the therapist a few days earlier to book an appointment. Yesterday she'd spent her first hour talking to the woman. Although Stephanie was nice enough, it was difficult for Tala to open up to her, to feel any connection with this person she had never met and whose face she couldn't see. Hopefully it would get easier.

The sound of gravel crunching beneath the wheels of a vehicle granted her a reprieve from her spiraling thoughts. Cole hung the dish towel over the oven door and smiled at her. "Try to have fun with this, okay? We may not be having the most traditional wedding, but I still want you to enjoy it."

"I will." Tala followed him to the front door. When Cole held the screen door for her, Cassandra slipped inside. A garment bag hung over one arm and the strap of a large leather bag over the other. "Hi, Cole. Tala." When her gaze landed on Tala, her smile was warm and friendly. "Nice to officially meet you." She hefted the garment bag higher on her arm and held out her hand.

Tala shook it firmly. Although she had prepared herself for it, no hint of the hostility she'd seen on Cassandra's face the first time she'd come to the ranch lingered there now.

Cole took the bags from Cassandra and nodded at the stairs. "Tala, do you want to do this in your room?"

"Sure." Tala headed up the steps. Cassandra followed her into her bedroom, and Cole came after them, laying the garment bag carefully on top of the colorful quilt before setting the other bag next to it.

"I'll leave you both to it." He offered Tala another encouraging smile before he left.

Tala closed the door and turned around. The woman in front of her wore a fitted, navy jacket over striped dress pants and appeared to have stepped directly off the pages of a magazine. Tala narrowly resisted the urge to glance down at her T-shirt and yoga pants. Of all the things Cole had thought to purchase for her, dress clothes hadn't been among them. Not that she'd needed them. Not before tonight, anyway. "This is really good of you, Cassandra."

"It was my pleasure, honestly." The woman in front of her sighed. "Could we talk for a few minutes before we get started?"

"Of course." Tala gestured to the rocking chair in the corner. "Please, sit."

Cassandra sat down and crossed her long legs gracefully. Tala perched on the edge of the mattress. Her guest wrapped slender fingers around the arms of the chair. "First of all, please call me Cassie. All my friends do."

"All right, Cassie."

"Secondly, I need to apologize to you for what I said the last time I was here."

Tala shook her head. "No, you don't. You were concerned about Cole, and I completely understood that."

"Still, it was a terrible thing to say, and I regretted it the moment it came out of my mouth." She ran a French-manicured fingernail along the grain of the oak. "I've been trying to figure out where that even came from, and I realized I was jealous." She looked up and met Tala's gaze. "But I understand now that I was clinging to something that never existed. It wasn't Cole's fault. He told me he wasn't feeling it between us, but I didn't want to hear it."

"Cassie…"

She held up a hand. "It's all right. After seeing him that night, I was able to let go of any illusions regarding the two of us. They were keeping me from seeing someone who actually might be the person I'm meant to be with. Someone I work with who's asked me out a few times. I finally said yes, and we're having dinner on the weekend."

"That's so great, Cassie. I hope and pray that works out for you."

"Thank you." She tilted her head. "So, can you forgive me?"

"If there's anything to forgive, then yes."

The words appeared to ease the tension shimmering around the woman. "Thank you." Cassie leaned forward a little. "I understand what Cole sees in you, Tala. And I hope that you and I can become good friends."

"I'm sure we will."

"Good." She clapped her hands together lightly. "Would you like to see the dresses?"

"I'd love to."

Cassie jumped up and strode around the end of the bed. She stopped on the far side in front of the garment bag and unzipped it. "Cole suggested blue to match your eyes, and I think that suggestion is right on. Your eyes are incredible."

Tala wrapped her arms around herself. It was her looks—her eyes, specifically—that the men who came into her room always commented on, if they took notice of her at all. Everything that had happened to her the last few years had been because men found her attractive. It would have been far better for her if they didn't.

Cassie let go of the dress she'd been about to lift from the bag. "You don't like comments like that, do you?"

Tala mustered a weak smile. "Not really, no."

"I get it. If it helps, when Cole talks about you—which he does pretty much non-stop—he rarely mentions your looks. He talks about what kind of person you are, the things he loves about you like your compassion and sense of humor."

"That does help. Thanks."

"Good." Cassie touched Tala's elbow briefly. "Let's choose your wedding dress, shall we?" She reached for the dress she'd been about to lift a moment before.

Choose my wedding dress. The thought sent a thrill through Tala.

"I brought three of them to pick from." Cassie spun around, holding the first dress in front of her. The short, royal-blue dress had cap sleeves and was covered in a layer of lace.

"Oh, Cassie. It's beautiful."

Cassie laid it on the bed next to the garment bag before carefully removing the second dress and holding it up. This one was a lighter blue and sleeveless. It was also covered in lace, and the back of the skirt fell lower than the front.

"That one is gorgeous, too." How was she supposed to decide?

Cassie laughed as she set the second gown beside the first one. "Like I told Cole, I'm pretty much a professional shopper.

I'm glad we have similar tastes." She reached for the third dress, lifted it from the bag, and held it in front of her, swishing her hips from side to side a little as she faced Tala. "Last one."

Tala pressed her fingers to her mouth. The dress was breathtaking. A richer blue than the other two, the sleeveless gown criss-crossed over the chest and was cinched at the waist by a broad band of material. Below the waist, the skirt fell in soft, flowing folds past Cassie's knees. A decorative, faux diamond swath sparkled across the waistband, adding a little tasteful bling to the dress. Fit for a bride.

"This one, right?" Cassie grinned.

Tala nodded. "They're all beautiful, but this one is …" No word seemed strong enough to capture her feelings.

"Perfect?"

"Yes, absolutely perfect."

Cassie held it out. "Want to try it on?"

"Definitely." Thankful she had showered after coming in from the barn, Tala took the hanger from Cassie and carried the dress to the small ensuite bathroom. For a moment after she'd hung it on a hook, she stood gazing at it. Then, not wanting to keep Cassie waiting, she quickly removed her clothes and tugged the gown on over her underthings. It fit as though it had been made for her.

Tala swished from side to side as Cassie had done. The skirt flowed around her legs like water. She swallowed the lump that had risen in her throat. When had she last worn a dress? She didn't have one among her things at Brady's house and had rarely worn one in the years before that. Junior prom, maybe? She had been taken right before her senior year, so that was the only prom she'd attended. Tala had thought that dress, the one Felicity bought for her when she took her and Rose shopping for the dance, was the most beautiful she'd ever seen, but the dress in her memory seemed cheap and gaudy compared to the elegant gown that swirled around her now.

Tala ran her fingers through her hair before returning to the bedroom.

Cassie drew in a quick breath. "Tala. You look stunning." Her eyes met Tala's. "I'm sorry, but you do."

"It's okay. I do feel stunning in this gown. Almost like …"

"A bride?"

She faced the floor-length mirror on the wall next to the bathroom. "Yes. A bride."

Cassie came up behind her and rested her hands on Tala's shoulders. Peering past her, she gazed into the mirror. "That's because you are a bride, Tala. And you are marrying a wonderful man who, even if he is incredibly good at seeing past your appearance to who you are inside, will still not know what hit him when you start down the aisle in this dress."

Warmth seeped into her cheeks. Tala had been careful since arriving here not to dress in any way that could be considered provocative. Not that any of Cole's choices had given her that option. The clothes he'd chosen were practical and comfortable, which was exactly what she wanted. Still, it might be nice, for once, to show him how well she could clean up.

"Here." Cassie's fingers slid from Tala's shoulders as she strode to the bed and opened the leather bag. "I figured you wouldn't have much in the way of accessories, so I threw in a few of my things." She tugged two pairs of shoes from the bag and held out a pair in each hand, dangling from her fingers by the straps. "Do you like either of these?"

One of the high-heeled pairs was black and the other a shimmering silver. They were both gorgeous, but Tala pointed to the silver pair. "Those look the most wedding-y."

Cassie held them out. "I agree. They'll match the bling on the waistband."

Tala took one of the shoes and braced herself on the wall as she slid it onto her left foot. It was maybe half a size too big, but she could make them work. After sliding on the second shoe, she turned to the mirror again. The shoes were a perfect match with the dress, although Tala felt a little wobbly in them. "I haven't worn heels in a while. I'll need to remind myself how."

Cassie grinned as she stuck the black shoes into the bag. "You have a couple of days to practice." She withdrew a velvet box and carried it over to Tala. "With the diamonds on the dress, my suggestion is to keep the jewelry simple." She lifted the lid. An array of sparkling pieces glittered in the box.

Tala stared at them. "I can't use your jewelry. What if I lose something?"

Cassie waved a dismissive hand. "It's all insured and replaceable. And it can be your something borrowed. Please. I want you to use it. It isn't doing anyone much good sitting in a box on my dresser."

Tala examined the earrings. A pair of dangling sapphires surrounded by diamonds—fake, she hoped—caught her eye. They would look amazing with her dress. "Hold on." She went over to her dresser and removed the tiny studs she normally wore. When she came back, she carefully lifted one of the earrings from the box and slid the post through the hole in her ear. When she had both on, she held her hair in one hand and turned her head from side to side. "They're so pretty."

"They're perfect. Will you wear your hair up for the ceremony?"

"I hadn't really thought about it."

"You should, to show off the earrings. Do you know how to put it in an updo?"

"I can figure something out."

"Why don't I come an hour early on Wednesday and do it for you?"

Tala met her gaze in the mirror. "I can't ask you to do that. You've already done so much for me."

"I'd like to. I grew up with three sisters, and we did each other's hair all the time. I haven't seen them in ages, so it would be fun to play with hair styles again." The wistful note in her voice caught at Tala's heart.

"I understand. I had two foster sisters who were like real sisters to me, and we did each other's hair as well. I haven't seen either of them since"—her voice caught a little—"well, in years."

"Sounds like we both need this." Cassie smiled at Tala's reflection.

"All right, if you're sure you don't mind." She twisted her hair around and held it up at the back of her head. "Although there won't be many people to see it, it might be fun to wear it up for a change."

"Even if there were a hundred people there, it would only matter if Cole saw it."

That was true. Tala let go of her hair as she turned around. "I don't know how to thank you for all this."

"You don't have to. It's what friends do, right?"

"Yes, it is." Tala reached for Cassie's hand. "Still, thank you."

"You're welcome." Cassie squeezed her fingers before letting go and carrying the velvet box to the bed. She slipped it into the bag and closed it, then returned the two dresses Tala wasn't wearing to the garment bag and zipped it shut. "I have a long day tomorrow, so I think I'll go. But I'll be here early on Wednesday."

"All right. I'll change and be right down to say goodbye." Tala opened the bedroom door and held it as Cassie walked into the hallway.

After she'd gone, Tala changed quickly, leaving the dress hanging on the back of the door. When she came down the stairs, Cole and Cassie stood in the entryway. If Tala had had any lingering apprehension about the two of them, the warm look Cole gave her as she approached would have banished it immediately.

"How did it go?"

"Great. Cassie has impeccable taste. She found the perfect dress."

"Good." Cole pulled open the door for Cassie. "Thank you again for doing that."

"It was my pleasure." Cassie flashed them a smile before stepping onto the porch. "See you both on Wednesday."

After she left, Cole closed the door and turned to Tala. "So you had fun?"

"I did, actually. You were right; Cassie is lovely."

"She said the same about you. And she's right."

Tala wasn't sure what to do with the fact that his words, and the way he was looking at her, were sending flocks of butterflies fluttering through her stomach. She cleared her throat. "I think I'll go put everything away and get some sleep."

"All right." Cole moved out of her way so she could get to the stairs. "Sweet dreams, Tala."

Somehow she knew they would be. "You too." She smiled at him before heading to her room. When she walked in, a small bag on the floor next to the bed caught her eye. Tala walked over and picked it up. The logo on the side, from a well-known lingerie shop—drew warmth into her cheeks.

What had Cassie done?

The warmth intensified when she set the bag on the mattress and reached inside to pull out a silky, steel-blue negligee and robe. A small white card lay in the bottom of the bag. Clutching the garments to her chest, Tala sank onto the bed and flipped over the card.

For when you are ready. Your friend, Cassie.

Tala set the card on the bedside table and carried the garments over to the full-length mirror. She held them up in front of her. That night in the hotel room, before she'd escaped with Cole, she had vowed never to wear lingerie again. These were nothing like the trashy pieces Brady had made her wear, though. They were long and elegant, and the material slid over her fingers like blue-tinged liquid silver.

Would she ever be ready to wear them?

Tala had no idea. She took one last, lingering look in the mirror before folding the garments, returning them to the bag, and sticking it in the back of a drawer behind a pile of T-shirts.

Only time would tell.

CHAPTER THIRTY-ONE

Cole straightened his tie for the eighth time, not sure, even now, if the door to the cabin would open and Tala would come in, willing to marry him. The chapel was as ready as he was for the ceremony to take place. He'd chosen evening because he wanted the space to be lit by candles and twinkling lights around the rafters, as soft and warm and glowing as it had been the night he first brought her here. And it was.

Vases stood on every available surface, filled with the bouquets he'd purchased in town. Soft music played in the background. The minister stood in front of the small table set up beneath the cross on the wall. And Lake had arrived thirty minutes earlier, thrown his arms around Cole in greeting, and then settled on the bench closest to the front to wait for the arrival of the bride. Cole had asked him to video the wedding so he could show Grams sometime. When it was safe for her to come see them.

Cole glanced at his watch. Again. 7:10. The wedding was supposed to start at 7:00. Would she show up? Cassie hadn't come into the chapel yet, either. No doubt the two of them were still getting ready. Or maybe Tala had changed her mind and Cassie was driving her somewhere Cole would never be able to find her. These long, interminable minutes, like the stretch of time he'd waited for Tala's answer after he'd proposed, told him as much now as they had then. He desperately wanted to marry her. If she had left after all, he wasn't sure what he would ...

The cabin door swung open, and Cassie entered, walked up the aisle, and sat on the front bench opposite Lake. She offered Cole a warm smile, which loosened the tight knots in his shoulders a little. His attention swung to the door. Tala stood in the opening. The sight of her literally stole the breath he'd been about to take. He couldn't tear his gaze from her as she strolled up the aisle toward him.

The dress Cassie had chosen was gorgeous. Diamonds on its waistband and the jewels dangling from Tala's ears beneath her hair—pinned up in a style he'd never seen on her—caught the candlelight and twinkled like the stars she loved to wish on so much.

The smile she gave him when she reached him eased all the fears that had assaulted him before she entered the building. It took everything he had not to reach for her, to only smile back before they both faced the minister. She spoke briefly on the sanctity of marriage, words that were largely lost on Cole as his focus was stolen over and over by the woman at his side. He and Tala repeated the vows the minister spoke. When it came time to exchange the rings, Cole fished them from his pocket and handed one to her. The brief contact needed for him to slide the band on her finger and for her to work the ring onto his were the only touches that passed between them.

"And now, by the power vested in me by God and the province of Ontario, I pronounce that you are husband and wife." The minister reached for their hands and held them in hers. "What God has joined together, let no person separate."

She squeezed their fingers. "May God bless you and your marriage and give you many happy years together." With a beatific smile, she released them.

Cole would never be able to express to her how grateful he was that she'd taken a potentially awkward moment and turned it into something poignant and meaningful. Someone clapped him on the back, and he turned to accept Lake's congratulations. Cassie rose from the front pew and came forward to offer Tala a hug, and with that the ceremony was over. Tala was his wife. He glanced over his shoulder to see how she was doing, but nothing in the eyes that met his, the blue deeper than ever—brought out by the shade of her dress—suggested that, with this step in their relationship finalized, she felt any regret.

The minister laid out the paperwork for the four of them to complete, and then she gathered up the forms and tucked them into her bag. Cole walked her to the door of the cabin. When they reached it, she rested a hand on his arm. "I'll file these tomorrow and let you know when you can pick up the certificate from the church."

"Thank you."

"I'll be praying for you and that sweet wife of yours. The road ahead may be difficult at times, but never forget that you don't walk it alone. And if either of you ever needs to talk, my door at the church is always open."

Cole covered her hand with his. "We'll remember that. And we'll remember your kindness in doing this for us."

"It was my privilege." With a final squeeze, she released him and slipped out the door. Cole waited until she started her car before he closed the door. When he turned, he nearly bumped into Lake, who'd been standing behind him. His friend stuck out a hand, and Cole gripped it. "Congratulations, man. I'm genuinely happy for you and Tala."

"I appreciate it. And I appreciate you driving up here to be a witness for us. I should have mentioned this before, but you're welcome to spend the night in the guest room."

"Spend your wedding night in the house with you and your new wife? For some reason, that thought never crossed my mind." Lake clasped Cole's upper arm. "I'm not going to drive back until morning, don't worry. I've booked a motel room in town."

"Okay. If you're sure."

"Believe me, I am. It was good to see you. Let me know if there's anything you need, and I'll keep you apprised of any developments in Toronto. Hopefully the trial will begin soon. When that's over, you and Tala will be free to live your life without having to look over your shoulder all the time."

"That does sound good."

"Take care, brother. Of yourself and your beautiful new wife."

"I will." Cole tugged the door open again and held it until Lake had descended the porch step. Before he could close it, Cassie came up behind him. "I'm going, too. But thank you for inviting me today, Cole. It was a beautiful ceremony. I'm thrilled for you and Tala."

"You are?"

"Yes. And I'm looking forward to getting to know Tala better. She invited me to come for a visit soon."

"That sounds good."

"Be happy, okay? That's all I want for you."

"Thank you." Cole's eyes sought out Tala over Cassie's shoulder, and a smile crossed his lips. "I believe I will be."

"Good. See you soon." She did up the belt on her long, red coat before ducking out into the night.

Cole closed the door and turned around. Tala had knelt on the bench in front of the cross and clasped her hands on the top of it. His throat tight, Cole went to his wife and lowered himself to his knees beside her, clasping his own hands on the wooden railing as he sent up a prayer for the two of them. When he spoke, he kept his voice low and reverent. "Are you okay?"

Her eyes glowed in the candlelight. "Yes. More than okay."

When she rose, Cole stood as well. "Are you ready to go home, Mrs. Blacksky?" He paused. "Or do you want to keep Tangalou? It's your decision, of course."

"I like the sound of Tala Blacksky, if it's all right with you."

It was far more than all right. Sharing his mother's and Grams' surname with her made it feel as though they had truly been joined together, if in name only. For now. "I'd really like that."

"Good. And yes, I am ready to go home."

They started for the back of the chapel, blowing out candles and unplugging the mini lights as they went. When they reached the door, Tala stopped. "Thank you for making this so special, Cole. The chapel was incredibly beautiful."

"You were incredibly beautiful."

She offered him a shy smile as she grasped the skirt of her blue dress and swished it from side to side. "It's the dress. Cassie did an amazing job picking it out."

"I agree that she did. But it isn't the dress."

Tala let go of the skirt, and it rippled into place. "Then thank you."

Cole had avoided complimenting her appearance since the night they'd met, guessing that she wouldn't be comfortable with him commenting on her looks. And he didn't want her to think that was all he saw when he looked at her. Tonight, though, he couldn't help himself.

She didn't seem to mind. This once.

"What do you think, dinner and then a popcorn-and-movie night?" Normalcy was likely what she needed the most, and it would remind him that, while so much had changed between them tonight, in certain ways nothing had.

The relieved smile she gave him confirmed her slight worry that, despite his reassurances, he may have forgotten that. "Sounds wonderful. We can even watch *Casablanca* again if you want."

He shot her a sideways glance as they stepped onto the porch. "Really?"

"Yes." She crossed the wooden slats with a soft swish of material around her legs. "I don't think anything can bring me down tonight, not even the greatest but possibly the saddest ending to a movie ever."

Which, he reflected as he fell into step beside her, was the most encouraging sign yet that Tala was as happy as he was that the two of them were now bound to each other for life.

CHAPTER THIRTY-TWO

Cole tugged on his old boxing gloves and danced around a little, warming up his muscles. When he was ready, he laid into the punching bag his dad had hung in one of the empty stalls for him to practice on when he'd been on the boxing team in high school. Being around Tala, close to her but not able to touch her, was getting to him even more than he'd thought it would. Taking out his frustrations on the punching bag helped.

They'd been married nearly a month. As he had promised, they'd carried on with life the way they had before they got married. They had breakfast before spending a few hours in the stables or painting the cabins. Tala spent a lot of time perusing the books in his dad's study, and he often found her curled in an armchair in front of the fire reading. They cooked dinner together most nights, and Tala was starting to develop more confidence in the kitchen. They often watched a movie in the evenings, the bowl of popcorn still on the couch between them. And then they went to bed.

Alone and in separate rooms.

Although Cole fought the constant desire to reach for her,

other than a brief glance in his direction occasionally that he couldn't quite interpret, Tala hadn't made any effort to let him know she felt the same way. So Cole reminded himself—over and over—of the vow he had made to her, to Grams, and to God to be patient and wait until they were on the same page. If they ever were.

He hammered away on the bag until drops of sweat trickled between his shoulder blades. Then, after a final flurry of blows that relieved most of the pent-up tension he'd been wrestling with all day, he swiped the sleeve of his T-shirt across his forehead and pulled off the gloves. He hung them on a nail before grabbing the flannel shirt he'd tossed over the top of the stall and carrying it over to the sink. Cole splashed water on his face and arms, dried them with the towel hanging over the edge of the sink, then shoved his arms into the sleeves of the flannel shirt and did up the buttons.

A slight crunching in the straw behind him caught his attention, and he turned around. Tala leaned against the wall outside Cocoa's stall. How long had she been standing there, watching him? His breath caught at the look on her face. The same look he'd seen flit across it briefly sometimes and thought might be desire—although he usually chalked that up to wishful thinking. At the moment, she'd let her guard down and wasn't attempting to hide her thoughts. Which didn't help him keep the feelings he'd been trying to repress under control. At all.

Cole clutched the edge of the sink, trying to appear casual but needing the support. "Something on your mind?"

Would she tell him? So far she'd proven herself incapable of lying when she did speak, but she could also keep information to herself, if she didn't want to share it, like no one he'd ever known.

"I was wondering…" Tala bit her bottom lip.

"Wondering what?"

She shot a look at the barn door. Was she considering fleeing? *Stay with me. Don't retreat.* Her gaze returned to him, and she lifted her chin. "What it would feel like to touch your arms."

Cole almost laughed. Definitely hadn't seen that coming. Maybe he and Tala weren't on completely different pages like he'd started to suspect. He let go of the sink and slowly undid the buttons on the flannel shirt, his eyes locked on hers. He'd thought she would, but she didn't look away. "You don't have to wonder, darlin'." He undid the last button, tugged off his shirt, and threw it over the edge of the sink.

Would she come to him? For a moment she didn't move. Then she closed the space between them one small, deliberate step at a time, stopping in front of him. Cole stayed perfectly still, afraid the slightest motion would spook her. She ran her hands slowly over his biceps. Cole swallowed. He'd imagined what it would be like, her fingers passing gently over his skin, but the reality was far more powerful than his mind had conjured. Her touch was light and left a tingling warmth in its wake.

For a few seconds, she rested her fingers on his upper arms, a small smile playing across the lips he couldn't tear his gaze from. Then she lowered her hands. "Thank you."

My pleasure, while true, didn't feel like an appropriate response. "You're welcome." Everything in him longed to pull her to him, but he refused to take advantage of the moment she had created. "I am your husband, you know. You can touch me any time you want."

She glanced away. How could she, after everything she had been through, still seem so innocent? Shy, even. To keep from breaking his resolution not to touch her, he reached for his shirt.

"Is there anything you want?"

Cole left the shirt where it was. It felt like a loaded question. He wanted lots of things, but he was terrified of frightening her away by telling her what they were. He probed her blue eyes. *God, help me. Give me the words to say. I don't want to push her away. And I don't want to break my promise.* "If you are asking if I think you owe me anything, then the answer to that question is now, and will be every single time, no."

She nodded at that, slightly. Cole was about to make a second attempt to retrieve his shirt when she spoke again, more softly this time. "Then you don't want to touch me?"

He almost laughed again. Could anything be further from the truth? *Help me.* "I definitely did not say that. Only that I will never touch you or accept anything from you if I think you're offering because you believe you owe me something. Never."

His words seemed to release something inside her, something that had been restricting her ability to draw in air. Her shoulders relaxed, and she took a long breath. When she stepped closer, his own ability to breathe grew restricted. "If I don't believe that, will you tell me what you want?"

Thinking clearly was becoming increasingly difficult. Cole sent up another plea to whoever might be listening. "I will if you want me to. But only if we make it like that game you used to play with your foster sisters, when you wished upon a star."

Her lips quirked. "And what exactly would that look like in this context?"

"I'll tell you what I want, but I'll put it in the form of a wish that you are absolutely free to grant or not."

Tala bit her lower lip again, clearly mulling over the suggestion. "All right."

Cole studied her face. Although her walls were often—understandably—firmly in place, he could usually read her pretty well. He didn't detect any hesitation in her voice or her gaze, which met his steadily. "Are you sure?"

"If you haven't realized it yet, if I say it, then I'm sure."

That was good enough for him. "All right, then. I wish that I could touch your"—he paused and her eyebrows rose a little—"face."

Amusement sparked in her eyes. "My face."

"Yes." He waited a beat before adding, "You can say no if you want to."

Tala's smile erased the last of his concerns. "No, it's all right. You can have your wish."

Cole lifted both hands to her face, barely grazing her skin as he moved his fingers over her forehead, her eyelids, her cheeks. Her shallow breaths were warm against his palms as he ran his thumbs along the path of her cheekbones. Like her fingers had been, her face was soft and smooth, and he closed his eyes, reveling in the feel of it under his fingertips. When he opened them and traced her bottom lip with one finger, the eyes fixed on his darkened. For a few seconds, he cupped her face in his hands, his thumbs stroking her cheeks, then he reluctantly let her go.

Cole had been with women before, but nothing in his previous experience had prepared him for the power of those few seconds of touch—not when her fingers had touched his arms or when his had brushed over her face. Electricity sparked so strongly he could practically feel the pulse, but it was more than that. Something much more intense passing between them, as though they were connecting on a level far deeper than merely physical.

Finally, Tala stepped back and the spell was broken. Cole was almost glad. Having no frame of reference for what had happened between them, and given their very complicated situation—and everything she had been through—he hardly knew how to deal with the feelings that coursed through him. Did she feel the same way? Judging from the weak smile she flashed him, she did.

He expected her to flee to the safety of her room. Instead, she stood her ground, her eyes not leaving his. "Will you make another wish when you want something?"

God, help me. Was this a test? Was there a right or wrong answer to that question? "If I did, would you make one, too?"

"I might."

Cole decided to go for it and, as Grams would say, let the chips fall where they may. "All right, I will, but I have two conditions. One, that you also make wishes when you want something, and two, that you promise you will say no if I ever wish for anything you're not comfortable with. If I think you've broken either of those rules, the game will be over."

In a lot of ways, it was a dangerous game, but they *were* married. Whether or not their union was conventional, Cole hadn't taken those vows lightly, and he wouldn't treat her, her feelings, or her body lightly, either.

"Agreed." The fact that she didn't hesitate before she said the word released a lot of the tension from his taut muscles. The game was on, then. "I'll go start dinner."

It took a moment for him to force his thoughts from the pact they'd made to mundane talk of food. "Sounds good."

Tala smiled again, as though she knew he needed the reassurance. Which he did. When she was gone, Cole leaned against the sink. What was that? Would whatever it was make things better between them or worse? He had no idea. When the trembling in his legs eased, he pushed away from the sink and tugged on the flannel shirt. If he didn't think he should go in and help with dinner, he'd return to the stall and go a few more rounds with the punching bag before heading to the house.

Maybe more than a few.

CHAPTER THIRTY-THREE

Tala carried the pot with the melted butter over to the large bowl on the island and drizzled the hot yellow liquid over the popcorn. It had been a week since she'd asked Cole if she could touch him. Even now she could hardly believe she'd done it. She only had because she'd spoken to the therapist, Stephanie, before heading out to the barn. While she still wasn't completely comfortable opening up to the woman, Tala had shared what happened with Desiree and how helpless she had felt as Brady dragged her friend away. Stephanie acknowledged that, given the way Brady had treated her, it was understandable that Tala would have difficulty being assertive. She challenged Tala to practice intentionally advocating for herself before they spoke again.

Seeking comfort after the reminder of the night Desiree was taken away, Tala had headed to the barn for a few minutes with Cocoa before dinner. Instead, she found Cole, washing at the sink. With the therapist's challenge still echoing fresh, she'd taken the woman's advice before she had a chance to talk herself out of it.

And she wasn't sorry.

Tala set the pot in the sink and fluttered her fingers over her face. Days later, she could still feel the light touch of his skin brushing over hers.

He hadn't made a wish since. Was he waiting for her to make one? He'd promised never to push her to do anything she wasn't ready for, so it was possible. As much as she appreciated that, she wouldn't be opposed to him letting her know if there was something he wanted. Especially since he'd told her she was free to say no.

Maybe tonight.

Those evenings, watching a movie together, she was intensely aware of his presence, his nearness. When they sat across from each other at the island or the table, or worked side by side in the barn, she had other things to focus on. She could keep her thoughts occupied with the task at hand, whether it was eating or mucking out a stall, and she always had something for her hands to do. When they sat next to each other with only the bowl of popcorn between them, no matter how good the movie was, her thoughts strayed constantly to him and how easy it would be to reach out and touch him as she had the week before.

Enough. Tala shook her head to clear it of thoughts she shouldn't be having. Although, as Cole had pointed out, he *was* her husband. Spinning away from the counter, she snatched the bowl of popcorn and strode to the living room. Cole was sliding a video cassette out of its cardboard holder. When she set the bowl of popcorn on the middle couch cushion and dropped onto the end one, he slid the tape into the slot of the VCR and walked over to her.

Tala studied him as he approached. He was smiling, but his eyes held an intensity she couldn't quite decipher.

Cole lowered himself to the coffee table, his knees an inch or two from hers. "I'd like to make another wish."

The words she'd been hoping to hear sent her heartrate

racing. "All right."

"I wish that, while we're watching the movie tonight, we could hold hands."

The wish was so sweet it would have taken someone much stronger than she was to have refused it. Besides, it was an innocuous enough request. Holding hands with a man, with someone she knew and trusted, wasn't scary, right? Had she ever done it before? Not that she could remember. "Okay."

He grinned. "Okay." The movie title flashed across the screen as he stood, came around the coffee table, lifted the bowl of popcorn out of the way, and sat on the middle couch cushion next to her. The room was softly lit, with only the light of the lamp on the table at the far end of the couch, the flames flickering behind the woodstove door, and the blue glow of the television to lift the darkness. Cole balanced the bowl on his leg and then reached for her hand. The strong fingers wrapping around hers for the first time, engulfing them in his, filled her with such a strong sense of security and … *home* that a lump rose in her throat.

Tala transferred her attention to the screen, trying to bring her emotions under control. "*Gone with the Wind?*"

"Yep. Have you seen it?"

"I don't think so." Felicity had mentioned the movie and told Tala and Rose and Jae they should all watch it one night, but they hadn't done it before …

Cole squeezed her fingers gently. "Are you okay?"

Tala nodded. She could feel his gaze on her, warm against her cheek, but she kept her eyes on the screen. For years she had worked hard to hide what she was feeling, but it was becoming harder and harder to do so with him. As time passed, the knowledge that she could trust him, that nothing bad would happen if he saw deep inside her, gradually tempered her ingrained fear. Replaced it with a warmth as comforting as the fire blazing in the stove.

Cole rubbed his thumb often over the back of her hand. Each time, the movement sent tingles of heat skittering across her skin and up her arm. So much for an innocuous request. Although the movie was good, her focus was drawn again and again to their clasped hands. The feelings that coursed through her—so many feelings—nearly overwhelmed her. If she had somehow fooled herself into thinking she could live with him—marry him, even—and be content to be around him night and day without wanting to draw closer, she was rapidly coming to see that it was going to be far more difficult than she'd imagined.

Around the time Scarlett married her second husband, Tala stopped fighting what she was feeling and gave herself over to enjoying the sensation of his hand holding hers. When the final credits rolled, she turned her head against the cushion to look at him. "That was a long movie."

In the glow of the table lamp, mischief gleamed in his dark eyes. "That was by design."

"Oh." Tala couldn't repress a smile.

"Did you like it?" Cole still held her hand in his, and Tala made no move to try and free it.

"I did, actually. Quite a departure from your dad's usual taste."

"That's true. The video was pretty old. Maybe it was even one my mother picked out." A thoughtful look crossed his face.

Tala squeezed his fingers lightly. "What do you know about her?"

"Only what my grandmother told me, since my dad never spoke of her. According to Grams, she was a beautiful free spirit, creative, kind. And she loved to laugh."

His words—and the melancholy in his voice—tugged at Tala's heart. Like him, she'd lost her mother early. But she had their years together to hold as precious memories in her heart. How sad to have never known the loving touch or care of a mother. Especially when his father had been so cold and distant. The sudden urge to wrap her arms around him and pull him close, offer what had been withheld growing up, consumed her. "She sounds lovely."

"I think she was." He set the nearly empty bowl of popcorn on the coffee table and ran his free hand over her knuckles, sending more shivers tingling through her. "What do you remember most about your mother?"

Tala closed her eyes, picturing her sweet mother's face. "She also loved to laugh. She worked hard and was often exhausted, but she took time every evening to have dinner with me and to ask about my day and tell me about hers. She could turn pretty much anything that had happened into a funny story, and we usually ended up laughing our way through dinner. What I remember most, though, was her deep faith." An image of her mother, head bowed over their food or sitting in the armchair by the window early in the morning, her Bible open on her lap, sent sorrow and gratitude for the gift of faith drifting through her, and Tala opened her eyes.

Cole was watching her. "She sounds lovely, too."

"She was." Tala mentally closed the book of remembrances of her mother before she descended into a sadness that would overshadow the sweetness of this evening. "I'm sorry you don't have those kinds of memories."

"Me too." He lifted her hand and kissed the back of it and then offered her a sheepish look as he lowered it to his knee. "Sorry. That over-stepped the boundaries of my wish a little."

Tala grinned. "That's okay. It means I can push the boundaries the next time I make a wish."

"Which I hope you do. Soon."

The quiet words ignited a rush of fluttering wings in her stomach, and Tala pressed her free hand to it.

Cole took a deep breath. "It's late. I guess we should get

some sleep."

"I guess we should."

He held her hand a few seconds longer before slowly releasing it. After nearly four hours of his touch, her skin felt suddenly cold as Tala pulled her hand into her lap.

Cole reached for the popcorn bowl. "You go on up. I'll wash the dishes since you made the popcorn."

Tala didn't have the energy to argue. "Okay, thanks. See you in the morning?"

"I'll be here."

His usual response filled her, as it always did, with a mixture of comfort and anticipation as she made her way across the living room.

For a long time after she had climbed the stairs to her room and gotten ready for bed, she stood in front of the window in her room, gazing up at the brilliant night sky. The north star, twinkling brighter than the rest, reminded her of her foster sisters, and the deep sadness she'd held at bay while she was with Cole wove through her. Where were Rose and Jae now? Were they alive? If they were, was it possible they could be gazing at the same stars and thinking of her? *Jesus, watch over them. If they are alive, keep them safe and help us to find each other again someday.*

Her fingers rested on the top of the lower window frame, and Tala studied them, clinging to the memory of Cole's strong hand holding them. *And be with Cole. Help him to see that, although he didn't receive the love he needed from his parents, you love him and can fill that void in his life. And maybe I can too, a little.*

Tala closed her eyes, allowing the peace that flowed through her as she prayed to settle in her soul. She'd make a wish in her game with Cole soon, as he'd told her he wanted her to do. But for now, her prayer was the strongest wish she could make on his behalf.

CHAPTER THIRTY-FOUR

Cole waited days for Tala to make another wish. Not knowing when she would or what it might be was driving him a little crazy, but he prayed for patience, which did seem to help. The feel of her hand in his during the movie night that already felt like months ago had been so right, so powerful, that he'd barely been able to let her go. And he hadn't been wrong about their game being dangerous. Every wish granted made it more difficult to go back to not touching her.

But he'd promised. He had spoken to Grams a couple of times since the wedding and each time affirmed his commitment to wait for Tala to be ready for more.

Cole yanked open a bag of chips and dumped it into a bowl. When he carried it to the living room, Tala was already there, studying the movies lining the shelves built into the wall on either side of the TV.

Cole set the chips on the coffee table and walked over to stand next to her. "Anything appeal to you?"

She shot him a sideways glance.

"A movie, I mean," he clarified.

"Oh." Tala pulled *Harvey* off the shelf. "How about this

one? Felicity loved Jimmy Stewart, but I don't think I've seen any of his movies."

"Sure. That's one of his best, so a good place to start." Cole stuck the video into the VCR. When he started toward the couch, Tala had already taken her place at one end. Should he return to his old seat at the opposite end? That felt like a giant leap backwards, which was a discouraging thought. Before he could make up his mind, Tala bit her lip like she always did when she was trying to decide whether to say something.

Cole stopped next to the coffee table. "What is it?"

"I might be ready to make another wish."

Finally. "Please do."

"I wish that you—"

"Granted."

Tala let out a short laugh. "You haven't heard the wish yet."

"It doesn't matter. Whatever it is, you can have it."

"Hmm." She gazed at him, amusement flickering in her eyes. "I may need to give this a little more thought, then."

"Take all the time you need." He rounded the coffee table and settled on the arm at the far end of the couch.

After a moment, she said, "Actually, I think I'll stick with my original wish."

"Which is …?"

"That you would give me a foot rub while we watch the movie."

A foot rub. He could definitely live with that request. "Done."

"Really?"

"Absolutely." His only regret was that she hadn't chosen a longer movie. Where was *The Sound of Music* when he needed it?

Suppressing a grin, he lowered himself onto the couch. The opening credits were already rolling, so he patted his leg. "Give me your feet."

Tala stretched out on the couch and rested her ankles on his leg. Cole slid his fingers under the bottom of her yoga pants until he reached the top of one of her socks. Strictly speaking, he didn't *have* to run his fingers along her skin as he lowered the sock, but since she hadn't removed them herself, he was going to consider that an invitation to take them off however he saw fit. She didn't offer any kind of protest, so … permission granted.

Cole draped her sock over the arm of the couch and wrapped the fingers of both hands around her small foot. She'd showered after they came in from working in the stables, and the faint scent of lavender soap drifted from her skin. Cole took a deep breath as he started to massage her feet. Tala closed her eyes and let out a small moan.

It was quite possible neither of them would get much out of the movie tonight.

He worked on her right foot for half an hour before repeating the actions he'd taken to remove her first sock on the left one. Her eyes were still closed, but her breathing hadn't deepened. If anything, it was as shallow as his. Which was interesting.

He spent as much time on her left foot as her right and then massaged her ankles and an inch or two up her leg before finishing. Pushing the boundaries with the wish again, but since it was her wish this time and not his, that was allowed. Wasn't it? When he finished, he rested his hand on the tops of her feet and settled in to watch the second half of the movie. Tala didn't pull away, only opened her eyes and turned her head on the cushion to face the TV, and they watched the end of *Harvey* in silence.

Only when the last credit had rolled did she peer down the couch at him and smile. "That felt amazing."

"Good." Cole reached for one of her socks before she could pull her feet away. He slid it over her foot and up, then adjusted her pant leg over it before doing the same with the other sock. Then he squeezed her feet with both hands before letting go. Tala sat up.

Cole gestured to the TV. "How did you like the movie?"

She wrinkled her nose. "I pretty much zoned out during the first half, but the second half was good. Very funny. I really like Jimmy Stewart."

"Me too. He was one of my dad's favorites, and I think that rubbed off on me."

"We might have to watch this one again sometime so I can catch the first half." Tala yawned and covered her mouth with one hand.

"Yeah. I admit I was also a little distracted."

When she lowered her hand and glanced at him, he screwed up his courage and added, "Maybe more than a little."

"Me too."

The two words, offered almost shyly, ignited fresh hope in Cole. Tala reached for the bowl, but he shook his head. "Leave it. I've got it."

"Okay, thanks. That foot rub did me in, so I think I'll call it a night."

"I'm going up soon as well. I'll see you in the morning."

"I'll be here."

The assertion—one he'd made often to her but that she hadn't, until tonight, given him—wormed its way deep inside Cole and settled in. He smiled at her before she crossed the room and disappeared into the hallway.

Cole reached for the bowl and carried it to the kitchen. Tonight had felt like forward movement, not backwards as he'd feared. He'd take every moment like that with her he could get and be thankful that, yes, she was here and would still be in the morning.

As long as that kept being true, he would really try to stop wishing for more.

CHAPTER THIRTY-FIVE

Tala ran the brush along Cocoa's side, reveling, as always, in the warm, musty smell of the horse. Christmas was a week away. She'd really wanted to get something for Cole but didn't want to ask him to pick it up himself. Or use his money. After searching her bedroom and the guest room for ideas a couple of weeks ago, she'd found something that might work. Last night she had stayed up late working on the gift for him, so her eyes were heavy today despite the three cups of coffee she'd consumed before coming out to the barn.

The sound of boots thudding along the cement walkway sent an instinctive frisson of fear sizzling through her that evaporated as soon as Cole appeared in the opening of the stall.

"Ever been on a snowmobile?"

Tala's eyes widened. "No. Not many opportunities for that in the city. But I've always wanted to ride one."

He picked up the gloves she'd set on the shelf outside the stall and held them out. "No time like the present."

Tala grabbed them and followed him outside. She'd heard the loud roaring of a motor earlier but thought it was the snowplow Cole used to clear the laneway. Instead, a snowmobile was parked outside the door. A trailer was hitched behind it, and Cole had tossed a tarp and an axe into it. Tala scrutinized the load as she pulled on her gloves. "Should I be concerned that you're taking me out to the middle of nowhere with a tarp and an axe?"

He laughed. "I'll tell you what they're for as soon as we get to where we're going."

"Which is …?"

He handed her a helmet. "A surprise."

"Hmm." Tala tugged the helmet over her hair.

Cole put one on as well and then swung a leg over the snowmobile. "Are you okay to ride behind me? You'll have to hold on to me or you'll go flying off."

She offered him a wry grin. "I'll make it my wish for today."

He chuckled. "Granted."

Tala stepped onto the runner and then slung her leg over the long black seat, settling in behind him and wrapping her arms around his waist. The day was mild for December, and brilliant sunshine reflected off the snow. Tala squinted. She might need to add sunglasses to the shopping list. Cole turned the key, and the engine roared to life. Gripping the handlebars, he eased the snowmobile forward and guided it around the side of the barn, past the ice-coated pond. As soon as they were clear of the corral and outbuildings, he yelled, "Hang on!" over his shoulder. The words were torn from his mouth, so she barely caught them. The snowmobile lunged forward.

Exhilaration poured through her. The machine sped so fast across the fields she felt almost as though they were flying. Keeping a tight hold on Cole, she lifted her head and let the wind whip past her cheeks. The trees at the edge of the field passed by in a blur. Tala clamped her lips together to keep from letting out a whoop of pure joy at the feeling of freedom.

Too soon the snowmobile slowed, and Tala leaned sideways to peer past Cole. They had arrived at the woods she'd seen from a distance lining the far end of the field. He brought the machine to a halt and turned it off. "We'll have to walk from here."

Tala hopped off the snowmobile.

Cole clambered off after her. "What did you think?"

She ran gloved fingers over one of the handlebars. "That was the most amazing thing I've ever done."

"I thought you'd like it."

"Like it? I loved it. Only it was way too short."

"We can take a longer ride next time. Today we have a job to do."

"What's that?"

He didn't answer, only tromped through the snow to the trailer, lifted the axe, and then grabbed the tarp he'd folded into a square and tucked it under his arm.

Tala planted her hands on her hips. "You're not going to tell me?"

"If I told you, it wouldn't be a surprise, would it?"

"I guess not." Adrenaline still coursed through her, and she had no trouble keeping up with Cole as they walked side by side into the forest. Thankfully, the snow wasn't nearly as deep here under the cover of the trees. Tala kept her eyes on the ground, watching for roots that might trip her up.

"Look out." Cole snatched a branch out of her path before she walked into it. He held it for her until she'd passed by and then let it snap back into place.

"Thanks." Tala lifted her gaze to keep an eye out for twigs that might poke her in the eye or slap her across the cheek. Had she ever walked through a forest before? Not that she could remember. The closest she'd come was strolling past small groupings of trees in the city parks in Toronto, which was a pale echo of this escapade. The crunching of their boots in snow and the chirping of the birds were the only sounds disturbing the hushed stillness of the woods.

After several minutes of walking, they emerged from the area of the forest filled with bare-branched oak and maple trees into a patch of evergreens.

Tala pushed aside a prickly branch. A patch of snow slid from the needles to land with a soft thud at her feet. "They look like Christmas trees."

"That's because they are. At least, one of them will be. Whichever one you choose."

"I can pick a Christmas tree for us?"

"Yep. Good surprise?"

She held a hand to her chest. "The best."

"Have you ever picked out a tree?"

She shook her head. "My mom and I could never afford a tree, so we'd string lights and hang a few ornaments on a plant in our apartment. Felicity used real boughs to decorate the mantelpiece, but she had an artificial tree we put up every year, so I've never had a real tree."

"Then it's way past time." Cole swept an arm across the clearing. "Go ahead. Take your time and find a good one."

Hardly able to believe this was happening, Tala wandered among the trees. She passed several that might be okay, but, as soon as she set eyes on a tree that stood a little off to the side, she knew it was the one. "That's it."

Cole had been walking silently behind her, allowing her the freedom to choose on her own, but he came up now to stand next to her. "Good one. Great shape and the needles look healthy. And it's a balsam fir, which gives off the best Christmas smell. Perfect choice."

His words of praise washed over her like warm water,

despite the snowflakes drifting through the air around them. "Now what?"

"Now we chop it down." He lowered the axe he'd been carrying propped on his shoulder and eyed the trunk a moment before stepping closer and hacking into it. As he'd suggested, the slightly sweet, woodsy fragrance filling the air recalled Christmases with Felicity, Jae, and Rose. Tala closed her eyes and breathed deeply, indulging in the memories that for so long she had forced from her mind.

She opened her eyes when she heard a cracking sound. Cole swung the axe once more and the tree toppled to the ground. He spread the tarp next to it, and between them they rolled the tree onto it. "Can you carry the axe?" He held it out.

Tala took it and hefted it to her shoulder, the way he had carried it. They started back the way they had come, Tala following the footprints they'd made on their way in and Cole dragging the tree along the ground behind him. When they emerged from the woods, she set the axe in the trailer and helped Cole lift the tree in after it. "Can we decorate it tonight?"

"Sure. We'll set it up as soon as we get home and then let it sit for a few hours. Should be ready to put the lights on after supper." He nodded at the snowmobile. "Want to try driving?"

Tala whipped her head toward him. "Really?"

He grinned. "Really. We're only going across an open field—you can't get in too much trouble."

"Then yes!" She snagged the helmet he held out and shoved it on her head before hopping onto the snowmobile. Cole climbed on after her and gave her a quick lesson in how to get the snowmobile going and guide it home. He spoke into her ear, his breath warm on her cheek, his arms circling her waist. She swallowed. Whose wish was this now?

When he told her to, she turned the key in the ignition,

closed the choke, hit the start button, and the machine roared to life. Tala glanced over her shoulder. "Hang on!"

Cole's arms tightened around her as Tala pushed on the throttle. The machine leapt forward. She let off on the throttle a little, until they were moving at a steady pace, then increased the pressure. She didn't have the nerve to get the machine up to the speed Cole had, but still they flew across the field. Tala hadn't thought any feeling could approach the one she'd reveled in while riding on the back, but the power of being in control was a rush she had never known.

As they drew close to the pond, she eased up and guided the snowmobile around the barn before bringing it to a stop. After turning off the engine, she spun around on the seat. "That was amazing."

Cole let go of her and climbed off. "Fantastic driving. You're a natural."

Tala slid off and removed her helmet. "Can we do it again sometime?"

"Of course. There's plenty of winter left. We can go out lots."

She handed him the helmet. He'd pulled his off, and he set them both on the seat of the snowmobile and gazed at her a moment. Tala ran her fingers through her hair. "What is it? Do I have helmet hair?"

Cole reached out and trailed a gloved finger along her bangs, sweeping them from her forehead. His eyes locked on hers. "You look perfect."

Tala's breath caught at his intense look.

When he spoke, his voice was low and soft. "I wish that I could kiss you."

Yes! Everything in her longed to shout the word, to tip her head back and allow him to ... Her stomach lurched. A wave of revulsion crashed over her, as instinctive as the fear that had shot through her at the sound of tromping boots in the barn. A montage of images flashed through her mind, of all those men in the hotel, strangers, pawing at her and trying to kiss her...

She wrapped her arms around her waist, willing the images from her mind. *It wouldn't be that way with Cole. He isn't anything like those men.*

His features softened. "It's okay. You're not ready."

"I ..." The words lodged in her throat when she tried to explain.

"It's all right, Tala. Really. That's the rule, remember? You can't agree to anything you're not comfortable with, or the game will be over." He inclined his head toward the trailer. "Can you help me take the tree into the house?"

"Sure." The word came out in a raspy whisper. Misery seeped through her, dousing the exhilaration of the last couple of hours. What was wrong with her? She wanted Cole to kiss her, had wanted that for a long time. Why, when the moment came, did she have to react so strongly against it? What must he think of her?

Her cheeks burned as she trudged after him. He grasped the trunk and waited for her to lift the top of the tree. They carried it to the house in silence. Cole held the screen door open as they transferred it into the hall and wrangled it through the living room door. "Lay it down here." He gestured toward an open area in front of the bay window. When they'd set their load on the floor, Cole unwrapped the tarp. "Let's prop it against the wall for now. I brought the boxes of decorations down from the attic earlier. The stand's in one of them, along with the lights and decorations, so I'll have to go through them to find it before we can set it up."

Tala offered a perfunctory nod.

"Tala."

She forced herself to look at him.

"It really is okay. I'm not upset."

Tala rubbed her forehead with one hand, hoping her gloves would prevent him from seeing that her fingers were trembling. "I know, it's just ... I think I'm getting a headache."

Concern flickered across his face. "Why don't you go lie down? There's a bottle of aspirin in the medicine cabinet if you want to take one. If you're feeling better in a couple of hours, we can eat and then decorate the tree."

The excitement at the thought had diminished, but she didn't want him to know that. "Okay. I'll see you later."

Without waiting for a response, she turned and fled to the sanctuary of her room. After tossing her coat and gloves on the chair in the corner and toeing off her boots, she stumbled to the window. The snow covering the fields sparkled in the waning sunlight like the diamonds on the blue dress she'd worn on her wedding day. It was too bright for stars to appear. Still, Tala touched her fingertips to the cold glass.

What a disaster she was. She'd known the trauma of the past would occasionally trespass all over the happiness she'd discovered on the ranch with Cole. But the ferocity with which it had encroached on the moment the two of them had shared, a moment that might have been the perfect end to the most thrilling afternoon of her life, shocked her.

Stephanie the therapist was going to have a field day with this one the next time Tala talked to her. Maybe she'd even make it into a psychology journal with Tala's case study. Her eyelids fluttered shut.

Cole had said all the right words, but did he mean them? Or had she done irreparable damage to the beautiful yet fragile relationship the two of them had gradually woven together since they arrived at this place?

Jesus. Tala opened her eyes and pushed her fingertips harder against the icy designs on the glass. What did she want to ask? For Cole to understand? To forgive her? That she would be able to let go of everything that had happened to her and move on with her life? She had prayed that, over and over, and in many ways she had seen that prayer answered. The first steps of it, anyway. Still, the trauma she'd undergone wasn't about to disappear into thin air.

Clearly.

Give me peace. Please. And Cole, too. Help us to work through this. As it so often did when she asked God for it, a whisper of peace did work its way through her. She'd talk to Cole. As her therapist had advised, Tala would be honest with him about what she was feeling and what had held her back. And hopefully, when she did, they would be able to put what happened behind them and keep moving forward.

CHAPTER THIRTY-SIX

Cole dropped onto the couch. Propping his elbows on his knees, he lowered his face to his hands. What had he been thinking? He'd had no intention of making that wish this afternoon. But Tala's enthusiasm, her wide-eyed wonder, had gotten to him as it always did. When she tugged off the helmet and gaped at him, her blue eyes huge and bright with exhilaration, he could think of nothing except how much he wanted to take her face in his hands and press his lips to hers.

All those weeks of being patient, of not pushing her, had been obliterated in a few seconds of utter weakness. Would they be able to move forward from here, or would they find themselves at ground zero again?

With a heavy sigh, Cole pushed to his feet. What was done was done. When she felt better, hopefully they could talk about it. His heart heavy, he trudged to the kitchen. Tala had enjoyed the steaks they'd grilled the night he proposed. He could toss two of them on the barbeque along with a couple of baked potatoes and then make a salad. If her headache went away, maybe they could enjoy a nice dinner, make their way onto even footing again.

When he finished preparing the food, he returned to the living room. After digging through two of the three boxes of Christmas decorations, he found the stand and maneuvered the seven-foot tree into it. He still hadn't heard anything from upstairs, so he tugged the strings of lights from the third box, untangled them, and wrapped them around the tree before dropping onto the couch again. The tedious part was done; he'd save the decorating until Tala joined him.

As though the thought had summoned her, he caught the sound of her light tread on the stairs. His stomach tightened a little as he waited for her to appear. When she did, she offered him a tentative smile as she crossed the room.

Cole slid to the edge of the couch. "Are you feeling better?"

"Physically, yes. But I do want to talk to you about what happened earlier." Tala sank onto the coffee table in front of him. "The thing is, when I was working for Brady, men tried to kiss me sometimes. Not all of them. Not even most of them, since that wasn't really what they were there for. But I always attempted to avoid it. It felt far too intimate, too much of a violation for a man I didn't know, who had paid to be there, to do that with me. I trained myself to watch for any sign that a man might be thinking about it so I could head him off. It became an instinct, something my body responded to without my brain even thinking about it. Today, when you said you wished you could kiss me, I wanted to say yes. So badly. Then that instinct took over and my body reacted violently. Not because of you but because of my past." She gazed at him under her long, dark lashes. "Can you understand that?"

The familiar rage that roared through Cole whenever he thought about what her life had been like, what she'd had to do, what disgusting, perverse men had done to her, ignited deep in his gut, but he willed it away so he could stay calm. "I do understand, actually. That makes perfect sense."

"Then do you think you can forgive me?"

He leaned forward, resting his forearms on his knees. "Forgive you? Tala, there's nothing to forgive. You didn't do anything wrong."

"I feel as though I did. Like I hurt you or made you feel that I wasn't drawn to you. That I haven't wanted to make that wish myself for a long time. And that isn't true. It's not even close to true."

Cole was afraid to move. What was she saying?

Before he could come up with a response, she shifted closer. "In fact, I'd like to make that wish now. If it's okay with you, that is."

"Umm, it's quite a bit more than okay." He searched her eyes. At least, it was if she really meant it and wasn't forcing herself to do what she thought he wanted. He couldn't detect any hesitation in them this time—the opposite, in fact.

Tala wrapped a warm hand behind his neck, pulling him to her. She touched her lips to his, gently at first, then more urgently. Cole slid his fingers along the sides of her face. The faint floral scent of her soap swirled around her, and he breathed it in, reveling in the fragrance and in the feel of her soft mouth on his. When she ended the kiss—far too soon for him—his head was spinning, and every sense was tingling wildly.

For a few seconds, his brain refused to engage enough for him to form a coherent sentence. Finally, he managed, "Was that ... all right?"

Her light, slightly breathless laugh eased any worry. "More than all right. It was everything I knew in my head it would be and more."

It had been even more than he'd thought it would be as well, which was saying something. Tala straightened. Although her body hadn't touched his, she'd been close enough that he'd felt the warmth of her along the length of him, and a sudden coolness gripped him. Everything in him longed to pull her to him and kiss her again, but his grandmother's warning voice rang in his head: *I said patience, Cole.*

He cleared his throat. "Are you hungry?"

The amused look she gave him sent heat creeping up the back of his neck.

"For food, I mean. I made dinner for us."

"I thought I smelled steak when I was coming down the stairs."

He nodded. "I barbequed."

"Then what are we waiting for?"

Personally, he was waiting for his legs to be strong enough to carry him to the kitchen. "Before we go"—he managed to stand and make it to the wall to pick up the cord he'd left for her to plug in—"do you want to do the honors?"

Her eyes lit with that inexplicable glow that he was so irresistibly drawn to as she crossed the room. "I'd love to." With a dramatic flourish, she leaned down and stuck the cord into the outlet. The tree flared to life on the strength of the hundreds of twinkling bulbs Cole had twined through and around the branches.

Tala drew in a quick breath and covered her mouth with her fingers. "Cole. It's incredible."

"It was your pick. We can come back after we eat to add the decorations."

She turned to him, her eyes glistening like they had the night he'd asked her to marry him. "Thank you."

"For what?"

"For being so understanding and so patient. And for giving me one of the most incredible days of my life. Actually, for giving me a lot of the most incredible days of my life."

"Every single one of them has been my pleasure. You've given me the best days of my life, too. And I'm looking forward to many more."

A slight shadow flickered across her face and disappeared so quickly he wondered if he had imagined it. Was she thinking about Brady?

Determined not to allow anything to mar the beautiful place they'd gotten to after their brief rough patch earlier, Cole inclined his head in the direction of the kitchen. "Shall we?"

When she started along the hallway, he followed her, breathing a prayer as he went that, if God was listening, he'd help them to keep moving forward with their relationship. And he tacked on a plea that the threat Brady continued to pose might soon be neutralized, so nothing could stand in the way of them having countless more incredible days like the one they'd shared today.

CHAPTER THIRTY-SEVEN

Christmas morning dawned exactly the way it should. When Tala climbed out of bed and padded across the cold floor to stand in front of the window, huge white flakes of snow drifted from the low-hanging sky.

Smiling, she dressed quickly and headed downstairs to warm up in front of the fire. The woodstove did a better job than the ancient furnace at keeping the farmhouse warm, but by morning the flames had died out, and the upstairs had grown frigid. The sight of the tree they'd decorated a week earlier twinkling in front of the window sent a surge of joy rippling through her. Almost as much as the appearance of Cole, clutching a tray with two steaming mugs and two plates loaded with food as he strolled into the room.

"Good morning."

"Morning. And Merry Christmas." She settled on the couch as he set the tray on the coffee table.

"Merry Christmas to you." He held a mug out. Tala wrapped her fingers around the warm ceramic. He'd already stirred up the fire and added wood, and flames danced behind the glass.

Cole sat at the other end of the couch. Tala shifted around to lean against the arm, facing him. "Breakfast smells so good."

"I made coffee cake and omelettes. That was always Christmas morning breakfast around here when I was growing up." He nodded at the tray. "Help yourself."

Tala set the coffee on the table and picked up both plates. Leaning forward, she held one out to him, and he took it with a smile. "Thanks."

"Thank *you*." She inhaled an appreciate sniff. "I am definitely not keeping my promise to contribute to the cooking around here."

His eyes gleamed. "We all have our strengths."

"Hey," she protested.

Cole laughed. "I'm kidding. We can pick up our cooking lessons after Christmas. For today, you can relax and enjoy it."

"I'm sure I will." Tala stuck a forkful of eggs, ham, and cheese into her mouth. Closing her eyes, she let out a sigh of pure bliss.

Cole snickered. "I'll take that as a compliment.

Tala opened her eyes. "You should. This is incredible."

"What kinds of Christmas traditions did you grow up with?"

"My mom and I kept things simple. We never had a lot of money, but she always found a way to get me a gift I loved. And I usually made something for her. We'd eat pancakes, and then we'd read the Christmas story from the Bible. Even though we didn't have much, she always made it a special time. Felicity did as well. She loved Christmas and kind of went crazy with decorating, baking, buying gifts, and having people over. On December 13th, she started reading from a children's book called *Star Light*. Every evening for twelve days, she'd read a chapter and one of us would add a piece to the nativity set on the mantel. On Christmas Eve, Felicity laid Jesus in the manger to complete the scene."

Cole snagged a piece of omelette with his fork. "I like that."

"Me too. It was really powerful, bringing the story to life that way."

"We should buy a Nativity set sometime and see if we can find that book."

The thought of following Felicity's tradition—one she had shared with her husband before he died—filled Tala with a deep joy, as though she was carrying on her foster mother's legacy. A lump rose in her throat. "I'd love that."

"Me too." Cole smiled before sticking the omelette into his mouth. "What else did you do?"

"On Christmas morning, the four of us gathered around the tree, and Felicity read the same story my mom used to. Then we took our time opening our presents. As soon as we were done, we went to a drop-in center and helped serve a turkey dinner."

"That sounds like a perfect day."

"It was. I had only three Christmases with her, though, before I ended up at Brady's. And, of course, Christmas Day there was no different than any other day." Bitterness threatened to snake around her insides again, but she shoved it away. Today was a day for joy, not sorrow.

Cole set down his fork. "I'm sorry, Tala. I hope we can make our own traditions over the Christmases to come."

"I hope so, too." She finished the last bit of omelette on her plate and broke off a piece of coffee cake to pop into her mouth. After washing that down with the coffee, she set the plate on the tray and hopped up. "I have something for you."

Cole set his empty plate on top of hers. "You do?"

"Yes." Tala hurried to the tree and grabbed the bag she'd stuck behind it the night before. She carried it to the couch and held it out to him.

Cole took it, a bemused expression on his face. "How in the world did you get me something?"

"Open it and I'll tell you."

She held her breath as he reached into the bag and pulled out a long, red, knitted scarf. His eyebrows rose. "How did you …?"

"I made it." Tala sank onto the couch. "I wanted to give you a Christmas present, but I didn't want to ask you to buy it, so I wasn't sure what to do. Then one day, when you were in the barn, I was snooping around in the guest bedroom looking for ideas, and I found a bag with wool and knitting needles on the closet shelf."

Cole ran his fingers over the scarf. "Who taught you to knit?"

"No one. I went on the computer whenever you weren't around and looked up YouTube videos. It's not very good, but it was the best I could do with what I had." The scarf had come out uneven, but maybe it wasn't a terrible first attempt. It was soft anyway and would hopefully keep him warm.

"Are you kidding?" Cole wrapped it around his neck. "It's fantastic." When he lifted his head, she stilled at the look in his eyes. "I don't think anyone has ever made anything for me. My dad always got me something practical, like a backpack for school or a fishing pole. And Grams bought me something fun, but she was never big on sitting around making things. This means more to me than anything you could have purchased."

Her throat tight, Tala nodded. "Good. I'm glad."

"I have something for you as well."

She shook her head. "You shouldn't have bought me anything. You've done so much for me."

"Actually, I didn't buy it." Cole went to the tree, reached into the branches, and pulled out a small, wrapped present.

Tala's fingers fluttered to her throat when he carried it over and held it out. What could he possibly have gotten her? She slid a nail under the tape at one end of the present and carefully peeled a piece of the paper loose. She hadn't been given a gift in more than eight years, and she was determined to savor every second of opening this one. At last the paper fell onto her lap, revealing a small velvet box. Tala slowly lifted the lid. A sparkling diamond ring rested between two folds of velvet, and she drew in a quick breath. "You got me a ring?"

Cole nodded. "It was my mother's. I found it in her dresser drawer a few weeks ago and knew right away I wanted to give it to you."

"Cole. I don't know what to say. It's the most beautiful thing anyone has ever given me. But do you really think I should get your mother's ring?"

"Of course. I checked with Grams, and she assured me my mother would have wanted you to have it." He slid a little closer. "Okay if I put it on?"

When she nodded, he took the box from her, withdrew the ring, and then set the box on the coffee table. Tala held out her left hand, and he took it and slid the ring onto her finger until it rested against the band. For a few seconds, he continued to hold her hand, the warmth of his fingers seeping into hers. The flock of butterflies that always seemed ready to take flight at the slightest of touches or looks from him rose in her stomach.

When he did release her, she swallowed hard before lifting her hand to admire the sparkling diamond. "It fits perfectly."

"Somehow I knew it would." He inclined his head toward his mother's Bible on the table at the end of the couch. "Do you want to read that Christmas story your mom and Felicity used to?"

"Would you? I'd love to hear you."

"All right. You'll have to tell me where to find it, though." He reached for the well-worn book and flipped it open.

"It's in the book of Luke, closer to the back of the Bible than the front. Chapter two."

It took him a minute to leaf through the thin pages to the right spot. Tala settled more comfortably against the cushions and listened as he read the old, familiar chapter. She hadn't been sure, when she'd thought about what this day might bring, whether the two of them would be able to make it very special. Cole's deep voice reciting the story she loved brought back so many good memories, though. She couldn't imagine how the day might have been any more special, any more meaningful.

Her heart full, she listened as he read to the end, thanking God as he did for the gift of that baby in the manger and for all the other unexpected gifts she had received since the night Detective Cole Blacksky came into her life.

CHAPTER THIRTY-EIGHT

Her own scream jolted Tala awake. She bolted upright, her heart skipping and pounding against her breastbone, long strands of hair plastered to her cheeks. Tala tossed off the covers and clambered out of bed. The wooden floor grounded her as the cold seeped into the bottoms of her bare feet. She stumbled to the window and flung open the curtains.

A bright moon beamed in the night sky, illuminating the field of white spread before her. She dug a fingernail into the sprinkles of frost on the glass, tiny tendrils of ice dropping onto the sill. The full moon looked so tranquil, so calm as it peered down on the world, as though nothing traumatic was happening on this little planet. If she could go there, somehow, maybe she would be safe.

Behind her, a light tapping sounded on the door before it creaked open. "Tala?"

"He's coming for me." Her voice came out flat, emotionless, belying the terror still raking sharp claws across her skin.

"No, he's not." Cole's footsteps thudded across the floor, stopping a few feet behind her. "He can't leave his house, Tala. You're safe here."

How many times had he said those words to her? For the first time, they didn't carry calm along with them. She shook her head.

"I would die before I let him hurt you."

She closed her eyes. "I think that might be what I'm most afraid of."

"I promise you ..."

She shook her head again, vehemently. "Don't. Don't make a promise you might not be able to keep."

When he didn't answer, she opened her eyes and gazed up at the millions of stars blazing across the sky. So many wishes ... She slid a trembling finger through the frost to land on the largest one she could see. "I wish ..."

Cole stepped closer. "What? What do you wish?"

"That you would hold me." She turned to face him. "Would you mind?"

"Mind?" He closed the space between them and gathered her into his arms. "I thought you would never ask."

Tala rested her cheek against his chest, the steady thudding of his heart beneath his T-shirt assuaging her fear. He hadn't made another wish or touched her in over a week, since he'd held her hand on Christmas morning to slide his mother's ring on her finger. She'd missed the feel of him so much it scared her.

She had no idea how long they stood in front of the window, his strong arms and the warmth of his body slowly, slowly loosening the sharp talons of horror that had held her hostage in the throes of the dream. She and her therapist had discussed her complicated feelings around a physical relationship with Cole. Stephanie was doing her best to help Tala work through those feelings.

Being in Cole's arms was helping a lot more.

Finally she stopped shaking, and he stepped back and held out his hand. "Here."

She slid her fingers into his, and he led her to the bed. When she sank onto the edge of the mattress and smoothed the front of her mauve T-shirt, he reached for the bottle of water on the nightstand and handed it to her. Tala took a sip of the cool liquid before setting the bottle on the table. Then she swung her legs onto the bed and stretched out.

Would he take that as an invitation? She contemplated him. *Was* it an invitation? Brady had taught her how to use her skills to comfort the men who came to her. Could Cole do that for her?

He only hesitated a second before he grasped the sheet and blankets and tugged them up to her throat. After tucking her in, he rested his bent fingers on her temple a moment. "Sleep. I'm not going anywhere." He backed toward the rocking chair in the corner.

"You don't have to stay." The words were weak. She should insist he go to his own room and try to get a few more hours of rest himself, but everything in her wanted him here. If he left, the dark shadows would close around her again, coming for her like she knew Brady would.

"I know." He offered her a small smile before tugging the afghan from the arm of the chair and spreading it over his lap.

Tala didn't protest further, only closed her eyes. She hadn't thought she would be able to sleep, but the nightmare had drained her of all physical and emotional strength. The sound of Cole's soft, steady breathing a few feet away kept the fear at bay, and she slowly allowed exhaustion to carry her into a few hours of reprieve.

Cole snatched a few minutes of sleep here and there, but, for most of the four or five hours he spent in Tala's room, he propped his elbow on the arm of the rocking chair and rested his head on his hand, watching her. She appeared to have sunk into a dreamless sleep—*Thank you, God*—but oblivion eluded him.

What had she meant when she said Brady was coming for her? Did she somehow know something Cole didn't? Had God given her a glimpse into the future, a way to prepare herself, or was the lingering terror of her dream playing games with her mind?

Whichever it was, Cole needed to be more vigilant than ever. He could check in with Lake more often, and he would drop into the police station next time he was in town, give them an update on the situation here. He should have been doing that all along—keeping him and Tala on their radar—but he'd allowed himself to believe they were safe here and didn't have to remind anyone they might need assistance at some point. That had been foolish and arrogant, and he would rectify that as soon as possible. Today, even.

Another thought barged to the forefront of his brain, one that had niggled in the recesses of his mind since the night he'd helped Tala escape. Why had Brady gone to the hotel? Had he somehow figured out who Cole was? Ice formed in his chest. If he had, it was only a matter of time before he discovered Cole had a connection to this place. The fact that he'd changed his last name would only delay the inevitable. And they'd already given Brady a lot of time.

Tala hadn't closed the curtains after her sojourn at the window, and, by 8 am, rays of sun fell across the bed, rousing her. When she stirred, Cole straightened. She opened her eyes and gazed at him a moment, as though attempting to figure out why he was there, in her room. Would she remember her dream?

A small smile crossed her lips. "Good morning."

"Morning." Cole lifted the afghan from his lap and folded it.

"Thank you for staying. It helped a lot."

"It was no trouble. I wanted to be here." Cole draped the blanket over the arm of the chair. "How are you feeling this morning?"

"As soon as I have coffee and maybe go for a ride on Cocoa, I'll be fine."

Did she have any recollection of the dire prophecy she'd made about Brady? In case she didn't, Cole wasn't about to bring it up. "I'll let you get ready, then." He stood and crossed the room.

"Cole?" Tala sat up, clutching the quilt to her chest.

"Yeah?" One hand on the doorknob, he faced her.

"What I said about Brady, that wasn't only because of my dream. It was something stronger than that. A gut feeling, I guess, that's partly based on what I know about him but partly on a deeper instinctive sense that I can't explain. I only want to make sure we're as prepared as we can be so that, if something happens, we're not caught off guard."

He nodded. "I still don't think there's any way he can discover where we are. Or that he could then escape and travel five hours undetected to get here. But I do respect your instincts. You know Brady a lot better than I do, unfortunately, so I don't want to discount your feelings on this. I promise I will take more precautions and be more alert than ever. And I'm praying."

Her shoulders relaxed. "That means a lot to me."

"To me, too." He tugged open the door. "I'll see you downstairs."

Cole returned to his room. As desperately as he could use a cup of coffee, he needed even more to analyze what had occurred in the night. When Tala had gone to bed, it had taken every bit of strength he had not to try to make something happen. He'd even wondered if she was issuing an invitation when she lay down and looked up at him. Did that mean something? Was she ready for their relationship to grow deeper?

Patience, Cole. Grams' words rang in his ears as they so often did.

I'm trying, Grams. Honest. It would have been easy last night. He suspected Tala would have been receptive if he had kissed her or attempted to take things further. She'd been distraught, though, and afraid. Even though they were married, it wouldn't have been right for him to take advantage of the moment.

He rubbed the side of his hand across his forehead. It was too much to wrap his mind around when he was so tired and worried about her. A shower would help wash away the cobwebs that draped themselves thickly over his brain. That and breakfast and a few hours of manual labor in the cold barn might enable him to figure out what he needed to do to keep Tala safe. Calling Lake would be a good start. The two of them could discuss strategies. Lake was one of the smartest guys Cole knew. Maybe he'd be able to come up with a better plan than Cole had so far. Something foolproof.

He winced. There was no foolproof plan. Even if Brady was being watched too closely to be much of a threat, nothing was stopping him from sending a couple of his hired guns to do his dirty work for him. Maybe they should think about moving somewhere else. Although it had been almost four months since they'd fled Toronto, and there'd been no sign that Brady had tracked them here, it could happen any time. More and more people had to have seen Cole in town. Any loose talk spoken in the vicinity of someone on Brady's payroll—and no doubt they were everywhere—meant word would get back to him.

Cole would go to town today and invest in a few more

locks for the doors. It wasn't likely that anything would keep Brady or his Neanderthals out for long—not with the type of firepower they would bring onto the property.

Still, making the place more secure might buy him and Tala time to call for help if and when they found themselves in desperate need of it.

CHAPTER THIRTY-NINE

Tala's bedroom door was open. Cole had thought she would be asleep by now. He might have been, except that he'd realized when he got to his room that he had forgotten to bring a glass of water up with him. Had it been open when he'd walked past on his way to the kitchen? Not that he could remember. A movement inside the room caught his attention, and he stopped. Tala sat on the stool in front of the dresser, brushing her long, dark hair, her back to the door. She was humming softly, and he leaned a shoulder against the door frame, attempting to identify the song. Before he could, her eyes met his in the mirror, and she stopped brushing.

Cole pushed away from the frame and walked across the room to stand behind her. "Here." He lowered his glass of water to the dresser and held out his hand.

She set the brush on his palm.

When he lifted it to her head, he caught a glimpse of her reflection, and his hand stilled. She wore a long, silvery-blue robe that had definitely not been in the bag of items he'd purchased for her the day they arrived at the ranch. Where had that come from? Cole struggled to return his attention to the task at hand—and to remember how to breathe.

He ran the brush lightly through the hair that hung halfway down her back. Since he hadn't made an official wish tonight—or for a couple of weeks now, wanting to give her space after the night he'd led her to the bed and then slept in the chair in her room—he tried not to touch her, but the strands of hair that brushed across his knuckles were soft, and his stomach tightened. "That was a beautiful song. What was it?"

"Something my mother used to sing to me. An old hymn, I think."

Maybe that was why it rang a far-off bell for him, since Grams had taken him to church as a kid. For a couple of minutes, he concentrated on running the brush through the long strands, until they fell in soft, shimmering waves. When he slid his fingers under the thick tresses to lift them free of her shoulders, his fingers lightly grazed her neck. Tala's gaze met his in the mirror again, and he let her hair fall down her back and handed her the brush. "You should get some sleep."

"Wait." Tala set it on the dresser and turned on the stool to face him. "I ... have a confession to make."

Not wanting to tower over her, Cole sat on the end of the bed, his knees inches from hers. This close, he glimpsed soft lace lining the top of the gown she wore under the robe and forced himself to lift his gaze to her face. "What's that?"

"I, uh, left my bedroom door open on purpose. I heard you walk by and go down the stairs, and I wanted you to stop on your way back."

His heart rate picked up. "Why?"

She twisted her fingers in her lap. "When you asked me to marry you, I told you I didn't know if I would ever be ready for us to ... be together."

A faint smile crossed his lips. "I remember."

"The thing is, I want us to be. Only..."

"Only what?"

The breath she drew in was shaky. "It's never been a good experience for me, ever. Often it was violent or aggressive, and it always felt cheap and dirty. I'm struggling with getting past that, with believing that it could ever be anything else."

God, help me. Give me the words. His stomach unknotted slightly. "I promised you I would wait until you were ready, even if you never were, and I meant that. However, I do want you to know that it wouldn't be like that with us."

"How do you know?"

"Because with all those men it was sex. With you and me, it would be making love. And that's completely different."

Tala tilted her head, her hair splashing over the silver-blue arm of her gown. "How?"

Cole rubbed the back of his neck and sent up another urgent plea for the right words to say. The idea of a healthy, loving physical relationship between a man and a woman had been horribly tainted for Tala, and he longed to restore that for her the way she deserved, even if he felt woefully inadequate for the task.

"You don't have to talk about it if you're uncomfortable."

He lowered his hand. "I'm not uncomfortable talking about it with you. I just ... I was praying, actually, for the right words." The candle he'd given her flickered on the bedside table, releasing the scents of coconut and warm ocean breezes into the air. Cole took a deep breath, inhaling the calming warmth of it. "Sex is a purely physical act that any two people can perform even if—and you know this as well as anyone—they don't care about each other or know each other's names. Even if they hate each other. Sex focuses on taking, not giving. It's about self-gratification, not meeting the needs of the other person. It can be bought and sold." He hesitated before adding, "And it can be forced."

Tala flinched. He was describing her life since she'd been abducted, he knew, a fact that nearly killed him on the rare occasions he allowed himself to think about it. "Love making is the opposite. It can only happen between two people who care about each other, who love each other. It's about giving, not taking. It's knowing what the other person wants and needs and doing everything you can to make sure they get that. And while, yes, it does involve the sexual act, it's much more than two people connecting on a physical level. They're connecting on an emotional and spiritual level as well—so deeply and inextricably that the Bible describes it as the two of them becoming like one person."

Her eyebrows rose slightly, and he smiled. "That's right. I read the Bible. More since I met you than I have in my life." Her eyes had softened. Was he getting through to her? He had no desire to talk her into anything she didn't want to do. He only longed to show her that sexual intimacy wasn't always ugly, violent, or self-serving—that between the right people and in the right context it was a beautiful thing. Even, he was willing to allow, a gift from God. "That's the kind of relationship I want us to have—so close that we're like one person."

Tala ran her fingers along the tie of her robe.

Cole studied her. The desire to bare his heart to her as he so often yearned to rose again. Although he waited for it, the wall that had risen, stopping him the first time he wanted to tell her how he truly felt—in the chapel before he proposed—was gone. He touched the sleeve of her gown with his finger. "And I believe we can be that close because I love you, Tala."

She bit her lip. "You do?"

"Yes." He'd felt that love so strongly, for so long, it seemed to him that every time he looked at her or touched her, she had to hear it over and over. Still, he needed to say the words. "I love you with all my heart. I would never have asked you to marry me if I didn't."

Her eyes searched his as though testing the truth of his words. When she smiled, his shoulders relaxed. She believed him. "I love you, too. Or I would never have said yes."

Joy flowed through him, deeper even than when she had agreed to marry him. "Then, whenever you are ready, I truly believe it will be very special, very powerful with us." He started to get up, to give her time to think about what he'd said.

She stopped him with her fingers on his knees. "I am."

He glanced at her hands and then up at her, needing to know exactly what she was saying. "You are what?"

"Ready. I want to make it my wish."

"Are you sure? Because—"

She leaned in and kissed him. The familiar scent of lavender drifted on the air. Cole closed his eyes and breathed it in. Breathed her in. His arms ached to hold her, but he kept them at his sides, letting her take the lead. After a moment, she pulled back, a small smile on her lips. "You should know me well enough to know that, if I say it, I'm sure."

Cole's heart thudded wildly. Was she being honest—with herself as well as with him? He sensed calm in her sapphire eyes—and something else. The same thing he'd seen in them the day she summoned the courage to tell him she wondered how it would feel to touch his arms. The tightness in his muscles eased.

Tala stood and held out her hands. When he placed his in hers, she drew him to his feet. Cole let go of her and slid his hands along her jawline and into her hair. He kissed her forehead, her closed eyelids, her cheeks, retracing the path his fingers had followed the first time he touched her. He moved slowly, giving her time to adjust. Or to realize she wasn't as ready as she'd thought she was.

When he reached her mouth, Tala's lips against his were as warm and soft as her skin. She responded eagerly to his kiss.

With trembling fingers, Cole loosened the belt around her waist and slid the robe from her shoulders. It fell to the ground behind her with a swish of shimmering silk. He lifted his head and searched her eyes. Not until they crinkled slightly at the corners and she clasped her hands around his neck did he bend down, lift her into his arms, and carry her to the bed.

Then, for a long time, no words were needed between them at all.

CHAPTER FORTY

Cole ran a finger over Tala's arm, absently drawing designs on her bare skin.

"I think it's over."

He froze, his fingertip still touching her arm. Over? Did she regret what had happened between them? Would she pull away from him? Insist on leaving like she almost had before he'd asked her to marry him? How could he possibly live without her now?

When he didn't move, she turned onto her back to gaze up at him. "The game, I mean." She burst out laughing as she touched a finger to his cheek. "You should see your face."

He grasped her finger and pressed it to his lips. "Don't ever scare me like that again."

She laughed again, lightly, the sound sending warm tingles racing over his skin. "I'm sorry. I didn't think about how that might sound. I only meant that I think we've gone about as far as we can with the wishing game."

"Oh, I can think of a few more wishes," he said, teasingly, before leaning down to kiss her gently on the lips.

She took his face in her hands. "Thank you, Cole."

"For what?"

"For showing me there is another way."

Part of him had still worried he had pushed her too hard or somehow, inadvertently, added to her trauma in some way. Her soft words blew away the last of his trepidation like dandelion seeds in the wind. He hoped and prayed that what had happened with them had been as different from anything she'd experienced with another man as day was from night. It had been different than anything he'd ever experienced, and he knew why. This time it was right, the way it was supposed to be. And it had been far better than anything he could have possibly imagined. Which meant that any lingering impression he had of God being a disapproving authority figure standing, arms crossed, in the sky somewhere, determined to ruin all his fun, had to go. 'Love is always the other way, darlin'."

She lowered her hands, and Cole ran his finger over her arm again. "How do you say that in your mother's language?"

"Say what?"

"Sweetheart, or darling, something you'd call the person you love."

"Oh." She had a tiny dimple to the right of her mouth that he'd never noticed until this moment. "*Mahal*. It literally means *love*."

"*Mahal*." He kissed her shoulder.

Tala bit her lip.

"What is it?"

"I know I've more than used up my wishes for the day..."

Cole tapped her nose with one finger. "Yes, you have. But if you hadn't, what would you wish for?"

"That you would stay here all night with me."

Cole tipped his head from side to side as though debating. "We'll have to get a judge's ruling on that." He stopped moving his head. "The judge has ruled that you are allowed a second wish."

"Are you sure?" Her face had grown serious, but she couldn't hide the dancing in her eyes. "You can say no if you want to."

Cole laughed. "Oh, I think we both know that is never going to happen."

Tala turned onto her side, her back to him. "You *are* remarkably agreeable when it comes to this game."

He wrapped his arms around her and pulled her close. "Tala." He couldn't seem to stop saying it. "Such a beautiful name."

"It means *star*, which is why I chose that nickname. I didn't want Brady to know my name, but I didn't want to lose it completely, either."

Cole's arms tightened around her. He'd give anything to be able to erase the last few years from her mind so she'd never have to think about Brady or anything that had gone on in that house of hell again. Or be affected by it. While he couldn't do that, he would do everything in his power to give her new memories that might, someday, so overshadow those dark years that they would fade to a distant fog in her mind, as ethereal and impotent to do damage as a fine mist.

"My last name, Tangalou, means *light* or *illumination* in Tagalog, my mother's language."

"So, your name literally means *star light*, like in the song."

"Yes. That's why my mother sang it to me so often. For years I thought she had made it up for me, until I found out it was a well-known children's song."

Cole rested his head on the pillow. "You mentioned once that you sang it with your foster sisters. Can you tell me about them? And how you ended up in foster care?"

She sighed.

"It's okay. You don't have to if you don't want to."

"No, I do. I've been wanting to tell you about that for a while. It's hard to talk about though."

"Take your time."

She nodded, her hair soft against his chin. "I never knew my father. When my mother first came here from the Philippines, she worked as a nanny to make money to send to her family. The father of the children she was taking care of took advantage of her, and one day she found out she was pregnant."

"How old was she?"

"Eighteen."

"What did she do?"

"She told my father, and he was furious. He fired her and kicked her out of the house."

Cole closed his eyes. How could his wife possibly show the level of trust in him that she had shown tonight after so many men had abused her and her mother? *That could only be you, God. Thank you for not letting her be destroyed by all she's been through in her life. She is a walking miracle.* "I'm sorry."

"She didn't talk about that time very much, but I'm sure it was incredibly hard. Thankfully, she was strong, and she found another job, this time as a cook in a women's shelter. Not only did she not have to deal with men there, but the management and the women were very good to her. They gave her a room and made sure she had prenatal care, and they also helped her after I was born. We were there until I was five, when she got another job cleaning hotel rooms during the day while I was in school. That paid a lot more money, so she could afford to get us an apartment."

"You got that from her."

"What?"

"Strength."

She was quiet for a moment, then she nodded. "She passed along her faith to me, which is where her strength came from.

No matter what she went through, she never lost that. It only grew stronger over the years, even when she …" Her voice broke.

Cole touched his forehead to the back of her head. "Are you sure you want to keep going?"

"Yes." She rested a hand on his arm. "She was diagnosed with breast cancer when I was thirteen. She had chemo and radiation, but they caught it too late. She died right after my fourteenth birthday."

It hurt for Cole to draw in a breath, his chest ached so badly for that young, grieving girl, suddenly alone in the world. "And you went into the system."

"Yes. Children's Aid came for me right away. They took me to a place that wasn't great. Not terrible, but one of the daughters in the family clearly didn't want me there, and she did what she could to make my life miserable. Thankfully, I had a wonderful social worker. I didn't want to say anything about what was going on, but she could see I wasn't happy, so she found me a place with a woman named Felicity Greenman."

A smile had crept into her voice. Clearly that placement had been better. Although something had happened when she was seventeen…

"Next to my mother, Felicity was the most wonderful woman I'd ever known. She had been married once, but her husband had also died of cancer. Since she'd always wanted children but hadn't had any before he died, she chose to open her home to those who needed a family. I was the first foster kid to come to her after her husband's death, arriving on Christmas Eve. She took in two other girls a few months later. Rose was fourteen, like me, and Jae was a year younger. We hit it off right away and became like sisters."

Cole smiled, picturing the three of them together.

"Felicity's house was one of those old ones with wide,

padded window seats. We'd sit on one of them almost every night and stare up at the sky, making wishes on the first bright star we saw. For a couple of years, everything was pretty much perfect. Felicity was a trained counselor, and she helped us work through stuff from our past. Then she started having health issues. For a long time, they didn't know what was wrong with her. Then one night she woke up in excruciating pain. I called an ambulance, and they took her away. When she came home, she gathered us in the living room for what she liked to call a family meeting. She told us she had advanced kidney disease, but the doctors were doing everything they could for her. She tried to sound upbeat and positive, but it was clear she was worried. Someone from CAS met with her the next day. When he left, she told us everything would be okay, but she was pale and shaking. Clearly the visit had concerned her. After she went to bed that night, my sisters and I had a family meeting of our own."

She was trembling. Cole rubbed his hand up and down her arm, trying to impart comfort and warmth. "Tala, please …"

"No. I need to finish." She drew in a shuddering breath. "In spite of her reassurances, we knew Felicity was dying. Rose and I were seventeen and Jae was sixteen, so CAS would come and get us, likely soon, and we would be separated. There was no guarantee we would end up in good places, so we made a reckless, ill-conceived plan to leave that night, to find a place where the three of us could hide out. I'd be eighteen in six months and Rose in eight months, so if we could avoid being caught before then, we'd be safe."

Cold dread crept over Cole as he realized what was coming, but he didn't speak. Clearly, she needed to tell her story, so he would listen to every word, as much as it caused him physical pain to hear it.

"We didn't last six months. We didn't even last the night. We snuck out of the house at two in the morning. We'd walked four blocks before a white van slammed to a stop beside us. I'd seen that van around our neighborhood before, and it always gave me the creeps, as though someone inside was watching us, but they'd never approached us. This time, the side door slid open, and four men jumped out. I screamed at Rose and Jae to run, but I didn't have time to see if they did because two of the men headed straight for me. Before I could move, they grabbed me and dragged me to the van. One of them held a cloth over my mouth with terrible-smelling wet stuff on it, and that's all I remember until I woke up in Brady's house."

Her skin had gone clammy and cold. Cole whispered in her ear, "Enough, Tala. Enough for tonight," and she nodded. He kissed the top of her head. "Can you sleep?"

"I think so."

"Good." Cole tugged the quilt up to her chin before wrapping his arm around her again. "Rest. I'm not going anywhere."

The trembling that had gripped her finally eased, and her breathing deepened. For hours after she'd fallen asleep, Cole lay there, listening to her soft exhalations, breathing in the faint lavender scent of her, and praying for God to help him let go of the intense hatred he felt for Brady so he could give Tala all the love that she deserved.

CHAPTER FORTY-ONE

Tala dried the last of the dishes and peered out the kitchen window. The ranch was caught in the grip of a vicious February snowstorm. Pellets pinged against the glass, and she could barely see the faint glow from the barn windows. Cole had gone out to do a final cleaning of the stalls and make sure the horses had food and water for the night. He'd only been gone half an hour, and already she missed him.

It still caught her off guard, how strong her feelings had grown for him in the months they had been here. She hung the towel over the handle of the stove and glanced out the window again. Cole would likely be awhile yet. Was it cold in the barn? The temperature had plummeted, driven by a merciless north wind that had swept the storm into their area. Maybe she should go out and help him so the chores would be done faster and they could return to the fire and a movie.

With a curt nod, Tala strode down the hall and snatched her purple winter coat off the hook on the wall. She tugged on her hat, gloves, and boots and then flung open the front door and stepped onto the porch. A gust of wind shoved her back a step, and she had to grasp the doorknob tightly to keep it from being torn from her hand. She wrangled the door shut and turned toward the stairs. The wind drove snow into her face, and she narrowed her eyes to slits. This might not be a good idea.

Berating herself for being tempted to retreat to the warm house when Cole was out in the cold barn alone, she made her way to the top of the stairs and descended to the walkway, buried now beneath at least a foot of snow. Keeping her eyes firmly on the glow from the barn windows, Tala struggled through one step after another, her boots sinking nearly to their tops. The bitter wind wrapped icy fingers around her lungs, choking off her air. The fifty yards between the house and the barn felt like miles as she made her way slowly toward that faint light in the distance.

After five more minutes of struggling through drifts, Tala paused to catch her breath. She'd never encountered temperatures like this. Probably should have grabbed her scarf, but it normally only took a couple of minutes to walk to the barn. The glow from the stable windows broke through the heavy snow. She sent another look over her shoulder at the house. She appeared to be about halfway. Might as well keep going.

Tala fixed her eyes on the light ahead of her. With snow swirling all around, every other marker—the trees, fields, cabins, truck—had disappeared behind a thick haze of white. She took a couple more steps forward. A sudden gust of wind drove her back a step. She regained her balance and sought out the glow from the barn window.

It had vanished.

Tala drew in a quick breath. Had Cole finished and switched it off? She needed that light to guide her. If it was gone, she had to return to the house. Tala whirled around, searching for the light on the porch or spilling from the windows.

Nothing.

Where were the house lights? A sick feeling struck her. Had the storm intensified so much that not even the light from inside the barn or house could penetrate it? She turned again, toward what she thought was the barn. A wall of white met her gaze. Was she even facing the barn? No matter which direction she turned, she could see only white. Completely disoriented, Tala fought a surge of panic. Cole had to finish up in the barn soon and would need to walk close to her to get to the house. All she had to do was stay where she was, and he would find her.

Except that the snow swirling around her was so thick that if he passed by more than a couple of feet away, they wouldn't see each other. "Cole." She called his name as loudly as she could, but the wind grasped it and swooped it into the air until it was lost in the night. "Cole." She tried again. The heavy snow blanketed the words, silencing them as effectively as it had silenced all other noise but the rush of wind driving hard pellets of ice into her cheeks and forehead.

"Cole." The word was nearly a sob as she sank to her knees. Another gust of wind battered her. How long could she last out here? Already the skin exposed to the elements had gone numb. She sat in the snow and bent her knees to her chest, crossing her arms on top of them so she could bury her face and protect her skin from the ferocious wind. *Jesus, help me.* Everything in her longed to start walking and hope she would bump into either the barn or the house, but if she missed either by even a foot, she could wander across the open fields and Cole would never find her.

She lost track of time as she huddled in the yard. Every couple of minutes she called out Cole's name, but the word never seemed to travel more than an inch or two from her mouth before being extinguished. He wouldn't hear her over the roaring of the wind. If he went into the house and didn't see her downstairs, he might assume she was taking a nap in her room and not go looking for her for hours. By the time the storm died down and he realized she wasn't inside, it would be far too late.

Her eyelids felt so heavy. She should fight the drowsiness tugging them down, but she was too tired. Maybe she could close them for a moment, gather up her energy, and then try calling Cole again. Her eyelids fluttered shut. A strange sensation, like a blanket being wrapped around her shoulders, crept over her. Tala relaxed into it. Yes. She needed to rest. Just for a moment.

A distant sound tugged her from near sleep. What was that? She strained into the howling storm, trying to catch it. Then she heard it again, a little closer this time. Her name. Cole was looking for her. She tried to summon the energy to call back, but the word came out in a raspy whisper.

"Tala."

She heard it again. More clearly this time. He was coming closer. She couldn't let him walk past her, or he might never be this near her again.

Summoning the last bit of strength in her body, she called out, "Cole."

He said her name again. Suddenly he was there, crouching in front of her, the scarf over his face flashing red as he scooped her into his arms and carried her to the house, his boots sinking into the deep snow over and over.

Cole shoved through the front door and into the living room. The rest of the house was in darkness, but firelight flickered off the vines and roses twining across the wallpaper, casting a warm glow over the room. Cole carried Tala to the couch and set her down. She shook violently, and, when he started to undo the zipper of her coat, she grabbed his hand to stop him. "It's wet, *Mahal*," he said, his voice gentle but with a thread of urgency. "We need to get you into dry clothes."

She was too cold and exhausted to argue and let her hand

fall to the couch. Cole tugged off her coat, hat, and gloves. "Here." After dropping his scarf and coat on the floor, he removed his thick sweater, pulled it over her head, and then wrapped a blanket around her. "I'm going to grab more blankets. I'll be right back."

His sweater smelled like hay and horses and woodsmoke, and Tala held the sleeves to her face and breathed in. She stared into the flames dancing behind the glass of the woodstove. The fire looked so warm, but it wasn't beginning to penetrate the deep chill that had settled in her core, making her entire body tremble. Her teeth chattered painfully, but she couldn't get them to stop.

In less than a minute, Cole was back, his arms laden with blankets. He wrapped them all around her. Then he dropped onto the coffee table, worked one of her arms free, and rubbed it with his hands. His frantic movements belied the calm look he was clearly forcing. Beneath his ministrations, pinpricks of pain poked into her skin. As unpleasant a sensation as it was, she was pretty sure that was a good sign. He massaged her fingers for a few minutes before tucking the arm he'd been working on beneath the pile of blankets and reaching for her other one. When he finished rubbing it vigorously, he pulled off one damp sock and began massaging her foot. At first, she could barely feel his fingers on her skin. Then, as feeling slowly returned, the pain grew nearly unbearable.

Tala bit her lip, trying not to cry out.

"Does your foot hurt?"

"Yes," she stammered, through still-chattering teeth. "That's a good thing, right?"

He managed a grim smile. "Yes, in this case pain is good." The intense prickling slowly eased as he worked on the other foot. Tala had no idea how long he had been rubbing life back into her limbs, but slowly, slowly the intense cold that had seized her inside and out began to release its hold, and warmth worked its way through her. Cole tucked the blankets more tightly and took her face in his hands. "Can you feel this?"

Tala nodded. Her cheeks prickled like her hands and feet had, but they gradually thawed beneath his touch.

"I'm going to make tea and grab you a dry pair of socks. I'll be as quick as I can."

"Tea. Socks. Good."

Cole kissed her forehead before disappearing into the hallway. Tala turned her head toward the woodstove, the heat of the flickering flames finally reaching her. After a few moments of relishing the fire and the weight of the mound of blankets, she closed her eyes and gave in to the comforting heat.

Cole's heart lurched when he came into the living room, carrying a tray with the tea pot and mugs, a clean pair of his thick work socks tucked under his elbow. Tala had fallen asleep. Was that safe? Would he be able to wake her?

He set the tray on the coffee table and sank down next to it. "Tala?" He grasped her shoulder and shook her lightly.

It took a few seconds—during which an almost paralyzing fear ensnared him—but she finally opened her eyes, blinked, and offered him a drowsy smile. "Hi."

Cole's eyelids dropped shut briefly. "You really need to stop doing that to me."

"Doing what?"

"Scaring me. I was worried about you falling asleep, that I might not be able to wake you."

His hand still rested on her shoulder, and she reached up

and covered it with hers. The soft palm felt warm on the back of his hand, and a little of the fear eased. "I'm fine to sleep now. I'm not freezing anymore. In fact, I'm toasty warm, thanks to you."

"Good." Reluctantly, he pulled his hand from beneath hers so he could pour her a mug of tea. "Can you sit up?" He set the pot on the tray and helped her get upright and then tucked a couple of pillows behind her back.

"Thank you."

Cole handed her the cup before reaching under the blankets and sliding the socks onto her feet, testing the temperature of her skin as he did. Both feet felt warm and dry, and a little more of the tension evaporated from his muscles. He waited until she'd taken a few sips and then touched the blankets covering her knee. "What were you doing outside?"

"I thought I would come out and help you in the barn. I …"

"You what?"

A sheepish look crossed her face. "I missed you."

If he'd been tempted to allow his fear to metastasize into anger at her for taking such a reckless risk, the possibility slipped through his fingers at the sweet admission. "I was scared to death."

"Me too. I know it wasn't smart, going out in the storm, but it wasn't that far, and I kept my eyes on the light shining through the barn windows."

He winced. "Then the power went out."

"I guess so. All I knew was that the light disappeared. Then, when I turned to go back to the house, I couldn't see light there, either. All around me was white, and I suddenly didn't know what direction I was facing. I was scared to move in case I wandered into a field."

Cole blew out a breath. "You did the right thing, staying where you were. I don't even know how I found you, except that I begged God to help me, and then I nearly tripped over you."

Tala let go of the mug with one hand and wrapped her fingers, hot from the ceramic, around his. "I'm sorry I put you through that."

He sighed. "You didn't mean any harm. You've never been out in a storm like that. You couldn't have known how easy it would be to lose your bearings."

"How do you find your way back and forth?"

"There's a rope tied to the wall outside the barn door and another one attached to the front of the house. If you ever need to go from one building to the other in a bad storm, take the rope with you and don't let go of it. I'll show you tomorrow, although …"

"Although what?"

"I'd rather you stay in the house next time, where you're safe and warm, city girl."

Tala gave him a crooked smile. "You know what? I don't feel like a city girl anymore."

Cole reflected on everything she'd been doing since she got here—mucking out stalls every day, chopping wood, riding Cocoa, driving a snowmobile. "I guess you're not." Even so, she might feel like a country girl now, but she still wasn't used to life in northern Ontario. Dangers also lurked here, even if they were different from the ones she'd faced in Toronto.

Tala squeezed his hand. "What is it?"

He twined his fingers through hers. "I was thinking about how close I came to losing you. I …" His throat thickened, and he cleared it. "I don't know what I would do if something happened to you." The thought of it shook him, more than he would have believed possible a few short months ago. Everything was different now, and he couldn't imagine his life without her. Didn't even want to think about her being torn away from him without warning.

Like my mother was from my father.

The revelation sparked a deeper empathy for his dad than he had ever felt. No wonder his father had struggled to go on with his life, to allow himself to love another human being as much as he had loved his wife. The pain of her loss must have been excruciating.

Tala's eyelids drooped, and he reached for the mug. "Why don't you rest? I'll bring in more wood to stoke the fire, and then I'll sleep in the armchair. The rest of the house will be too cold until the furnace comes back on."

She didn't protest when he took the tea, only relaxed against the pillows. Cole tucked the blankets around her and watched her for a few minutes, hesitant to go until her eyes closed and her breathing grew deep and even.

Then he forced himself to leave her to bring in more wood to keep the fire going through the night. After sticking several pieces into the stove—enough for flames to roar behind the glass when he closed the door—he sank onto the armchair. Although he'd told her he would sleep, Cole sat there for hours, listening for the sound of her breathing and praying that tonight was the last time he'd ever have to deal with the overwhelming terror that he might have lost her forever.

CHAPTER FORTY-TWO

Sometime before dawn, he'd clearly given in to the exhaustion—emotional and physical—because Cole was gradually roused from a deep stupor by the enticing aromas of coffee brewing and bacon frying. He opened his eyes. Tala was gone, the blankets folded neatly on the couch. And she was cooking, which meant she had to be okay.

He climbed the stairs, changed, brushed his teeth, and splashed a little cool water on his face to chase away the last of the haze. The house was warm, so the power must have come on in the night. Cole ran a comb through his hair before heading to the kitchen, anxious to see Tala and make sure she had emerged from her near disaster unscathed.

The bright smile that greeted him when he came into the kitchen did a lot to push away the lingering shadows. Tala stood in front of the stove, a spatula in one hand. "Good morning."

Cole rounded the island and pulled her to him. "Morning. How are you feeling?"

She tipped her head to gaze up at him. "Good. Warm."

"Warm is good."

"Yes, it is. I don't think I'll ever take it for granted again."

Cole let her go. "That smells great. What can I do?"

She pointed to the table with the lifter. "Sit. Everything's almost done."

He wandered over to the table. She'd set their places already, and a carafe of coffee sat on a hot pad. Cole filled his mug with the steaming liquid. He watched her as she worked, sliding the spatula under the eggs and transferring them onto his plate before adding several pieces of bacon. He tried to imagine the kitchen, this house, his bed—which they'd shared since their first night together—without her presence and couldn't do it. Didn't want to do it. Thank God she had agreed to marry him.

He meant the fervent prayer. Even if Cole had ignored him most of his life, God had given him far more in the woman in front of him than Cole had ever dared to hope for. He leaned back as Tala set the plate of food in front of him and then returned to the stove for hers.

"This looks amazing."

"I know, right?" Tala sounded delighted at her own accomplishment. "I think I'm finally getting the hang of this cooking thing. Which is good"—she set her plate on the table and grasped his hand—"because I wanted to make this to thank you for last night."

"I didn't do much."

"Cole. You saved my life."

He squeezed her fingers. "You saved mine first." He meant it. He hadn't even realized, until he met her, how shallow and meaningless his existence had been. She'd breathed life and light into it. He'd never be able to thank her for the myriad of ways she had made his life better simply by being her. And by choosing him.

Her smile was warm. "I guess we're even, then."

She laughed and chatted as she ate, as though she hadn't had a brush with death the night before. Maybe her years of living with the constant threat of violence had inured her somewhat to the gravity of her life ending. His throat tightened, and he took a sip of coffee to ease the ache.

A strand of hair had come loose from her ponytail, and she tucked it behind her ear. When she did, Cole caught a glimpse of an inch-long scar on her temple. He'd noticed it before but never asked her about it. He set his mug on the table and reached over to touch it lightly with the tip of his finger. "How did you get this?"

Her smile faded. "That's a long story."

He glanced at the window. "Given the amount of snow we got last night, neither of us is going anywhere."

Tala stood, picked up their empty plates, and carried them to the sink.

Cole grabbed their mugs and the coffee carafe and followed her. After returning the pot to the coffee maker, he leaned against the island. "You don't have to tell me if you're not ready."

She set the second dripping plate in the rack before turning off the tap and facing him. Cole reached for the towel hanging on the oven door and handed it to her. She wiped her hands and tossed it on the counter. "No, I need to."

"Okay. But if you want to stop any time, you can."

She drew in a quivering breath. "It happened three years ago, during my night of ice."

Cole blinked. She'd said those words before, often, in her sleep. The nights she woke up screaming or crying out, her long hair damp against her cheeks. What did it mean?

Tala rubbed trembling fingers over the jagged line on her head. She'd just been through another trauma—he shouldn't have pushed her to tell him about that scar. "Tala..."

"I'm all right. But please don't interrupt, or I won't be able to get this out."

He nodded.

Tala grasped the edge of the counter on either side of her, knuckles white. Cole tried bracing himself for what he was about to hear, although he suspected the attempt would be futile.

"I had a customer one night, a kid. It was his eighteenth birthday, and his dad had bought him an hour with me. To make a man out of him, Brady said. The poor guy was so nervous. I chatted with him for a bit, trying to get him to relax. After we'd talked about our favorite movies, food, that sort of thing, he asked why I was doing this. He seemed to genuinely want to know, like he actually cared. I knew I shouldn't do it, but somehow the whole story came out, how Brady had forced me into this life, that I couldn't leave. As soon as I finished, I knew I had made a terrible mistake. The kid's eyes had gone huge, and he looked completely horrified. He mumbled something about how he couldn't do this and fled."

Cole's chest constricted. That could not have gone over well with Brady. Had he hit Tala in the head with something? Questions poured through him, but he was determined to honor her request not to interrupt.

Tala rubbed her palms over the front of her navy pants. "The guy told his dad everything, and his father went straight to the security guard outside my hotel room to complain and demand a refund. The guard contacted Brady, who instructed him to take me to the house immediately. He told him to let me know he would be dealing with me shortly and not to leave my room."

Her voice shook a little. *God, help her.* His wife had clearly suffered unimaginable horror. Cole suspected he was about to be given another glimpse of exactly how much, whether he wanted to or not.

From what he knew of Brady, and by the way she was clutching the counter now, only God could have helped her get through whatever retribution Brady had meted out that night, and only God could help her now. *Please* ...

"Brady made me wait for hours, until shortly before dawn. Suddenly the door to my room burst open. Two of his henchmen stormed in and dragged me out of bed and down to the basement. I'd never been taken there, but I'd heard rumors ..."

Her entire body shook. Everything in him longed to go to her and pull her into his arms, shield her from what was coming, but he couldn't. She needed to get it out, and—if it killed him—he would listen in silence to every word.

"When we got to the bottom of the stairs, Brady stood in the middle of the dimly lit space, his arms crossed. He was clutching something that looked like one of those billy clubs that British police carry. A sink a few feet away had a bucket of water in it. And bags of ice piled next to it."

Ice? Cole's eyes narrowed. He had no idea what Brady had planned to do with that, but the image alone was making him as cold inside as Tala had been last night when he'd carried her into the house. He wished he could cross his own arms to ward off the chill, but, if she had to go through this, experiencing every bit of it over again, so did he.

"The men stripped off my clothes and tied my wrists to a ring hanging from the ceiling."

A white-hot flame sparked deep inside Cole, driving out the cold. The sniveling, pathetic coward. Brady had to be over two hundred pounds, nearly twice Tala's size. And he'd still recruited two of his soulless bullies to take her clothes and restrain her, so he could do whatever he was about to do. What kind of man did that to a woman? He gritted his teeth.

The kind of man he'd gladly rip the arms and legs off, given the chance. Or maybe he wasn't a man at all but a demon straight from hell.

"When they finished, Brady walked over to me, really slowly, like a lion advancing toward its prey. When he reached me, he stuck the end of the club into my throat and lifted my chin, so I had to look into his eyes. They were as hard and cold as that ice, and in that moment I truly believed I would not survive what was about to happen." Her voice had gone flat, clinical, as though she was distancing herself from that basement and whatever had gone on there. Good. Cole prayed she could, that she wouldn't feel everything she had felt that night. He wasn't sure, if she did, that she would be able to maintain the grasp on her sanity that somehow she'd been able to until now.

Or that he would.

"He said, 'You broke my number three rule, Starr. *Never tell.* That means you've earned a night of ice.' I had no idea what that meant, but before I could give it much thought, he hit me in the stomach with the club."

God, help me. The silent cry that echoed through him roused a distant memory. He'd cried out to God before, when he was a kid and he'd reached for his dad and been rejected. Again. Had God heard him then? Did he hear him now? The flames licking up his insides eased a little, so maybe. "Tala." He couldn't let her go through this, relive another second of it.

She shook her head, and he pressed his lips together. He didn't have a choice. She'd tell the story, and he'd listen—even if it ripped them both apart. Maybe being ripped apart was the only way to be put together again, to be healed. *God, please. Help us both.*

"He hit me over and over. I'll spare you the details except to say it only took a few blows to start feeling as though I was being burned alive. After a while—I have no idea how long—I passed out. Darkness surrounded me, coming for me, and I gave into it gladly, knowing it was the only way to escape."

Tala closed her eyes. When she opened them, the look in them told Cole this wasn't over yet, that not even unconsciousness had ended her torment. The knots in his stomach constricted until it took everything he had not to lean forward in an attempt to ease the pain.

"I was shocked awake by a bucket of ice water being thrown over me. When I opened my eyes, coughing and sputtering, Brady's men stood in front of me. One of them held an empty bucket, the other clutched one that was still full. I wasn't sure why, since the first one had been plenty to shock me awake, but then the guy with the empty bucket tossed it aside and grabbed a handful of my hair to tilt my head back. The other man slowly poured his bucket of water over me. With ice cold water streaming over my face, I couldn't breathe for at least thirty seconds. But I could think. And it struck me then what I was facing—hours of torture, likely, with no chance of release unless I died. Even then I suspected Brady would find a way to resuscitate me and keep going.

"And I understood why the girls had spoken in whispers about the basement—how, whenever they had used the term *night of ice*, they'd done so with a look of sheer terror on their faces and immediately glanced around to see if anyone had heard."

Stinging bile rose in Cole's throat. *God, they water-boarded her.* Even with all the terrible things he'd imagined her going through since Brady took her captive, nothing he'd thought of had come close to her reality. His fists clenched on his thighs.

"Even now, words seem so weak, so incapable of conveying the horror of what was happening—the shame and vulnerability of being naked in front of those men, the utter helplessness of knowing I was completely at their mercy, that they could do anything they wanted to me and nothing and no one would stop them, the fear ..."

Cole pushed away from the island. He had to go to her, had to hold her. She shook her head again. It nearly destroyed him, but he slumped back. *God* ... He didn't even know what to ask for anymore.

"I knew Brady wanted something—for me to scream or cry, to confess what I'd done and beg for forgiveness—but I couldn't. Even at the time I knew that was making things worse, but I couldn't do it. I kept thinking about all the girls he'd brought there, all the others he had tortured and humiliated, everyone he would drag down in the future, and somehow I knew that, if I lied and told him I was sorry for breaking his *number three rule*, I would let all of them down. I would allow him to win, make it easy for him to do this over and over."

She touched her fingers to the scar on her temple absently, as though she didn't realize she was doing it.

"At one point Brady was shouting at me about the rules, and he grabbed the bucket and tossed the water on me himself. Only I wasn't unconscious at the time, and I jerked my head. The bucket slammed into my forehead. I should have gotten stitches, I'm sure. Blood dripped from the wound for a couple of days after that, but of course I didn't get any medical attention at all."

The room spun around Cole. How in the world had she survived? She had to have had broken ribs, maybe internal injuries or a concussion. The flame inside him heated to an inferno.

"I don't know how long it went on, and I have no idea how many times I blacked out. I do know that, when one of the men was cutting me down, I glanced over and the bags of ice were gone. When they dragged me upstairs and threw me onto my bed, it was late in the morning, so I had to have been gone from my room for hours. I stayed in bed for a week before one of the other girls told me my clock was back on the fridge."

His brow furrowed. "Your clock?"

"Yeah. We had a small kitchen on our floor with a full-size fridge. Each of us had our own clock fridge magnet that was set to our next appointment, so we always knew when it was. I could barely walk to the kitchen to see what the clock said. He'd given me two hours' warning, which was generous for him."

Cole could barely draw in a breath. If she'd sustained injuries like that in the real world, she wouldn't have been out of the hospital for weeks. In Brady's world, a week was long enough before he sent some strange man into her room to throw himself on top of her and...

His stomach heaved, and he only barely avoided throwing up the breakfast she had made by drawing in several slow, deep breaths, his inhalations so ragged they scratched like sandpaper along his windpipe.

Tala stumbled over to grasp his upper arms. "Don't."

"Don't what?" The words came out in an agonized whisper.

"Hate. It won't hurt Brady if you do. In fact, he'd laugh if he knew. It will only burn and eat away at and eventually kill you. Like poison."

"How can you not?"

"Jesus," she said, simply. "Do you know that after he was whipped, nailed to a cross, and was dying a slow, horrific, agonizing death, he looked down at the people who were torturing him, mocking him, and asked God to forgive them? When I'm holding on to anger or bitterness, I think about that. It's the only way I can let go of it. I'm not strong enough not to hate on my own."

This from the girl who hadn't broken under hours of

torture. Still, it was one thing not to scream. It was another not to hate. Cole took her face in his hands. "I can't promise I won't hate him, or that I won't rip his head from his body if I ever see him, but for your sake, I'll try."

"That's all I ask." She rested her hands on his hips. "You know, he also had his clothes stripped away. Jesus."

He stroked her soft skin with his thumbs. "No, I didn't know."

"He understood how I felt that night. And he was there in the basement with me. I felt him. He was always with me—every time a man came into my room or Brady hit me or another girl disappeared. And God spoke to me, too, through beauty. There were always moments of beauty, even in the midst of all the horror."

"Like what?" Cole lowered his hands. He couldn't imagine beauty surviving in a place like that.

"My room had a window, high up. I couldn't reach it to look out, but I could see the branches of a tree outside. Every season brought a gift—buds bursting out of their shells, thick green leaves with birds flitting between them, the stunning colors of fall, snow drifting softly from the sky to land on the bare branches and glisten in the moonlight. All of it even more breathtaking in contrast to the ugliness on my side of the window. The beauty of creation resonated deep inside me, as though God was using it to reach through the glass and let me know he saw me, that he hadn't abandoned me. It gave me hope that one day there would be beauty in my life again, and that hope helped me to survive."

It was all too much for him to process. Cole wrapped his arms around her and held her tight, until they both stopped shaking and the heat that had burned inside him since she'd started telling her story subsided enough for him to take a breath that didn't cause physical pain. "I'll never let anyone hurt you again. I promise."

Tala didn't answer, only drew in a shuddering breath. She wasn't wrong—he couldn't really make that promise. Still, in this moment he meant it.

He would die before he let anyone touch a hair on her head again.

CHAPTER FORTY-THREE

Although he'd only snatched a couple hours of rest after rescuing Tala from the storm, Cole struggled to sleep that night. Thoughts of what had happened to her, her *night of ice*, assaulted him relentlessly. He would have tossed and turned if he hadn't been so worried about waking her. Finally, when the thick darkness outside the window lightened a little, he gave up and eased off the covers. After quietly tugging on a pair of jeans and a T-shirt, he slipped from the room and stumbled to the kitchen. His throat was dry, and Cole filled a glass with water from the tap and then, without thinking, opened the door to the freezer above the refrigerator.

His gaze fell on the two blue plastic trays filled with ice cubes, the sight of them hitting him like a punch to the gut. No wonder Tala had refused ice in her water the first time he'd offered it. He couldn't leave these in the house for her to see. The heat that had billowed through him the night before rose again, and he grabbed both trays and stalked to the door. He tugged on his boots with his free hand, shrugged into his coat, and then yanked open the door and stormed outside. By the time he reached the dumpster behind the barn, his breaths were coming in short, angry gasps.

Cole held a tray in each hand and turned them upside down to bang them on the edge of the dumpster. Fury seized him, and he continued to smash the trays against the metal rim of the trash container long after the tiny squares of ice had flown from them. Finally, completely spent, Cole tossed the trays into the receptacle, propped his elbows on the rim, and lowered his face into his hands.

"Oh, God." He moaned the words without thinking and then jerked his head to stare at the slate-gray winter sky, watery pink along the eastern horizon. "I don't understand you." He flung the words heavenward. "I've tried to, since you're important to Tala and Grams, but I'm really struggling." He slammed his palms against the metal rim of the container. "If you were there with her that night, like she believes, why didn't you stop it? Are you that weak, or are you simply not as loving as Tala believes? If I'd been there, nothing would have kept me from tearing those guys apart with my bare hands." He smacked the rim again. "She's the most incredible person I know, and she loves you and trusts you completely. How could you let her suffer like that?"

No answer from on high. Big surprise. Cole folded his arms on the rim and dropped his head on them.

He stayed that way for a long time, the sour smell of the dumpster drifting up his nostrils, until a gust sweeping in from the north brushed the back of his neck. With a heavy sigh, he lifted his head. And froze.

The watery pink lining the eastern horizon had transformed into the most brilliant sunrise he'd ever seen. Oranges, fuchsias, and yellows stretched across the sky below a band of gray. Set against the dull, cold slate, the beauty was so intense that he not only saw it but felt it inside him. Was that what Tala meant by the beauty of creation resonating deep in the soul?

The wind that had swept over him carried with it an early hint of spring, of the damp earth along the side of the barn sheltered from the storm and buds struggling to form on branches. Birds wakened by the dawning of the sun chirped loudly in the trees around him. Every one of Cole's senses was filled with something that sent pleasure rippling through him, along with a feeling he couldn't name. Hope, maybe? That hope she had talked about beauty and light providing for her, helping her to survive? Maybe it was, because it quelled the anger roiling in his chest.

"All right." He clutched the edge of the cold metal dumpster with both hands. "I still don't fully understand you." He gazed at the brilliant colors stretching across the sky. "But I do know I can't go on this way, half in and half out. So, I'm in. I can see that, even if you didn't stop what was happening to her, you did bring Tala through all that. Please don't stop. She needs you. And I know now"—he exhaled a long breath—"that I do as well. I need you to give me wisdom, some idea of how to help her. I'm feeling my way along in the dark here. And not only with Tala, but for a long time before I met her. All my life, maybe. But I want what Tala and Grams have, and that's you. If you're willing, if you'll take me, then I give myself to you. Do what you want with me."

The same calm that filled him when he stared at the cross in the chapel wafted through him now. Cole tapped the top of the dumpster with his palms a couple of times, took in one last glimpse of the sunrise, and then turned and made his way to the house. He couldn't put his finger on what had changed, but—as it had at his father's grave—something did feel as though it had given a little inside. Like when his words had seemed to remove a restriction for Tala that day in the barn, so she could breathe easier.

And he felt stronger, which was good. As Lake had said about Tala, Cole would need to be. A thought as cold and stinging as the wind and ice he'd battled when trying to find his wife in the storm shivered through him now.

Somehow he knew that he and Tala would both need to be strong if they hoped to make it through whatever lay ahead.

CHAPTER FORTY-FOUR

The storm that Tala had gotten lost in had dumped a couple of feet of snow on the farmyard, snow that was melting fast in the warmth of the sun. It was only late February, though, and Cole had cautioned her not to be fooled—winter was far from over. Tala lifted her face to the sun as she stepped out of the chapel. The peace she always felt after being in the beautiful space Cole had created for her suffused her now, bolstered by the low, comforting call of a mourning dove in the barn.

More than by the phone conversation she'd had in the chapel. Tala sighed. She and Stephanie had talked eight times now. While the woman was kind and knowledgeable, and it had helped a little to discuss some of her issues with a professional, it felt as though the two of them had gone about as far as they could together.

A drop of cold water landed on her cheek as she walked beneath a low-hanging branch on her way to the barn. She swiped it off as she pushed another branch, glistening with ice, out of her path. The sight of the ice clenched her chest a little, but not as much as it would have before she'd told Cole the story about Brady taking her to the basement. As hard as that had been to recount, it had also helped. Telling him what she had been through and seeing the love and acceptance in his eyes, even the anger he tried to hide from her, allowed her to release something she kept locked inside.

Entering the stables offered Tala almost as much serenity as being in the chapel did. The commingled aromas of hay, leather, and horses had become a scent headier to her than the most expensive perfume, and she stopped and drew in a deep breath.

A shovelful of straw and manure landed in the wheelbarrow a couple of feet in front of her, and she wrinkled her nose. That smell she had never quite gotten used to, although it was familiar now and kind of comforting in its own way. Cole stepped into the doorway of a stall, leaned a shoulder against a post, and grinned. "Sorry about that."

Tala made a face at him. "I doubt you are."

He chuckled as he leaned the pitchfork against the wall. "How did it go?"

"It was okay."

"Just okay?"

The hint of despondency in his voice hurt. He had hoped talking to Stephanie would help Tala deal with her past, and she hated disappointing him. She wouldn't lie to him, though. "She's nice, but talking to someone I don't know, whose face I've never seen, isn't doing much for me."

"I get it. I wish it was safe for you to see someone in person."

"Me too."

"Hopefully soon." He kissed her on the forehead. "I'll go dump this load, and then we can have lunch."

"Sounds good." As Cole lifted the handles of the wheelbarrow and headed for the back door, Tala wandered over to Cocoa's stall. The big horse whinnied softly and nudged her palm with a velvety nose. Tala grabbed one of the apples Cole had set on the railing and offered it to her. As always, the feel of the horse's lips brushing over her skin made her smile.

She rubbed the star shape on the horse's head until she heard Cole's boots tromping along the cement walkway. He lowered the empty wheelbarrow to the cement and swiped his arm over his forehead. "Ready to go?"

"Yep." She followed him to the door and into the bright sunshine. As they crossed the yard, Tala glanced at the spot where she'd sunk to her knees during the storm. She'd come out the next day, when the wind and snow had finally stopped pummelling the area, and could see the faint marks, not quite fully filled in, where she had sat, less than fifty feet from the barn.

Pushing the thought from her mind, she traipsed up the walkway she and Cole had shoveled free of snow a few days earlier.

"It's nice out. Want to sit a few minutes?" He nodded toward the swing at one end of the porch. When they'd settled on it, Cole reached for her hand. "I've been thinking a lot about the story you told me last week about the ice."

She nodded.

"I told you once that no one can force you to testify against Brady, and I meant it. If it's too hard for you, going over all that again, you don't have to. You can refuse."

A big part of Tala wanted to take the out. Bella—Carmen, that is—would still testify, and maybe one or two of the other girls, now that they were away from the house. But maybe not. It made her sick that Brady could go free because the women who were able to testify to the things he'd done couldn't bring themselves to. Although she also got it. "I have to do it. Brady needs to pay for everything he's done. More than that, he has to be stopped so he can't hurt anyone else. And I doubt the other girls will speak up, partly because they're too terrified of him."

"Partly?"

Tala clutched the chain of the swing. How could she possibly explain? She drew in a breath. "When I was in the house, mostly what I felt for Brady was fear. Also hatred, although I prayed about that a lot and tried to let it go, since I didn't want to become as hard and bitter as most of the other girls. I believe God answered my prayers and kept me from losing myself to that hatred, but I felt other things for Brady, confusing things. He was an expert at mind games, and that got to all of us at times."

When Cole spoke, his voice was gentle. "How do you feel about him now?"

For a moment, she didn't answer, and then she met his gaze. "That's a difficult question to answer. I need to tell you about something else that happened in the house that might help you understand."

"Okay." He gripped the wooden arm of the swing, as though bracing himself for another story like she'd told him last week. In some ways, this one was more horrifying, although it didn't involve violence.

"A couple of years ago, I was getting ready to go to work one night when one of Brady's men knocked on the door. He told me Brady had instructed him to bring me to his room, which never happened. I could think of only two reasons Brady might issue such a summons: either to punish me for some infraction I couldn't remember committing or"—she studied their clasped hands, resting on Cole's leg—"he wanted me to … service him before I went to the hotel. That didn't usually happen, either. Other than the first few days or weeks after a girl was brought to the house, when he personally took on the job of conditioning her, Brady didn't typically use us that way. Still, I couldn't think of any other possibilities. The invitation wasn't optional, so I went with the man, trying not to panic.

"He didn't drag me along, only walked beside me, which was also strange. And he told me Brady said to let me know I wasn't in trouble. I didn't entirely trust that. It was a favorite ploy of his, making us think everything was fine so that we'd let our guard down before he exploded in fury."

Cole's fingers squeezed hers, but he didn't speak, which Tala appreciated. She took another, slightly shuddering breath. "When we reached Brady's room in a different wing of the house, the guy rapped lightly on the door. Brady opened it right away. He was smiling, and he reached for my hand and tugged me into the room. He told the man we weren't to be disturbed, and then he locked the door. Which made me think that I was definitely there to do something for him.

"He must have known that was what I was thinking because the first thing he did was take both my hands in his and tell me tonight wasn't about him, it was about me. He said he'd been hearing a lot of good things, and he was really happy with me."

Tala ran her fingers up and down the cool links of the chain, keeping herself there, on the porch with Cole. "I still didn't trust what was happening, but someone brought us food and we had dinner together, with wine and everything. When I hesitated before drinking it, he took a sip from mine, so I'd know it hadn't been drugged."

She stole a look at Cole. He was frowning, as though he was wondering, like she had in that room, what Brady's end game might be in giving her a night like that.

"What happened after dinner?"

"Brady took me out on his balcony to see the view of the city. It was incredible, something I could never catch a glimpse of from the window in my room. While we were out there, he told me I was special to him. That he knew he was hard on me, but only because he needed to teach me to do what he said, because that was the only way he could protect me."

Cole's features hardened a little. "Then what?"

"He was so kind, so gentle. It had been almost seven years since anyone—a man, anyway—had spoken a kind word to me or told me he wanted to keep me safe. It cracked something inside me, and I started crying. I tried not to because we got in trouble for it, but I couldn't help it. I told Brady I was sorry, but he said it was okay to cry that night, and he held me while I wept."

Cole's eyes closed for a couple of seconds, as though the image of the two of them standing there, Brady holding her close, was too much for him. She understood that. Even at the time, wildly conflicting emotions had roiled through her.

Cole's knuckles were white around the arm of the swing, but, when he spoke, his voice was steady. "Then what happened?"

"When I stopped crying, he took my hand and led me into the ensuite bathroom off his room. He had a sunken tub in there, and he ran the water for me and lit candles. Then he told me to take as long as I wanted, and he left the room. I was still leery about everything that was happening and apprehensive about taking off my clothes, but the lure of a hot bath was too strong. I stayed in that tub for almost an hour, and for the first time in years I was able to forget what my life was like now.

"I finally got out and dressed and went into his room. He came over to me, still smiling, and asked how that had been. I told him it was heavenly, and he laughed. He said I could go to my room and sleep, that I was off for the rest of the night. He also warned me about telling anyone what had happened that evening, although he didn't need to. I knew he wouldn't want the other girls thinking he had that side to him, even if it was all an act for my benefit, which I knew it was."

A few shards of rust had come off the chain. Tala let go of it and brushed her palm over her jeans.

"Even believing that, those couple of hours in his room completely messed me up. Which I know now was his intent. The kindness he showed me, after years of abuse, was likely some form of psychological torture or brainwashing. I kept telling myself that, but still I found myself sucked into it, reliving that time in his room over and over in my mind."

She stared at the flecks of rust scattered across her jeans like tiny splatters of blood. "So when you ask me how I feel about him, I mean it that it's extremely difficult to answer. I hate him. I'm terrified of him. I'm drawn to him. A small part of me wants to protect him while a much larger part wants to destroy him. And all of that is tangled up inside me like strands of DNA. I have a hard time separating any one feeling from another." She tugged her hand from his to press her fingertips to her temples. "He lives inside my head now, and I don't know if I will ever be free of him."

"You will be."

Tala lowered her hands. "How do you know?"

"Because you're getting help. None of the feelings you described are surprising—Brady deliberately cultivated them. But just as they were planted in you, they can be dug up by the roots. Maybe the woman you've been talking to isn't the right one for you, but as soon as it's safe, we'll find you the best therapy we can. It won't be easy, and it may take a great deal of time, but I'll be there for you every step of the way."

Another bit of the wall around her heart crumbled to dust. "Thank you for that. Despite what I told you, I *am* going to testify against him. I have to."

"I get it." Cole ran a finger down her cheek. "Thank you for sharing that with me."

Tala nodded. "I want you to know I have absolutely no

love for him. I couldn't. I know better than anyone how evil he is and the cruelty he is capable of."

"I believe you."

She rested her head on his shoulder, and Cole slid an arm around her and pulled her close. As long as she had God and Cole on her side, Tala was pretty sure she could invoke the strength to do anything.

Even take the stand and, with Brady watching and listening to every word, tell the court exactly what he had done to her and the other women in the house. As confusing as her feelings toward him might be, she was determined to make him pay for the suffering he had put every one of them through.

No matter what it cost her to do it.

CHAPTER FORTY-FIVE

Cole stabbed the off button on the phone and tossed the device onto the island. Although he'd hoped to be able to get on with the PD in Elliott Lake, he hadn't expected to be offered a job so soon. Only part time, but that suited him fine. The farm expenses were covered, and the Toronto PD hadn't complained yet about the groceries he charged to the card Lake had given him. Still, they couldn't live on that forever, and Cole didn't want to dig too deeply into his savings. Giving up his apartment in Sudbury as well as officially quitting his job there were next on his agenda. He'd thought severing those ties might be a little harder, but it only confirmed his commitment to staying on the ranch with Tala, a thought that filled him with excitement for the future.

That excitement was tempered by the thought of telling her he would be gone from home a few shifts a week. How would she feel about that? Personally, he hated the idea of leaving her. Although Lake continued to assure him Brady was being closely monitored, the threat persisted in the back of Cole's mind. And it had to hover in Tala's as well.

She wandered into the kitchen and went straight for the

coffee maker, as usual. Despite his trepidation about telling her his news, he couldn't stop the smile that crossed his face as he watched her. She'd become an early riser so she could go out to the stables in time to help him with the chores, but it clearly wasn't natural timing for her. Her ponytail was slightly askew, and her eyelids were heavy as she walked toward him, clutching her blue, polka-dotted mug to her chest. She looked so adorable that he couldn't resist sliding his hands along her jaw when she reached him and greeting her with a lingering kiss.

Months of keeping himself from reaching for her, from touching her, had left him with a deep appreciation for the freedom to do so now—a gift he didn't take lightly. "Good morning."

She offered him a smile that faded as she studied him. "What's wrong?"

She'd become as adept at reading him as Grams, which Cole found equally disconcerting and comforting. He kissed her again, lightly this time, before reaching for his own mug. "Nothing's wrong, exactly."

She took a sip of coffee, as though she needed to fortify herself before probing further. "Has something happened?"

"I got a call from the police department in Elliott Lake a few minutes ago. They offered me a part-time job."

She nodded, slowly, clearly processing everything that might involve. "That's great, Cole."

"It is?"

"Well, yeah. I mean, you've been off work for a long time. I get that you need to go back. And Elliott Lake's a lot closer than Sudbury, right?"

"Yes, that's the good part. It's only ten minutes to the station from here. Are you sure you'll be okay alone though?"

A shadow flickered across her face, but she banished it

quickly. "Of course. I feel safe here, and it's only part time." She gazed into her mug. "Will you work nights?"

"Not often, I hope. I told them I much prefer days. It sounds as though they'll try, although, as the new guy, I can't expect them to do me too many favors."

"Of course not. Either way, it's okay. I'm capable of being here on my own."

"I'll check in with Lake regularly, make sure Brady's still under surveillance."

She nodded.

"I'm also going to put extra locks on the doors. The hardware store didn't have any alarm systems in stock, but I asked them to order one. I should be able to pick it up in a week or two. And here"—Cole set the mug down again and strode over to retrieve the box he'd set on the counter next to the fridge—"I got you this the last time I was in town, in case the job panned out." He handed her the small white box. "It's a disposable phone, like the one we've been using. Much safer because there's no chip in it connected to you, so no one can directly track you through it."

She took it from him and lifted the lid. "This is great, thank you. I do feel better knowing I can reach you if I need to."

"I've already programmed my cell number into it, as well as the station number. You can hit one to go straight to me or two to go to the reception desk, and they can page me if for some reason you can't get me on the cell. Hit three if you need to call..."

She looked up from studying the device she'd removed from the box. "If I need to call who?"

He blew out a breath. "911. Highly unlikely, but you never know."

Tala set the phone on the counter. "Sounds like you've thought of everything."

"I've tried. I don't like leaving you, though."

An impish grin crossed her face. "Think of it as Rick leaving Ilsa. It's for the greater good."

He let out a short laugh. "I'm glad to see you've come around on that. Although it's not quite the same. I'm not leaving you forever—only three or four times a week, and I'll head straight home the second my shift is over."

"I'll be here waiting for you."

The words, and the way she was looking at him, were so sweet that he buried his fingers in her slightly mussed hair and captured her mouth with his again. His job didn't start for a couple of days, and he planned to make every minute he had with her before then count.

The chores could wait.

CHAPTER FORTY-SIX

Telling Cole about the night of ice and the evening she had spent in Brady's room may have lifted a little of the load Tala carried, but it had also stirred up long-repressed memories that had given her nightmares for three straight nights. Whenever they started, Cole wrapped his arms around her and held her close, cutting them off and dulling the sharp edges of horror that always accompanied them, but still she struggled to return to sleep.

This evening, tired and restless and putting in time while Cole took a shower after coming home from his second day shift in Elliott Lake, she dropped onto the armchair in front of the fire with a heavy sigh. The disposable phone Cole had given her sat on the coffee table next to the laptop, charging. She kept it plugged in with an obsessive determination to make sure it was always ready in case she needed it. The two days he'd been away at work had been okay, but tomorrow he was scheduled to work all night. Cold dread crept through her whenever she thought about spending the long hours of darkness that comprised the early-spring nights here all alone.

She stared at the screen. Fully charged. That reassured her a little, and she leaned forward to set it on the table and then stopped. Could she …? Tala glanced toward the living room doorway. Cole had told her no one could track her through this phone. Still, she suspected he wouldn't be in favor of what it had crossed her mind to do. It was highly unlikely Rose would have the same cell number she'd had eight years ago, even if she was alive and able to receive messages. But what if she did? All Tala wanted to know was if her foster sisters were okay. She couldn't remember Jae's number, but Rose's had stuck in her head. She wouldn't tell her sister where she was, even if she did manage to get a message to her, which was unlikely. Nothing bad could happen from a simple text, could it?

She shot another glance at the doorway. The fact that she felt the need to hide what she was doing from Cole told her she absolutely shouldn't do it, but her finger was drawn, almost against her will, to the keypad button. She tapped it, and the screen filled with numbers. Did she dare? Her desire to know if her sisters were all right was too strong. Before she could change her mind, Tala tapped a quick message to Rose. *It's me. I'm okay. Need to know if you and J. are, too. Let me know.*

The second she sent it, panic filled her. Tala hit the home screen button to hide her activity and then tossed the device onto the coffee table, her fingers burning where they had touched it. *Relax.* No one could trace her phone, and nothing about that message would give a stranger a clue about who— or where—any of them were. Still, it took several deep breaths for her heart to slow enough that the pounding in her ears eased.

Tala reached for the laptop, hoping that scrolling through a few mindless entertainment stories would drive away the lingering wisps of darkness—remnants of the dreams and of the impulsive act she'd committed.

News headlines flashing across the top of the screen captured her attention. What was happening in the world felt so far removed from Tala's life with Cole on the ranch that for a few moments the fact that the news was so readily available on the Internet didn't register. When it did, her eyes widened. Was it possible? She stared at the screen. She'd searched online for Rose and Jae but hadn't found a trace of either. Until this moment, it hadn't occurred to her to look up Desiree. Did she want to know? Her stomach knotted. No, she didn't. But she had to. Bella had survived. Was there any chance Desiree had, too?

Tala typed in a news station and a date. She scanned the headlines, but none of them hinted at the story she was looking for. After trying a few other dates following the first one, a headline popped up, slamming into her like a fist.

Unidentified Body Found by Jogger on Shore of Lake Ontario

The picture below it, of a woman lying partially submerged in the water, her face turned away from the camera, stole the breath from Tala's lungs. The woman's arm lay on the sand, charm bracelet wrapped around her wrist, palm up as though in supplication. Had Desiree been begging Tala, even in her last few seconds of life, to help her?

The room spun around her. No matter how hard she tried, she couldn't draw in enough air to push back the dizziness. Everything in her screamed to stop looking, to close her eyes or exit the site, but she couldn't tear her gaze away.

"Tala? What do you want for dinner? I was thinking—" Cole dropped to a crouch in front of her and touched her arm. "What is it?"

She couldn't answer. It took everything she had to keep drawing in one shallow breath after another.

Cole scanned the screen. His shoulders slumped as he

cupped her chin to turn her gently to face him. "You knew her."

Tala nodded.

"Here." He took the laptop, set it on the coffee table, and reached for her hand. When she stood, her legs shaking, he led her to the couch and tugged her down beside him. "Can you tell me about her?"

She drew in a quivering breath. "Her name was Desiree, and she was in the house with me for a couple of years. A few months ago, rumors were circulating that she was pregnant. I couldn't sleep that night, worrying about it, so I got out of bed and started for her room, hoping we could find a way to either solve the problem before Brady heard about it or get her out of the house somehow. Brady and two of his men beat me to her."

She pulled her feet onto the couch and wrapped her arms around her legs, like she had that night. "When they dragged her into the hall, she called out for me. She begged me to help her." Her voice broke, and she buried her face in her hands.

Cole wrapped an arm around her, and she rested her head on his shoulder. His hair was damp from the shower, and he smelled of soap and a faint cologne. The scent and feel of him drew a little of the horror from her. After a couple of minutes, she lifted her head. "I tried, Cole. I tried so hard, but Brady threatened to take me to the basement if I didn't stay out of it. I shouldn't have listened to him. I should have—"

"Tala." Cole shifted onto the coffee table in front of her and grasped her upper arms lightly, waiting until her eyes met his. "There was nothing you could have done to stop it. You know that, right? It wasn't your fault."

Her throat ached. It had to be her fault. Ever since that night, she had blamed herself for being so paralyzed by Brady's threat that she had abandoned Desiree. Was there really nothing she could have done? She pushed through the haze in her mind, reliving those terrifying moments. If she had left her room, what would have happened? Could she have fought off the three men? Of course she couldn't have. Which meant that, if she had tried to interfere again, Desiree would still have been killed. Tala might have been as well, if Brady had made good on his threat.

Which he would have.

Cole's brown eyes remained fixed on hers. "Nothing that happened was your fault. Nothing."

Shudders rippled through her like aftershocks from a massive earthquake. Could she believe that? Believe it wasn't her fault she'd been taken that night or that her sisters might also have been? That she couldn't have saved Bella any more than she could have saved Desiree? That she hadn't deserved to be beaten by Brady for telling that kid the truth about her situation?

Cole ran his hands up and down her arms. "You're the strongest and most amazing woman I know. Somehow you survived everything that happened to you and kept shining this incredible light. And I'm sure that you've shone that light on everyone you have ever encountered. You couldn't have saved them, but you did make their lives better. You gave them hope. And you let them know they weren't alone."

Tala clenched her arms against her stomach as everything she had held herself responsible for in her lifetime strobed through her mind. Her father's abandonment, her mother's and Felicity's deaths, what had happened to the other girls in the house ... could she finally lay all that down? Accept that she hadn't caused any of those things, that she'd only been fighting to survive and to try in some small way to help those around her, like Cole said?

Something cracked deep inside—the vault where she kept all the pain and the tears and the suffering, hers and those of everyone she had ever cared about. That night in Brady's room, a hairline fracture had appeared, but Cole's words, his tenderness, threatened to rupture it completely. Panic gripped her. If she started crying now, she might never stop. "Cole, don't."

The words came out as a desperate plea, but he only shook his head. "No. I'm not letting it go. Not this time. I mean it, Tala. You've never made anyone's life worse, only better. Mine most of all." He captured her face in his hands as though willing her to hear him. "It's time to let go of the lie that you are to blame for the pain, yours or anyone else's."

The vault gave way then. Deep, wracking sobs tore through her as everything she had repressed rushed to the surface and spilled out. Cole returned to the couch and pulled her to his chest. Although she'd fought it, the weeping helped, as if she were being washed with cool water inside and out.

She had no idea how much time passed before her tears were finally spent. For several more minutes she stayed in Cole's embrace, his heart beating strong and steady against her ear. Finally, she sat up and brushed a hand over his denim shirt. "You're all wet."

"It doesn't matter." Cole wiped the tears off her face with his fingers. "Will you tell the court what you saw, with Desiree?"

The question lifted more of the weight off her shoulders. She couldn't help Desiree then, but she could now, by doing everything possible to put Brady and the men who had taken her from the house that night behind bars. "Yes. It was so horrible, what they did, and so unnecessary. They could have called"—her head jerked—"the doctor."

Cole brushed the hair from her face. "The doctor?"

"Yes. Brady had a doctor come to the house sometimes. Obviously, he paid him well for his silence, but if you could get him to testify ..."

"Do you know his name?"

"Brady called him Archer, but I don't know if that was his first or last name."

"That's good, Tala. That could really help."

"I hope so."

"It will." He ran a finger under her eye, swiping away the last of the moisture. "Every day more and more evidence is mounting. And Lake says the trial is scheduled to begin in a month. Brady will be sentenced and locked up for the rest of his life. Then all this will be over. You will be free."

Cole sounded so sure of that, so certain. Tala wished she could be as well. But she knew Brady. Maybe, someday, his sins would catch up to him. But he wouldn't go down without a fight. Before he was stopped for good, he would make sure that everyone who had betrayed him and helped bring down his empire paid a terrible price for doing so.

Especially her.

CHAPTER FORTY-SEVEN

Cole's phone vibrated. He read the text—a response to the message he'd sent Lake a few minutes ago—and set his cell phone on the kitchen counter so he could grab his water bottle from the fridge. He hated working nights. While they tried to accommodate him and had given him mostly days, this was the third time he'd been scheduled to go in at 11 pm. Fortunately his new boss knew about the situation with Tala and Brady. The chief had agreed that, if she needed Cole to come home, he could go. Even so, he'd feel better once he was able to pick up the alarm system and get it installed.

Light footsteps sounded on the linoleum behind him, and he grabbed the water bottle off the top shelf, closed the refrigerator door, and leaned against the kitchen counter as Tala walked toward him. Her hair was loose and hung down the back of her red T-shirt. Her blue eyes, fixed on his, were intense, and he swallowed hard when she stopped a few inches in front of him. "Ready to go?"

Cole pulled her to him, not sure if he had the strength to leave her tonight. He kissed the top of her head. "I have everything I need, but no—I'm not ready to go."

She lifted her head. "Why not?"

"Because I don't want to leave you."

Tala slid her hand behind his neck and pulled him down. When she touched her soft lips to his, he closed his eyes and drew her closer. After ending the kiss, she gazed up at him, her fingers still warm against his skin.

"If that was supposed to make it easier for me to leave, it didn't work."

"It wasn't." Her smile was mischievous, and it took everything he had not to pull her to him again. One more kiss like that, and he would definitely be arriving at work late tonight. Something that wouldn't look good when he'd only been working there a few weeks. Tala stepped back. "You'd better go."

"I guess." Clutching the water bottle, he pushed away from the counter. "Is your phone charged up?"

"Always."

"Good." Cole reached for her hand. "Walk me to the door?" He didn't let go until he'd grabbed his jacket off the hook. "I'm sorry I have to leave."

"Don't be. You need to work. Just come home as soon as you can in the morning."

"You know I will." He kissed her again, lightly this time. "Lock the door behind me."

"Of course." The words sounded confident, but her eyes were more honest than her voice. Cole paused, studying her. Apprehension flickered in their depths, and light creases raked across her forehead. She wasn't as cavalier about him leaving her alone all night as she was clearly trying to sound. He touched her arm. "I heard from Lake a few minutes ago. He confirmed that nothing is happening with Brady. He hasn't left the house."

"That's good to hear."

His news didn't seem to comfort her as much as he'd

hoped. "Do you want me to call in? Stay home tonight?"

The two seconds it took her to respond told him a lot, but she shook her head. "No, of course not. You need to go to work. I'll be fine for a few hours."

Cole was torn. Everything in him wanted to stay with her, but he had made a commitment to the local police department. They needed him as well. And Tala could call if anything happened. Although, given Lake's update, it wasn't likely.

"Are you sure?"

"Yes."

Which may have been the first time she had outright lied to him. Unease stirred in Cole's gut. He shot a look out the door. The ranch was dark and still. No reason to suspect anything could go wrong. Still, he couldn't shake the disquiet. "All right, then. Call if you need me, and I'll come right home." He stepped onto the porch.

"Cole?"

He glanced back. "Yeah?"

"Be careful."

Was that why she seemed so tense tonight? She was worried about him? "Always."

She smiled faintly and closed the door. Cole waited until he heard the click of the locks before striding to his car. As hesitant as he was to go, he did need to work. And they couldn't let the very low threat of Brady finding out where Tala was keep them from living their lives. That was only handing him the kind of power over them they were both determined not to let him have.

Even so, if he was offered the chance to come home early, Cole was absolutely going to take it.

Tala hadn't wanted Cole to leave for work any more than he had wanted to go. She missed him when he wasn't there, and she couldn't stop the trepidation that rolled in like the tide as darkness entombed the old farmhouse. Restless and knowing she wouldn't be able to sleep if she went upstairs right away, she watched a movie—*Roman Holiday* this time. After the credits rolled, she read awhile in the living room, reluctant to leave the warmth and comfort of the fire and the table lamps she'd turned on all around the room. When the words started to blur, she finally slipped a marker between the pages and set the book on the end table. She checked the sliding glass doors and the front and side entrances, making sure they were securely locked, and then wandered into the kitchen. Her gaze fell on an object on the counter, and she froze. Cole's cell phone. If he didn't have that, she wouldn't be able to contact him if…

Pushing away thoughts of what could happen that she might need to call him about, Tala forced herself to draw in a few deep breaths. *It's okay. I have his other number.* If she needed him, she could call his work, and he would be here in ten minutes. Besides, Laken had confirmed that Brady was still in his house, so why was she worried? Her tight muscles loosening slightly, she made her way up the stairs and into her old room. She'd spend the night in here, since Cole's door didn't have a lock. If she could fall asleep, it would be morning before she knew it. She shot a look at the clock radio next to her bed. 1:40. A few more hours and he would be home.

Tala brushed her teeth and washed her face. On the way to the dresser to get her pajamas, she took a detour and meandered over to the window. The quarter moon cast a pale silver glow over the farmyard, reflecting off the snow-covered fields. She pressed a finger to the north star, twinkling brightly in the sky. *Help me not to be afraid. Even when Cole isn't here, I'm not alone. You're with me. Don't let me forget that.*

A slight noise from downstairs paralyzed her finger against the glass. *What was that?* For a few seconds, panic held her in place. Then a thought struck her, and she lowered her hand. The noise hadn't been loud enough for someone breaking through locked doors. It had to be Cole, returning for his phone.

A thrill shot through her. Maybe he'd even gotten off early and come home to stay, which had happened one other time when he was working nights, since it was usually quiet in town in the early morning hours. Spinning away from the window, Tala crossed the cold wooden floor, unlocked and flung open her door, and hurried down the stairs. "Cole?"

He didn't answer. Tala reached the bottom and glanced at the front door. Still closed and locked. If Cole had come home, he hadn't entered the house that way. Or maybe he'd slipped in, grabbed his phone, and gone back out, not wanting to wake her.

She crept along the hallway. The house was silent. Either she'd imagined the noise, or it had been Cole coming and going. Either way, she needed to calm down. Everything was fine.

She checked the side door. Also locked and closed, with no sign of forced entry. She compelled herself to take a deep breath as she headed for the kitchen.

Cole's phone was gone. He must have come home, grabbed it, and left again. A stab of disappointment shot through her. She should have come down as soon as she heard something, and maybe she could have caught him. The sight of him, the feel of his arms around her, even for a minute or two, would have given her the strength to face the few hours until daylight. For some reason, this night felt more foreboding than usual. While she'd been a little uneasy the other nights he'd worked, she hadn't felt this fearful. What was it about tonight that …?

Ice-tinged air wafted by, and she wrapped her arms around herself, her red T-shirt little protection against the draft. A cold as intense as the one brushing over her skin calcified her insides. Why was cold air drifting through the house?

Tala stared down the hallway in the direction of the laundry room. Another frigid gust brushed over her, sending chills rippling along her skin. The back window Cole had showed her as a secret way to get into the house was open. Tala swallowed. Had Cole forgotten his key and come in and out that way to get his phone? If so, why had he left the window open? Maybe he'd only exited a moment ago and stopped to check phone messages and hadn't had a chance to close it yet. Which would mean that he was still on the property.

Tala took a step forward. Then something caught her eye, and she stopped and slowly turned to stare at the refrigerator. The bone-chilling cold spread through her chest and stomach and along her arms and legs. Her brain struggled to comprehend what she was looking at.

A clock magnet stuck to the front of the fridge.

CHAPTER FORTY-EIGHT

"All units. Armed robbery in progress." The dispatcher gave an address, and Cole's partner for the night, a young cop named Karen Hill, turned the key in the ignition. "That's a couple blocks away. Let's go."

Cole set the paper cup in the holder and fastened his seat belt as Officer Hill drove out of the coffee shop parking lot. He flicked on the lights and siren and then grabbed the door handle as they tore along the street and wheeled into the liquor store lot. "There." He thrust a finger in the direction of a young guy in a hoodie sprinting between cars. His partner drove as close to the suspect as she could, and Cole jumped out. Officer Hill squealed away, screeching to a stop at the end of the row the kid sprinted along. The suspect veered left, in Cole's direction. Cole reached deep for an extra burst of energy and propelled himself forward. When the kid emerged from between two parked vehicles a few feet ahead, Cole closed the space between them and leapt onto his back, bringing the guy to the pavement. Bills and coins from the kid's hoodie pocket scattered across the concrete. Cole yanked the perpetrator's arms behind his back and held them for his partner as she arrived, breathless and tugging a pair of handcuffs from her coat pocket. In seconds, she had snapped the cuffs around the kid's wrists, and Cole hauled him to his feet.

His partner frisked the kid while Cole read him his rights. Grasping the guy's elbow, Cole led the young man toward the back passenger-side door of the squad car. Elliott Lake was a quiet town, its population largely seniors, so this was the most excitement he'd encountered since taking the job.

He hadn't been a beat cop for a couple of years, not since making detective, but he didn't mind it. Except for the fact that it was keeping him from being home and doing the job he most wanted to do—keep Tala safe. How was she? He pondered that as he and his partner drove to the station. His wife was one of the strongest people he knew, but she could give in to fear occasionally, like the time he left her on the deck to barbeque. Although she hadn't protested when he told her he needed to return to work, he'd caught her trepidation when he kissed her goodbye tonight, and it had dug deep into his chest.

His phone hadn't vibrated during the first three hours of his shift, so hopefully she was okay. Officer Hill wheeled the car into the parking lot of the small police station and parked near the door. After they processed this guy, maybe Cole would give Tala a call, see how she was doing.

Until he heard her voice, he wouldn't be able to shake the sense that he had made a terrible mistake, leaving her to come into work tonight.

Tala stared at the clock, trying to grasp the ramifications of seeing it on her fridge. The hands were set to two o'clock. If it had been twenty to two when she started to get ready for bed, it had to be nearly two o'clock now. Which meant her next appointment—with Brady, this time—was imminent.

Tala tried to swallow, to force herself to think, but her throat had gone completely dry. She strained to hear any sound that would let her know where Brady or the men she knew he would have brought with him might be, but she heard nothing. *My phone.* She'd left it next to her bed. If she made it to her room and locked and barricaded the door, she could call Cole. She might be able to hold off any intruders for ten minutes, until he arrived with the police. Breaking for the stairs, she raced up to her room. She closed the door quietly and turned the lock before glancing around. Her phone wasn't on the bedside table. Had she set it somewhere else? She tried to claw through the panic to remember what she had done when she came into the room earlier.

Tala scrambled around to the far side of the bed and yanked back the quilt and sheet. No sign of the device. Had she left it downstairs?

"Looking for this?"

If there was any warmth left in the blood flowing through her veins, Brady's stone-cold voice drove it from her. Tala closed her eyes for a couple of seconds. *Help me, Jesus.* She turned around. Brady stood in the doorway of the bathroom, holding up her phone. He'd shaved his beard, and he looked younger and somehow even deadlier.

She jumped as a fist thudded against her bedroom door. *Cole.*

A cruel smile twisted across Brady's face. "No, it's not your knight in shining armor. He's still at work—we checked before we decided to pay you a visit. We have hours to become reacquainted before he gets home, don't worry."

Brady crossed the room to the door. Her pulse thundering in her ears, Tala shot a look at the window. If she could get to it while his back was turned, open it and jump out, maybe catch that tree branch she'd thought she might be able to reach if she tried, she could climb down and get to the farm truck before any of the men were able to reach her. Cole always kept the keys to the old vehicle above the visor ...

She ran for the window and shoved her palms under the frame of the lower half. It moved up a couple of inches, but before she could shove it again, iron fingers grasped her arm and yanked her away from the glass. The brilliant north star was the last thing Tala saw before Brady jerked her around to face him.

"Where do you think you're going, my little star? We're not finished here, you and me. In fact, we're only getting started." He wove his fingers deeper and deeper into her hair as he spoke. When he had a firm grasp, he yanked her head backwards. Tala bit her lip to keep from moaning as flames shot across her scalp. He leaned in close, his breath hot against her cheek. "Did you really think you could cross me and get away with it?"

When she didn't answer, he released her and brushed a strand of hair from her face. Somehow the gentle gesture was far more terrifying than his violence.

Her knees were weak, and Tala shoved a palm against the windowsill so she wouldn't collapse. "How did you know to come to the hotel room that night?"

"Your guard called me. Something about your client raised his suspicions."

"So he tipped you off and you killed him?"

"*I* didn't kill him. *You* did. The second you crawled out that window, you sentenced him to death."

The knife he could always stick between her ribs dug deep and twisted. Tala struggled to keep her features even, so he wouldn't see he was getting to her.

His smirk suggested she wasn't successful. "It took a bit of work, but we used the hotel security footage to figure out your *client* was actually Detective Cole Blacksky. We were working on connecting him to this place. Likely would have done it soon, but then you did it for us."

Her eyes narrowed. "What do you mean?"

His smile was mocking. "I mean that you practically issued me an engraved invitation."

"How?"

"Last week, when you sent a text to Raine. I have her too, you know. I've had her since the night you came to me."

Her eyelids fluttered. Raine? That must be the name Rose had given him when she arrived at the house. But which house? Rose hadn't been with Tala, so where was he keeping her?

Brady let out a cold laugh. "That's right. I have another house. One your cop friends, who aren't nearly as smart as they think they are, know nothing about. Raine's there now, alone. As soon as I'm done dealing with you, that's where I'm headed. And when I get there, she'll pay the price for your betrayal, too."

"Brady." Not Rose. She'd been through so much in her life. She pretended to be tough but could be reduced to tears at the sight of a baby bird fallen from its nest or a mother yelling at her child in the grocery store. She had the softest heart of anyone Tala knew. At least, she had eight years ago. What had her time in Brady's service done to her? "Don't hurt Raine. Please. I'll do whatever you want me to do."

"You'll do whatever I want you to do no matter what. And Raine *is* going to suffer. I've made sure of that. If I don't come back for any reason, the house will be destroyed. The Bird has a finger on the trigger as we speak. As soon as I give the signal, it will all go up in smoke."

What did that mean? Was Brady planning to blow up the

house with Rose inside? Tala's stomach churned. And who was The Bird? She shook her head to clear it. It wasn't impossible that Brady was making all this up to add to her torment. She couldn't let him distract her, especially since she could do nothing about what he'd told her. Still, she had to keep him talking. If she could delay whatever he planned to do a little longer, Cole might come home early and stop it. *Or Brady will kill him.* The thought nearly paralyzed her again, but she forced it from her mind. A movement to the left of Brady caught her eye, and she glanced over. Two huge men stood inside the door, arms crossed. Six and Four. The two thugs who worked for Brady and were as big and as cruel as he was. Of course.

She returned her attention to the man who had made her life a living hell. "I used a burner phone. How did you trace it?"

Brady shrugged. "That made it a little more challenging, but not much. Burner phones can't pinpoint an exact address, but close enough. To a communication tower in Elliott Lake, anyway. Then it was a simple matter of sending someone to watch for your *Detective Blacksky*—Brady said the name as though it tasted like poison on his tongue—to come to town, which he did a couple of days ago. My guy then followed him home, reported your location to me, and I made the arrangements for our little reunion."

"How did you get out of the house without alerting the police?"

"Anything's possible if you know the right tech guy and have enough money. Which, thanks to you, I did." His gaze traveled the length of her and back up. Tala repressed a shudder at the lewd expression on his face when his eyes met hers again. "I've kept a separate account for all the money you and that body of yours made for me over the years. I used that money to buy my freedom and to track you here. Essentially *you* paid for this night with *me*, which is beautifully ironic, don't you think?"

Brady still gripped her arm, sending throbs of pain pulsing along the length of it. She was helpless against the three of them. With Cole gone, they could do anything they wanted to her, and she couldn't do a thing about it. She was in God's hands now. That thought sent a tiny bit of courage seeping through her, and the debilitating terror eased.

Brady's cold eyes probed hers, confusion clouding his for a few seconds. He'd always been able to read her, to know her thoughts as soon as they crossed her mind. He had to be able to see that she wasn't as afraid as she'd been seconds before.

He thrust her in the direction of the two men. "Enough talking. Bring her."

The men each grabbed one of her arms, as tightly as Brady had, and she clenched her teeth, refusing to give the three of them the satisfaction of hearing her cry out. Brady pushed past them and stalked from the room. The two men hauled Tala into the hallway after him. Where were they taking her?

It didn't particularly matter. Whether they took her somewhere on the property or drove her to another location, what awaited her was a long night of torture and, unless God chose to intervene, her death.

Brady was right. No one crossed him and got away with it. Although she'd allowed herself to believe, for a few glorious months, that she could, deep down she had always known that one thing Cole had told her—repeatedly—was a lie.

She wasn't safe here.

CHAPTER FORTY-NINE

It took a while to get the guy booked and into a cell for the night. When they finished, Cole twisted his arm to glance at his watch and grimaced. 2:20 in the morning. Better not try to call Tala. As much as he would love to hear her voice, it would be selfish of him to disturb her if she had fallen asleep.

If anything was wrong, she'd have let him know. Hopefully he hadn't missed the notification if she had tried to call or text. He reached into his pocket but couldn't feel the device. A sick feeling struck him. Had he left it somewhere? A vision of it on the kitchen counter flashed through his mind. Oh man, he'd set it there when he grabbed his water bottle from the fridge. Had he walked away and left it after Tala walked in? It wasn't impossible, since she'd distracted him pretty effectively. What if she had been trying to reach him?

Cole strode to the front desk. A woman with blond hair caught up in a messy bun smiled as he approached. "Hi, Detective."

"Hey, Lori. Anyone call here for me tonight?"

"Nope. I'd have let you know as soon as you came in."

A fist compressed his gut. No news was supposedly good news, but something didn't feel right.

Lori tilted her head. "Problem?"

"I forgot my phone. I'm toying with the idea of running home to get it, but I don't want to leave Officer Hill on her own."

"Why don't you check with the chief?"

Cole's eyebrows rose. "He's here?"

"Yeah. He said he couldn't sleep, so he came in to get paperwork done. He's in his office working, but he won't mind you dropping by."

"All right. Thanks." Cole strode down the hallway, stopped outside the chief's door, and rapped lightly. He had no idea why, but his apprehension about Tala was deepening into something stronger. She'd have phoned the station if something was wrong, wouldn't she? Unless she couldn't. The fist clenched tighter.

"Come in."

At the chief's terse invitation, Cole twisted the knob and pushed open the door. "Sorry to disturb you, sir."

The chief waved a hand, dismissing the apology. "What can I do for you, Detective?"

"I just realized I forgot my cell phone at home. As you know, it's imperative for the person I'm protecting to be able to get hold of me. I'm thinking of taking a break and driving home to grab it, if it's okay with you."

"You brought in the guy from the liquor store?"

"Yes. Officer Hill and I got him processed."

"Great." The chief glanced at the pile of paperwork on his desk. "You know what? I can't see anything much happening tonight. McDonald can go out with Hill if there's an issue. Why don't you head home and not worry about returning? I'll call if I need you."

Cole wasn't about to wait to be asked twice. "All right. Thanks, Chief."

The chief nodded. Cole stepped into the hallway.

"Blacksky."

Biting back his impatience, Cole turned. "Yes, sir?"

"You're doing good work here. I'm sure it's a lot quieter than you're used to, but we're happy to have you on board."

Cole offered him a tight smile. "Quiet works for me right now, sir." He left the office and headed for the parking lot nearly at a run. Tala was likely fine, but—given the way his stomach had clenched into a tight knot that was making it hard to breathe—he would get to the ranch as quickly as possible so he could see for himself.

Brady's men hauled Tala down the porch steps and across the front yard. Tala tried to drag a foot through the gravel, to leave a sign showing Cole where they had taken her, but Six yanked her arm to jerk her forward. Brady reached the barn and flung open the door. The men dragged her inside and onto the cement walkway running between the horses' stalls. Cocoa whinnied softly, and the terror that had whirled around Tala like the snow and ice pellets the night she lost her way in the blizzard eased further. Somehow, even though the horse couldn't do anything to help, her gentle presence made Tala feel she wasn't completely alone. *Don't leave me.* She sent up a fervent prayer, reminding herself that God was with her, too.

Four let go of Tala's arm, and Six flung her toward Brady, who'd stopped a few feet before Coal Miner's stall door.

Brady backhanded her across the cheek, directly below her right eye. Tala stumbled against the wooden wall, the shocking pain of it reverberating through her. She braced herself on the wall outside an empty stall. Coal Miner whinnied loudly and tossed his head. Something on the far side of the barn caught Tala's eye, and she glanced at the sink where she filled the buckets for the horses. Bags of ice were stacked on the floor. The billy club Brady had used on her that night in the basement lay on top of the pile.

No. God, no. Anything but that.

Through the windows lining the far wall, Tala caught a glimpse of stars sparkling against the night sky. *I wish ...* She drew in a long, slow breath before facing Brady. He was going to kill her. Maybe there was nothing she could do about that, but, if Cole came home while they were still here, they would kill him as well. She might be able to prevent that, at least. If she could antagonize Brady enough, he might skip the preliminaries and go straight to the ice. Maybe he'd even lose it and kill her quickly. As soon as she was dead, it was possible the men would leave, and Cole would be spared.

She met Brady's cold, amber stare steadily. "You are such a coward, Brady. You always have been."

His face darkened as he took a step toward her. "Shut your mouth, Starr, or this will go much worse for you."

Worse than a night of ice? She almost laughed. "Why? Will you sic your brainless lapdogs on me, the ones who have to be told what to do like mindless children? Get them to do your dirty work for you because you're not man enough to do it yourself?"

Tala braced herself. Even then, when he bent his arm and drove it under her throat, hard enough to shove her against the rough wooden stall door, the searing pain in her neck and head sent electrical shocks pulsing through her entire body. He increased the pressure until she couldn't draw in a breath. Good. *Jesus, let this end now.*

Darkness crept across her field of vision. Just before

unconsciousness could sweep her into oblivion, Brady yanked his arm away. Tala held both hands to her throat, gasping for air as she slumped against the wall.

Brady grabbed her upper arms and yanked her to her toes. "Nice try. You'd like that, wouldn't you, for me to kill you right now, quickly and painlessly. Well, that's not going to happen. I've been fantasizing about this night for months, and I plan to enjoy every second of it." He let go of her and cupped her chin, forcing her to look up at him. The eyes probing hers remained hard, but his features softened slightly. "You were always my favorite. Do you know that?" His hand slid from her chin to her hair, and he rubbed a strand of it between his fingers. "So beautiful. I would have kept you with me forever if you hadn't betrayed me."

Tala worked up enough saliva to spit in his face. "And I would choose death over being in your disgusting presence one minute longer than I have to."

A cold smile crossed his face as he slowly wiped the spittle off his cheek with the sleeve of his black T-shirt. "That, my little star, can easily be arranged."

Grasping her elbow, he hauled her to the far side of the barn, stopping a few feet from the sink. "But we won't rush it. We have a few hours, so we'll take this nice and slow." He jerked his head toward the pipe running the length of the barn above their heads. "Since apparently you need me to tell you what to do, boys, here are your instructions. Take off all her clothes, and then find a rope so we can tie her hands to the pipe here. After that, the four of us will get down to business."

CHAPTER FIFTY

Cole pushed the accelerator nearly to the floor in a desperate attempt to get home. Although it normally took him ten minutes, tonight he turned into his long, winding driveway seven minutes after leaving behind the streetlights of town.

No doubt Tala was fine, and the uneasiness propelling his mad dash was only his mind conjuring imaginary scenarios based on her apprehension earlier. Still, he wouldn't relax until he saw her. As soon as he reached the end of the stone pathway leading to the house, he slammed to a stop, killed the engine, and then jumped out and strode for the front door. After flinging it open, he hurried inside. "Tala?"

The house was silent. Not surprising, since it was 2:40 in the morning. Tala was likely fast asleep, and his tearing through the house yelling her name would only terrify her. Forcing himself to calm down, he climbed the stairs and strode along the hall to their room. The door was slightly ajar, and he pushed it open and walked inside. No one was there, and the bed was neatly made. Had she decided to sleep in her old room tonight? His didn't have a lock on the door. She might have returned to hers where she'd feel safer when she was alone. He stepped into the hallway.

Something's wrong.

The air in the hall was still and heavy, as though something had happened. But what?

When he reached Tala's room, she wasn't there. The covers had been pulled back, so maybe she'd slept for a bit. Had something woken her? Cole checked the washroom. No sign of her. He took a step toward the door, but a movement snagged his attention. The lace curtains billowed into the room on a frigid gust of wind. The glass was raised a few inches. Cole frowned. Why would she open the window on such a cold night? He lowered the pane before leaving the room and bounding down the stairs. After checking the living room and study, he made his way to the kitchen.

When he jogged into the room, it was freezing. Cole spun toward the laundry room, his heart skittering in his chest. The back window was open. Had someone broken in? Lake had assured him that Brady was still in his house in Toronto, but what if he was wrong? It wasn't impossible for someone who knew what they were doing to remove an ankle bracelet without triggering the alarm. If Brady had been able to do that, he could have slipped out of his house without being seen, and the PD would have no idea he'd left the premises.

Which would mean he could be anywhere.

Cole scanned the kitchen, desperate for a clue as to where Tala might be. The sight of the clock magnet on the fridge struck him like a hard fist to his kidneys. Brady had escaped somehow. And he was here. Or had been. Somehow he'd tracked Tala to the ranch. But what had he done with her? The thought of the dark, damp basement below chilled him as thoroughly as if he'd been splashed in the face with a bucket of ice water like she had been. Brady wouldn't have taken her down there, would he?

Cole yanked open the door off the kitchen, hit the switch to flick on the dim light, and tromped down the stairs. "Tala?" If she was alone down here, he didn't want her afraid that the approaching footsteps might be Brady or any of his minions.

No reply. Cole hit the dirt floor and did a quick visual sweep of the space. Empty. That fact offered him scant comfort as he raced up to the kitchen. If Brady had taken her somewhere, how would Cole find her in time to stop him from carrying out whatever nefarious plans he had for her? Shoving those thoughts aside so he could think clearly, Cole started along the front walk.

A glow from the barn windows drew his attention, and he started for the large outbuilding. A black SUV was parked along the far side of it. *They're still here.*

A mix of dread and relief poured through him. He'd left his gun in the car. Should he go back for it?

"Brady, no!" Tala's sharp cry from inside the barn, the same words she'd called out at night so often, shattered the silence. Cole abandoned every thought except that he had to get to her. When he reached the wooden door, he grasped the handle and wrenched it open.

A hulking man stepped into the doorway inches in front of Cole. Before he could move out of the way, the man's fist slammed into his jaw. The blow sent Cole staggering back a few steps. As he waited for the world to stop cycloning around him, another man joined the first one, and each of them grabbed an arm and hauled him into the barn. They dragged him to a chair in the center of the wooden floor and threw him onto it. One of the men held his arms behind his back as the other tugged a plastic tie from his pocket. Cole struggled against the strong grip holding him in place, but he couldn't free himself before the man who had hit him wrapped the tie around his wrists and the center wooden rung of the chair and pulled it tight. Straining against the restraints only resulted in the plastic digging deep into his wrists. Cole abandoned the effort with a groan of frustration.

When he looked up, Brady stood a few feet from him, towering above Tala as he held her in front of him with his arm wrapped firmly across her chest. They hadn't taken her clothes this time, and she still appeared to be okay, except for a smear of blood on one cheek, below her right eye, and red marks on her arms and neck that clenched Cole's hands into fists behind his back. "Let her go, Brady."

The big man laughed. "I don't think so. Starr and I have unfinished business, and we're going to finish it here, tonight. I'm glad you've crashed the party, though—it's always more fun to have an audience. The dilemma for me is whether to kill you first, in front of her, or kill her in front of you before finishing you off. Either way, should be a good show, right, guys?"

The man who'd met Cole at the door laughed while the second man nodded. From the corner of his eye, Cole caught a glimpse of a pistol sticking out of the jacket pocket of the one closest to him. If his hands weren't tied ...

He met Brady's cold gaze. "I called the police—they should be here any minute."

"Is that so? And how did you call them, on this phone?" Brady pulled Cole's device out of the pocket of his jeans. "Or was it that one?" He nodded at Tala's phone sitting on a nearby bale of hay before tossing Cole's over to join it.

Cole gritted his teeth. Obviously, Brady was as aware as he was that no one was coming to help them. He and Tala were on their own. The sink caught his eye, and he glanced over. A bucket sat in it, and another one lay on its side on the floor, bags of ice piled next to it. His eyes swung to Tala's. They held a mixture of fear and anger that broke his heart as much as it gave him hope. He was useless here, but, if she got mad enough, maybe she could do something, distract the men somehow, long enough for him to free himself. He wouldn't give up. Not yet.

"You set yourself up with quite the situation, Detective." Brady's tone was mocking. "Living way out here in the middle of nowhere with your own private whore to do whatever you want to, whenever you feel like it." He let go of one of Tala's arms and cupped her chin, forcing her head up to face him. He leaned down and pressed his lips hard against hers. Tala struggled but couldn't free herself.

Cole fought his restraints. "She is not a whore." He ground out the words. "Leave her alone and untie me. Face me like a man instead of the pathetic coward you are."

Brady straightened. "Ah, it's like that, is it? You've fallen for her. I get it. Starr certainly has a way of charming men. Lots and lots of men, in fact." He ran a finger along the neckline of Tala's red T-shirt. "But I assure you, she is most definitely a whore. One of the best I've ever had. Her loss cost me a lot of money, which I fully intend to take out of both your hides tonight. Before I do, let's have her give us a little demonstration of her many talents."

He cupped her chin again. "You broke my number two rule, Starr. *Never try to leave.* Which means you have earned yourself another night of ice. And you broke my number one rule, *never betray me.* The minute you did that, you signed your death warrant and ensured that you will never walk out of this building alive. I've changed my mind, though. I will let you take your clothes off yourself this time. What do you say—one more show, for old time's sake?" He let go of her and nodded at her shirt. "Nice and slow so we can all enjoy it. Then the boys and I will have a little fun before we get on with the task at hand."

Tala didn't move. Cole's heart thundered against his ribs. *God, no. Stop this. Please.* "Don't do it."

Brady lifted his gaze over her shoulder and inclined his

head in Cole's direction. The massive goon who'd hit him in the doorway lumbered around to the front of the chair and drove a fist into Cole's stomach. He bent forward as far as his bound wrists would allow, gasping for air.

Tala lunged for him. "Don't hurt him. I'll do it." She dropped to her knees in front of the chair. Her fingers slid down his arms until they reached his hands, and she pressed something small and cold against his palm. Cole closed his fingers around it as the thug who'd hit him grabbed her elbow. He hauled her to her feet before shoving her at Brady.

He caught her as she stumbled toward him. "Clothes off. Now. Any more hesitations and your boyfriend will suffer the consequences."

When he let her go, Tala grasped the hem of her T-shirt and slowly lifted it over her head.

Ignoring the pain that pulsed through his gut, Cole clenched his teeth until they ached to keep from groaning her name. He wouldn't give that to Brady, even now.

"It's okay, Cole." Her voice had gone soft and sultry, like it had that first night he'd gone into her hotel room. "Brady's right. I'm very good at this. In fact, watch me. I'm going to crush it." She swayed slowly, side to side, as she twirled the red shirt in one hand. She tilted her head, so slightly the three men watching her didn't appear to notice, or maybe they thought it was part of her act. Only Cole caught the motion, and he followed it to the side of a stall three or four feet from her where he'd propped the shovel after mucking out the stall that day.

The fog of horror muddling his thoughts cleared. Tala did plan on crushing it. Literally. *Only way to handle a snake.* His eyes met hers, and she offered him a small smile. The men standing next to him were fixated on her, their attention off him completely. Cole worked the blade open on the tiny jack-knife she'd pushed into his hand and wrangled it into position, clutching it as tightly as he could in his fingers. If he dropped it, chances were good that, even if she could get to the shovel, she wouldn't be able to take out all three men before one or two of them stopped her. She needed his help, and he couldn't let her down. Not if either of them hoped to survive this. He shoved the blade against the plastic tie and started to saw, keeping an eye on Brady's men in his peripheral vision.

Tala ran a hand over her bare ribs and stomach beneath the pale blue sports bra she wore. Cole sawed harder. She tossed the T-shirt in Brady's direction. He caught it and crossed his arms, pressing the shirt to his chest as he stared at her, appearing to be transfixed by her movements as she undid the button of her jeans.

Although there was no music, Tala moved as if she could hear the rhythm in her head, gradually working her way closer to the shovel. Cole shot another glance at the two men. One of them whistled, and the other called out, "That's it, baby," as she lowered the zipper on her jeans. Neither of them paid him any notice whatsoever.

With a last, hard cut of the knife, the plastic tie fell into the straw beneath Cole's chair. Tala's eyes met his, and he nodded. The shovel was within her grasp, and she grabbed it. Hefting it in both hands, she spun around, swinging it with all her might and catching Brady across the side of the head before he had a chance to uncross his arms.

Cole vaulted off the chair. Before either of the men could move, he'd snatched the gun from the pocket of the one who'd plowed his fist into his gut, fired the weapon at him, then swung it toward the other man. He'd grabbed his gun, but Cole got off another round before the guy could take aim and fire. Both men dropped like rocks onto the wooden floor.

Cole whirled around. Brady lay on his back on the straw-strewn floor. When he moaned and started to sit up, Tala lifted the shovel above her head and brought it down hard. Brady collapsed onto the floor, blood pouring from his nose and a deep cut on his chin.

Cole checked the two men. He'd shot them both in the chest at point-blank range—neither of them was going anywhere. He flipped the safety on and shoved the gun into the back of his jeans as he crossed the floor to Tala. When he reached her, he pulled her into his arms and held her tightly against his chest. She was trembling, and he cupped her head with one hand. "Are you okay?"

She nodded against his uniform shirt. After a moment, he held her out at arm's length so he could judge for himself. "Are you sure?"

Her laugh ended on a sob. "I think you know me well enough to know—"

"I do know you." He pressed his lips to hers. They were trembling, too, as much as the night he'd carried her in from the cold. It would take a lot longer for her to warm up this time, but she would. Tala was a survivor. She would recover from this, and he would be there to help her every moment.

When he let her go, she rubbed her hands up and down her arms. "We should tie Brady's wrists in case he wakes up."

"Good idea." Cole tugged a set of handcuffs from his jacket pocket.

Tala did up her jeans and pulled the red shirt over her head as Cole shoved the unconscious Brady onto his side and reached for his arm.

"Take his shirt off before you tie his wrists." Tala's voice had gone hard.

Cole contemplated her a moment. He had a pretty good idea where she was going with that. He shrugged. If it helped her deal with the trauma Brady had put her through, he was all for it. Setting the cuffs in the straw, he grasped the bottom of Brady's long-sleeved black T-shirt and yanked it over his head.

"Can we cuff him to that?" Tala pointed up.

Cole followed her gaze as he tossed the T-shirt away. The heavy metal pipe he'd installed to carry water to the animals hung a few feet above the stalls on lengths of chain. If they could get Brady to his feet, they should be able to raise his arms above his head far enough to lock him into one of the chain links with the cuffs. It wouldn't be easy, but if it helped Tala, Cole would swing the man from the top of a flagpole. "I think so."

"Wait." She knelt beside him. As he watched, she tugged off Brady's boots and socks and then undid his belt and the button and zipper of his jeans. Cole leaned back on his haunches and didn't interfere as she worked off the rest of Brady's clothes and threw them across the barn floor. When she finished, he crouched in front of Tala's tormenter. Thoughts of everything Brady had done to Tala—everything he had forced her to do—sent rage-induced adrenaline coursing through Cole. Enough that he was able to toss Brady over his shoulder. Heaving to his feet, Cole staggered a couple of steps. Brady had a good twenty or thirty pounds on him, and he was dead weight at the moment.

Cole regained his balance and maneuvered Brady below the pipe. Tala dragged the chair Cole had been tied to across the floor, set it next to her former captor, and climbed up on it. Cole lifted one of Brady's arms. She grasped his wrist, slapped one of the cuffs around it, and reached for his other arm. With Cole lifting him as high as he could, she managed to pull both arms up to the chain and snap the second cuff through one link and around Brady's other wrist.

Breathing heavily, she jumped off the chair and moved to Cole's side. Cole studied the handcuffs and chain, now supporting Brady's full weight. Cole had made sure to securely install the chains from the ceiling so the pipes could never fall on any of the animals. They should hold, even if Brady struggled against the cuffs. And if they didn't, the pipe would likely come down and smash him on the head, which would take him out again anyway. If all else failed—Cole ran a finger over the butt of the weapon he'd stuck in his jeans—he wouldn't hesitate to do whatever he had to do to protect Tala from the monster who had terrorized her and so many other women. It was pretty clear the man had no weapon hidden anywhere on him that he could use to defend himself or hurt either of them.

Brady groaned.

Tala's blue eyes met Cole's. "Should we call the police?"

Cole smiled grimly. "Probably." He didn't move toward either of their phones.

"I don't want you to get into trouble." She walked over to the sink and turned on the tap. "Maybe you should wait outside."

"And miss all the excitement? Not on your life."

As water filled the bucket, she reached for a bag of ice and ripped it open, pouring most of the bag into the cold water. When the bucket was full, she turned off the tap, wrapped the fingers of both hands around the handle, and carried it over to Brady.

Cole didn't envy Brady what he was about to face. He didn't feel sorry for him, either. The man deserved every bit of whatever was about to happen.

Tala let go of the handle with one hand and slid her fingers under the bottom of the bucket. Then she heaved the contents directly into Brady's face, washing away the blood flowing from his nose and chin.

He reared his head and sputtered water. Tala tossed the bucket aside and grabbed the night stick from the pile of bags, grasping it tightly in both hands. Cole stepped back, not wanting to get in her way. This was her show. His only job was to make sure Brady was never able to hurt her again. Although Cole doubted she'd need his help with that.

Brady blinked rapidly, as though trying to orient himself. He glanced down at his naked body before turning hate-filled eyes on Tala. "You filthy—"

"No." Her voice was as cold as the ice lying in the straw at Brady's bare feet. Still clutching the club in one hand, she stalked to the work bench and snatched the roll of duct tape Cole kept hanging on a nail above it. She strode back and handed it to him. "Cover his mouth please, Cole. I don't want to hear a word he has to say."

"With pleasure." Cole snatched the towel from the edge of the sink and used it to swipe the water off Brady's face. Then he ripped off a long piece of tape, tucked the roll under his arm, and slapped the strip over his mouth, smacking it down in a few places for good measure. Brady glared at him over the top of the silver tape.

Cole stepped out of the way again. Tala advanced on Brady slowly. When she reached him, she dug the tip of the stick into his throat. "You broke *my* number one rule, Brady. *Never treat human beings like cattle to be bought and sold.*" She dug the end in a little deeper to drive home her point. "I believe that means you've earned yourself a night of ice."

Brady glanced at Cole. The enraged cockiness was gone from his eyes, replaced with stark fear as the reality of his situation sank in. Cole lifted his shoulders. "Don't look at me. After what you did to her, I'll haul buckets of ice water over to her all night if that's what she wants."

Tala raised the club, clutching it in both hands. "It doesn't feel good, does it, Brady, being stripped naked and tied up and facing a severe beating you can't do anything to stop?"

Brady said something Cole couldn't make out. Obviously

Tala couldn't either, as she ripped the tape from his face. "What was that?"

He jerked his head as skin ripped off with the tape. "I said no," he mumbled.

"Oh." She slapped the tape over his mouth again and lifted the club. Brady winced and shoved against the wood floor with his bare feet, attempting to get out of her way. His bound hands kept him from moving far.

Tala stepped closer, her face in his. "Everything in me wants to use this club to beat you senseless. Nothing would give me greater pleasure than hitting you until you passed out and then throwing bucket after bucket of ice water in your face, like you did to me. Cole wouldn't stop me, would you, Cole?"

He shook his head. "Nope."

The fear in Brady's eyes intensified.

"Neither would your friends over there." She jerked her head toward the men Cole had shot. Brady's eyes darted in that direction before settling on her face again. "And since you took our phones so we couldn't call the police, they're not coming, either. Which means you are on your own. And you are completely at the mercy of someone you treated worse than garbage for eight years. Someone you abused and tortured and forced into having sex with strange men for money that went straight into your pocket. And someone who had to sit by and watch while you did the same thing to other girls she cared about. Which puts you in a really bad position, doesn't it?"

She reached for the tape but stopped when he forced out the word: "Yes."

"Most of all, someone who watched you coldly and cruelly deal with two women for committing the crime of getting pregnant while under your supposed *protection*. Remember Bella and Desiree, Brady?"

He swallowed hard and nodded. Fresh blood dripped from his nose and chin onto his chest.

Tala pulled the night stick back a little as though preparing to whack him in the head with it. "If for nothing else, you deserve to be beaten to a pulp for what you did to them. And you deserve to have water slowly poured over your face so you can't breathe. To feel the intense terror of knowing you likely won't survive what you are going through, and that, even if you do, you will be going to prison for the rest of your life. Don't you?"

Brady yanked on the cuffs and tried to move out of her reach, but the chain held him in place.

"Don't you?" Tala's voice rose.

He nodded again.

For a long moment, she stood there, club in position to rain blows over his head. Finally, she lowered it and stuck the tip under his chin again, hard enough to force him to look at her. "I want to do that, Brady, hurt you like you have hurt so many. The only reason I'm not going to is that you are a human being created in the image of God, and, for that reason alone, you have the right to be treated with dignity. A right you stripped from me and all the other women you forced to work for you against their wills. I'm leaving you for God to deal with. I will, however, gladly testify about everything I experienced and witnessed in that house. Should be enough to make sure that you never breathe free air again. Or hurt another woman." Tala lowered the stick to her side. "Call the police, Cole."

A brief spurt of disappointment was doused quickly by an intense admiration for her courage. Cole nodded and made his way to the bale where Brady had tossed their phones. Before he could make the call, sirens sounded in the distance. Someone had notified the police already. Lake, likely. Cole checked his text and call records. Yep, a whole bunch of frantic messages from his friend. Whoever had been watching Brady's house must have figured out—finally—that he was no longer there and reported his escape.

Cole shoved the device into his back pocket. Tala had dropped the club in the straw, picked up the bucket, and carried it over to the sink. She grabbed a bag of ice, ripped it open, and dumped the contents into the sink with a furious shake of the bag.

Cole took the opportunity to step in front of Brady and drive a fist into the man's gut. Everything in him longed to beat the man unconscious, but he stopped himself after one blow. Brady groaned and bent forward as far as he could. Cole grabbed the hair at the back of Brady's head and forced his head up until their eyes met. "That was for everything you have ever done to my wife." He leaned closer and hissed, "Far, far less than you deserve, but, like her, I'll leave the rest to God. I would not want to be in your shoes when you face him one day. I promise you he will demand an accounting for everything you have done to those girls he loves, every single thing he has seen you do. And he will make sure justice is fully meted out to you and every other lowlife rodent like you who has gotten fat and rich on their suffering."

Brady's face paled, but otherwise he didn't respond. Cole had surprised himself with the words that came out of his mouth. Did he really believe in a God who had seen everything Brady had done and who would personally reckon with him and every man like him one day? Cole didn't have to think about it long. Absolutely, he did. He couldn't put his faith in any other kind of God than that.

Cole strode over to help Tala empty the rest of the bags. When they finished, the sink was three-quarters full of ice. Cole switched on the hot water to melt it. Tala leaned against him. She was shaking, and he wrapped an arm around her and drew her close.

The wailing of sirens grew louder. Cole kissed the top of Tala's head before checking on Brady. His head hung low, drops of blood still sliding down his chest and stomach.

Cole stroked Tala's hair, the love he felt for her so intense it hurt his chest. As much as she had to have longed to beat Brady as brutally as he had beaten her and others, she'd proven once again how strong she was by choosing the much harder path.

She had shown him mercy.

The sirens grew deafening, nearly drowning out the sound of multiple vehicles approaching the barn and screeching to a stop. In seconds, the chief burst through the wooden door, flanked by four officers, all with guns drawn.

"Wait here. I'll talk to them." Cole let Tala go and stepped in front of her slowly, keeping his hands in sight. Although the cops knew him, they weren't aware of everything that had happened here and would be on full alert. Any sudden movement could cause a trigger-happy rookie to fire off a wild shot or two. "It's okay. The situation is under control."

The chief studied him a moment before lifting his hand. "Holster your weapons."

Once they had all complied, Cole strode toward the chief. Two EMTs came into the barn carrying a stretcher, and he waved a hand toward the two men on the ground. They headed over and set the stretcher on the ground, feeling for pulses. Cole was pretty sure they wouldn't find any.

The chief stuck his Glock into his chest holster and let his jacket fall over it. "Everybody okay?"

"Tala and I are. Brady's men are dead. Brady took a couple of blows to the head and face with a shovel. He'll need medical attention, but it shouldn't be anything life threatening."

The chief peered past him at Tala. "You sure she's okay?"

"Physically, yes. She's shaken up, but she's strong."

"Good." The chief swiveled his head to stare at Brady. He pursed his lips before swinging his gaze to Cole. "I'm going to need a full account of everything that's gone on here tonight."

"Of course. Okay if Tala and I come to the station in the morning? She's been through a lot tonight."

The chief hesitated. "Come in first thing."

"We will."

His boss gestured toward Brady, who hadn't looked up since the police entered the barn. "Get him down from there and then cuff him again."

Two officers started for Brady. "Should we put his clothes on, Chief?"

The chief slid a glance at Cole. "Nah. They'll only have to take them off again at the hospital. We'll throw a blanket on him in the car."

Brady didn't resist the man who climbed on the chair and unlocked the cuffs or the one who snapped them around his wrists again. Every bit of fight seemed to have been knocked out of him. Whether it was the blows he'd taken to the head or the fear of a beating or anything either of them had said to him that did it, Cole had no idea. Whatever the reason, the man appeared completely and utterly defeated as the two officers grasped his elbows and led him toward the barn door.

Cole shot a look at Tala. She was carefully watching everything that was going on. Hopefully it would help with her healing to see her tormentor revealed for what he truly was after his thugs, his weapons, and even his clothes had been stripped from him—the sniveling coward Cole had accused him of being.

Right before they stepped outside, Brady rallied enough to glance over his shoulder at Tala. "I can get a message to The Bird anytime I want," he said, his voice low and mocking. The officers tugged on his arms, and the three of them disappeared out the door.

Cole frowned. The Bird? What did that mean? From the stricken look on Tala's face, and the way she swayed slightly before steadying herself against the wall, she had some idea, anyway.

He turned to the chief. "Can I take her to the house?"

"I guess so. We'll be here for a while, but I don't think you need to be." He inclined his head toward the two men on the ground. One already had a white sheet over his face. As they watched, the EMTs transferred the other one to a stretcher and prepared to do the same with him. "I take it that's your work?"

"Yep." Cole reached behind him and tugged the pistol out of his jeans. He offered it to the chief, handle first. "I got this off one of them; my weapon's still in my car."

The chief took the gun from him, his gaze lingering on Cole's red, chafed wrists. "I'm getting more and more curious about what went on here tonight."

"I'll tell you everything in the morning, I promise."

"Yes, you will." The chief clapped him on the shoulder. "Take good care of her, Detective. And yourself."

"Yes, sir." Cole dipped his head before making his way to Tala. He switched off the hot water tap before holding out his hand. "Ready to go home?"

She drew in a long, slow breath before sliding her fingers into his. "Yes, let's go home. But there's something I need to tell you as soon as we get there."

CHAPTER FIFTY-ONE

Tala's fingers trembled in his as they climbed the stairs to the front porch. Cole pulled open the door and held it for her. "Are you sure you want to talk tonight? Maybe it would be better to get some sleep first."

She shook her head. "No, I need to tell you this now. In a few hours, it might be too late."

"Okay." He caught her fingers in his again and led her to the living room. A gust of cold air brushed past them, and, as soon as she sank onto the couch, he let go of her. "I'll be right back." She nodded, and Cole strode to the laundry room. He slammed the window closed. When they went into town in the morning, he would pick up a lock to put on it to make sure no one ever got into the house that easily again.

When he returned to the living room and sat next to her, she turned to face him. "It's my fault that Brady tracked us here."

"What do you mean?"

"That phone you gave me—I used it a few days ago to try and send a message to Rose, one of my foster sisters. She didn't respond, but Brady told me he has another house the

PD doesn't know about, and Rose is there, although she goes by the name of Raine." She ran her hands up and down her bare arms. "He'd kept her phone—he kept all our phones so he'd know if someone tried to contact us—and he intercepted the message when I sent it. He told me that, when he was done with me, he planned to finish taking out his wrath on her."

Cole tugged the blanket from the back of the couch and draped it around her shoulders. "I don't blame you for trying to contact Rose. I'll let the PD know what Brady said, and maybe they can find his other house through her phone. Although ..."

"What?"

"It's unlikely Brady would keep the phones on-site, or the PD would have used them to find any girl who'd been reported missing. He likely has them off most of the time and probably keeps them in a secure location. Still, it's a lead for them to follow up on."

"So you'll contact Laken?"

Cole leaned forward to grab the phone he'd retrieved in the barn and stuck into his back pocket. "Yeah. He's tried calling me about twenty times, and I'm sure he was the one who sent the police here as well, which means they must have figured out Brady escaped from the house."

"There's something else." Tala's voice quivered.

"What's that?"

"Brady told me the house Rose is in could go up in smoke, that someone named The Bird has his finger on the trigger. He told me he could get a message to whoever that is whenever he wants to. Do you think he has it wired to explode?"

Ah. That explained Brady's cryptic threat. "Could be. Or he might have been messing with your head again. In case he wasn't, I'll let Laken know that, too, so he can take the bomb squad in with him if they discover the location. What's Rose's last name and cell number?"

"Galway." Tala recited the number, and Cole texted it to Lake so he'd have the information in writing. In seconds Lake texted back a confirmation of receipt along with the urgent question: *Are you both okay??*

Cole responded that they were fine, that Brady was in police custody and Cole would call Lake tomorrow to fill him in on everything that had happened. Then he slid the phone into his pocket and stood. "It's done, *Mahal*. Laken will take care of it. Neither of us can do anything more tonight, so let's try and get some sleep."

She nodded and took the hand he held out. Neither of them spoke as they made their way upstairs. As they approached the main bathroom, Cole tugged on her hand. "Here." She followed him in, and he let go of her and opened the medicine cabinet door. He pulled out antibiotic cream and the box of bandages, setting both on the counter before grabbing a few tissues and dampening them with warm water. Tala leaned against the counter as he gently swiped the dried blood from the small cut beneath her eye, applied a thin layer of cream, and covered it with a bandage. "Did he hurt you anywhere else?" He worked hard to keep the anger out of his voice, but, when her eyes met his, he knew he hadn't completely done it.

She gestured to her neck. "He shoved his arm against my throat when I goaded him into it."

Cole's eyebrows rose as he tipped her chin back to examine her. "You goaded him? Why?"

"I thought if I could make him angry enough, he might kill me quicker."

Cole let go of her. He'd ask why in the world she would want that, but he knew the answer. If Cole hadn't arrived home early, Brady would have drawn out Tala's torture for hours. A fast death would have been the best thing she could have received at his hands. Heat coursing through his chest, Cole cupped the back of her head and tugged her to him, as much to comfort himself as her. For several minutes they stood that way until finally, reluctantly, he let her go. She badly needed sleep.

"What about you?" She ran a finger along his jawline.

Cole's gaze flicked to the mirror above the sink. He'd almost forgotten about the slug he took to the jaw, although it was already darkening and, now that she had drawn his attention to it, throbbing. His gut ached too, but none of that mattered. She was safe. "I'm fine."

"It's starting to swell. You need some"—her finger stilled on his face as her gaze locked with his—"frozen peas."

He caught the faint flicker of humor in her eyes—not quite her usual spark, but far more than he'd expected to see for a long time—and shook his head slightly. Only Tala could joke after everything she had just been through. "I'm okay. All I need is to go to bed and hold you in my arms for a few hours."

"Granted." Tala offered him a small smile before going down the hall to get ready for bed. When she returned to his room in her purple pajama bottoms and black T-shirt, Cole was sitting up in bed, leaning against the headboard. Tala settled on the edge of the mattress next to him. "I need to talk to you about one more thing before I can sleep."

Cole wasn't sure how much more he could take. But if she needed to talk, he'd listen. He reached for her hand. "What is it?"

"It's what Brady said about me tonight, when he called me a—"

"No." A pang shot across his chest. "Don't say that word. That is not what you are."

"But it is a role I played." Tala worked the edge of the blanket with her fingers. "When I was first abducted and taken to Brady's, the hardest part was the feeling of complete and utter powerlessness. The idea that anyone could do anything they wanted to me was reinforced over and over those early days by Brady and his men.

"After days—or maybe weeks, I lost track—of this *conditioning*, I started to believe what they were telling me, that I was only as valuable as the pleasure I could give them. I began to accept the truth that I was so used and abused now that it didn't matter if I kept living that way. *What's one more?* was the question I repeatedly asked myself as they started sending different men into my room."

Cole fought to keep his fury under control, especially when he caught another glimpse of the barcode tattoo on the inside of her wrist. As soon as possible, they were going to look into having that removed.

"One day, I mouthed off to one of Brady's men, Three, I think, or maybe Five."

"Three?"

"Yeah. We were never told their names, so we numbered them to keep them straight. That day, Three lifted his arm to backhand me. Brady shouted, 'Not her,' and the guy didn't hit me. Brady sent me to my room and told me to watch my mouth or next time he wouldn't stop the man, but it was too late—he'd revealed his hand. I was valuable to him. And I wasn't powerless."

Cole kept his gaze fixed on her, desperately trying not to think about everything she had gone through but to focus only on what she was trying to tell him.

"Being good at what I was forced to do put me in high demand among his clients. Which gave me a small measure of power and allowed me to occasionally help the other women. He wasn't lying tonight—I was the best at what he made me do. God forgive me."

Her voice broke, and Cole pressed her hand to his chest.

"You were doing what you had to do to survive. God knows that. He saw what was happening to you, and he knows your heart. I don't believe there is anything to forgive, but if there is, he will forgive you. He *has* forgiven you."

For the second time that night, the words coming out of Cole's mouth took him by surprise. How had he become so sure of who God was and how much grace and mercy he had to pour out over the ones who loved him, who trusted in him despite their horrific situations? He felt as though he'd been wearing a blindfold his whole life and that somehow, in the months since he'd brought Tala here, that blindfold had been torn away. For the first time in his life, he saw God clearly. He wasn't some cold, hard father who demanded obedience and excellence in exchange for a grudging word of approval.

He didn't love people because of anything they did; he loved because he *was* love. He couldn't be or do anything else. Grams had taught him that, although Cole hadn't fully assimilated that truth until Tala became part of his life.

Which meant that, whether or not Cole had ever earned his father's approval, God loved him.

As a son.

Ngwis.

Tears pricked his eyes, but he blinked them away. Tonight was about his wife, not him.

Tala gazed at him. "How can you sound so sure?"

"Because I am sure. I'm as sure about that as I am that I love you, which is saying a lot." He lifted the back of her hand to his lips. "I hope and pray you can be as sure one day."

He released her and lifted the blankets next to him. "For tonight, you only need to rest. Brady's behind bars, and he will be for a very long time. You don't have to be afraid anymore."

Tala rounded the footboard to climb into bed next to him.

Cole wrapped his arms around her, and she laid her head on his chest. "I don't know if I remember how to not be afraid."

"That's what I'm here for." He tightened his hold. "Whenever you forget, I'll remind you. Always, for the rest of our lives."

CHAPTER FIFTY-TWO

The chief kept them at the station for several hours, asking them to repeat every detail of their ordeal several times. Cole knew it was necessary, but the lines of exhaustion around Tala's eyes, the way the fingers she'd rested on the table trembled a little as she relived her encounter with Brady, nearly drove him out of his mind. All he wanted was to take her home, close the door, and shut the world out for a few days. Or weeks.

He checked his phone periodically but heard nothing from Lake about Rose or Brady's other house. Every time he glanced at the screen, Tala looked at him, her eyes filled with hope that faded when he shook his head.

Finally, the interrogation ended. When they arrived home, Tala hung up her coat and then gripped the post at the bottom of the stair railing. "I think I might lie down for a bit."

"You should. Sleep as long as you need to."

"Will you wake me if you hear anything from Laken?"

"I will, I promise." Cole leaned in and kissed her. "Rest. I'll make dinner while you're taking a nap."

The ghost of a smile flitted across her face. "That sounds like a good deal for me."

"You've earned it." He watched as she trudged up the stairs. The thought of how close he'd come to losing her—one he hadn't allowed to settle in his mind until now—stabbed through him. *Thank you, God, for being with her when I couldn't be. And for compelling me to leave work early and go home.* If he hadn't left his phone at home, if he hadn't listened to that gut feeling, Cole couldn't even think about what might have happened. What he would have found when he arrived home at the end of his shift.

Hoping to distract himself, he wandered into the living room and grabbed the laptop. He'd do a little research, see if he could find anything on her foster sister, Rose Galway. He entered everything he could think of into the search bar but came up empty. Cole blew out a breath. Now what? He felt helpless to do anything to help track her down from here. Hopefully Lake would have news for him soon. Another thought occurred to him. He couldn't remember the last name of her second foster sister, Jae, if Tala had ever told him, but he did recall she'd once mentioned that her foster mother's name was Felicity Greenman. That wasn't a terribly common name. Maybe he'd look her up, see if he could find a funeral announcement. Like it had helped him to go to the cemetery and say goodbye to his father, it would likely be healing for Tala to visit Felicity's graveside.

Cole searched the web for a few minutes until an article caught his eye and he clicked on it. After reading it, he sagged against the couch. Wow. Not what he had expected to find. He did a little more research, eventually managing to track down contact information for the author of the article. Cole sent an email and then closed the laptop, set it aside, and went to get started on dinner.

As soon as he walked into the kitchen, his eyes fell on the clock magnet, still stuck to the front of the fridge. The inferno that had gradually cooled since yesterday roared to life as he stalked over and snatched it off. What kind of sick freak did that to another human being? Cole carried the thing in the tips of his fingers down the hall and out the front door. He likely shouldn't be touching evidence like this—something that Brady or his henchman might have left fingerprints on—but there was proof enough they'd been on the property. This horrific reminder of Tala's past he was going to destroy so that she never had to see it again.

Cole tossed the magnet onto the stump and then snatched up his axe. He raised it over his head and brought it down on the magnet. Over and over he chopped until the heinous thing lay in a hundred tiny pieces and the fury coursing through him had waned slightly.

"Okay, okay, you got it. It's dead."

The soft voice behind him spun Cole around. He lowered the axe to the ground as Tala walked toward him. Her voice held the barest hint of laughter. Would this woman never cease to amaze him?

"I'm sorry. Did I wake you?" He shot a sheepish glance at the stump. Not the quietest activity he could have found to do while she was trying to rest.

Tala shook her head, her hair swishing across her back. "I couldn't sleep." She held out her hand. "Mind if I take a few whacks?"

"Be my guest." Cole held the handle out to her and then stepped away, giving her room to swing.

Tala hefted the axe and brought it down on the tiny black and white pieces, until it was pretty much impossible to tell what the object of their wrath had once been. After a few minutes, she lowered the axe head to the ground. "I know I still need professional help, but chopping things up has got to be at least as therapeutic as that."

Cole reached for the axe. "So is going for a ride. Want to take the horses out before dinner?"

Tala's face lit up. "I'd love that."

He set the axe in the woodshed, swept the tiny pieces of the magnet into his palm, and fell into step beside her as they strolled toward the barn. Even though he wasn't touching her, Cole could feel her tensing as they approached the building. Still clutching the pieces of magnet in one hand, he captured her fingers in his other one. "You don't have to go inside. I can saddle both horses and bring them out to the corral."

For a few seconds, Tala didn't respond. Then she pushed back her shoulders. "No, I need to go in. The longer I wait, the harder it will be."

"All right, then, we'll do it together."

The tension radiating from her eased a little. "That sounds good."

Cole held up his fist. "First I need to throw this in the dumpster behind the barn."

Tala nodded and walked with him around the back of the building. When they reached the dumpster, Cole let go of her. He sprinkled the pieces all around the bin and brushed his hands together to swipe off the last of the bits. "There. You never have to see that thing again."

"I'm very glad to hear it."

Cole rested his forearms on the top of the dumpster. "You know, the morning after you told me about your night of ice, I carried the ice cube trays out here and demolished all the cubes before tossing the trays into the dumpster after them."

Her eyes widened. "You did?"

"Yeah. I was so angry with God for allowing you to go through that. I came very, very close to turning my back on him for good because I couldn't believe he cared about anything that was going on down here. Then I looked up, and the most gorgeous sunrise I'd ever seen had spread across the sky. I actually felt it, deep inside me. Like you said that day about the beauty of creation resonating in your soul. And it seemed as though God had painted the sky those brilliant colors just for me. To show me that he'd heard my prayers and was here with us. And that he had always been with you. That morning changed everything for me." He lowered his arms and faced her. "It opened my heart, allowed me to truly love God." He brushed a strand of hair, damp from her exertions, away from her face. "And you."

Tala smiled up at him. Cole lowered his head and found her mouth. He had no words to tell her how much he loved her. How terrified he had been the night before when he'd been sure Brady was about to end her life in front of him. He hoped that she could feel it in his kiss, in the thumbs caressing her soft cheeks.

When he finally lifted his head, the sapphire eyes that had captured him the moment she'd first turned her gaze on him in the hotel room glowed with a light he was only beginning to understand. Like the stars she was named after. From what Cole could remember from the one astronomy course he'd taken in college, their light came from nuclear fusion deep in their core. And a source of light far greater than he could comprehend shone from her core as well, lighting her from within.

"Wow." Tala breathed the word, grasping his forearms as though she was a little unsteady on her feet. Which Cole completely got.

The sun had drifted toward the horizon, and for a long time they stood in each other's arms, watching as soft tendrils of red and orange and yellow deepened into a blazing display across the sky. It was here, where Cole stood holding the woman he loved, that God had revealed himself to Cole. He wouldn't have thought it likely, but this patch of earth—surrounded by overgrown weeds, the slightly sour smell of garbage drifting on the air—would now always be, for him, a piece of sacred ground.

CHAPTER FIFTY-THREE

Exhausted by the events of the past few days, Tala slept late the next morning. When she woke, Cole's place next to her was empty, and she glanced at the alarm clock beside the bed. Almost 10 am. She hadn't slept that long since the first day or two she'd arrived here.

Tossing off the blankets, she hopped out of bed, padded across the floor, and went to her old room to shower and get ready for the day.

Twenty minutes later, she traipsed into the kitchen. Her heart tripped a little in her chest at the sight of Cole, leaning against the island watching her as she came through the door. He held out her blue mug, and Tala bounded over to take it from him. "Good morning."

"Morning."

Clutching the mug in both hands, Tala took a sip. "I thought you'd be in the barn."

"I was, earlier. But I wanted to be here when you came down because I have something for you."

She tilted her head, her ponytail swishing across her arm below the sleeve of her blue T-shirt. "News about Rose?"

Hope geysered through her, doused quickly when Cole shook his head.

"No, sorry. I texted Laken earlier, but they haven't found the house yet. Or figured out who The Bird might be. No reports of any bombings in the city, either, so it's looking more and more like Brady was simply trying to get into your head. Although Laken has come across several reports of bombings in the city over the last few years, and he is looking into whether any of them can be tied to Brady."

Her shoulders slumped. "Thanks for keeping in touch with him."

"Hey." Cole slid his fingers under her chin and tipped it up until she met his eyes. "They have a big team on this. Something is bound to happen soon, and Laken will let us know as soon as it does. If your foster sisters are alive, we'll do everything we can to find them."

"Okay."

He let her go. "In the meantime, it occurred to me that I never gave you a wedding present."

"Well, ours wasn't exactly a conventional wedding. I didn't get anything for you, either."

"Still, I wanted to do something for you, so …" He reached for her hand. "It would be easier if I showed you."

Tala set her mug on the island and followed him to the living room. What could he possibly have gotten her? He'd already given her so much, a whole new life. She couldn't think of a thing she might need or want beyond what she had here, with him.

They reached the doorway of the living room. As Tala followed Cole into the room, a woman who had been sitting in an armchair in front of the fireplace rose to her feet, joy splashing across her face. "Tala."

Tala stopped abruptly, gaping at the woman. It couldn't be. "Felicity?" She whispered the word, afraid that saying it out loud might make it not true. Might make this apparition in front of her disappear. How could her foster mother be here, standing in front of her, when she had died years ago?

With a small cry, Tala hurtled across the room and flung herself into Felicity's arms. Her foster mother laughed as she took a step backward. She wrapped one arm around Tala's shoulders and cupped the back of her head with her other hand, the way she had so often done when Tala was a young, scared girl living in a strange house with people she didn't yet know would become her family.

After a moment, Tala stepped back and reached for her foster mother's hands. "How …? When …? I thought …"

"You thought I died. I know. Here." Felicity guided her to the couch, and Tala sank onto it.

Cole took the chair where Felicity had been sitting. Tala looked over at him. "You did this?"

"When you were napping yesterday, I went online to see if I could find any mention of your foster mother. Based on what you told me, I thought I was looking for an obituary. Instead I found a number of articles written by Dr. Felicity Greenman. The first one I clicked on, written less than a year ago, was about loss and grief. I knew I had the right person when she mentioned her heartbreak over losing the three girls she considered her daughters. Her website had contact information, so I messaged her and told her you were here."

Felicity clasped Tala's trembling fingers. She studied the woman who had been a second mother to her. How old would she be now, early forties? She had a few wrinkles around her eyes and across her forehead, but she looked strong and healthy. How was that possible?

"As you can see, I didn't die. Shortly after you and Rose and Jae disappeared, a family member offered to donate a kidney to me. The transplant was successful, and I have been well ever since."

"Do you know anything about Rose and Jae?" The geyser spurted hope again, dashed by the sadness that flickered across Felicity's face.

"No. I've searched for the three of you for years, but it was as though you had vanished from the face of the earth. I tried to cling to hope, to keep believing that one day I would see you again, but until your wonderful husband here"—she inclined her head toward Cole—"contacted me yesterday, I had nearly given up. As soon as I got his message, I packed a bag and drove to Elliott Lake. I spent the night in a hotel and came straight here an hour ago. I couldn't wait another minute to see you, my sweet girl."

Tala's eyelids fluttered shut. All those years, that lost time with Felicity, everything they had been through, it had all been for nothing. She opened her eyes. "I'm so sorry we left."

Felicity sighed. "As broken-hearted and terrified as I was, I did understand. You were all so young, and I know you believed there was no hope for me, that you would be separated. I've agonized for years over how I could have done or said something differently so you wouldn't have felt the need to run away."

Tala lifted the back of her foster mother's hand to her cheek. "I wish we hadn't. I've wished that every day since."

"We can't change the past, dear one. We can only look forward to the future and what it holds for us."

Tala lowered their clasped hands to her knee. "Can you stay?"

Felicity glanced at Cole, and Tala followed her gaze. Cole nodded. "She's going to stay with us for a while—a long while, I hope. I'll fix up the large cabin for her. In the meantime, she can have the spare room upstairs."

Tala swung back to Felicity. "Really?"

Felicity smiled. "If it's all right with you. I gave up my practice when I was ill and then heartsick over your disappearance. I now write articles for various magazines and journals, which I can do from anywhere." She rested her free hand on Tala's arm. "I want us to make up for lost time. And Cole has shared a little of what you've been through. I think I may be able to help if you're willing to open up to me."

The hope that Tala had barely clung to during her time with Brady flared to life. While meeting with Stephanie had helped a little, the thought of being able to talk through everything she'd gone through with someone she already loved and trusted, someone she'd believed she had lost forever, filled Tala with deep joy. "I'd love that."

Felicity patted her arm. "It's settled, then. I'll have my things packed and shipped here, and we can begin this new chapter of our lives." She let go of Tala. "I'll get my bag from the car. When I come in, if you wouldn't mind showing me to my room, I'll freshen up. After that, maybe you can give me a tour of the ranch."

"I'd be happy to." She stood and watched as Felicity walked across the room and disappeared into the hallway. When she was gone, Tala whirled to face Cole.

He grinned. "Good present?"

"The best present ever. I can't believe Felicity is alive and staying here with us. Are you sure you're okay with that?"

Cole closed the space between them and took her face in his hands. "Tala, she's your family. Of course I'm okay with her being here. If it makes you happy and helps you with your healing journey, then I am one hundred percent for it."

She stood on her tiptoes to press her lips to his. "You've already made me happier than I ever dreamed possible. All of this is more than I could have imagined."

"But no more than you deserve." He kissed her again, lightly. "And you've made me happier than I ever dreamed possible, too."

The screen door creaked again, and Cole let her go. "Show Felicity to her room, and then we'll give her the grand tour."

Tala started for the hallway. *Thank you, Jesus. For remembering my name. For remembering me.* If she had ever doubted, she knew now that he had never forgotten her. That he'd been with her every moment of the last eight years, and he always would be.

The future that, from the moment Tala had been taken by Brady's men she had never truly believed she would have, stretched out before her now, as bright and beautiful as the stars in the sky.

A NOTE FROM THE AUTHOR

Dear Reader,

Tala's story is very dear to my heart. Although it is hard to read at times, the reality is that this is not only Tala's story, it is the story of countless women—and men—around the world at this very moment.

For me, human trafficking always felt like something far away, something that happened in other countries. Then, a few years ago, I attended a women's conference in Ottawa, Canada's capital city. The speaker addressed this issue, including statistics that clearly showed that the evil of sex trafficking exists everywhere, including my own country. In fact, the woman told us that if we were staying in a hotel that night—which I was—she could practically guarantee that somewhere in the building a girl was being trafficked. I will never forget the impact of those words—they felt like a direct hit to my heart. I certainly did not sleep well that night, aware of what could be happening somewhere in that hotel.

Since that day, this story has been slowly forming in my mind. Many other Christian authors are also penning stories of women being forced into slavery. I believe this is much more than a mere trend—this is God laying these precious people on our hearts, compelling us to put faces and names, even fictional ones, to these souls who represent those who are being used, abused, and tossed away every single day.

Dear ones, if you feel at a loss to know how to begin to respond, start with prayer. As Tala said about her wish for Cole, prayer is the most powerful weapon we can wield on behalf of another human being. Pray for every person being held in captivity, and then ask God if there is more that He would have you do. Donating to a reputable organization dedicated to freeing modern-day slaves is a powerful step to take. And those organizations can also help if you want or feel called to become even more involved.

It is important to be alert to what is going on around you and aware of the signs that someone in your vicinity might be being trafficked. The Canadian Centre to End Human Trafficking has released a comprehensive list of trafficking indicators that everyone should be familiar with. Read that list here: www.canadiancentretoendhumantrafficking.ca/signs-of-human-trafficking. As well, the Canadian Women's Foundation has developed a simple hand signal that anyone in trouble can use to silently ask for help. Check out the signal here so you know what to do if you see someone making this sign in person or on video: https://canadianwomen.org/signal-for-help

God has not turned his back on these women. He sees them. He is with them always. And one day, He will ensure that perfect justice is meted out to those who have done such irreparable, unspeakable harm to these beloved children of His.

Join me in praying for that day.

Sara

ABOUT SARA DAVISON

SARA DAVISON is the author of four romantic suspense series—The Seven Trilogy, The Night Guardians, The Rose Tattoo Trilogy, and Two Sparrows for a Penny, as well as the standalone, *The Watcher*. A finalist for more than a dozen national writing awards, she is a Word, Cascade, and Carol Award winner. She currently resides in Ontario with her husband Michael and their three mostly grown kids. Like every good Canadian, she loves coffee, hockey, poutine, and apologizing for no particular reason. Get to know Sara better at www.saradavison.org and @sarajdavison.

You can also find Sara on Amazon, BookBub, Goodreads, and Facebook.

ACKNOWLEDGMENTS

Always and above all, to the One who gives the stories, who put every star into place, and who engraves our names on the palm of His hand.

To Michael, my kids, and my extended family—for putting up with all the angst, doubts, joys, second-guessing, and the challenge of trying to be creative when the world is going crazy. I literally could not do this wild writing life without you in my corner. I love you all.

To my dear friend, brilliant wordsmith, and master editor, Deb Elkink—I have no words to express my gratitude for your generous gifts of time, knowledge, and endless encouragement. My stories are better because of you.

To my amazing Mosaic sisters. I am so thankful to God for the gift of each one of you. May He use your stories to bless and impact many as they have done for me. And to our beloved Mosaic readers—your support of our work blesses each of us more than we can say. May God bless each of you richly and remind you every day that you are worth more than many sparrows.

TITLES BY SARA DAVISON

THE MOSAIC COLLECTION: NOVELS
Lost Down Deep
Written in Ink
Every Star in the Sky

THE MOSAIC COLLECTION: ANTHOLOGY STORIES
"Taste of Heaven"
(in *Hope is Born: A Mosaic Christmas Anthology*)
"Ten Bottles of Sand"
(in *Before Summer's End: Stories to Touch the Soul*)
"Sixty Feet to Home"
(in *A Star Will Rise: A Mosaic Christmas Anthology II*)
"I'd Like to Thank the Academy"
(in *Song of Grace: Stories to Amaze the Soul*)
"Star Light"
(in *The Heart of Christmas: A Mosaic Christmas Anthology III*)

THE NIGHT GUARDIANS SERIES
Vigilant
Guarded
Driven

THE SEVEN TRILOGY
The End Begins
The Darkness Deepens
The Morning Star Rises

The Watcher

UPCOMING
Forged (2022)
Book Four in The Night Guardians Series

DISCUSSION QUESTIONS

1. Cole buys practical items Starr will need, but he also makes a few additional purchases—a candle, a lighter, three large bars of chocolate, and two novels.

If you found yourself in a strange place with none of your belongings, what three things (beyond basic necessities) would make you feel most comfortable and at home?

2. At his father's grave, Cole reminds himself that "he hadn't come here to try and figure out what his dad's religious beliefs might have been. He'd come here to unload on the man lying six feet beneath his feet."

Have you ever gone to the cemetery and talked to a person who had been in your life when they were alive? What did you talk about? Did it help? If you haven't, but you have unresolved issues with someone who is gone, what would you say to them if you had the chance?

3. Starr's questions about Cole's father get him wondering if "his dad had kept a desert of emotional distance between them only because he was afraid of loving someone else that much and possibly losing him, too."

Have you ever suffered a loss that made it difficult for you to trust or love again? Were you able to get past that? If so, how?

4. When Starr asks Cole if he minds if she says grace before they eat, he is shocked. "She believed in God? The last few years hadn't driven her faith in a benevolent being from her? How was that possible?"

Do you believe it is possible to go through something as horrific as Starr experienced and still hold on to your faith? Have you ever been through an extremely difficult or painful experience? Did it push you away from God or draw you closer? In what ways?

5. In one of his early prayers, Cole shot a look at the ceiling and hissed, "Can you hear me? If so, could you possibly direct a little of that wrath and judgment of yours Brady's way? If anyone on earth deserves a smiting from almighty God, it's that pathetic excuse for a human being. If you could make him pay for everything he did to those girls, to Starr, that would be really great."

Is there a Biblical justification for the idea that God would unleash wrath and judgment on someone like Brady? Do you believe that it is okay for believers to pray for that? Why or why not?

6. Cole witnesses such a spectacular sunrise that he feels as though it is a message from God. "Set against the dull, cold slate, the beauty was so intense that he not only saw it but felt it inside him. Was that what Tala meant by the beauty of creation resonating deep in the soul?"

What do you think of this idea? Do you believe God speaks to us through nature? Have you ever had an experience like that? Describe what it was and how it made you feel.

LET'S CONNECT!

Let's Connect!

I would love to connect with you further. You can find me at the following places:

Website (where you can subscribe to my short, monthly newsletter): www.saradavison.org

Twitter: @sarajdavison

Facebook: @authorsaradavison

If you've enjoyed or been moved by *Every Star in the Sky*, please consider leaving a review. Your words bring hope and encouragement to the author as well as to other readers. Thank you!

COMING SOON

TO THE MOSAIC COLLECTION

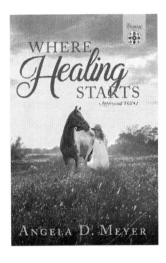

Joanna and Blake Hannigan grew up in an angry home and made an all-for-one pact–them against the world–in order to survive. Now that pact may keep them from what they each long for.

While doing community service for shoplifting, Joanna's walls begin to come down. She wonders if she does have something of value inside of her, but still full of bitterness, she can't get off the path to self-destruction.

Will a near death experience put her on the road to redemption?

Blake refuses to accept the consequences for putting his brother-in-law in the hospital. He runs from the law and does the unthinkable.

In the face of impending disaster, will Blake's choices lead to healing?

Unless the siblings realize their pact can't save them, they may not find the One who can.

Made in the USA
Middletown, DE
10 March 2022